CONVICTION

THE SOPHISTICATES SERIES

• Book Two •

CHRISTINE MANZARI

This book is a work of fiction. Any references to historical events, real people, or real places are used ficticiously. Other names, characters, places, and events are products of the author's imagination, and any resemblance to actual events or places or persons, living or dead, is entirely coincidental.

To My Dad —

You taught me to always be true to myself.

You are my hero.

1

The Rink

The ringing was loud in The Rink, echoing through the darkness, bouncing off the concrete walls, and shattering the silence into a million invisible pieces. Out of habit, I reached into my pocket before I remembered that I'd lost my phone days ago. I hadn't seen it since Monday night when I used it to email Cleo. I tried using Stanley's phone to call and find it, but the battery was obviously dead and it was nowhere to be found. I kicked back the covers and sat up slowly, hearing everyone else around me getting up as well.

"Will someone pick up that damn phone before I start twitching?" Quinnie complained.

I briefly dropped my head in my hands before running my fingers back through my tousled hair. Quinnie during the day was a headache. Quinnie 24/7 was a complete and utter pain in the ass. I hoped this mission would be over soon. Everyone was getting cranky, including me, although I seemed to be able to hide it better.

After Cassie's rescue, Professor Younglove sent me back to The

Rink with a team of Deviants to see if we could find anything that might lead us to where Delia Younglove and the Others, the unauthorized twins of the Deviant Dozen, might now be located. This errand had been a lot less successful than the first mission to The Rink. The only thing we'd done in the last two days was go through every inch of the abandoned building and catalog our findings, which in all honesty were nothing more than leftover junk from the roller rink's glory days. The only things that had been left behind were the militaristic bunk beds in the middle of the rink, loose wires where surveillance cameras must have once been, and the food in the pantry and kitchen. The first thing I did was throw out all the food—it would have been too easy for the Others to poison it, much like retreating villagers burned their fields and homes when invaded by enemy armies.

The team of Deviants that Professor Younglove sent along with me consisted of Quinnie, Eva, Sadie, Marty, and Dexter. They had been expecting some glorious battle between us and the Others when we arrived at The Rink, but instead we'd done nothing more than battle cobwebs and dusty storage areas. I didn't really mind. It was better than what I was normally asked to do when on a mission, but given a choice, I'd rather be back at the Academy with Cleo.

But if I couldn't be at the Academy, I'd be happy just to have my phone back. I had no idea what happened to it and I kept expecting it to turn up. It hadn't. The stupid thing disappeared just like the Others.

The unidentified phone finally stopped ringing and I heard Stanley's voice offering a groggy greeting. Then silence.

"Ozzy, it's for you," Stanley said from somewhere in the darkness.

Cleo

2

Kind of Feels Like Déjá Vu

The flashing of the emergency light in the corner of my room and the persistent wail of an alarm forced me awake. My legs were tangled in my blankets and I was covered in sweat from another nightmare. I'd been having bad dreams more frequently ever since the confrontation at The Rink with the Others. I wasn't getting much sleep anymore and the sleep I did manage to get was spotty at best. Groggy from my interrupted sleep and confused by the incessant scream of the alarm, I was still trying to puzzle out what was going on, wondering what I was supposed to be doing, when a voice began to echo through a speaker that was near the flashing light. Had that light always been there? Funny how I never noticed it before. Then again, I'd never been awakened in the middle of the night by a flashing siren either.

I tried to focus my thoughts enough to listen to the announcement coming out of the speaker. The voice giving the directions was Professor Younglove's.

"All cadets report to the dining hall immediately. I repeat, all cadets report to the dining hall immediately."

I climbed out of bed, grabbed the green hoodie that was slung over my desk chair, and slipped it over my arms as I hurried out of my room and into the hall.

"There you are!" Arabella said, catching up to me. Arabella, of course, looked like she had been up for hours. Her hair was long and straight, dyed in black and white horizontal stripes. Her makeup was picture perfect as well. I hadn't looked in the mirror before leaving my room, but I was confident that I probably had a massive case of bed head and sleep-crusted eyes. Not for the first time, I was jealous of Arabella's deviation.

We followed the rest of the cadets, a river of plaid pajamas, tangled hair, and a chorus of yawns, flowing down the steps and through the halls toward the dining hall.

"What do you think is going on?" Arabella asked a little too cheerfully.

"Don't know and don't care. I just want to sleep." I wasn't a morning person, or a middle of the night person for that matter.

"They better let us out of the morning run for this," Arabella muttered. "Some of us need our beauty sleep." She looked over to me and then added, "Clearly, some of us need it more than others. Good God, girl, don't you own a hairbrush?"

I glared at her. "It's the middle of the night and alarms are going off. I didn't stop to primp. For all we know, this place is on fire."

Arabella grunted. "We can only hope."

When we entered the dining hall, we quickly spotted Sterling, Wesley, and Theo and made our way over to them.

Theo winced when he caught sight of me. "Looks like you were rode hard and put away wet, Cleo."

I made an obscene gesture at him, but he merely laughed and patted my overly knotted hair. I pushed his hand away and he laughed again.

Sterling scanned the room, looking at all the confused cadets who were milling around nervously. "Anybody want to guess what this is about?" he asked, folding his arms over his chest.

"Maybe it's some sort of new training drill," Wesley suggested.

Just then, the doors swung wide open and Dean Overton careened into the dining hall like a boulder rolling down a mountain. The sea of cadets parted and scurried to get out of his way as Younglove followed in his wake, her clothing fluttering around her spare frame and a folder in her arms rustling in a whisper of loose papers. They stopped when they reached the middle of the hall and I had a severe case of déjá vu. It wasn't a good feeling.

Dean Overton waited until the chatter died and all eyes had made their way to him. "There has been another terrorist attack," he announced.

There was a spattering of concerned muttering that the dean silenced with a hard look and a raised hand.

"A few hours ago, there was an attack on Andrews Air Force Base in southern Maryland. A large number of aircraft were destroyed."

The room erupted in a chorus of worried questions as everyone looked around at each other. Another terrorist attack? Everyone knew what this meant. Not all of the cadets would be returning to their beds tonight. For some, St. Ignatius and all its distractions of work detail, team sports, and formals would be nothing but a memory by morning; a memory replaced with the realities of a

Sophisticate Mandate future—a life in the military.

"How many?" a brave soul up front asked.

I wondered the same thing. How many cadets would be leaving this time? Maybe me. Maybe this was it. The thought was a frightening one and I instinctively gripped my elbows, crossing my arms over my chest. Knowing that I wouldn't even have a say in the matter if my name was called made me feel completely helpless.

"How many planes were lost?" the same voice clarified before Overton could respond. I was momentarily startled, surprised that I'd misunderstood the original question. I should probably feel guilty that I was more worried about my own safety than that of the people on the base. Seriously. How could I not be worried about that? After all those lives lost during *Wormwood* and recent terrorist attacks, how could I not have even thought of the victims of this attack?

Dean Overton's small, piggish eyes found the speaker. "All of the aircraft that were in the air for training exercises were destroyed," he explained. "And all those that went out to check on the ones that were lost were also destroyed. Even the helicopters. Many that weren't even in the air were destroyed. Air Force One is nothing but a pile of burning metal right now."

This revelation spurred another round of anxious chattering, but the dean ignored it.

"Since the response team we sent out a few weeks ago for the casino bombing and building collapse is still in Nevada, we'll need to send a new team out to help the military with this catastrophe. When your name is called, step forward. You'll be leaving immediately."

He began to call out names from a list and with every name, I worried if it would be someone I knew taking that final exit through the doors of the Academy.

"...David, Oxenford, Diana Oxenford, Drake Oxenford, Ethan Oxenford, Felicity Oxenford, Hector Oxenford, Jerome Oxenford, Justine Oxenford..."

I relaxed when I realized that all of the names being called were those of cadets three years older than me and my friends. They were set to graduate from the Academy later this year. I didn't personally know any of them, but I still felt the pang of guilt as I watched them slowly make their way through the crowd, far from eager to have their names called. A group of approximately fifty bedraggled cadets walked in a daze toward Dean Overton and then were unceremoniously led out of the hall. The mood was somber and quiet, the silence broken randomly by the sounds of stifled sniffling. I might not have known any of the cadets called, but as I looked around, it was obvious that they had left friends behind. The grieving was starting. Reality was finally setting in. Being a Sophisticate had its benefits, but eventually, we would all pay dearly for the right to have those benefits. Did it matter if we were stronger, faster, and smarter when in the end, we had no freedom to choose our own futures?

Younglove stayed behind briefly to address the remaining cadets.

"As you can see, the Program is still in high demand. You may go back to your rooms, but let this be a reminder that your training is imperative." Her eyes scanned the room and stopped meaningfully on me and my group of friends. "Time to master your skills," she said.

Then she tucked her folder into her chest and left the hall, leaving behind a silent, and slightly frightened, room full of teens. The same thought was on everyone's mind—Am I next?

Ozzy

Just Hanging Around

Another terrorist attack. This one too close for comfort.

Younglove had been irritated that my phone was missing and that she had to call Stanley to get a hold of me to relate the bad news. But in the end, she was just relieved to be able to provide a lead on her sister, Delia, and the Others. She wanted to find them as much as I did. Younglove's briefing on the situation had been short but clear—most of Andrews Air Force Base was destroyed or currently still on fire. Base officials didn't know what happened. No planes, missiles, tanks, or any other form of attack had been observed. Things just started exploding and dropping out of the sky—the sky that was nearly within spitting distance of Washington D.C: the sky that suddenly seemed as poisonous as the waters of *Wormwood*.

It was as if the base was attacked by phantoms.

That's exactly what someone would see who didn't know what to look for. If you didn't know to expect a Deviant, you'd never see them coming.

"How do we know Delia and the Others were there?" I asked Younglove as I moved around my temporary bunk, gathering all of my things and stuffing them back in my bag.

"Captain Jefferson called me to ask why my sister and the Deviants had been sent to the base. Apparently, they came right through the front gate posing as the Dozen. While I was on the phone with him, the attack began."

"Does he know what we're capable of? What the Others are capable of?"

"He does now."

I finished packing my bag and zipped it shut. "Does he have anyone else down there that can help us?"

"No, there are no Sophisticates or Hounds currently stationed there aside from him. But we're sending a team of Sophisticates from the Academy to serve as backup for you. Headquarters will probably send a contingent of Hounds, but you will get there before they arrive. Do you want me to send the rest of the Dozen as well?"

A selfish part of me wanted to agree just so I could be with Cleo again, but the logical part of my brain reasoned she was safer at the Academy. How could I convince Younglove to keep her there without raising suspicion as to why? Younglove already warned me to keep my romantic distance from Quinnie. Everyone always assumed that Quinnie and I were an item, and I never bothered to correct the assumptions in the past because I didn't care. Even now, I let people think whatever they wanted because it was easier to disguise my feelings for Cleo when people were looking elsewhere. Avoiding romantic entanglement with Quinnie had never been a problem. I'd grown up in the same Universities as her and she was like a sister; a very annoying little sister.

Cleo was another story. I was drawn to her and I'd fallen hard. In the dojo, she was strong and fearless—taking down Sophisticates who were much bigger and stronger. In the classroom, she was relentless—learning languages as easily as if she were learning the lyrics to a song. In her friendships, she was loyal and dedicated—creating her own family within the Program, even though her real one had been taken from her. I was also a sucker for the rebellious side of her—the girl that broke into top-secret Program files, the girl that stood up to the Others for her friends, and especially the girl that threw a perfectly good dress out a window in a fit of rage. No one had ever noticed Cleo like I had because she was always in Cassie's shadow, and only too happy to be there. She didn't crave the limelight, she thrived in the shadows. I saw her for who she was because I lived in the shadows, too.

The problem was that I was expected to be the leader of the Dozen with no emotional attachments to anyone in the group. That way, I would have no qualms about leading them into danger. The current situation was just proof that I couldn't be the leader the Program wanted me to be. Instead of agreeing to have the Deviant Dozen at full force, my first instinct was to protect the person I cared about the most.

No. Cleo couldn't come.

"No," I said. "I think it's best if you keep some of the Dozen at the Academy as a protection measure. We don't know what Delia's plans are, but we do know that she wants Cassie back. This could be a distraction to pull away your strongest defenses so that she can attack the Academy. The Sophisticates you're sending should be enough. How many can I expect?" I didn't really think that Delia was going to attack the Academy, but I wanted Younglove to think that it was a possibility so that she'd keep Cleo at St. Ignatius where she'd be safe.

"Fifty-three. All final year cadets. They're already on their way."

"Good," I replied, mentally trying to decide whether those odds were going to be good enough. "We'll be leaving immediately. I'll be in touch when I know more." I hung up the phone and tossed it back to Stanley. "We're leaving in three minutes," I called to everyone.

"I found this in my stuff," Quinnie said, tossing a familiar phone on top of my bag. "I don't know how it got there." A smug grin broke across her face before she turned and walked away.

***

My phone was dead, of course. I shoved it into my duffel bag as I opened the passenger side door of the SUV. I didn't bother with plugging it in to charge because it would only serve as a distraction. Right now, I needed to focus on the task at hand—how was I going to keep myself, Stanley, five Deviants, and fifty-three other Sophisticates alive while stopping Delia and the Others? It wasn't going to be easy. It probably wasn't even possible.

Andrews Air Force Base was located in Maryland, a few miles southeast of Washington D.C. It was only an hour away from The Rink, but knowing that the Others had been there and were probably responsible for the attack, the trip felt like it took hours. Andrews wasn't one of the biggest or most active bases in the country, but it was close to the Capital and home to Air Force One. It seemed that Delia Younglove wanted the Others to be seen and blamed for the attack. The question was, why?

At the entrance gate, the guard on duty briefly spoke to Stanley, who was driving, before thrusting his flashlight into the interior of the SUV to check out who was inside. There was a lot of grumbling as sleep-deprived eyes were momentarily blinded by the bright light. Finally, the guard was pushed to the side as a familiar Hound came to the driver's side window. When he saw me, he nodded in approval.

"You guys got here fast. Good. Let's get you through the gates so I can get you out on the tarmac to investigate."

I recognized the Hound, Tony Jefferson. He was relatively young for a captain, but he was one of the original Hounds of the Program and Stanley was in total awe to be in the presence of a Program legend.

"Have they left the grounds?" I asked, ignoring the fact that Stanley was staring slack jawed at Captain Jefferson. "If they were seen leaving, we probably need to start following their trail as soon as possible."

"They're still on base," Tony replied.

"How do you know? This place is huge. They could've escaped in any number of ways. They're not exactly normal Sophisticates."

"I'm well aware they're not normal," the captain said, his gaze briefly touching each of my fellow occupants. "But they're still here. We know where they are and we have them surrounded, but I've given the order not to engage them yet. Damn," he said, glancing around the interior of the van again, "they look just like you."

"Exactly like us?" I asked. I'd seen a few of the Others, but hadn't seen my own double yet.

"Exactly," the captain confirmed. "Actually, there is one difference."

"What's that?"

"No tattoos," Captain Jefferson answered. "I noticed that when I was watching the footage. The one that looks like her," he said pointing to Quinnie, "had her arms bare and she had no markings on her forearms. I noticed tattoos missing on all of the ones that didn't have their forearms covered."

I hadn't thought about it before, but it made sense that the Others wouldn't be tattooed. The tattoo was part of the Program. The Others weren't even supposed to exist.

"And they haven't attacked you or tried to escape?" I asked.

"No. They're inside the hangar for Air Force One."

"I thought Air Force One was destroyed."

"It was, but we were training a new crew. It was on the runway so the hangar was unharmed."

"What happened to the crew?"

"They'll survive. The explosion that incapacitated the aircraft took out the tail. The crew was able to evacuate before the plane was totally destroyed."

"And Air Force Two?"

"It's in the hangar."

"Do you think they plan to steal the plane? Is that a possibility?" I asked Jefferson.

"I guess that at this point anything is possible, but I doubt they would. It'd be too easy to track and even easier to shoot down." The captain frowned. "It seems like they're waiting for something. My guess is that they're waiting for you."

"Why do you say that?" Stanley asked, finally getting over his speechless admiration of the legendary Hound.

Captain Jefferson turned to look at Stanley. "Just a gut feeling. Professor Younglove explained that you all have something they want."

"You mean Cassandra Dracone?" I asked.

Jefferson nodded. "I'm not sure what they plan to do, but this message," he said, gesturing to the base behind him where dark smoke coiled into the pre-dawn sky that flickered with the flashing lights of emergency vehicles, "This message is for you, I think."

"Well, let's not keep them waiting any longer," I replied. "Let's go see what they want."

***

The Air Force One hangar was a massive, imposing structure with its own runway. It was shaped like a hexagon and at each of its six points it boasted huge pillars that were the size of silos. Military vehicles were scattered around the building with their lights flashing; men were hiding behind barricades with their weapons drawn and pointed in the direction of the immense, white fortress. The bay door that led to the runway was open, a gaping maw of light that beckoned to the waiting soldiers with the illusion of safety and security. The surviving presidential plane was visible through the doorway as were several objects that appeared to be hanging from the interior ceiling.

I surveyed the building as I waited for the contingent of Sophisticates from the Academy to show up.

"Still no word?" I asked the officer in charge.

"Not a peep," the man, whose name was Captain Cheswick, confirmed. "They've made no contact, nor any additional acts of aggression. I still don't understand why we don't go in there and capture them. There are only about a dozen of them." The glare that he gave Captain Jefferson, who was easily fifteen years his junior, was more than unfriendly. It was clear that despite their similar titles, Captain Cheswick was bitter about the fact that Captain Jefferson's Sophisticate status gave him the higher rank and the power to call the shots.

"These are no ordinary terrorists," Jefferson explained. "You send your men in there and I doubt any would make it out alive."

"And you think these kids can do any better?" he asked, staring at me and the rest of the Deviants with disgust.

"I know they can," Jefferson growled. "And this order isn't just coming from me, it's coming from the Program. From the very top."

Cheswick huffed in annoyance.

I continued to stare at the objects hanging inside the hangar, ignoring the testosterone-fueled pissing contest between the captains.

"What are those things suspended from the ceiling inside?" I could just barely make out what looked like a few dozen lumpy forms that were slightly swaying back and forth.

Cheswick glanced toward the open bay door. "Hostages."

Hostages? Well, that certainly complicated things.

Cleo

4

Top Five Days

Sleep was not my friend. Every time I thought I might be able to drift off, my eyes were drawn to the emergency light in the corner as part of me expected another alarm to pierce the quiet of the night. I couldn't stop thinking about the terrorist attack and whether the next incident would have my name called, or worse, the names of my friends.

Friends. Just thinking the word made my chest ache.

Cassie woke up from her coma on Monday and I still hadn't been allowed to visit her. It was now Thursday, although just barely. She was still in the infirmary recovering from the physical and emotional torture she endured at the hands of Delia Younglove and the Others at The Rink. It didn't seem fair to be kept apart from her, and frankly, it was starting to piss me off. If I could see for myself that she was okay, I knew it would relieve some of my worries. I remembered how difficult my first day at the Academy had been and I was positive that if Cassie could just see a familiar face, it would help her recover.

Maybe if Ozzy was here, he'd be able to persuade someone to let me in to visit my best friend, but he wasn't here. He'd been sent on a mission just a few short hours after Cassie regained consciousness and I hadn't see him since.

I sat up and retrieved the note from my dresser that I found on my pillow Monday night. It had been hastily written and was barely legible, both because of the writing and the wrinkled paper. I smoothed it out across my thigh, greedily reading the words, hearing them in his voice.

Roasting Creamsicle,
I know that you're upset you're not part of this mission, but I'm relieved. Without Quinnie around, I know you'll be fine while I'm gone. I'll do my best to get back as soon as I can because I can't wait to continue what we started this morning. Definitely one of my top five days ever.
Ozzy
P.S. Please be careful in weapons class. Remember, aim the sharp end at the enemy.

I smiled and shook my head. He was romantic and sweet, and yet he couldn't resist a smartass comment. I wondered if he missed being in weapons class as much as I missed him teaching it. It just wasn't the same when he wasn't there to guide my body where it needed to go. When his hands were strong on mine and his breath was warm against my neck as he leaned close to show me proper technique—those were the times that I really appreciated my absolute incompetence with weapons.

Roasting Creamsicle. I sighed in acceptance. Out of curiosity, I lifted the note to my nose to see if there was any lingering scent that I could identify as Ozzy's. Nope. It smelled like paper and ink, nothing else. I read the note again, savoring every hastily scrawled word, the letters confident and dark—just like Ozzy.

Since sleep didn't seem to be in my future, and I was desperate for something to make me forget the middle-of-the-night-events, I pulled my laptop to my bed. Like an addict, I reread the emails that Ozzy and I sent to each other a few days ago.

——————————————————————-

Subject: Top Five Days
Date: Mon, 30 Oct 11:37
From: Clementine
To: Osbourne

Master of Weapons,
I received your note. The one you left on my pillow. It seems that once again, you have been trespassing in my room. Surely you know that's not allowed. I'm happy to hear that time spent with me is ranked among your top five days. I would like to know what your other four days are so I have a measurement of comparison of just how fabulous I truly am.
Anxiously awaiting your reply,
Cleo
P.S. It occurred to me that if I had a better weapons instructor, I would know which end of the weapon to stick in the enemy. Perhaps I need more personal instruction.

Subject: Four Days

Date: Mon, 30 Oct 11:46

From: Osbourne

To: Clementine

Surely you know the other four days all belong to you as well. There is no comparison.

P.S. Don't you worry, I plan to give you very personal instruction when I return. Now get to sleep. You have a hard enough time with the morning run when you've had enough rest.

Subject: Sweet Dreams

Date: Mon, 30 Oct 11:53

From: Clementine

To: Osbourne

I'll nod off as soon as I can think of something worth dreaming about.

Subject: Go to sleep

Date: Mon, 30 Oct 11:55

From: Osbourne

To: Clementine

I will just have to invade your dreams then. Go to sleep, I'll be waiting for you.

For all his arrogant and confident coolness, Ozzy could really turn on the charm. I didn't know if it was just to entertain me, or if he actually meant it, but I decided I didn't really care because I liked that he wanted to charm me.

That was the last email Ozzy sent, a promise at 11:55 on Monday night to meet me in my dreams. But it never happened. At three in the morning on Tuesday, my email program pinged one more time. The message was from Ozzy's address, but when I opened the email, there were no words. My screen was filled with a picture of Ozzy and Quinnie. He was asleep, his left arm flung out to the side, Quinnie's head nuzzled against his bicep. It was clear that she was taking the picture herself. Quinnie's smile was smug and the middle finger she held out to the camera said everything that the email lacked in words.

I was confident that Ozzy was unaware that Quinnie was in his bed that night, but it was an image I couldn't get out of my mind. I didn't write back to him because I wasn't sure what to say. I kept waiting for him to realize what happened and to call or email me to explain things.

He hadn't. He was with Quinnie and I was alone in my bed at the Academy with nothing but a raging case of insecurity for a companion. My jealousy wouldn't allow me to fall back to sleep so I spent the rest of the night struggling to keep the anger at bay.

It wasn't an easy battle. The blanket smoldered a bit, but at least I didn't actually set anything on fire.

Yet.

Fall Out

The reinforcements from the Academy finally arrived and I was glad they seemed awake, even if they all appeared terrified. No matter how many classes on weapons and strategy a Mandate cadet may have taken, nothing could have prepared them for the carnage they witnessed upon entering the front gate of the base. They drove past the wreckage of the planes that were still ablaze. They saw the ambulances and rescue crews still working to free injured soldiers from twisted, smoldering metal. They saw black bags zipped up with hidden horrors inside. And now, they were here, staring at a hulking monstrosity of a building where the people responsible for the attack waited behind a shield of dangling hostages. The cadets were rightfully afraid and they still didn't even know the truth about what those people could do to them.

I led my group of Deviants and Sophisticates to an area far behind the military barricade that was set up around the hangar. I wanted to be well away from the possibility of being overheard by any of the soldiers nearby. As I stared at all the expectant faces I recognized from my last few years at the Academy, I felt it was only fair to give them the truth. I hadn't asked Younglove whether I was supposed to reveal the secrets of the Deviant Dozen, but there was no way I was going to let these young men and women walk into a confrontation with the Others without knowledge. It'd be their most important weapon.

"Inside the hangar," I said, pointing to the building beyond the flashing lights, "there are a dozen people who are responsible for this attack." Excited whispering broke out as the cadets realized they had the advantage in numbers. "Don't get ahead of yourselves," I said a little louder, calming down the chatter that was rippling through the group. "Just because there are more of us, it doesn't mean this will be easy. They have dangerous skills."

"We're Mandates. We all have dangerous skills," someone said with a laugh.

I paused until the cadets were done half-heartedly congratulating themselves on their superiority. "Yes, you're all terrifying. And I'm sure any handful of you could've caused planes to fall from the sky." I looked around at all the young, naive faces. "These people aren't Sophisticates. They're not even Mandates; they're much worse. They're human weapons with no remorse and no Program to control them. And, they're going to look familiar to you."

I explained the situation, taking the time to make sure that the cadets were aware of what each member of the Deviant Dozen could do and that the Others not only looked like the Dozen, but wielded the same skills: Cleo's explosions, Quinnie's electricity, Arabella's preternatural strength and flexibility, Sterling's speed, Theo's and Wes's unnatural vision, Sadie's agility, even my perfect aim. I exposed the Dozen in all their horrifying truths, peeling back the carefully protected secrets with words that sounded unbelievable even to my own ears. A cadet up front raised his hand.

"Yes?" I asked.

"You're joking, right?"

"I wish I was."

"People can't just make things explode and toss around electricity like superheroes. Not even the Program can play God. I mean, yeah, you have good aim, but come on," the large cadet looked down at Marty. "You expect me to believe knives just appear out of his skin?" The Sophisticate's gaze found Dexter next. "And he spits acid?"

"Yes."

The cadet crossed his arms. There was always a doubter in every crowd.

"Marty," I said. "Devon looks like he could use an extra weapon. Think you can help him out?"

Marty smiled in response. "No problem."

He raised his arm as a black needle-like object appeared on his forearm and grew until it was the size of a large spike. He flicked his arm forward and the blade flew from his skin and embedded itself in the trunk of a nearby tree. Two more quick flicks of his arm and Marty had produced two other black blades of different sizes. He looked at the cadet who was now staring wide-eyed at the tree. "I wasn't sure what size you preferred," Marty taunted.

Sophisticates began to back away from Marty and the rest of the Deviants, giving us plenty of space and wary looks.

"Oh, for shit's sake," Quinnie snapped. "What a bunch of pansy asses! This is what Younglove sent for help?" she asked as she gazed around the group in disgust. "If we wanted to hurt you, you wouldn't be standing here all healthy and looking like the bunch of cowards you are." She forcefully dropped her arm downward and a miniature bolt of lightning jumped from her fingers and blasted the earth near her feet, sending a shower of dirt and burnt grass into the air around her. Cadets jumped back again.

"Not helping," I scolded Quinnie quietly. "Now," I said loudly, "as I was saying, our main purpose is to capture the Others so that they can be questioned by the Program, but don't hesitate to incapacitate or even kill them if it means your safety. They're already responsible for several fatalities this evening and I don't want to add any of your names to the list. There will be nearly twice as many Others as there are Deviants tonight since half of the Dozen are back at the Academy. We're going to be at a disadvantage, even with the help of the rest of you."

"So what's the plan?" someone asked.

"We walk in through the front door. No sense trying to sneak up on them because they have a Theo and a Wes."

"What does that mean?" a cadet asked.

Quinnie rolled her eyes. "He just finished telling you what Theo and Wes could do, Liam. I'm not saying you're stupid, but you have really bad luck when it comes to using your brain."

"And I'm not saying you're a bitch, but you're a bitch," Liam countered.

"Enough!" I interrupted. Did the Program really think I could lead Sophisticates into battle? It was like herding pissed-off cats. Working alone was so much easier—not necessarily better, just easier. "Look," I said, trying to be patient. "Theo and Wes are like walking security cameras. We can safely assume there are two

Others that can do the same thing. There's no point trying to sneak up on them because they already know we're here and they're waiting for us. They know they're outnumbered, but they don't care. They're not scared, but you should be."

***

I led the Deviants into the open bay of the hangar and waved for the rest of the Sophisticates to stay just outside. At this point, they were more of a liability than anything, but I wanted there to be witnesses and at least some measure of protection for the soldiers stationed outside. I had no idea what Delia Younglove wanted or if I was going to make it through this encounter unscathed. If my group of Deviants couldn't stop the Others, I wanted to give the rest of the soldiers outside a fighting chance. Fifty-three Mandates was better than nothing.

I knew there was a chance I could die tonight. At least I could feel good about my decision to keep Cleo far from the danger. I'd spent so long trying to figure out how to protect her from the Program and what they wanted to use her for, it never occurred to me that I might have to protect her by leaving her behind. I was no martyr, though. I wasn't going to sacrifice myself for the Program. I was going to do my best to protect my team and the rest of the innocent people on base, but I also had every intention of getting back to Cleo.

As I strode confidently into the huge building, I looked up at the hostages who were dangling in large nets hung from the ceiling. Many were dressed in fatigues and most of them were conscious, reaching through the holes of the nets, begging for my help. I passed under a woman in a business suit whose bun was disheveled. Black smudges of make-up streaked down her cheeks, ragged confessions of her frightened tears.

"Help me," she begged. "Please, I have children. Don't let me die."

I wanted to offer her words of comfort, but I was on the hunt now and I couldn't allow myself the distraction of compassion. I couldn't see any of the Others yet, but I knew they were there. I could smell them. I could sense them. But the scents of the Others, which I recognized from The Rink, were intermingled with those of the many hostages. I assumed that was part of their strategy—to confuse my tracking abilities.

"Stop right there, Osbourne," a voice echoed through the cavernous building. It was Delia Younglove, her voice easily recognizable.

I raised my fist, halting Quinnie and the rest of the Deviants behind me. The only living people I could see were the hostages suspended from the ceiling, their sobs echoing brokenly in the bright room.

"We won't be staying long," Delia said. "So there's no use getting worked up and making things messier than they need to be. We just wanted to pass along a message."

"I think we got your message loud and clear," I said, looking around. Aside from the Air Force Two plane that survived the earlier attack, there were two dark SUVs with tinted windows at the far end of the building. Delia's voice was coming from that direction.

Delia laughed. "Oh, really? And what message is that, Tracker?"

"You have power and you're not afraid to use it. I already know that. What I don't know is what you want."

"Oh, that's easy," Delia purred, stepping out from behind one of the SUVs just far enough that I could see her face. "I want Cassandra back."

At the sight of Delia, my fingers twitched, instinctively reaching for my gun. She was far away, but not far enough. I could still easily put a bullet through her forehead and end it all right here. But I knew that the Others probably had at least a dozen weapons already trained on me, the Deviants, and the hostages. And not all of the weapons would be gunfire. I still remembered the fireballs from The Rink. I couldn't start a war in here and risk so many lives if there was a possibility that it could have a better outcome. I just had to be patient.

"Now, now," Delia admonished. "Don't be so eager, Tracker. If you reach for your weapon, Euri will blow your head off before you even get your gun out of its holster."

I glanced to where Delia was pointing and saw a familiar face behind the barrel of a gun that was pointing directly at me. My duplicate was crouching behind the landing gear of the plane. It was like looking in a mirror. Actually, it was like getting a glimpse of what my victims must see in the last moments of their lives—merciless green eyes without an ounce of regret, ready to do what they were ordered to do. I could tell Euri was good at following orders. I was good at following orders, too.

I turned my gaze back on Delia. "Cassandra's not here with us right now, she's still recovering from her last visit with you."

I'd meant to speak calmly, but remembering the torture I'd seen Cassie put through, I just couldn't seem to keep my composure. My mouth was rigid and the words had to fight their way past my teeth. I didn't want to just kill Delia, I wanted to wrap my hands around her throat and watch the life drain out of her eyes. For

Cassie. For Cleo. For all the hostages hanging from the ceiling, begging for their lives. For all the victims outside that were zipped up in black body bags.

I was both exhilarated and disgusted with my urge to kill. Sometimes I felt like it was too hard to hold onto my humanity when I was dealing out death so often. Every time I pulled the trigger, a part of my soul shriveled up and died. At what point would I finally say "no" to the Program and "yes" to my conscience? At what point would I finally choose to become just a man and not an assassin? It was so easy to be the killer, and at the same time it was so hard.

Delia interrupted my thoughts. "I'm well aware she's not with you, Tracker. However, she will be delivered to me, under the conditions that I set. The longer I have to wait, the more places I will attack. This and the casino in Vegas are just the beginning."

The casino in Vegas? She had to be bluffing.

"You're lying. The casino bombing occurred long before Cassie was ever taken by you."

"The casino bombing had nothing to do with Cassandra. My soldiers needed a training exercise and Vegas needed a dose of reality. People like that have no idea what those of us in the Program have been forced to sacrifice. They think only of their own pleasure, not of the suffering of others." Delia swiped the hair away from her face with the back of her hand.

"What are you training for?" I asked, knowing I wouldn't get a straight answer, but hoping to get a clue about Delia's intentions.

"Revenge. We're training for my revenge," Delia said simply. "Enough questions. I will be contacting the Academy to let them know how I would like Cassandra delivered to me."

"Why not just tell me now?" I asked. I wished that I knew for sure where the rest of the Others were. The only one I could see was Euri. I knew that capturing them was likely no longer an option. If they were willing to bomb a casino and kill innocent people on a military base, they were nothing less than terrorists. The first lesson I learned as a Deviant was that the Program didn't negotiate with terrorists. They terminated them. Or rather, I terminated them.

The sneer that slipped onto Delia's face was lethal. "Because you are part of the message."

Delia ducked behind the car and even though he was far away, I heard Euri shifting. I reacted immediately.

"Down!" I yelled, turning and tackling as many of the Deviants behind me as I could.

I fell to the ground on top of Quinnie as a bullet ricocheted off the concrete floor where I'd just been standing.

"Get off me!" Quinnie yelled as I shifted and reached for my gun. I rolled with her in my arms as another bullet hit close by.

"I'm trying to protect you," I growled as I pushed her backwards and swiveled around into a crouch, pulling my guns out of their holsters. I fired off four shots with my right hand, aiming for the tires of the SUVs and hitting them with my usual precision. With my left hand, I fired toward the plane, forcing Euri to duck behind the wheel for protection.

"Are you too stupid to take cover?" Quinnie spat, jumping in front of me as the doors to the SUVs opened and the Others exited the now disabled vehicles.

I tried to push Quinnie behind me again, but she defiantly moved farther in front of me, her hands moving in front of her body like she was doing some sort of interpretive dance. A thin, electrical field materialized in front of her, spinning outward from her hands.

"What are you doing?" I asked, unsure whether I should keep shooting. Euri fired a series of shots at Quinnie and the bullets hit the bright blue swirl of crackling electricity and deflected back toward him. He dove out of the way as a bullet hit the wheel of the plane, causing it to hiss ominously.

"Electromagnetic force field. My body is the electrical field and my hands are creating the moving charges for the magnetic field. I was reading about it in a book Younglove gave to me—say hello to your own personal Lorentz Force. You should be able to fire through it, I'm only deflecting from the other side of the force field. Of course, that's my theory. I haven't had a chance to test it out yet."

I was surprised that Quinnie not only knew a word as long as electromagnetic, but that she knew what it meant as well. I wasn't surprised that she could create the force field, just that she understood it. Quinnie was usually more interested in the color of her nails than in physics—or any other class that took time from her rigorous beauty schedule.

I didn't wait for any further explanation. I could hear Younglove yelling at the Others to follow her out of the hangar since the SUVs were disabled. They were on the run and I knew we had to act quickly. Euri was trapped, hiding behind a wheel of the plane, unsure whether he wanted to risk my aim. Sharp black blades came hissing past me as Marty tried to flush Euri out of his hiding place. The blades embedded in the side of the plane or clattered noisily along the concrete floor near him, but none found their mark. Euri called for backup just as a volley of fireballs exploded against Quinnie's bright blue shield. She grunted with each strike and the swirling electricity flickered briefly before the motion of her hands brought it back up to strength.

I sighted down the barrel of my gun, finding Persephone half-hidden behind one of the SUVs. I had a perfect shot of her forehead and the red light danced eerily along the skin above her eyebrows. Her eyes raised upward as if she could see the light on her skin. Then she looked back at me and smiled. My finger lightly rested on the trigger. I knew I had to pull it, but I couldn't make myself do it. I knew killing her was the right thing to do. So many people had died at her hands tonight and in Vegas, but...she looked just like Cleo. There was a sliver of doubt in my mind that made me incapable of doing what I knew I should. Before the Others, I'd never felt doubt or hesitation on a mission. When there was a target, I pulled the trigger. Always.

My heart hammered in my chest, fear and anxiety making my hands shake with uncertainty. All I could see was Cleo's face at the end of the barrel of my gun. And even though I knew it was really the face of a cold-blooded killer, I couldn't take the shot. My brain was telling me that the girl on the other side of the hangar was Persephone, but after years of watching Cleo from afar and slowly becoming fascinated with her, I couldn't seem to make my heart see the truth. I told myself that the beautiful, brown-haired girl with fire on her fingertips wasn't Cleo. Deep down I knew that no matter how much they looked alike, they weren't the same person, but my heart couldn't accept it.

"Shoot her!" Quinnie screamed as another fireball shattered against her stormy shield of electricity. Flames roared over the edges of the force field and Quinnie dropped to the ground as the shield disappeared. Persephone grinned at me and threw another fireball as she ducked behind the SUV. I just managed to shove a limp Quinnie to the side as a mini explosion tore a hole into the floor barely ten feet away. The force of it knocked me down, showering me with chunks of broken concrete.

I quickly regained my footing, ignoring the stinging pain from the blast's shrapnel. As soon as I saw Euri make a break for the door, I aimed at his leg and took a shot. He fell to the ground, screaming in frustration. He pointed his gun at me, and then seemed to change his mind. He raised his arm and shot at one of the hostages close to him. His perfect aim sheared the rope that held the net aloft and the woman inside crashed to the ground in front of him, shielding him from my fire. Euri knew he could've taken a shot at me, but he also knew he would've taken another hit in return. The only hope he had was to protect himself with a hostage.

Euri pushed himself to a standing position, favoring the leg that I'd shot. He was holding the woman to his chest as a shield, the gun pressed firmly against her skull as he threatened her into shuffling toward the open hangar door behind him. Euri definitely knew what he was doing because I couldn't find an open target. To kill him, I'd have to kill his shield.

I stalked forward, careful not to put myself too close to Euri in case he decided to aim his gun at his hunter instead of his hostage. Reaching the open bay door, he pulled the woman with him and then ducked through, pushing her back inside once he was lost in the darkness. The sounds of explosions outside were accompanied by tremors that rocked the building. I could feel the vibrations through the ground as I stumbled forward.

I ran across the hangar toward the door, darting behind objects for cover, not sure whether Euri was waiting outside for me to run headlong into a trap. I could hear footsteps behind me and I quickly chanced a look back to see that Marty and Dexter were following me. Quinnie was still lying limp on the ground and Eva and Sadie were standing next to her—their guns drawn, looking for danger. Quinnie's electrical force field was gone and she looked like she was unconscious.

The sounds of gunshots and engines roaring to life outside spurred me to run recklessly across the remaining distance of the building. When I reached the open door, I peered cautiously out into the darkness and saw the tail lights of two vehicles far off in the distance; too far for me to make a successful shot with my pistol. I could have made the shot with my sniper rifle, but it was still packed away in the SUV.

Frustrated, I looked around and saw bodies littering the ground near the perimeter where the soldiers had been stationed. Small fires fed hungrily on the wreckage where blackened concrete barriers had been blasted apart. It looked as if several vehicles were missing from the barricade that had originally surrounded the hangar.

Captain Jefferson came running toward the doorway, but then slowed as he eyed me and the gun hanging at my side.

"Osbourne Dracone, Sophisticate 76547, Assassin 93," I said, rattling off my identification so that the captain would know it was me and not an imposter. Although, come to think of it, Delia Younglove likely had given all of our personal information to the Others to use anyway. Remembering what the captain said earlier about missing tattoos, I pulled my sleeve back and showed him my forearm, complete with Sophisticate tattoo.

The captain nodded. "They got away," he explained. "Stole two SUVs and disabled the rest."

"Disabled?" I asked, tearing my gaze from the captain to look in the direction where the retreating taillights had gone.

"When they came out, all hell broke loose. Lightning strikes, balls of fire, and some kind of liquid that burns." He looked around. "My men took cover. The Others stole two vehicles, and when the soldiers tried to start their cruisers to go after them...nothing. All these cars are dead, they won't start."

"All of them?" I asked, noticing for the first time that the head-lights were all off and that dark shapes were crawling in and out of the vehicles, apparently trying to bring them back to life.

"Dead. Just like the planes," Jefferson explained.

Ozzy

6

A Baker's Dozen

I couldn't stop thinking of what the base must have been like a few hours ago when, without explanation, planes started plummeting out of the sky into the unyielding ground below. The attack could have come in any number of ways. Eva's twin could control radio and sound waves, so it was possible that she used her skills to interfere with the navigation systems of the aircraft. Maybe it was a combination attack between Eva's and Cleo's twins. I didn't put it past Persephone to use fireballs to disable the planes and vehicles. Even Quinnie's twin, Elysia, could have used her electrical skills to cause havoc. Whatever form the attack had taken, I was sure it had been horrific and terrifying for those involved.

For the first time, I began to see the ways in which the Program planned to use the Deviant Dozen. How easy it was for a handful of teenagers to completely destroy a military base with no more than their bodies and minds.

Human weapons indeed.

My head throbbed as I considered how the attack might have been orchestrated. Defending against something like this had never even been considered as a possibility. The Deviant Dozen were meant to be a tool to use, not something to defend against. The rules had completely changed and the Program was unprepared for the mess they had made. There was no question that it was the Program's mess because clearly, the Others were some sort of byproduct of the Deviant Dozen.

"Do you think they're already off base?" I asked Captain Jefferson.

"I called the front gate, but there was no answer," Jefferson explained. "I think the perpetrators have already left the grounds."

"Can the vehicles they stole be located?" I asked, ignoring the visions that were now plaguing me.

"Yes, we can track them. Would you like to go after them or should I have a team sent?"

"I'll go," I said. "I'm sure they'll ditch the vehicles, but I'd still like to go search for clues. Let me gather up the rest of the Deviants and make sure they're all okay."

"Sure."

"I'll be leaving the rest of the Sophisticate cadets here to assist you with cleanup and additional defense."

"I appreciate that," Jefferson said. "We could use the help."

It didn't escape my notice that the Mandates of St. Ignatius were slowly being spread out across the country to clean up the destruction that Delia was leaving in her wake. Whether the Program realized it or not, I knew it was all part of Delia's plan—her revenge. She was weakening us.

I started walking back to the brightly lit hangar, but turned to face the captain again. "Did you lose anyone when the Others escaped?" My eyes roamed over the area where bodies were scattered across the scorched earth. I noticed that medics were now tending to those dark shapes with the help of handheld flashlights.

The captain's mouth pressed into a hard line before he spoke. "I'm not sure yet, but after what they did earlier tonight, I doubt that we made it out of this unscathed." His eyes were fiercely dark, glittering with fury. "You have to find them."

"I will," I promised.

"And kill them," Jefferson demanded.

I nodded.

Even knowing what they had done and knowing what they planned to do, could I really find the resolve to kill other teens who looked like my friends? Could I really kill someone that looked like me? I'd already proven that I couldn't be trusted to even maim Cleo's twin, let alone kill her. Besides, the Others were just kids.

I was in trouble. For once, I didn't think I could do what I'd been designed to do. I couldn't eliminate the threat.

It seemed the assassin had finally found his conscience.

***

Just inside the door to the hangar, I found Marty and Dexter watching as I finished my conversation with Captain Jefferson.

"They got away?" Dexter asked.

"For now. How is everyone?" I noticed that the rest of the Sophisticates finally entered the building and were working at getting the hostages safely lowered from the ceiling. I made my way over to Quinnie, Eva, and Sadie. Quinnie was now sitting up, her head resting in her hands. She looked like she was going to be sick.

"How do you feel?" I asked, kicking the side of her expensive trainers with the toe of my boot.

She looked up at me through her knotted hair. "Narfy."

"Has she been talking nonsense since she came to?" I asked Eva.

"Narfy," Eva repeated. "Nauseous...barfy...narfy. I suggest you and those expensive boots back away."

I didn't back away. Quinnie might look like she was going to vomit, and she might even need to vomit, but she had too much willpower and pride to ever do something as humiliating as throw up in front of everyone. It'd be too much of a sign of weakness and Quinnie never showed weakness. I knew my shoes were safe.

"That was amazing what you did with the force field," I said, instead.

"You don't have to tell me that, I was there." Quinnie moaned, dropping her head between her knees.

"You must be sick if you can't even come up with a proper insult," I replied.

Quinnie lifted her head just long enough to glare at me and give me the middle finger.

"Ozzy," Dexter called, "there's something here you should see." He was crouched on the floor in front of a teenager with blond hair who was sitting in the middle of a collapsed net.

I left Quinnie to her misery and moved to stand behind Dexter's shoulder to inspect the boy, who looked like he was about my age.

"Who is this?" I asked.

"One of the hostages. He said he was brought here by Delia."

The boy's hair was a shaggy golden yellow that fell across his forehead. He was staring at the floor and looked just as frightened as the rest of the hostages.

"What's your name?" I asked.

"Rune."

"Rune? Is that a first or last name?"

The boy shrugged. "I don't know. That's just what they called me."

"Why were you with Delia?" I pressed.

"I...I don't remember." The boy's eyes darted around the room as if looking for escape.

"Where are you from?"

"I don't remember that either."

"What *do* you remember?" I snapped. The boy cringed and I regretted my tone immediately. I was used to dealing with cocky Sophisticates. This boy looked terrified.

"I remember being tied up and gagged in the back of an SUV, but I don't know how I got there and I have no idea why I'm here or who I am." His eyes couldn't seem to find the courage to meet my gaze and he neurotically twisted a handful of the net in his grip. I could see that there were bruises around his wrists and what looked like another one across his right cheek.

"Stanley!" I called out to the Hound who was organizing the rescue of the hostages.

Stanley gave a few remaining directions to the group of cadets around him and then jogged to my side. "What's going on?"

"I need your phone to send a message to the Academy."

Stanley handed over his phone and I sent a text to Professor Younglove with a quick explanation of what had transpired.

"Rune," I said. When the boy looked up, I took his picture with the phone, but before I could text it to Younglove, the phone rang. She must have been waiting for my message.

I answered it. "Professor."

"They got away?" She was irritated.

"Yes, but we're using GPS to track the vehicles they stole. The Deviants and I plan to leave as soon as we finish here at the base." I briefly told her about the interaction with Delia and the Others.

"So, she did all this merely to give us the message that she wants Cassandra back?" Younglove was doubtful.

I didn't blame her. It was a lot of trouble to go to, and a huge risk to take, when she could have just claimed responsibility for the Vegas casino attack and made a threat over the phone. Delia exposed herself and the Others recklessly by attacking Andrews Air Force Base.

"That's what she said," I responded. "And she's prepared to continue with attacks until she gets what she wants."

"I see. Did she say why she wants Cassandra?"

"Not exactly."

Younglove's tone became curt. "Well, what *did* she say?"

"Only that she wants revenge."

"Revenge..." The word hung in the air, but Younglove didn't bother to finish her thought.

"Do you know why she wants revenge?" I asked.

There was a moment of silence. "You've met my sister, haven't you, Osbourne?"

"Obviously."

"And you've met me."

"Clearly."

"We were part of the first attempts at genetic modification for the Deviation project. My sister and I were among the few trials that survived. The experiments were not as successful as the

Program hoped. There were side effects—some worse than others. Delia was always angry at our parents for giving us to the Program, and at the Program for using us as guinea pigs, but I thought she had moved on and accepted things the way they were. She seemed to enjoy her position at the University. I always knew she was angry, but..."

"She wants revenge on the Program for what they did to her," I said. I had to admit, I didn't blame Delia at all. I hated the Program for what I was forced to do even though I was a successful experiment. Delia Younglove, leader of the psychotic group of Others, was the poster child for experimentation gone wrong. She had every right to be pissed.

"That would be my guess. And I'm guessing that she is obsessed with Cassandra because she is exhibiting the skills that Delia was intended to possess. As I mentioned, Delia's genetic modification was a failure and there were unwelcome side effects." Younglove's voice was part disappointment and part understanding. I wondered, not for the first time, just how trustworthy the Professor was. Blood was a strong connection. When push came to shove, would Twyla Younglove side with her sister or the Program?

"Do I have permission to use the Deviants to help me track the vehicles the Others stole?" I asked.

"Yes. You better get on your way. You probably won't find much. I'm sure she had this planned out to the very last detail."

"That was my thought too, but there might be something. Everyone makes mistakes, even Sophisticates. I have to at least check."

"Agreed."

"There's just one more thing I needed to get your opinion on before we leave."

"Yes?"

"One of the hostages, a teenage boy, was brought to the base with Delia and the Others."

"They brought a hostage with them? Have you questioned him?"

"I have, but he seems to be suffering from some memory loss. All he remembers is that they called him Rune."

"Is he a Sophisticate?"

"I don't think so, there's no tattoo. Maybe I could send you a picture and see if you recognize him. I don't know what to do with him at this point. I'm sending you the photo now." I pulled the phone from my ear and clicked a few buttons to send Rune's picture to Younglove. A few seconds later I heard a dinging sound come from my earpiece as the photo arrived on Younglove's phone. It was followed by a sharp intake of breath.

"I'll be there within two hours. Do not leave."

I looked at Rune who was now cautiously peering up at me through the jagged hair that covered his eyes.

"Who is he?" I asked.

"He's the last of the Dozen."

"That doesn't make any sense. Cassandra was number 12, she was the last of the Dozen."

"You don't understand," Younglove said excitedly. "The Deviant Dozen was the brainchild of Russell Baker, the man at the very top of the Program leadership. Before you were known as the Deviant Dozen, you were referred to as Baker's Dozen. Rune is number 13."

Cleo

Accusations

The one good thing about Quinnie going on the mission was that I didn't have to worry about her for a few days. No one to cast dirty looks my way during meals, no one to insult me during the workshop, and no one to taunt me in the locker room before derby practice. Quinnie-free days were great days. If only I could ignore the fact that Quinnie was with Ozzy, I'd be much happier. I couldn't stop thinking about the stupid picture.

"What do you think they're doing right now?" Arabella asked as we made our way to our first class.

"Who?"

"The Sophisticates that Dean Overton and Professor Younglove sent away last night."

"I don't know." I yawned my last word. I never managed to fall asleep again after the alarm, but I was at least smart enough to be grateful my name wasn't called.

"Have you heard from Ozzy?"

I shook my head. "Not since Monday night." I didn't want to admit to her just how much it hurt that he hadn't tried to explain the picture of him and Quinnie. He must have seen it, right? Had he changed his mind about me? Was Quinnie what he wanted now?

"Did you talk to Ms. Petticoat about seeing Cassie?"

"She said Cassie isn't ready to see me. They explained to her about the Others, but Ms. Petticoat said Cassie is having a hard time dealing with everything. She feels betrayed and is having difficulty with her deviation, so they're keeping her alone in the infirmary for now." I looked down at my feet and my voice dropped. "I just want to see her."

Arabella draped her arm over my shoulder. "You will soon, don't worry."

I nodded.

"Do you think Ozzy found anything at The Rink?" she asked, changing the subject.

"I hope so. I want Delia and the Others to burn for what they did to Cassie."

"Speaking of the Others, Sterling and I had an idea about them."

"What kind of idea?"

"We think they were failed experiments."

"It looked like they were pretty successful to me." Fireballs, whips of electricity, and well-aimed explosions. And that was just two of the Others. Who knew what the rest of them could do?

"No, I mean failed experiments as in we don't think they were meant to go full-term. Why else would they be hiding out in a run-down roller rink? If they were *meant to be*, they'd be here with us. We think someone completed an abandoned experiment. Eleven or twelve experiments, actually."

"Who? Delia Younglove?"

Arabella shrugged. "Maybe. I don't know anything about the woman, but she's definitely at the top of our suspect list. She appeared to be in charge of them. We need to do some research on our own. If Professor Younglove's sister is involved, we can't really trust the professor."

"Did you ever really trust her?"

Arabella shook her head, confirming my assumption. Although Twyla Younglove was far more acceptable as a mentor than her sister, Delia, neither woman was maternal or friendly, or even remotely trustworthy in my opinion.

"I'm going to talk to Professor Lawless, though. If anyone can give us some insight into this mess, it's him."

A sudden push from behind sent my backpack cartwheeling down the hallway right before I went sprawling across the floor after it. I slid a few feet before I hit the wall, my face absorbing the impact.

"Cleo!" Arabella was already at my side, trying to help me to my feet. "Are you okay? What the hell did you trip over?"

"Didn't trip," I answered, waving Arabella's helpful hands away. I pushed myself into a sitting position before dropping my head between my knees. My face was throbbing—a painful, pulsing, warning that something might be broken. Immediately, I noticed drops of blood splattering on the floor between my feet. Fabulous. My nose was bleeding. As I pinched the bridge of my nose and tilted my head back, I made eye contact with a guy who was large and angry. His thick head rested on his muscular shoulders like a boulder balancing on the edge of a rocky cliff.

"How long did you think you could avoid me?" he asked, fists clenched at his sides.

"I wasn't avoiding you," I answered in confusion. "I don't even know you."

That wasn't entirely true, I recognized him from weapons class. I was pretty confident his name was Mike. Or Mark. Or maybe it was Matt. It definitely started with an M. Whatever his name was, I had no idea why he was so pissed at me.

"Did you think I didn't see it was you? I'm not stupid, you know."

Arabella stood, raising herself to her full height—all five foot nothing of it.

"I don't know what your problem is, Michael, but I'll bet it's some kind of mental condition that's pretty hard to pronounce."

Ah. So it was Michael.

"You better have a good explanation," she continued, "or I'm going to rip you a new one." Arabella jammed her finger into his chest, and even though I was pretty sure it didn't hurt him, he flinched.

Michael took a look at Arabella and surprisingly, some of his rage seemed to disappear. Despite her diminutive size, no one really wanted to mess with Arabella. And with good reason. She had anger issues. If only they knew the full truth of the kind of damage she could do.

"She tripped me in the cafeteria," he accused, pointing a thick finger at me. "I dropped my breakfast."

"You're lying," Arabella huffed, dismissing his accusation. "I was with her at breakfast."

Michael stiffened, probably weighing the risks of tossing Arabella down the hall as well.

"I know what I saw." The words squeezed through his clenched teeth.

"It wasn't me," I promised. I gingerly stood up, keeping my head tilted back.

"It wasn't Cleo," Arabella repeated, stepping in front of me and staring Michael down like they were on a roller derby track instead of in a hallway between classes.

"I don't need anyone to explain what I saw with my own eyes." He peered over Arabella's head, catching my gaze. "If you ever mess with me again, a bloody nose will be the least of your worries." He stalked off down the hall and when he passed my backpack, he viciously kicked it. The lump of worn fabric slammed into the wall, bursting at one of the seams, spilling books and papers across the stone floor.

Great. My backpack was now in tatters. I could feel the burn of frustrated tears at the corners of my eyes. I hurried over to my ruined bag and started gathering all of my stuff while still trying to keep the nosebleed under control. Arabella handed me a tissue and helped me pick everything up before it was trampled underfoot by cadets hurrying to class.

"Don't worry, I can fix this," Arabella said before handing me the stack of papers and books she'd rescued. She folded the ruined piece of fabric and stuffed it into her own bag.

I wondered if anyone could fix all the broken pieces of my life as easily.

***

It was time for derby practice. Finally.

The sound of wheels humming across the polished wood was music to my ears.

Speed. Power. Grace. Pushing. Shoving. Chasing.

I needed to get lost in the frenzy of practice for an hour. I tried several times to track down Younglove so I could talk to her about Cassie, curious as to when I'd be able to see her again, but the professor hadn't been in her office all day.

When Arabella and I rolled out onto the track for warm-ups, however, Younglove was seated in her usual spot, only this time she had a laptop on the table in front of her. She didn't bother to look up when the team started circling the track. We knew what to do. Five minutes of intense skating around the track and Younglove only took her attention away from the small screen in front of her long enough to flip the switch to turn the obstacles on.

I was ready. I vaulted over a low bar and then neatly ducked under one at waist height. I was in the middle of congratulating myself for staying upright when Maya stumbled into me, knocking me to the floor.

"Sorry," Maya called over her shoulder. I was quick to notice it wasn't actually an apology. The word didn't agree with Maya's tone of voice, but I got up and brushed myself off. I'd accidentally taken out my own teammates before, too. It was the nature of the sport—accidents happened.

But, the next time around, Maya stumbled into me again, pushing me toward a bar that had just appeared out of nowhere. With a swift contortion of my body, I avoided the bar only to trip over another I hadn't seen. I ended up skidding across the floor on my knee pads and wrist guards for a few feet before Maya fell on top of me.

"Oh. Watch where you're going," Maya scolded, as if it had been my fault.

I glanced toward Younglove, but the professor was still absorbed with whatever was on her laptop and was oblivious to what was happening on the track.

"What's your problem, Maya?" I demanded, standing up.

"My problem?" Maya asked, innocently. "Oh, I don't have one." She glared at me and then jumped back into the rush of skating bodies.

The rest of my teammates took turns tossing glances my way as they skated past. When Arabella sped by, she slowed down enough to lift her eyebrows in confusion and hold her hands up in question as if to ask, *"What's going on?"*

That's exactly what I wanted to know. Maya and I never had an argument before and I couldn't think of anything I'd done recently to offend her.

For the rest of practice, I had one objective. Avoid Maya. It was a lot harder than I would've guessed. Maya was definitely making an effort to use her blocker skills on me. If Younglove had been paying any attention, she would've been furious that Maya was avoiding the strategy of practice to focus on one player so relentlessly. But the professor wasn't paying attention, at least not to roller derby, and I ended up spending more time than usual sprawled out on the track.

An hour later, in the locker room, I was having trouble getting dressed thanks to the multitude of bruises and injuries Maya had caused, and I was even more frustrated than I'd been before practice. So much for snuffing out my jealous anger with exercise. Practice did more harm than good and the mood in the room was tense. Everyone looked nervously between Maya and me as if expecting a fistfight to break out. Maya was angry and no one knew why.

"What was that about?" Arabella muttered as she pulled a black t-shirt over her head.

I glanced toward Maya and met her cold, angry gaze. Her hair was wild and free and every bit the image of her derby name, *Afro-de-she-smack.* I sat down on the bench and pulled on my shoes. "I have no idea, but she's starting to piss me off. Do you think she's mad about what happened to Katie at the formal? Do you think she blames me since I was Quinnie's target?"

Arabella huffed. "What? No. How could she?"

"I don't know, but I'm going to find out." I stood up and walked toward Maya who was now standing with her hand on her hip, watching me approach, her caramel colored eyes hard and threatening.

"Got a problem, Clementine?"

"Just you."

There was a collective gasp from the rest of the Damsels. I wasn't the aggressive type, and I was easily a foot shorter and at least thirty pounds lighter in muscle mass than Maya. It was one thing to battle it out on the track where one could use speed and agility for protection. It was another thing to tempt fate by antagonizing a behemoth like Maya. She wasn't the biggest girl on the team, but she was big enough.

Maya stepped forward, intimidating and close. I felt as if I'd been swallowed in her shadow, but I didn't flinch or step away.

"Do you want to tell me why you were bullying me on the track or is it a secret?" I asked.

"Stop flirting with my man. In fact, stay away from him all together." Maya's head dipped low, her face coming threateningly close. I could see the beads of sweat still clinging to the edge of her hairline, and I could sense Maya's body tensing as if readying to pounce.

"Who is he?" I asked, annoyed. This was ridiculous. I hadn't flirted with anyone.

"Don't get smart with me." Maya's fist clenched and her voice shook with anger.

"How am I supposed to stay away from him if I don't know who he is?"

I felt the sting of the slap long after I'd stumbled from the impact and fallen over the bench behind me. Tears sprang to my eyes involuntarily, but not because I was hurt or scared. I was furious.

"Don't mess with me," Maya sneered. "I saw you hanging all over him earlier today in the hall, trying to kiss him—even after he told you he was dating me. And then when I came over, you ran off like the coward you are. Quinnie was right about you. You're a boyfriend snatcher and you better watch your back."

Maya turned and walked off, pushing her way through the rest of the Damsels. Their dirty looks weren't for her though, they were for me. The girl code was clear—you didn't mess with your friend's man. And Maya was a friend.

Or rather, *had* been a friend.

Arabella looked down at me. "Ew. Were you really trying to kiss Bernie? If you're trying to make Ozzy jealous, there are much better choices." Arabella checked behind her to make sure Maya hadn't overheard. "He's dated nearly everyone on the girl's football team. You could catch something just by looking at him."

"No, I wasn't kissing Bernie. I've never even met him." I extracted myself from the overturned bench and went to fetch my stuff. "What is going on with everyone? First, Matthew said I tripped him and now Maya thinks I'm trying to steal her boyfriend. Is everyone going crazy? Or is it just me?"

"Michael."

"What?"

"Michael was the one who blamed you for tripping him, not Matthew."

"Oh, yeah. That's right. Michael." I shook my head. *Was* I going crazy? Why couldn't I remember that guy's name? I used to have such a good memory.

Arabella looked at me as if she was thinking the same thing, but instead she said, "Come on. Let's get to dinner."

As we made our way to the dining hall, I tried to come up with an explanation as to why there were two cases of mistaken identity in one day. Was someone trying to frame me? If so, who?

Persephone?

The name popped in my mind and I immediately dismissed it. I was in a military academy for the Program. There were guards and cameras everywhere. We probably had more security surrounding us than the President of the United States. There was no way Persephone would break into a high security Program facility merely to torment me. What would be the point of that anyway? No. Persephone was on the run with Delia and the rest of the Others.

And Ozzy was tracking them.

***

Back in my room, after work detail, I immediately went to the computer to check my email.

Nothing from Ozzy. Or Quinnie.

Regret and relief.

I obsessively checked my email in between homework assignments, even long after lights out. When it became clear that I could no longer stay awake, I allowed myself to drift off into an uneasy sleep that was peppered with nightmares and visions. Blond curls cascading over muscular arms. Blue whips of electricity singeing skin. Fire burning away fabric. Dark basements with dirt floors. Green eyes. Cats clawing faces.

Blood. Fire. Light. Dark.

Accusations.

There was no alarm the next morning. There was only an inhuman screeching accompanied by a fist pounding on my door. I rolled over to look at the clock. It was only 5:30 in the morning. I still had ten more minutes of sleep before I had to get up for the morning run. I sat up in bed, shaking off the nightmares, trying to make sense of the noise at my door.

"Get out here, bitch! Get out here now! You can't hide in there forever. You have to come out some time."

I recognized the voice. It was Maya. And there was no way I was going to open the door. Maya sounded even angrier than she had been in the locker room. If Maya wanted in, she'd have to break down the damn door.

Unfortunately, she probably could.

There was no way I could sleep through the battering of my door, so I got up to get ready for the run. I shivered as I slipped out of the covers and my feet touched the unusually cold floor. As the ranting and raving continued, I considered slipping out through my window to avoid a confrontation with Maya, who was becoming more belligerent with every passing second. Belatedly, I noticed that my window was already slightly open, which would account for my overly chilly room. I didn't remember opening it last night, but I'd been so tired I realized that I must have. I pushed the window closed, shutting out the crisp morning air as one last shiver rattled my tired shoulders.

I could now hear other cadets coming to my door, trying to calm Maya down. Was she still mad about Bernie and the flirting that never happened?

"What's going on?" It sounded like Arabella, but the voice was muffled from being on the other side of the door.

"Look what she did to my door!" Maya screamed.

Her door? I didn't do anything to anyone's door. I'd been in my room all night. I could feel my fingers tingling in response to yet another accusation. This was getting out of hand and I was determined to set things straight. I crossed the room and jerked open my door. Every cadet on my floor was standing right outside, looking down the hall to where Maya was now standing, gesturing at the door to her room. It was obviously defaced, and it wasn't just graffiti or whipped cream or any other practical joke. Maya's door was covered in some of the most awful words I'd ever heard or seen. Words of hate and prejudice—bigotry in full color.

How could Maya think I would do that?

Every mussed up head of hair in the hallway turned toward me to reveal looks of horror and disgust.

As I stared in disbelief at the door, Maya pushed her way through the stunned mass of pajama-clad cadets and crashed into me, wrapping her hands around my neck.

CLEO

8

RED-HANDED

The chair in Professor Younglove's office was just as uncomfortable as I remembered. It didn't help that my neck was sore, thanks to Maya's massive man-hands. Thankfully, even as disgusted as they were by the desecrated door and Maya's allegations, the other girls managed to restrain her and get help before things ended badly. And with my fluctuating moods, things could have gone very badly for Maya and everyone else if I had lost control.

I sat in the hard chair, waiting for Younglove to show up. It was Maya's word against mine. I hoped the meeting was merely a formality. There were no witnesses and surely Younglove wouldn't believe that I was actually capable of something so heinous. If Quinnie were around, it would have been easy to believe that she was setting me up somehow, but she was gone. I couldn't think of anyone else that would have done that to Maya's door.

The one good thing that I could get out of my current situation was that I would finally get to talk to Younglove and ask her about

Cassie.

If she ever showed up.

I was about to get up and look for her when the office door opened and Younglove entered. She looked disappointed and angry. Great. Clearly, she talked to Maya first. Younglove walked to her desk and stood behind it, glaring down at me. She had a thin, plastic box in her hand and she was tapping it methodically on the desktop as if considering what to say.

"Would you like to explain why you defaced the door of a fellow cadet with such hateful words? Not just a fellow cadet, a teammate. I thought that you and Maya were friends."

"We were...I mean we are," I corrected myself. "I'd never do anything like that. I was in my room all night."

Younglove's hands stilled and the box rested on the desktop as the silence in the room became heavy and accusatory. "Are you sure that's the answer you want to stick with?"

"I didn't do it," I said, defiantly. I wished I could come up with something eloquent and believable, but those were the only words that seemed adequate.

Younglove answered by opening the box she was holding and pulling out a disk. She slid it into her computer and then turned the screen around so I could see. At the click of a button on the keyboard, a video popped up on the screen showing a recording of a dormitory hallway.

I looked up at Younglove in confusion. "What's this?"

"Just watch."

I let my gaze drop from Younglove's face and back to the video on the screen. Within seconds, a sliver of movement caught my eye as one of the doors opened inward. My stomach plummeted into confused nausea as I watched myself step out into the hallway, wearing Academy plaid and carrying several spray paint cans. I then watched in horror as the on-screen Cleo crept down the hall and proceeded to spray disgusting words and images all over another door. Maya's door.

I didn't say anything—couldn't say anything—as the Cleo on the video finished and quickly retreated back into my room. I stared at the screen long after the door shut and only looked away when the professor finally turned it off.

I looked up at Younglove again. "I was asleep. I swear. I don't know what's going on, but I know I didn't do that. That wasn't me."

"We found the paint cans in your room."

"No."

Younglove walked around the desk to stand next to me. When she reached out and grabbed my elbow, I flinched instinctively. Younglove turned my arm slightly. "You have paint on your forearm," she pointed out, indicating a patch of red.

I stared at the dried paint in horror. *No.* "No," I said again.

"I'm disappointed in you Clementine. This kind of behavior is completely unacceptable and so unlike you. I know it's been a hard adjustment for you, but this is inexcusable. Your punishment will be severe."

Fear wrapped around my throat as tightly as Maya's hands had. "Are you going to whip me?" I whispered.

Younglove's lips pursed tightly before she answered. "You won't be punished that severely. But this will go on your record. For this offense, you'll clean Maya's door immediately, and then for the next week, you'll be doing her work detail in addition to your own."

I felt relief flood through my body, loosening the fear that had been holding my breath tightly in its grip. I didn't deserve to be punished. I knew I wasn't capable of what I saw on the video. I still wasn't sure exactly what it was I saw on the video, but at least I wasn't going to be whipped. I would do the extra work detail because I didn't really have a choice, but I was also going to figure out what was going on. Someone was trying to frame me, but who and how? And most importantly, why?

Theo was a genius with video, could he have made a video like this? He tormented Quinnie on behalf of Wesley. Was he now trying to punish me for not returning Wesley's affections at the formal?

No. Theo was my friend, wasn't he? I managed to stall my conspiracy theory thoughts long enough to notice that Younglove was still looking at me, waiting for a response. A response. What should I say?

"What is Maya's work detail?" It's all I could think to ask.

"She works in the kitchen. She cleans dishes, scrubs pots, and mops floors. You'll report there after your work detail with Ms. Cain."

I nodded, numbly. It wasn't the worst punishment possible, but it still sucked. Shelving books was much more preferable to scrubbing burnt food off of pots and pans.

It's only one week, I reminded myself.

"May I go?"

Younglove motioned to the door. "Clean Maya's door before you do anything else. You'll find cleaning supplies have already been brought up for you."

Embarrassment settled around my shoulders as I reached for the door handle. The other girls would see me cleaning the door.

They would know that Younglove had convicted me of the accusation.

Right before I slipped through the doorway, I remembered the reason I was glad to see the professor in the first place. I turned back around to find Younglove still glaring at me.

"How is Cassie?" I asked, hopefully.

"About the same. A little better. It's taking longer than expected for her to accept her new condition. I'm not sure when she'll be ready for the Deviation Workshop, but it probably won't be as soon as I'd like," she admitted.

There was a lump in my throat that I couldn't manage to swallow down. "When will I be able to see her again?"

Younglove considered me for a moment. "After your little stunt today, I imagine it'll be a while," she answered dryly.

A while? How long was that?

There were a million things that I wanted to say. I wanted to demand to see my friend, to be given a chance to explain things to her myself. I wanted to insist that I was innocent, that I wasn't capable of doing the things I was accused of doing. I wanted to scream that no matter how many workshops I went to, I'd never become the weapon the Program wanted me to be, that I would tame the beast that lurked within me. I wanted to beg for my freedom, to be thrown out of the world of Sophisticates.

But, I knew that my declarations and promises and pleas would fall on deaf ears. So I clamped the words behind my lips and slipped through the door and into the hallway. The one thing I learned from being in the Program was how to pick my battles and this was one I knew I couldn't win. I would take my punishment until I could prove my innocence.

***

I managed to finish cleaning Maya's door just in time for a shower before breakfast. As the other girls came back from the morning run, I endured a few vicious insults and a volley of indignant glares. Thankfully, I didn't have to deal with Maya, whose stuff had already been moved to a different floor so she wouldn't have to interact with me. Fingers red from scrubbing and cheeks still flushed with embarrassment, I stood in the shower, the water scalding my skin as I tried to wash away the smell of the turpentine. The smell lingered, just like the shame of Maya's allegations. Neither was likely to wash off any time soon.

Entering the dining hall, I was bombarded with whispered insults and angry stares. It was like walking through a gauntlet of pure loathing. It didn't take long for the rumor of Maya's door to get around. Under the hateful glare of so many people, I felt dirty and tainted.

Despite the fact that most of the Academy thought the worst of me, Arabella stayed by my side, giving the stink eye to anyone who looked at me the wrong way. I didn't like the idea that Arabella might fall in disgrace along with me, but there was nothing I could say to get her to keep her distance. She was loyal to a fault. When I finally got my food and made my way to the table, Sterling, Wesley, and Theo were already there—watching me with uncertainty. Actually, Theo was staring at his breakfast, seemingly only interested in whether to eat his waffles or bacon first. I set my tray down and took a seat.

"Did you really do it?" Wesley asked.

"Of course she didn't!" Arabella came to my defense immediately. "This is Cleo we're talking about."

"Right, I know." Wesley eyed me warily. "It's just..."

"I didn't do it," I repeated for what felt like the millionth time in the last few hours.

"I heard you're being punished," Sterling pressed.

"Where'd you hear that?" I asked, my appetite ebbing away with every denial I was forced to make. I hadn't even had a chance to tell Arabella the full extent of my punishment yet.

"Maya is telling everyone that you have to do her work detail for a week. She's pretty excited about it," Theo mumbled offhandedly between bites of his waffle.

I groaned. Would there ever be a day when I wasn't the center of gossip and rumors at the Academy?

"I would never even think things like that, let alone paint them on someone's door," I promised.

"Then why is Younglove punishing you?" Sterling asked. "It's not like she has proof. Right? How can she believe Maya over you?"

"She has a video," I admitted, looking up from the table and stealing a glance at Theo to see his reaction, to gauge whether this revelation was a surprise to him or not.

Theo's fork was suspended midway to his mouth. "She has a video? Of you?" He appeared as surprised as I had been. He was either a very good actor, or not involved. I wanted to believe the latter.

"She has a video of someone that looks like me," I corrected. "That person spray painted the door, but it wasn't me."

"Someone that looks like you? Who else could it be? You don't exactly resemble any of the girls here," Wesley pointed out, nodding toward one of the large female football players as she walked past our table.

"Persephone looks like me." I crossed my arms defiantly.

"Yeah, but she's on the run with the Others. There's no way she could break into the Academy. Aside from Headquarters, it's the most secure location in the Program." Wesley snorted. "Right, Theo?"

Theo nodded, but his attention had finally left his breakfast and settled on me. "Arabella could look like you. If she wanted."

"What?" Arabella's screech was so loud, every head in the dining hall turned to look at us.

"I'm not saying you did it," Theo said, a smug smile on his face. "I'm just pointing out the obvious. We're brainstorming, right?"

"No. You're being a suicidal asshole if you think I'm going to let you throw me under the bus for this."

"The video showed someone coming out of my room, not Arabella's," I said, defending the one person, aside from myself, that I was sure was innocent. "But I know I didn't do it either. I was asleep."

"Maybe you were sleepwalking?" Sterling offered. "You can't be blamed for something you don't remember doing."

"It's not that I don't remember doing it. I didn't do it," I said. Again.

I could see doubt in the expressions of Sterling and Wesley. I hoped they wanted to believe I didn't do it; that they wanted to come up with an explanation to exonerate me, even under the evidence of a video. But I wasn't giving them anything except for a worthless "I didn't do it" and the outrageous explanation that my evil twin broke into a high security compound just to frame me. I didn't dare tell them about the paint cans in my room or the patch of paint on my arm that Younglove pointed out. I felt that would've put the final nail in my proverbial coffin.

Theo looked thoughtful, but he didn't ask any other questions. He was uncharacteristically quiet. That worried me. He wasn't eating anymore, either. That really worried me.

"Cleo, of course we believe you. But if there's video..." Wesley's voice trailed off. He couldn't finish the sentence.

"It. Wasn't. Me." I was pissed. The heat that suddenly consumed me was overwhelming and it felt like my blood was on fire. My fork was bending and melting in my grip. I tossed it to the side.

"I have to go." I stood up.

"Way to go, dude, you totally pissed her off," Theo said. "If Cleo is too mad to pig out, you know it's bad."

I grabbed my untouched breakfast, stalked to the trash can, and hurled the entire thing, tray and all, inside. I couldn't even muster the effort to be offended by Theo's observation. I was disappointed because Sterling didn't believe me. And aside from Arabella, he'd been my one other true ally since the beginning. Ozzy was gone, Cassie hated me, and Sterling suspected me.

In my heart, I believed I was innocent, but in the eyes of everyone else I was guilty. There were Maya's accusations. And a video. And paint cans. And paint on my arm.

In their eyes, I'd been caught red-handed.

Cleo

9

Cleo's Monster

On the way to the Deviant Workshop, I was beginning to feel relieved that I'd made it through half the day without being wrongly accused of something. I found myself constantly on edge, expecting anyone who looked at me to blame me for something horrific. What I couldn't understand was why Younglove still insisted on holding the Deviant Workshop. There were only five of us available to take the class—Arabella, Sterling, Theo, Wesley, and me.

Younglove didn't let us off easy with reading out of books. Since the discovery of the Others, she explained that our physical training was imperative. It wasn't just a matter of perfecting our skills for the sake of offering the Program bigger and better weapons. We had to be bigger and better than the weapons that were already out there—the Others. As far as Younglove was concerned, we could read books on our own time. The workshop was time for action.

"The five of you are light years behind the rest of the Deviant members. I want you to spend the next few days working on your deviations and perfecting your skills. I have a feeling it won't be long before we're facing off against the Others again, and I want you to be prepared. All of you."

Younglove's gaze settled on me and I had the distinct feeling that the words were meant for me specifically. Everyone else could use their skills effectively and on command. I was the only one holding back. I was the only one with a beast inside; an uncontrollable monster that fed on fury. I'd been trying my best to starve it and I would continue to starve it no matter how difficult it was.

I stood in the back corner of the gym, far from the others, staring at a target. I wasn't putting any effort into destroying it. I had no intention of ever using my deviation again.

"I know what you're doing," Younglove said, startling me. She appeared out of nowhere.

"Just following orders," I responded, glaring at the target as if I was attempting to burn it to the ground.

"No. You're staring at that target and counting down the seconds until the workshop ends. Why don't you want to use your deviation? You're probably the most powerful Deviant in the entire group, and yet you deny your abilities. You need to be in control in case you face off against the Others again."

I bit the inside of my lip before answering. "I'm trying, Professor, but it's no good," I lied. "Maybe I'm defective."

"You're not defective. You know how to use your power, you're just reluctant to do so. You just have to start using it," Younglove ordered.

No, I don't. And you can't make me.

"I can't make you," Younglove said, as if she could read my thoughts. "But for your sake, you really need to."

I wondered if that was a threat. I felt the spark of annoyance fluttering in my stomach, but I ignored it. I refused to let it grow into the hot seeds of anger. That's exactly what Younglove wanted.

"Are you having trouble sleeping at night?" Younglove asked. "Bouts of depression? Hopelessness? Forgetfulness? Confusion?"

I could sense that Younglove was staring at me and I finally turned to meet her gaze. I was feeling all those things, but I wasn't going to admit that to her. What was her point anyway?

"Your deviation is part of who you are, Clementine. Since you've started exhibiting, I'm sure you've felt the need to use it more often than you actually have. If you deny the urge, you're denying your body and mind an aspect of yourself it needs to explore. It's going to affect your sleep, your mood, your memory, and even your actions."

"What exactly are you trying to say?" I asked.

"I think you really believe you didn't deface Maya's door."

"That's because I didn't."

"And yet there is video proving that you did."

"That wasn't me," I swore. "And I'm going to prove it. Somehow."

"You know what I think?"

I didn't, but I had a feeling she was going to tell me anyway.

"I think," Younglove went on, "that you did it and just don't remember. I've heard the rumors of other issues you've had with fellow cadets and I think these occurrences are your mind's way of dealing with the fact that you are denying yourself the release you need. Your body and mind are rebelling, putting you into situations where you will be faced with confrontation and forced to use your powers. You just need to let your deviation happen. Wouldn't you rather learn how to control it instead of letting it control you?"

"It's not controlling me."

The look on Younglove's face made it clear that she didn't agree, but instead of arguing she said, "I expect to see some results soon."

As she turned to leave, I hurried to move in front of her. "How is Cassie?"

Younglove looked down her nose at me and blinked a few times before answering. "She's learning to control her deviation. She understands the importance. You seem to be the only Deviant who doesn't." Then she turned and walked toward Wesley and Theo, leaving me feeling small and worthless.

***

The locker room was nearly empty when I got there for derby practice on Wednesday night. I was glad to have Arabella at my side, although I felt like a coward for not wanting to face Maya alone. I was relieved to discover that Katie was the only one there.

"Katie!" Arabella and I exclaimed at the same time. We rushed over to hug her, excited yet careful.

"How are you?" I asked, squeezing the bigger girl gently as if I might break her.

"They finally let you out of the infirmary?" Arabella said, pushing me out of the way to get a hug of her own.

"I'm good." Katie was subdued and her swagger was missing. "Look," Katie started, her voice lowering as she stepped closer to us. "Something strange is going on and I just want to know..." She looked around and then her voice dropped even lower. "What did

Quinnie do to me?"

I glanced at Arabella, wondering what to say. We weren't allowed to talk about the Deviant Dozen or our skills, but at the same time, I didn't want to lie to Katie either. When we didn't answer immediately, Katie started to cry. Katie. Crying. It was like the world had been turned upside down. The only thing that would've been more absurd was if Arabella had been crying.

"What did Younglove tell you?" I asked.

Katie's lips flattened angrily. Younglove hadn't given her a real explanation. That much was clear.

The door to the locker room opened forcefully and we looked up just in time to see Younglove enter as if she knew Arabella and I were moments away from revealing the big secret about the Dozen.

"There you are," Younglove said, capturing me with her glare and trapping me into silence. "Come." She hooked her finger at me and then retreated through the door and into the arena. I followed quickly. Younglove turned to face me when the door shut behind us. "I think it's best if you don't come to derby practice today. You and Maya were too much of a distraction yesterday. I thought you'd work it out on your own, but as your actions overnight proved, you aren't capable." She took a deep breath and then released it slowly as she surveyed me like a troublesome appliance. "Professor Peck is expecting you in ten minutes. You're excused."

Professor Peck? Could this day get any worse?

When I didn't move, Younglove's voice rang out harshly. "Now."

"Yes, Professor," I responded. I could feel the anger looming inside, threatening to billow up out of me with the violence of storm clouds in the summer. I turned toward the locker room and flung the door open hard enough for it to bounce off the wall behind it. I stalked past Arabella, snatched my backpack off the bench, and hurried out before I was forced to answer any questions. Great. Another hour with Peck. It was probably the worst punishment I could've imagined. For Peck, it was probably a dream come true.

I didn't go straight to Peck's classroom. I intended to use every bit of the ten minutes I had before showing up for my punishment. I took the long way around so that I could go past the infirmary, hoping to be able to stop in briefly and talk to Ms. Petticoat to find out how Cassie was doing. Younglove clearly wasn't going to give me any information.

I really needed to concentrate more on figuring out why I had been accused of things I was certain I hadn't done. It wasn't me. Was it? The thought was brief, but strong. Of course I knew I wasn't capable of doing any of those things. Not knowingly at least. But what if Younglove was right? What if by caging the monster inside, I was losing a bit of my sanity? I had to admit that controlling my anger was incredibly hard at times. It took a lot of concentration and willpower. Was I losing myself to the monster inside and not even realizing it?

I finally reached the hospital wing and I quietly pushed the door open, just enough to peek inside. "Ms. Petticoat?" I called.

When no one answered, I stepped in and quickly made my way to the office, a small room just to the right. The door was closed so I walked closer to peer through the window to see if Ms. Petticoat was inside. The desk was neat and sparse, as immaculate and sterile looking as the rest of the infirmary. A flicker of motion caught my eyes and I focused on the glass in front of me to see my reflection staring back at me.

No. Not reflection. *Reflections.* Not one, but two reflections of myself. One Cleo was wild-eyed and horrified, mouth agape. The Cleo reflected over my shoulder was grinning—a terrible smile. The smile of a monster. My monster.

It was terrifying. Like walking into a dark room and staring into a mirror only to see a nightmare. The possibility of seeing a face staring back at me in the dark had always frightened me. My first instinct was to close my eyes and that's exactly what I did as I stood in front of Ms. Petticoat's door. When I finally mustered the courage to open my eyes again, the monster was gone.

I once told Sterling that I couldn't run from the devil because I couldn't run from myself. It was as true now as it was then. I couldn't run from the power inside, or the anger that seemed to rule me, or the fact that I didn't know myself anymore. I couldn't run from the all-consuming worry that maybe everyone was right, maybe I was going crazy, maybe I couldn't trust myself after all. I knew I couldn't run.

But I did anyway.

***

"How was your date with Peck?" Arabella asked at dinner.

"I'm not going to be able to move tomorrow. It was worse than conditioning class because I was the only one there for her to torment," I complained.

"I've got a heating pad you can borrow tonight, if you need it," Arabella offered.

"I hope you have a full body model, because everything hurts."

She laughed and we ate in comfortable silence for a few minutes. I finally got the courage to ask the question that had been plaguing my thoughts since the workshop and my strange visit to the infirmary.

"Arabella, do you feel like you have to use your deviation on a regular basis? Like it's an itch you have to scratch or something?"

She sat quietly for a moment, considering my question. "I don't know. I like using it, but I've never really thought about it in the sense that I feel like I *have* to use it. Why?" Arabella tore into a breadstick like a dog gnawing on a bone.

"Just something Younglove said. She seems to think my refusal to use my deviation might be causing me some issues."

"Refusal? I thought you just couldn't control it," Wesley said.

"What kind of issues?" Sterling asked at the same time.

I turned to Wesley. "I can't control it, but I also try not to use it."

"What issues?" Sterling asked again.

I took a deep breath. "She thinks that by not using my deviation, it might be causing me to be a little unbalanced."

"Unbalanced?" Wesley repeated the word like he'd never heard it before and was seeing how it felt on his tongue.

"She thinks you're going crazy." Theo laughed.

"It's not funny." I was so sure that I was innocent of all the things I'd been accused of in the last few days, but was I really innocent? Could Younglove be right? Were my body and mind rebelling and making me do things I couldn't remember? Seeing a crazy reflection of myself and my monster in the infirmary window certainly wasn't a good sign. I knew that much.

"Is it true, though?" Wesley asked.

I glared at him. Even though I was starting to question myself, Wesley's lack of trust was really starting to irritate me.

It was 10:30 that night when I stumbled back to my room—heart heavy, body exhausted, and hands raw and waterlogged. I spent an hour with Professor Peck moving all the plate weights from one side of the gym to the other. There seemed no purpose behind it other than to wear me out. Or down. Yes, definitely to wear me down.

The rest of the night should've been easy enough with only dinner and work detail at the library, but then I had to return to the kitchen to do Maya's work detail. Ms. Goddard, the portly, red-faced woman in charge of the kitchen, led me over to the large sink without so much as a friendly greeting. Her curt orders were unintelligible, but I figured out pretty quickly what I was supposed to do.

Scrub. Scrape. Scour.

Sitting on my bed, I stared at my hands. The skin was raw and red, already dried and cracked. It was going to be a long week. How did Maya do this every night? I only had half an hour to get my homework done before lights out and right then, I wasn't sure I could coerce my hands to hold my pen to write, or my mind to concentrate. All I wanted to do was fall into bed, give in to deep sleep, and wake up to find out this was all a dream—the accusations, Maya, Cassie, the Academy, the dish scrubbing. I wanted everything back to the way it was a few months ago.

And then I remembered Arabella, Sterling, and Ozzy.

Well. Maybe I didn't want everything back to the way it was.

I pulled the laptop off my desk and onto my bed, intent on doing at least some research for my foreign language class with Professor Alcott before going to sleep. Instead, I found myself navigating to my email program. Nothing new. No emails from Arabella. Nothing from Ozzy.

I ignored the lack of Ozzy emails, determined not to be jealous, and started my research. I stayed up much later than I intended and was so drained that when I finally climbed between my sheets, I was sure that I would sleep heavily until it was time for the morning run. But when sleep overtook me, the nightmares invaded, poisoning my dreams and holding me hostage with my own fears and tainted memories.

It wasn't Persephone burning with anger and fueled by flames of hate this time. It was me. I had finally succumbed to the beast inside. I was a helpless prisoner of my nightmares, trapped inside the monster I'd become. Outside I was like Persephone, dealing death and destruction in an indiscriminate fiery hell, but inside...inside I was screaming for release and unable to fight or escape what I had become.

I was trapped inside the beast.

Ozzy

10

Rune

I was exhausted. We spent the last two days at Andrews Air Force Base and I was ready to go back home to the Academy. After an unsuccessful attempt at interviewing Rune, who insisted he couldn't remember anything, Younglove had him put through a battery of medical tests to confirm that his genetics were what she assumed. She was right. He had the same genetic modifications as the Deviant Dozen's thirteenth member, Sebastian. At least that's what the tests suggested. Rune hadn't been able, or willing, to perform his supposed deviation.

He claimed amnesia.

I claimed bullshit.

Younglove claimed he was valuable.

It was mid-morning on Friday before we left the base and headed back home. Unlike Younglove—I was distrustful of Rune and his supposed amnesia. Why would Delia bring a Deviant Other to the base and leave him as a hostage? Was he truly broken or was he a spy? Delia had to know that if she left Rune behind, he'd be taken to St. Ignatius. Clearly, she wanted him to be taken and I wasn't happy being forced to bow to Delia's wishes. But as Younglove pointed out, we couldn't exactly leave Rune behind. Threat or victim, he had to be taken into custody.

I glanced over at Rune, who was staring blankly out the window. His gaze was distant and he seemed distracted. Not just distracted, almost vacant.

Maybe he was as much a victim as Cassie had been. Who knows what kind of torture he might have been subjected to? Even if Rune was a spy, he was outnumbered at the Academy. Perhaps we could find out more information about Delia and the Others from him.

The SUV was quiet on the way back. After the interviews and debriefing, we spent most of our time helping with clean up at the base. Even with the fifty-three Sophisticates that the Academy sent to help, there was a lot of work to do. It had been two days of physical and emotional exertion with little chance for rest.

Everyone but Rune and I had fallen asleep by the time we finally entered Academy grounds. It was early afternoon and the sun glared down on the harsh lines of St. Ignatius from behind, casting the Academy as a dark silhouette against the bright, blue sky. In the shadows that spilled along the front of the building, at least a dozen Hounds waited. Victim or not, I was glad to see that Rune's arrival was being taken seriously. I just wished I knew if twelve Hounds guarding him would be enough.

I didn't have long to consider, though, before Rune was taken away by the bristling entourage of Hounds and professors. Just before walking through the main doors, Rune glanced back over his shoulder as if looking for support. I merely nodded at him before turning back to the Deviants.

"Return to your rooms until the meeting with the rest of the Dozen tomorrow morning. I suggest you get some rest."

"So, we're just confined to our rooms like prisoners?" Quinnie was regaining some of her energy and it seemed her irritating mouth was the first thing back to full strength.

"Standard procedure after a mission. Look at it as a free pass from your classes and work detail for today."

"So, that's it? Younglove's not even thankful for the job we did?" Quinnie whined.

"What did you expect?" I shook my head. "This is what you were designed to do. Success isn't rewarded, it's expected. We'll be lucky if we don't get punished for our failures. Delia and the Others got away, remember?"

"We rescued the hostages," Marty pointed out.

"Delia had no intention of keeping, or hurting, the hostages. The only thing we successfully did was to stay alive."

I slammed the door of the SUV shut and stalked up the steps and into the school. I wasn't used to failing missions; I was used to my perfect aim and perfect record. The last two missions with the Deviants had not gone well and it pissed me off. I desperately wanted to find Cleo and talk to her. Actually, what I really wanted to do was find a dark corner and kiss her senseless. But that would have to wait. If I went stumbling around the Academy in search of her, I'd be in direct violation of Younglove's orders to return to my room. I'd also be drawing unnecessary attention to the fact that Cleo was more to me than just another member of my team of Deviants. Seeing her would have to wait. I'd waited seven years to talk to her the first time. A few hours wouldn't be that hard. At least that's what I told myself.

In my room, I dug my phone out of the duffel bag where it had been since Quinnie returned it to me. I plugged it in to charge and collapsed on the bed. I was asleep before I could even kick my shoes off.

***

When I woke up, my room was so dark that I wasn't sure I'd actually opened my eyes. I reached over to the nightstand and fumbled around for my phone, clicking the screen on to see what time it was. It was a quarter after nine and I'd been asleep for nearly eight hours. I turned on the light and sat up in bed, checking to see if there were any important emails or messages sent while my phone had been missing. I smiled as I remembered the last email exchange I had with Cleo. I wondered what her response had been and if she had any idea how true it was that I dreamed about her, especially when I was away on a mission. Thinking about her was a comfort, something good to hold on to when I was doing the Program's dirty work.

Confined as I was to my room, the least I could do was email her. She should be out of work detail by now.

I opened the message thread with Cleo to see if she had written back. She hadn't. But a message had gone out to her from my phone later that same night—one I didn't send.

What the fuck?

Anger ricocheted through my chest as I realized that my phone had been missing because Quinnie purposely stole it after sending a picture to Cleo. It took all of my willpower not to smash the phone against the wall and hunt down Quinnie to confront her. A chill crept over me as I realized that Cleo had never responded. Surely she had seen the picture, but it had been four days and she hadn't written back or called.

The fury that had been raging through my body sputtered out as dread sank into the pit of my stomach. What if she was mad at me? I couldn't lose her faith again. I had just been able to make things right between us when I was sent away to The Rink.

Now, I'd been gone for almost five days, unaware that this picture existed and that Cleo had seen it. I couldn't bear the thought of losing her. If only she'd written back, I would know that she understood the picture wasn't from me, that it was just a vindictive prank of Quinnie's.

I fumbled with my phone, trying to dial Cleo's number with anxious, clumsy fingers. I had to start over twice until I got the number right. The phone rang several times before going to voicemail. I didn't leave a message because I couldn't think of what to say.

I waited five minutes, my knee bouncing out an anxious rhythm as I considered what to do. I tried calling again, but only got the machine.

Screw procedure. I had to see her. I had to fix this. I stuffed the phone in my back pocket, pushed open the window, and climbed out into the chilly night air. The clouds of my warm breath circled my head as I hurried down the side of the building and toward the tree outside of Cleo's window. In less than a minute, I was pushing open her window, which thankfully wasn't locked. I let myself hope that it was because she wanted me to come visit her. By now she knew that it was my preferred method of visitation.

Not only was Cleo not in her room, but it was just as dark as mine had been. It didn't even look like she had been back to her room since work detail. I decided to wait. I was already breaking the rules by being in her room, I couldn't exactly go skulking through the hallways looking for her. I might be the weapons instructor now, but even I had to follow some of the rules. Confinement after a mission was one of them. I turned on the desk lamp and sat in her chair to wait for her, not feeling my usual confidence.

***

I jumped into a standing position as the door opened forty-five minutes later and Cleo's familiar scent preceded her into the room. It was faint, but still there. Roasting creamsicle. Her big brown eyes found me immediately and for once she wasn't startled. She also didn't seem to be overly excited to see me. Her gaze was wary as she paused just inside the room, softly closing the door behind her.

"Where were you?" I asked, a touch of accusation in my voice. "You got done work detail at 9:00. It's almost 10:30."

"It's a long story." Cleo looked tired and I noticed that she was rubbing her hands. They were bright red and the skin looked cracked and sore.

"What happened to your hands?" I crossed the room and grabbed them, inspecting the raw skin. The dread in my stomach flared up into anger once more. "Did someone hurt you?"

Cleo pulled her hands out of mine and looked away as she walked to her closet and tossed her bag inside. "No. I have to do Maya's work detail for a week. Like I said, it's a long story. Right now I just want to finish my homework and get in bed."

Was she dismissing me? I caught Cleo's elbow and turned her to face me. She looked exhausted.

"We have to talk," I said.

She winced and looked away. It took her a few agonizing seconds to answer. "About what?"

"My phone went missing Monday night, right after I emailed you."

Cleo lifted her chin and let her eyes find my face, but she didn't say anything. Was that hope I saw in her eyes?

"Quinnie stole my phone. I was asleep when that photo was taken. I would never allow Quinnie in my bed."

Cleo exhaled in relief. "That's what I hoped."

"You were worried?" It killed me that she doubted me. Couldn't she tell how infatuated I was with her?

Cleo shrugged in response, unable to look me in the eye.

"She's just trying to antagonize you," I said.

"It's working."

"Don't let it."

"It's hard not to," Cleo admitted. "You two have history."

"Not that kind of history. We went to school together before I was sent here. I've known her for a long time, but she's like a sister to me. That's all."

"She doesn't feel the same way. She wants to be your girlfriend."

"The feeling isn't mutual." My voice was firm and I reached for Cleo's hands again and threaded my fingers through hers.

"But I heard..."

"Not all rumors are true. You should know that better than anyone, Cleo. Quinnie doesn't mean anything to me. Not that way anyway. Haven't I made it pretty clear how I feel about you?"

Cleo was quiet for a moment before she answered. "You're right, I'm sorry."

I felt awful. I didn't want her apologizing—she hadn't done anything wrong. She was the one that was being victimized by

Quinnie's jealousy.

"The infirmary," I said.

"What?"

"And the infirmary again. Your closet. The dojo. The King and Queen's seat."

"Ozzy?" Cleo asked. She obviously didn't know what I was talking about.

"My top five days. Every time I kiss you, it's one of my top days. Whenever your lips touch mine, you own another piece of my heart. You own me." I was still holding her fingers and when I pulled our hands to my chest, I released her fingers and pressed her palms to the area above my heart. "You own this," I said.

If I was being honest with myself, she owned me long before our lips had ever touched. Long before we had even met.

"You own me," I repeated, trying to catch her gaze. She finally looked up at me and her unfaltering gaze threatened to strip me raw.

"I think it's more like you're stealing pieces of me," Cleo admitted. "You're nothing but a cocky, trespassing thief. No matter how many times I lock that window, I always find you in my room." She smiled, letting me know the accusation was actually a compliment. "And no matter how much I hold on to my heart to protect it, you repeatedly disarm me and claim me bit by bit."

I felt my mouth hook up into the grin that I knew made her blush.

"Good. Mission accomplished." I pulled her into my arms, tucking her head against my chest, feeling my earlier fears ebb away.

Cleo's arms circled my waist, finding the patch of skin under my t-shirt just above the waistband of my jeans. Her fingers absentmindedly lingered on my sensitive skin, seemingly oblivious to their effect on me.

"Now," I said, trying to regain my composure, "tell me what's wrong."

Cleo told me about Maya's accusations about Bernie, the defiled door, the video, and her punishment.

"I swear I didn't do it," she said.

"Of course not," I answered thoughtfully. "You have much better taste than Bernie." My attempt at humor wasn't only to raise her spirits. I had to get my mind off the innocent exploration Cleo's hands were making along the skin of my lower back.

She rolled her eyes and tried to hide her smile. "I don't even know who Bernie is and I didn't do that to her door either." A small little crease wrinkled the skin between her eyes as she frowned.

"I believe you."

"You and Arabella are the only ones who seem to."

"What's Sterling's problem?"

Cleo shrugged.

"Well, don't worry about it. We'll figure out what's going on. We'll clear your name, okay?"

"Okay."

"I'm not going to let anything happen to you, Cleo." I reached up and tucked a stray chunk of hair behind her ear. That curl of hair was always escaping defiantly to hang into her eyes and I thought it fit her personality perfectly.

Cleo swallowed and laid her head back down on my chest. "You can't protect me from everything, Ozzy. This is the Program and I'm a Sophisticate. Being in danger has been my fate since they told me I was a Mandate, especially now that I'm supposed to be some kind of human weapon."

"I'll protect you," I promised. "From Quinnie, from all these lies, and especially from the Others."

Cleo was quiet for a moment, as if she wanted to believe me, but didn't think I could follow up on that particular promise.

"So, how did things go?" she finally asked. "With your search for the Others?" She seemed glad to have the opportunity to change the topic.

"It was a total failure. We searched The Rink for clues, but they were pretty thorough in their departure. We didn't find much. Actually, we didn't find anything but discarded food and old roller skating supplies. We were planning to return a couple of days ago, but Wednesday night changed everything."

"What happened Wednesday night?"

"Delia and the Others attacked Andrews Air Force Base. We were sent to capture them and take them into custody."

Cleo lifted her head off my chest. "They were responsible for the attack? I can't believe Younglove didn't tell us that. What happened?" She pulled back further so that she could inspect me closer, her hands running protectively over my arms and chest as if looking for wounds.

I liked that she was worried about me. Hell, I loved that she was worried about me, but I loved it even more that she was running her hands all over me.

She had no idea what she did to me. I tried to ignore the way my body was responding to her and instead I explained what happened, knowing that I was breaking even more rules. Technically, until the debriefing occurred with the rest of the Dozen, the information was still top secret.

I didn't care, though. I was never going to keep something from Cleo again. I knew that, however horrific the truth was, I would always have to tell her. I explained the confrontation we had with Delia and the Others, the rescue of the hostages, and the discovery of Rune.

"Wow. Number 13? That's...intense."

"I know. I don't like that he's here at St. Ignatius. I don't know what we should've done with him, but keeping him at the Academy where he can spy on the Dozen is not a good idea at all. You should've heard Younglove when she saw him. She was so excited; like she'd won the lottery."

"What do you think he can do?" Cleo asked.

"I have no idea."

We were both quiet for a moment.

"So, Persephone was really at the base? You saw her?"

"Unfortunately. Why?"

"I keep thinking that someone is trying to frame me. I would never do any of those things I've been accused of. It's almost as if..." She paused.

"As if what?"

"As if Persephone were here doing all of these awful things."

I hugged her tighter. "That seems like a logical idea," I admitted, "but Persephone was at Andrews Air Force Base with Delia and the Others."

"Oh," she responded.

"Persephone was also seen yesterday in Washington D.C. She was spotted with a few of the Others near the Washington monument."

"Did anything happen?"

"Not yet. A group of Mandates was sent to patrol the area, but there was no attack. Maybe the Others were just scoping it out, but now there are Mandates there to guard it."

Cleo bit her lip.

"Don't worry. We'll figure this out together. The good thing is that with Rune here, I think Younglove will be less inclined to send me out on any missions. I'm guessing she'll want as many Deviants around as possible until we know more about him. So thanks to Rune, I should be around more," I said, cradling Cleo's face in my hands before threading my fingers into her hair. I loved it when she wore it down. She closed her eyes and let her head fall back, indulging in my touch.

"Good," she said breathily.

"You have no idea. I have every intention of making a few more top days," I promised.

"Why don't we get started now?" Cleo asked, opening her eyes. She reached up and buried her fingers in my hair, pulling me down until my mouth was against hers. Her sudden bursts of passion always took me by surprise, which was why I spiraled out of control so easily when I was with her. Every time we kissed, it was like someone opened a floodgate and we were both swept away with the force of our desire for one another. Our mouths pressed together over and over again in feverish need.

Five days apart was way too long.

Cleo's lips were open in invitation, her breath hot and sweet, her tongue tracing a delicate path along my lips. When I kissed her back, she moved her hands to my chest and playfully pushed me backwards onto the bed. I fell across the mattress, leaning back on my elbows to look up at her. She stood at the edge of the bed, her hands on her hips, while she defiantly stared down at me. Her hair fell over her shoulders and around her face in bold waves as the light from the desk lit her up from behind. My eyes couldn't help traveling the length of her body to the hem of her pleated, Academy plaid skirt where it grazed the middle of her thighs, nearly begging my hands to come explore.

My eyes grudgingly found their way back to her face and I grinned. "I thought you had homework to do."

"I thought you planned to give me personal instruction. At least that's what you promised in your email earlier this week."

God. She was teasing me, and the tease was almost as exciting as actually touching her. Anticipation flared inside my chest and it took every ounce of restraint I had to not pull her down to the bed on top of me.

"I was referring to weapons class, Ms. Dracone," I teased back.

"Oh, I'm sure you have a weapon concealed somewhere, Professor Dracone," Cleo purred.

I groaned quietly and my body responded instinctively to Cleo's words—I liked hearing her call me Professor. I could almost feel the touch of her eyes as her gaze traveled leisurely along my face, chest, arms, and legs. I didn't move or try to touch her, I just let her look. Slowly, she climbed onto the bed, her knees on either side of my hips. She gazed at me triumphantly, as if she was in total control. I enjoyed the feeling of being at Cleo's mercy so I remained still, waiting for her to do whatever she wanted.

She gripped the edge of my t-shirt and pushed it up to my chin, trailing kisses up my stomach and over my chest, taking her time, making sure she didn't miss a spot. Her mouth and tongue were like a match igniting puddles of gasoline—my skin blazed at every place she touched.

I tried to pull her up and bring her renegade lips to mine, but Cleo shook her head and smiled impishly before going back to the slow torture of kissing and nibbling on my bare skin. Her fingers roamed along my legs and then across my stomach before wandering to the one place my body was begging for her to discover. Her hands knew exactly what I wanted and she gave it to me, touching me with just the right amount of pressure. A groan escaped my throat and finally Cleo's lips eagerly found mine, as if stealing my desire for her own.

I couldn't take it anymore. I reached up and flipped her onto her back, her hair spilling across the bed behind her in dark, soft waves. Without missing a beat, she reached up and peeled my shirt off and then tossed it to the floor. Her shirt came off next and my lips instantly found the bare skin just above the edge of her bra. Her roasting creamsicle scent was strong across the skin just under her throat and her chest arched up to meet my lips as I kissed her there. She was smiling and her hands were still caressing me, her fingers sliding along the inside of my waistband, driving me to the edge of my control. When she started to unbutton my jeans, I moaned in regret. I pushed back and stood, stepping away from the bed, breathing heavily.

Reluctantly, I backed away even further. I grabbed the back of my neck with my hands, giving them a place to be before they could reach out for her again. I had to get distance between us; the temptation was almost painful. If I didn't leave, we might do things we both might regret later. I knew for sure that a few more minutes of this and I wouldn't be able to trust myself to think coherently.

This wasn't the way I'd envisioned my first time with Cleo—

and I had envisioned it more times than I wanted to admit. She deserved something special, something different. Everything was happening way too quickly.

She continued to stare at me, her gaze tracing the contours of my body as if she were touching me.

"I have to go," I said.

"What?" she asked, her voice rising in question. She pushed herself up on her elbows, her body still deliciously on display. I bent over to get my shirt, tearing my eyes away from her.

"I have to go," I repeated.

"What's wrong?"

"I think that's enough personal instruction for one night," I said, stealing another greedy glance at her sprawled on the bed. I quickly moved to the window ledge, knowing if I didn't get far away from her soon, it might be too late. She was still lying on the bed smiling at me with that same sort of smile I had given her many times before.

My control was already slipping.

"One of these nights, Professor Dracone," she drawled, "I'm going to sneak into your room and you'll have nowhere to run and hide."

God. This girl was killing me.

"I dare you," I challenged. "Good night, Cleo."

I shut the window behind me and then quickly climbed down the tree and ran back to my room before I could change my mind and give us both what we really wanted.

CLEO

BUTTERFLIES

On Saturday morning, after the run, Younglove held the debriefing for the Deviants. Quinnie sat toward the front of the room and took every chance she could to cast superior smirks over her shoulder in my direction. I spent most of the time concentrating on staying calm so that I wouldn't be tempted to burn Quinnie's hair right off her hateful head. Despite the visit from Ozzy last night, I still hadn't forgotten that Quinnie sent me the picture. Arabella kept looking curiously at the tiny curls of smoke rising from the tips of my fingers, her eyebrows raised in question. I couldn't explain what my problem was without losing my temper, so I sat quietly, mentally going over my latest Arabic lesson to keep my thoughts calm.

I found it troubling that a few weeks ago I couldn't force my deviation to appear, and now it was almost a constant battle to keep my fury caged inside. I knew the abundance of anger I always felt wasn't normal and the fact that it could come with disastrous consequences was frustrating. Sometimes I felt as if my humanity was slipping away to leave behind a monster I didn't recognize. I wondered if Younglove was right—maybe suppressing my power was making me a little crazy. Maybe if I released it and let it out to play once in a while, I'd be able to control it more easily.

I expected Younglove to send us off to our classes after the debriefing was over, but she didn't.

"Now that you are all up to speed on the events of the last few days, I have someone I'd like you all to meet," Younglove said. She pressed a button on her desk phone and said, "send him in."

The door opened and a guy with shaggy blond hair entered, his shoulders slumped as he looked at the ground. He lifted his eyes briefly, just long enough so I could see that they were bright blue.

I assumed he was Rune, the boy that Delia Younglove left behind at the base. He didn't look very dangerous. Then again, I didn't look very dangerous either and I could easily set the entire room on fire with a small lapse in concentration. Apparently, Younglove felt that Rune was fairly harmless, because she grabbed his elbow and happily pulled him to her side as if she was the proud owner of a fancy new purse.

"This is Rune. He is the newest cadet at St. Ignatius Academy. I wanted you all to be the first to meet him since he'll be attending the Deviant Workshop with you. Ozzy will be his mentor for the time being and will be attending classes with him when not teaching weapons."

What the hell? Cassie had yet to be released from the infirmary and this guy, who had been with Delia Younglove and the Others for God knows how long, was now a cadet at the Academy? I didn't like it one bit. Especially since Ozzy was assigned as Rune's mentor. It was pretty clear that "mentor" really meant "bodyguard."

It was Quinnie who was brave enough to speak up. "How can he attend the workshop? It's for Deviants."

"Because he is a Deviant," Younglove answered. "As I explained to Osbourne, the Deviant Dozen was the brainchild of Russell Baker, the man at the very top of the leadership of the Program. Before you were known as the Deviant Dozen, you were known as Baker's Dozen. There were originally thirteen of you. Unfortunately, Sebastian Dracone, who was Rune's counterpart, didn't survive the exhibiting of his deviation."

"How come you never told us about Sebastian before?" Quinnie asked.

"Because he never mattered before. He was dead long before many of you came here."

"And Rune is a twin of Sebastian?"

"That's the theory."

In my opinion, Younglove was way too happy about the situation.

"What's his deviation?" Quinnie asked.

"Sebastian's code name was Pistol Shrimp," Younglove said, glancing at Rune to see if this revelation piqued his interest. It didn't. He was rolling a piece of lint between his fingers as if it was the most interesting thing he had ever seen in his life.

Sterling leaned over to whisper to Arabella, loud enough for me to hear. "I wonder if he'd trade code names with me. Pistol Shrimp has much more badassery to it than Hummingbird."

Arabella rolled her eyes before whispering back. "Pistol Shrimp sounds pretty stupid to me. What the hell does it even mean?" I thought I saw Rune twitch his head toward the whispered conversation, but when he neglected to actually look up, I figured I must have imagined it.

Younglove was still speaking, oblivious to Sterling and Arabella's whispered conversation. "Although Rune is unaware if he started to deviate before he suffered his memory loss, it is believed that he will have the same skills that Sebastian was designed to have. By using his hands, he should be capable of producing blasts of air that can stun or kill, much like a gunshot. In addition, he should be capable of producing loud noises that would incapacitate any living thing within a certain distance. As I said, he isn't aware if he has ever deviated, and his counterpart Sebastian did not survive the exhibition of his deviation, so we're not sure how effective he will be. We're not exactly sure why he was left at the scene of the attack as a hostage. It could be that he is defective and has no deviation at all."

I cringed at Younglove's bluntness, but Rune ignored it. The lint still captured his attention, as did a hang nail on his thumb. As I continued to watch Rune ignore the fact that everyone was talking about him, Sterling raised his hand.

"Yes?" Younglove asked.

"Are you sure it's safe to have him around? It sounds like his deviation is dangerous, especially since we don't know his intentions. Have you considered that he's lying about his memory loss and was sent here as a spy?"

Younglove's glare was so heated it looked like it could melt the skin right off Sterling's face. "We have considered every possibility."

I was surprised to find my own hand raising. Younglove seemed to be caught off guard as well. When the professor nodded in my direction, I asked, "If the Others are our twins, where did they come from? Were they stolen from the Program or created without the Program's knowledge?"

Younglove didn't answer right away. It was clear she was uncertain how much to share with us or whether she should share anything at all.

Finally, she said, "The Others were not approved projects for the Program. During the research and experimentation for the Deviation project, certain genetic alterations caused some unsatisfactory complications, which resulted in disastrous side effects and failed mutation for those test subjects that came before you. Sometimes it was death, and in other instances it was physical or mental imperfections. I myself don't understand the science behind it, but it was discovered that certain qualities could be isolated by splitting genetic material like twins—the good qualities in one, the undesired qualities in another. It's assumed that Delia must have stolen the discarded, undesired genetic material to create her own set of Deviants. If that is what actually happened, it's a miracle the Others survived at all.

"In any case, since the discovery of the Others, records are being investigated and people are being interviewed. We were recently informed that the unused, undesired genetic material of Baker's Dozen was slated to be disposed of by a hand-picked team of people. One of those people was Delia. Clearly, she didn't do what she was supposed to. According to what she told Osbourne, her main goal right now is revenge and we assume that she will use the Others as her own personal army to that end."

Arabella snorted. "Undesired genetic material? Are you sure we got the right Quinnie then?" She hooked her thumb toward Quinnie and smirked triumphantly.

There were a few snickers in the room that quieted down fairly quickly once Quinnie spun around, her hands and hair sparking like a damaged electrical wire.

"What?" Arabella asked innocently. "I'm just wondering. It would explain a lot."

The air around Quinnie hummed and Younglove was quick to step in. "Cool it. Both of you. We have enough trouble without fighting amongst ourselves."

"One more question," Sterling said, raising his hand.

"Yes?"

"What sport and work detail will Rune be doing?"

"For the time being, he will only be attending classes and the workshop. The rest of his time will be spent with Osbourne or the Hounds."

I cringed inwardly for Rune. Time with the Hounds. That was code for "prisoner." Another discreet look at him proved that he didn't seem to care either way.

"I think our meeting is done for the day," Younglove said. "You are all caught up to speed and, hopefully, this new information will encourage you to work a little harder on your skills. I guarantee you that the Others are prepared, and willing, to use everything at their disposal. As I mentioned, they are products of discarded genetic material—they are dangerous."

She looked around at all of us before letting her gaze settle on me.

"Our research suggests that some of the defects in the genetic mutation of the Others is their lack of humanity—an inability for empathy, guilt, or a general sense of right and wrong. Imagine a Deviant without a conscience. Immense power without a soul. No offense meant, Rune," Younglove said to the boy who seemed to be ignoring the conversation. "You may yet prove us wrong, but everyone should know what to expect. The Others were never supposed to be completed experiments and since they've been outside of the Program's control for the last seventeen years, we have to be prepared to expect the worst."

Rune didn't seem to have an opinion about the whole affair. When the meeting was adjourned, he followed Ozzy out of the room like a trained puppy. Life pretty much sucked for Rune, but at least the lucky bastard didn't have to go to work detail.

***

At lunch, Rune was with Ozzy when he arrived at the table where I sat with Arabella, Sterling, Wesley, and Theo.

"Does he have to sit here?" Arabella asked, motioning to Rune.

"I want to sit here and, unfortunately, he goes where I go," Ozzy said, setting his tray on the table.

I had to agree with Arabella. I knew it was cruel to not want Rune around, but no one felt comfortable around him. He was too much of an unknown. Younglove didn't seem to share this worry. Despite her warnings about the dangers of the Others, it appeared that she wasn't concerned about Rune. It wasn't Ozzy's fault that he was forced to have Rune as a shadow, so we'd have to put up with the strange new boy. For now.

"What are you doing the rest of the day?" I asked Ozzy.

"I'm scheduled to do some training with Rune after lunch," he said.

"What about later tonight?"

Ozzy looked at me, a smile playing across his lips.

I leaned in until my lips were against his ear. "I mean, much later," I whispered.

"Depends on what kind of offers I get," Ozzy responded quietly.

"Should I leave my window unlocked?" I asked. "Or should I visit you this time?"

He paused for a moment and I hoped he was remembering my threat to sneak into his room so he couldn't run away once things got interesting. "I don't think your climbing skills are that dependable," he teased.

"Oh, you'd be surprised what I can do with the right incentive."

Ozzy's expression didn't change, but I noticed the slight darkening in his eyes and I knew he'd gotten my message loud and clear.

"Would you quit whispering and flirting? The pheromones coming off you two is enough to make me gag," Arabella complained. "It's bad enough Theo's sitting here."

"Hey, what did I do?" Theo mumbled, midway through stuffing his face. Food was falling back onto his plate.

"See?" Arabella complained pointing to him. "It's like eating with a farm animal."

"Come on, Bella," Theo crooned. "I thought we were friends. Maybe I could whisper sweet nothings in your ear," he offered, scooting closer to her.

As the rest of lunch disintegrated into a battle of insults between Theo and Arabella, Ozzy leaned closer to me and whispered, "Leave it unlocked."

***

"What are you doing?" Arabella was nearly dragging me back to the dorm.

"Clearly, getting my ass dragged through hallways by an angry oompa loompa," I retorted, trying to pull my arm out of Arabella's hand. I knew it was a low blow and not at all warranted, but

Arabella's hair was a vivid green and at the moment she was a tiny, angry, force of nature with an unnaturally strong grip on my upper arm.

"Come on," Arabella growled. She pulled me up the stairs and down the hallway past my room. She stopped in front of a door with a skull crudely carved into the wood, unlocked it with her key, and then pushed me inside.

I'd never been inside Arabella's room and I wouldn't have been more shocked if I'd been shoved into a room full of vipers. I was in no way prepared for how girly it looked. The room was painted a pale turquoise and there were delicate, white butterflies all over the place, swarming across the walls and casting dainty shadows in their wake. There were even butterflies hanging from the ceiling at varying heights as if in flight. All of Arabella's furniture had been painted white and her bed was covered in a turquoise comforter that matched the walls.

"Wow," I said, sitting down on the bed in a daze. "This is so..."

"New."

"I was going to say creepy." I looked at Arabella. "Don't take this the wrong way, but this is a lot of freaking butterflies."

"And?"

"And it doesn't seem like you, that's all."

There was no humor in Arabella's voice when she laughed. "What do I seem like? I don't think I even know half the time." She walked over to the mirror and looked at her hair. As I watched, it morphed from the bright green, shaggy hairdo Arabella had been sporting all morning and turned into a smooth, sheath of teal that fell to the middle of her back. It almost matched the walls, but was much darker and bolder. She turned back to me. "But hey, we didn't come here to talk about me. We came to talk about you. Just what the hell were you doing at lunch?"

I rolled my eyes. "Come on, Arabella. You know I like Ozzy."

"I know, and so does nearly everyone else. But Rune didn't need to know. You've got to treat that boy like the enemy. As far as we know, he was sent here to spy on us and we don't need to go showing him all of our weaknesses. If I could hear what you were whispering to Ozzy, then he sure as hell could, too."

"You heard?" I could feel the warmth of embarrassment creeping up my neck and over my cheeks. I still wasn't used to the physical, and nearly animalistic, response I had to Ozzy whenever I was in his presence. It seemed to be getting stronger and more uncontrollable, but I hadn't realized it was so noticeable to everyone else.

Arabella shrugged. "Okay, I didn't really hear anything, but I didn't need to. It was pretty obvious what you were talking about since you were drooling all over each other. And now Rune knows that you both have at least one weakness—each other. You might not have noticed he was paying attention, but I did. Maybe he is just some dumb fool that has an annoying case of amnesia, but just be careful what you do and say in front of him, okay?"

"You're right," I agreed. "I wasn't thinking."

"Oh, you were thinking, just not about anything but Ozzy's ass."

"Arabella!"

"Am I wrong?"

"Of course. I was thinking about his biceps and abs, too." I laughed and Arabella's agitation finally cracked into amusement when she pulled a fancy pillow off the bed and threw it at me.

"You're hopeless."

"Me? What about you? You, the queen of all things black and spiky, live in a turquoise room filled with paper butterflies."

"They're not paper, they're acrylic."

"They're still butterflies and really, really girly."

"I'm a girl," Arabella retorted.

"Please. You're not this kind of girl. This borders on obsession," I said, standing up and walking around the room, ducking under low hanging butterflies. "Like big time obsession. I'm thinking some therapy is in order. Does Sterling know about this?"

"No. I told you, it's new." Arabella seemed a little shy now that I was evaluating her room.

"What possessed you to do this?" I inspected the butterflies near me and noticed they were all different. It looked like they were hand-carved and there had to be at least a thousand of them in the room.

"Possessed is a tad strong, I prefer the term 'inspired.'"

"Okay, what inspired you to fill your room with swarms of hand-made butterflies?"

Arabella, uncharacteristically, sighed in defeat. She walked over to her dresser and pulled something out of a box. She then handed it to me.

"Professor Lawless gave me this," she said.

I looked at the object in my hand—a thick gold chain with a circular pendant hanging from it. It was a locket made from a piece of turquoise and thin swirls of golden filigree. On top of the fancy network of gold was a golden butterfly.

"Lawless gave you this?" I asked. That seemed inappropriate.

"Open it."

Using my thumbnail, I opened the locket and a piece of paper fell out into my palm. Feminine handwriting curled across the page. It said: "We wanted to keep you."

I looked up at Arabella whose eyes were glistening with the beginning of tears.

"What is this?" I asked.

"It's from my parents."

"Your parents? How did Lawless get it?" Jealousy uncoiled in my chest like a sluggish, hungry, poison.

Arabella reached for the locket and paper and gently tucked the words back into their hiding spot.

"Apparently, our genetic donors are allowed to bequeath a gift to us. It's kept in storage and we're supposed to get it when we graduate from the Mandate or Vanguard programs."

I watched enviously as Arabella stored her treasure back in its box on the dresser.

"What do you mean they're supposed to give it to us?"

"Lawless said there's a huge storage room filled with this stuff, things meant for Sophisticate children. But that's all it is, just storage. It's never passed on. It just gathers dust forever."

"They never give it to us? Then why do they have it?"

"There's not supposed to be a link between donors and children, right? They can't give us this stuff without creating some sort of emotional baggage for us. Donors who actually think we'll get these items are foolish. It's just the Program's way of making the donors feel less guilty that they gave their child up in exchange for a shitload of blood money. It's to make them feel better, not us."

"But if we're never supposed to get them, why did you get yours?"

Arabella leaned against her dresser and shrugged. "Lawless

likes me. He knew about these and had access. Remember how I told you that he was the one who told me that my parents—I mean donors—were from Baltimore? He thought I'd want to have it."

I was silent for a moment.

"Do you think Lawless would get my item for me?" I asked. I didn't want to let myself get too eager. Lawless liked that I was a star student in his class, but I was certain that stealing Sophisticate items from storage came with a huge risk. I wasn't as close to him as Arabella was so I might not be worth the risk.

Arabella looked down at her feet and kicked the back of her shoe with the toe of her other one.

"I'm sorry, Cleo, but you don't have anything. I already asked him to check."

"I don't have anything? Not at all?"

Arabella shook her head, pity evident on her face. On one hand, I was grateful that Arabella thought to ask for my item, too. On the other hand, there was nothing in the storage room for me. Nothing. No ragged cardboard box with my name written on it with sentimental junk sitting in it. Just like there was no folder with my name on it in the Restricted Section.

I bit on my bottom lip and blinked my eyes several times, trying hard not to cry. I felt like my heart had been ripped in half. My parents didn't leave me an item, not even a letter or small message. Nothing. I'd read an article about parents who fought the Program for the right to keep their baby, and I'd been hoping it was about me. Clearly it wasn't. My donors couldn't even be bothered to leave me a small memento. They just took their money and ran.

Then it occurred to me—maybe they knew what kind of monster their child really was; maybe that's why giving me up had been so easy.

When I finally got my emotions under control, I asked, "Can I look at your locket again?"

Arabella nodded in understanding.

After dinner, I made my way to the library to do the first of my two work details of the night. I was lost in thought, obsessing over the video Younglove had of me defacing Maya's door. I was no closer to finding out what actually happened and it was driving me crazy. Although Persephone would be the perfect explanation, there was the fact that she'd been seen elsewhere in the company of Delia and the Others.

I also rejected the idea that Theo, video genius that he was, framed me in retaliation for my rejection of his brother. He seemed just as surprised about the existence of the video as I was. Besides, he was my friend.

Quinnie definitely had the motive to want to frame me, but she hadn't been at the Academy when it happened. That didn't mean she couldn't have orchestrated it, but I had no way of proving it, or an explanation of how she could have done it.

Arabella could have done it.

I mentally kicked myself in the head for that awful, random thought. Sure, Arabella could have easily used her deviation to make herself look like me, but she had no motive. She was the one person that stuck up for me since the accusations began. I tossed that ridiculous idea in a guilty pile of things I was embarrassed for even thinking.

"Did you get the message I sent you?"

Despite the fact that I was surprised, I resisted the urge to spin around at the sound of Quinnie's voice. If she wanted to attack me, she would've done it already. She was here to torture me, and I wasn't going to give her the satisfaction. I kept walking toward the library, but her footsteps echoed through the hallway as she followed me.

"I thought it was a really nice photo," she continued, "but Ozzy does snore in his sleep."

"Quinnie, I don't need a photo as proof that you're desperate and pathetic. I already knew that."

There was a slight buzzing sound and I spun around just in time to dodge a small streak of blue light that hit the wall behind me, leaving a tiny gouge in the stone and a pile of dust on the floor underneath. Quinnie's hair appeared to be floating as the sound of electricity continued to buzz around her.

"There are no cameras in this part of the hall, loser," she threatened.

Instead of cowering, like I might have weeks ago, I closed the distance between us, feeling the burn of my power flare through my body. Quinnie flinched at what I imagined must have been a blast of furnace-like heat that pulsed off me.

"Good. I've had enough bogus video footage pinned on me as it is. Younglove might have a hard time deciding which one of us started this, but it might be worth it to get a little payback. What do you say?" I allowed another blast of heat to roll off my body. In response, Quinnie sent jagged fingers of electricity snaking through the heated cloud. She was testing my resolve, but I didn't budge. We stood there for a few seconds pushing our deviations against one another without actually attacking.

Quinnie grinned as a bolt of her power streaked across the

space between us, snapping across my arm. It bit into my skin, leaving a welt, but I didn't flinch. I wouldn't give her the satisfaction. I meant to retaliate with another wall of scorching heat, but instead, a flame roared between us, catching the edge of her blazer and lighting it. Quinnie screeched and yanked the sleeves off her arms, wildly contorting her body until she freed herself from the jacket. She threw it to the floor and then stomped on it to put out the flames. I could feel my mouth hanging open in horror at what I did. I thought I had it under control, but my deviation almost set her on fire.

Quinnie stepped away from the smoking remains of the jacket, refusing to put her back to me. I didn't know what to say. There was a small part of me that wanted to gloat and tell her she deserved it, but I was afraid to let that part speak. Once I let the beast inside have the power of words, I might lose whatever control I still had over it. Quinnie continued to back down the hallway, her glare trained on me, her hands floating in front of her as if ready to ward off an attack.

"You owe me a jacket, bitch," she said just before she ducked safely around the corner.

I stared at the empty space where she had just been, trying to get my breathing under control. Then I picked up the burnt jacked and tossed it into the nearest trash can, hoping that this incident didn't come to Younglove's attention.

Cleo

12

Anticipation

I rushed back to my room after finishing Maya's work detail. When I opened my door, I was happy to discover that Ozzy was already there, lying on my bed, reading a book. He was wearing jeans slung low on his hips and a black button down shirt that had more buttons left undone than fastened. His sleeves were rolled up to his elbows revealing his tan, muscular forearms. I walked toward the bed and he continued reading, even when I dropped my bag noisily onto the floor.

"You're alone, I hope. No Rune?" I asked playfully, looking around the room.

"I got off babysitting duty at nine," Ozzy answered. "It's just me tonight, Desert Flower."

Perfect. "I'm going to take a quick shower. You'll be here when I get back, right?"

"I'm incredibly obsessed with this book I'm reading right now. I'll probably want to do nothing else but read it all night." He still hadn't looked at me, but there was a ghost of a smile tugging at the corners of his mouth.

"Really?" I asked, seductively peeling my jacket off and letting it fall slowly from my hands to the floor.

Ozzy swallowed, attempting to seem uninterested as he spared a quick glance at me. "It's a very interesting book."

"You're also reading it upside down," I said.

His eyes darted back to the book, *Al-Mawrid Al-Haddeeth*, the English/Arabic dictionary from my Arabic language studies class. It was right side up, but to someone who didn't actually know Arabic, it was hard to tell the difference.

"Gotcha! I knew you weren't reading that stupid thing." I laughed.

"Busted." Ozzy tossed the book to the side and started to stand. "Now that my cover is blown, there really is no reason to stay any longer." He stretched his arms over his head, feigning boredom.

I stepped forward, put my hands on his chest, and pushed him back down on the bed. Ozzy grinned, pulling me down with him. I struggled to get out of his grip.

"Seriously, don't go anywhere," I ordered him. "I have to go shower. I still smell like fish from washing all those pans."

"I love it when you talk dirty to me." Ozzy took another book off my desk and leaned back onto my pillows.

"There's more where that came from, just give me fifteen minutes." I grabbed my shower caddy and a clean set of clothes.

"Do you need any help?" Ozzy asked. "I'm really good with a loofah."

My face heated with the brief images that flashed through my head of me and Ozzy in the shower together. I wasn't sure I was ready to take that step. Besides, I knew he was just teasing. He was the one that was always cutting things off before they went too far.

"I think I can manage. Stay," I ordered before closing the door behind me and hurrying to the bathroom down the hall.

I was twisting my wet hair into a braid when I came back in the room ten minutes later. Ozzy was still on my bed, but he had new reading material—the book about Malaysian Fire Ants that Younglove had given me at the last Deviant Workshop. I sat on the bed next to him.

"Did you know that Malaysian Fire Ants build nests in leaves to protect their Queen? They fold the leaf over and around like an envelope and then seal it with a sticky substance," Ozzy asked.

"I didn't get to that part yet."

"I could read it to you, it's incredibly interesting," Ozzy offered.

I grabbed the book and tossed it to the floor. "I don't find origami all that interesting; especially when it's done by ants."

"That's because you've never seen any good origami." Ozzy sat up and grabbed one of my notebooks off of the desk. "Want to play a game?"

Sure, as long as it ends with kissing, I thought. "What kind of game?" I asked out loud.

"Two truths, one lie."

I raised my eyebrows in question. It wasn't exactly how I imagined the night unfolding, but it would still be time alone with Ozzy.

"How do we play?"

"You tell two truths and one lie and the other person has to guess what the lie is."

"That's not a very fair game, you'll win. You know everything about me."

"Not everything. Besides, here's your chance to learn all of my deepest, darkest secrets," he taunted.

I shrugged.

"What? Don't you want to get to know me better?"

"Yeah, but I'm at a huge disadvantage since you've been spying on me for the last seven years. Besides, I thought...you know, I thought we'd be doing other things. I brushed my teeth and everything."

"Well, that's your fault for thinking you were getting to first base." He scooted away from me as I playfully punched at his arm.

"First base? I'm not even getting up to bat!"

Ozzy laughed and positioned himself on the other end of the bed, facing me, but as far from me as he could get. I wanted to close the distance—climb onto his lap and kiss him until that self-satisfied grin of his was gone.

"I'll tell you what," he bartered. "When you guess the lie correctly, you can claim your prize."

"Which is?"

"Winner's choice. Whatever you want."

"What if I guess wrong?"

"You get nothing."

I considered the offer. "Deal. You go first," I said. I could do this. I took a criminal justice class at the University and one of the things we learned was to read body language and be able to deduce when someone was lying. It was a good skill to have in the business world. This was going to be easy as long as I paid attention.

"Okay, remember...two truths and one lie. Ready?" When I nodded, he continued. "I alphabetize all of my books...When I was ten, I wanted to grow up to be a trapeze artist...I hate chocolate."

Oh God. This was going to be impossible. Not only did Ozzy not have any "tells," but he wasn't even looking up. He was carefully ripping pages out of my notebook, tearing them into squares, and writing on them. I watched the pen scratch across the paper, leaving the strong, harsh marks I'd begun to recognize as his writing.

I thought about what he said. I'd never seen his room, but he was a control freak so it was entirely possible that he alphabetized his books. The weapons cabinet had become almost OCD in its organization since Ozzy took over as weapons instructor. That was definitely one of his truths. It was a toss-up between the other two comments, though. Trapeze artist or chocolate hater? Who didn't like chocolate?

"You can't possibly hate chocolate, that's your lie," I guessed.

"Wrong. I never wanted to be a trapeze artist when I grew up."

"You hate chocolate? That seems criminal. Chocolate is like heaven on earth. What made you invent a trapeze artist lie?"

Ozzy shrugged.

"I have to tell you, you're a little too good at lying. It's a bit worrisome."

"It's just a game," he reminded me. "But yeah, I never dreamed about being anything other than what I was—a Sophisticate with flawless aim. Weird, huh? I think I realized pretty early on that I didn't have many choices when it came to my future. Maybe that's why I exhibited so early."

"Wow. I thought this was going to be a fun game. You're going all serious and fatalistic on me. Way to be a downer." I gave him an exaggerated frown.

Ozzy laughed. "Sorry. It's the truth. Your turn."

"Okay. Let's see." I chewed on the end of my thumbnail and

stared at the ceiling while I scoured my brain for things he might not know about me. "I'm scared of boats...I hate wearing socks...I've read the *Great Gatsby* three times." I silently congratulated myself for my cleverness on that last one.

Ozzy was quiet for several moments as he considered my words. He took one of the papers filled with writing and started to fold it. I was mesmerized as his fingers pressed down along the creases he made. He finally answered, "I read your file so I know that you really are scared of boats. That's definitely one of your truths."

"Dammit! That story was in my file?" How embarrassing. I was eleven when I went on one of the rare field trips the Program had allowed the Sophisticates. We went down to the Inner Harbor in Baltimore for one of the Duck Boat Tours—a boat that could drive on land and cruise around in the water at the harbor. Every passenger was given plastic duck lips to annoyingly quack with for the entire ride. For an 11-year old, the duck lips alone were worth the trip. As the boat was skimming along through the harbor, I'd seen a real duck out in the water and wanted to pet it. I leaned too far over the edge, but I wasn't wearing a life preserver. In the time it took for Cassie to notify the driver and for the boat to turn around, I almost drowned. Later, I learned how to swim but the thought of getting on a boat still brought back memories of that day.

It made me feel incredibly vulnerable that Ozzy knew even that small tidbit of my history. It was like standing naked in the middle of a room and having no way to hide all of my flaws and insecurities.

Ozzy grinned. "Yeah, it was in your file. There were even pictures. You were cute as a waterlogged 11-year old."

I threw my pillow at him. "Fine. So what's my lie?"

"I notice you're not wearing anything on your feet right now, so your hatred for socks is also a truth. Your lie is that you've read the *Great Gatsby* three times. I'm going to guess that five times is closer to the truth."

I pouted and crossed my arms. "Was that in my file, too?"

"Ha! Was I right? Really? Five times? I should get two points for that." Ozzy chuckled as he started writing on another piece of paper. "No, that wasn't in your file. You're just predictable when it comes to your books. I think five times is your average for classics, am I right?"

"Right, but you don't have to be so smug about it. So, what are you claiming as a prize?" *I'm available.*

"I think I'll save all of mine up for later."

"All? Confident, aren't you?"

He looked up just long enough to give me a heart-stopping smile. "I'm always confident when it comes to you. There's no target I've researched more intensely."

I blushed.

"My turn," he said, releasing me from his gaze as he looked down at another square of paper. "I own a pair of leather pants...I caught a shark once when I was on an Academy fishing trip... I got to ride in the Oscar Meyer Weinermobile."

I bit my bottom lip. Leather? A shark? Weiner cars? None of those sounded possible. But at the same time, they all seemed possible. I still didn't know Ozzy all that well, so any one of them could be true. I sucked at this game. Ozzy was still folding and writing, creating a stack of discarded, folded paper.

"You never rode in the Weinermobile," I guessed.

"Nope. I have."

"Seriously? The Weinermobile is a truth?"

"It was my tenth birthday present from the Program, sort of like a prisoner's last meal request. Right before they shipped me off to the Academy, they told me I could have anything I wanted for my birthday."

"And you picked the Weinermobile?"

"I was ten," he reminded me. "And it was awesome. Definitely one of my top five days," he looked up from his pile of papers. "Until I met you."

His gaze was a smoldering caress that traveled across my face, paused at my lips, and then slid down the rest of my body, carefully following each and every curve.

"My lie was the shark. I've never even been fishing. I hate boats, too." His eyes met mine in soft understanding. "Your turn."

I reached over to grab one of the folded pieces of paper to see what he was doing, but he swatted my hand away. "Nope. You haven't earned that yet. Your truths and lie, please." He went back to looking down at the paper and writing.

"Ugh. Fine. I once ate an entire pizza by myself...I can fit a whole lemon in my mouth...I'm going commando right now."

The pen stopped moving and Ozzy cleared his throat. I knew I was gloating, but I didn't care. If he was going to force me to play this game, I was going to play dirty.

Ozzy looked up from the paper, his gaze traveling slowly up my legs, across my hips, along my stomach and chest, where it finally rested on my mouth. "You've never eaten an entire pizza," he declared.

"Seriously? How do you know that? Just how much have you

spied on me?" No way was I going to win this game.

His eyes flicked up to mine briefly before returning to my mouth. "I didn't know for sure the pizza was the lie. I guess I was just hoping the other two were true." He licked his bottom lip before biting it. "Are you really going commando right now?" His forehead creased in question.

Oh the things I wanted to do to those lips. "Well, you could always double check to make sure," I challenged him.

Ozzy's smile widened until his teeth were showing. "We work on the honor system here, Desert Flower. I'm pretty sure if I were to check your 'going commando' claim, this game would be over right now."

"Are you admitting you have no control when you're with me?"

"I think we both know *that's* a truth."

"So does that mean you're claiming your prize for this correct answer at the end of the game, too?"

"Exactly. My turn," he said, returning to his papers and the game. "I'm ambidextrous...I found twenty dollars in my jacket pocket this morning...I'm also going commando right now."

Ozzy was folding a paper in his lap, but he was looking up at me through the hair that had fallen across his eyes. I couldn't look away. I didn't want to.

"No way you found twenty dollars today," I said quietly.

He grinned and shook his head. "Wrong again. I've never gone commando before."

"No time like the present," I suggested.

"Guess one of my lies correctly and you can request that."

"You're such a tease."

"Anticipation is the best part."

"I'd have to disagree. Your lips on mine right now would be the best part."

"Two truths and one lie, please."

Sitting so close to Ozzy and his lips and his hands and his...everything...was like riding one of those spinning rides at the amusement park. Every time he looked at me with his intense gaze, my stomach flipped excitedly. Every time his lips eased into a smile, warmth rushed through me before settling low in my body. Every time he laughed, I wanted to make him do it again. My hands wanted to reach out and touch him and my lips ached to taste his skin. He was just out of reach, and yet so close it was painful.

Anticipation. That's what it was. That was the real game he was playing. Anticipation.

I decided to enjoy it for what it was. "All right, my turn I guess. I'm scared of the dark...The first thing I bought with my work detail money was a pair of jeans...I've never gotten to third base with a guy."

"You're scared of the dark?"

"That wasn't a guess, that was a question."

"The jeans was your lie. The first thing you bought was a journal," he explained. "Since when have you been scared of the dark? That's something I didn't know about you."

"You know about my journal? Snoop much, Snoopy McSnoop-erson? I didn't know my purchases were so interesting."

"Everything about you interests me. What about the dark?" he pressed.

"Being interested is no excuse for spying on me." I rolled my eyes and then took a deep breath. "I've been scared of the dark ever since the Ravens game."

He released his breath slowly. "Right. The kidnapping-that-wasn't-a-kidnapping."

I nodded.

"So, you've never gotten to third base, huh?" Ozzy changed the subject before it could get serious. "Do you want to?"

"Is that an offer or are you claiming your prize?"

"Neither. I'm just curious."

"And you're going to stay that way." I reached again for one of the folded papers and Ozzy blocked me.

"My turn," he said. "Ready?"

I nodded.

"I once shoved a marshmallow up my nose and it got stuck...I have an IQ of 163...I've gone skinny dipping before."

"No way your IQ is 163," I scoffed.

Ozzy stopped folding and raised an eyebrow at me.

"For real? That wasn't the lie? Your IQ is higher than mine?"

Ozzy grinned. "Sorry, Desert Flower. You're only two points behind me though."

"I challenge you to a rematch," I demanded.

"Would it be that bad if I was smarter than you?"

"No. I'm just not used to that being an issue," I admitted. Ozzy was so jaw-droppingly attractive, it didn't seem fair that he was a genius, too. "So what was it? The marshmallow or nudity?"

"I've never stuffed a marshmallow up my nose."

"Well, that's good. Tell me the story about skinny dipping," I urged.

"Maybe later, it's really not that exciting."

"Nudity is always exciting."

Ozzy's eyebrow lifted as he looked at me. He knew what game

I was playing and he was playing his game too, drawing out the anticipation as long as he could. He began weaving the bits of folded paper together and setting his finished products behind him. "One last round for you. Give me some truths and a lie."

I leaned back against my headboard, trailing the nail of my finger over my lower lip as I tried to come up with a way to win at least one round. "I had an imaginary friend named Gladys until I was six...I once dyed my hair blue...I dreamed about you last night, and you weren't wearing anything."

Ozzy's eyes darkened as he captured me in his gaze. "And just what was I doing in your dream while I wasn't wearing anything?"

"How do you know that's not the lie?"

"Because your imaginary friend's name was Juniper, not Gladys." Ozzy set the papers aside and leaned forward, crawling across the bed like a lion stalking his prey. As he came closer, I leaned back into the pillows. He didn't stop until he was propped over me, his lips in striking distance of mine.

"What was I doing in your dream?" he repeated, the huskiness in his voice raising goose bumps on my arms.

"Something similar to this." My voice was shaky, vibrating with the anticipation of his lips touching mine.

"Similar? Was it this?" he asked, bringing his mouth near the base of my neck, allowing the heat of his breath to skim along my collar bone. I let my head fall back giving him access to kiss me.

He didn't touch me.

"Or was it something more like this?" His breath trailed up my neck until his lips were near my ear. I shivered.

Then he whispered. "Or was it like this?" Ozzy lowered himself so close that he was within millimeters of touching his lips to mine.

My eyes were locked on his as his mouth hovered over mine, our ragged breaths mingling with the need to touch each other.

I moved slightly, trying to bring my lips to his and Ozzy jumped back, grinning. "Uh, uh, Desert Flower. You didn't get any questions right. Tonight I'm the one that gets to make requests. I believe I earned at least four."

"What do you want?" I knew my voice sounded needy, but I didn't care.

"I want you..." He paused.

Yes?

"...to put on that red dress for me," he said slowly.

"What?" That wasn't what I expected at all.

"I want you to go put on that red dress for me. I bought it. I want to see you in it," he repeated.

"Are you serious?"

"Dead serious. Last time you put it on, it was for another guy. I want you to put it on for me this time."

"I'm nearly begging you to kiss me and you want me to play dress up?"

Ozzy laughed. "Humor me. I promise I'll make it worth your while."

"Well, in that case..." I jumped up from the bed and hurried to the walk-in closet, closing the door behind me. I found the dress bag shoved in the back corner of the closet and pulled it out. When I opened it, the red fabric tumbled out. I'd forgotten just how beautiful the dress was. My pajamas were soon tossed on the floor and I was stepping into the dress and pulling the glittering, beaded strap up over my right shoulder. Smooth, red fabric hugged the curve of my hips, flaring out at my knees.

I was still struggling to zip it up when Ozzy called to me from the other side of the door. "Don't forget the shoes."

"Is that request number two?" *I hope he's not wasting a request on shoes!* I thought desperately.

"Of course not. The shoes are part of the ensemble. You almost done?"

"Just battling it out with the zipper." I bent my body nearly in half reaching for the zipper and yanked it up. "Ah! Done. I'm coming out now."

"Just a minute."

I heard a click from the other side of the door followed by soft noises that sounded like music. I unraveled my braid and ran my fingers through my damp hair, flipping my head over to try to give it some body. There was a knock on the closet door and I flipped upright again. "Yes?" I asked hesitantly.

"I'm ready for you."

My stomach clenched in excitement and I slowly opened the door, peeking around the edge to see what awaited me on the other side. When I caught sight of Ozzy, my hands fell to my sides and the door swung wide open on its own. He was standing in the middle of the room, wearing the same suit as the night of the Autumn Formal—black pants, black shirt, black jacket, and black tie. The same square of red silk was peeking out of the breast pocket of his jacket. His tousled hair had been somewhat tamed and his green eyes were bright with amusement. He was standing with his legs slightly apart and his hands clasped behind his back. My breath was tight in my chest as I realized how handsome and put together he was and how bedraggled I must look with no makeup and my hair damp and unbrushed. I fidgeted nervously with my hair, as Ozzy stood a few feet away, silently inspecting me from top to bottom.

"You look as stunning as I remember." His voice was low and appreciative.

Ozzy pulled a small bundle from behind his back and presented it to me. It was the pieces of paper he'd been writing on and folding while we played the game. He had fashioned them into a bouquet of origami flowers. There were five of them clustered together, a beautiful combination of fragile white paper and stark black handwriting. How did he assemble all those scraps of paper in the small amount of time I was in the closet? Was there anything he couldn't do?

"I take it back," I said. "I'm suddenly in love with origami."

"They're not the real thing, but they'll last longer."

I took the flowers from him and brought them close to my face, trying to read the words. "What do they say?"

"My thoughts about my top five days," he said. "In case you had any doubts."

"Oh." I wanted to sit down and unfold the flowers and read them all right away, but at the same time, I didn't have the heart to destroy them. "Thank you, I can't wait to read them," I said, carefully setting the flowers on my dresser. "So, you've got me all dressed up, now what?"

"Time for my second request." Ozzy tilted his head, his eyes locking on mine. "I want you to dance with me. And only me this time."

Something in my chest stirred at the way he looked at me. Wesley's possessive behavior the night of the Autumn Formal had made me want to swat him away like an annoying gnat, but Ozzy's claim on me made me feel lightheaded and breathless. I was beginning to accept that pretty much everything about him made me feel that way.

Ozzy held his hand out and I took it, desperate to finally be able to touch him. He pulled me against his chest and my hands easily found their way to the back of his neck, my fingers knotting into the soft curls of his hair. His hands rested on my waist while his thumbs lightly caressed my sides, sending chills through my body. We danced the first song slowly, barely moving, enjoying the luxury of being able to touch each other at our leisure.

Ozzy's fingers inched higher, reaching the bare skin of my back. He traced lazy circles on my skin while my fingers skimmed along the collar of his shirt before making their way down his shoulders and to his chest. I was about to let my hands venture into his jacket when the music changed. It had a Latin flavor to it.

"Have you ever danced salsa?"

"No. Cassie was the dancer, not me."

"Ah, so you're a virgin? My favorite," he teased. I smacked him, but his smile refused to fade. "Just move like this."

He grabbed my waist and helped me sway to the music the way he wanted. I watched his hips and feet and followed the sensual undulation of his body. It took the entire song for me to feel comfortable doing the steps, but when the song ended, another started and Ozzy took my hands in his.

"Don't think too much, just trust me." With the gentle guiding of his hands, he soon had me moving around comfortably. The first time he spun me, I giggled dizzily, but I was soon back in his strong grip and in time with the music—close to his body where I wanted to be.

I lost count of how many songs we danced to. The songs didn't matter. All I cared about was Ozzy: his hands, his eyes, his mouth, and the feel of his body flexing and moving with mine. He expertly guided me in smooth spins and steps song after song, leaving me breathless with anticipation, never knowing where my body was going until he put it where he wanted.

He pulled me close, caging me against him with his arms wrapped around my waist. His body pressed against me from thigh to chest, deftly moving in time with the music. I became greedy for the feel of him, running my hands up his back and pulling him even closer. He ducked his head down, running the tip of his nose along my collarbone, breathing deeply, before allowing his lips to finally make contact with my skin. When I felt the burn of his mouth at my throat, I sighed as if finally releasing the pent up hunger from an entire night of temptation and restraint. Ozzy slowed his dancing, barely rocking me in time to the music. He lifted his head from my neck.

"Ready for my third request?"

I nodded.

"I'll need a kiss goodnight before I head home."

"What? Already?" I'd been hoping for a kiss, but I wasn't ready to give him the goodnight one just yet.

"It's 2 a.m.," he pointed out. "The morning run is only a few hours away. So, do I get a kiss goodnight or what?"

I reached up, buried my fingers in his hair, and pulled his head down to mine. The moment our lips met, it was as if all the suppressed desire from the night exploded through us. Our bodies responded instinctively, carried by the force of our hunger for each other. Heavy breaths echoed between us as our lips found each other over and over again. His hand was on my lower back, roaming down the swell of my backside to the top of my thigh. My fingers found their way inside Ozzy's shirt, and were soon climbing across the muscles of his stomach on their way to his chest. I trembled as Ozzy's thumb traced along the edge of the back of my dress. Our hands and fingers and mouths were everywhere, frantic to be unleashed on one another. I could feel Ozzy's heart thudding heavily in his chest and I knew mine was echoing the same delirious beat.

Ozzy pulled away. "Christ," he swore, bringing his hands up to my face to run his thumbs across my lower lip. "I don't want to leave."

"Then don't."

"If I stay, I won't be able to stop."

"Then don't," I urged, biting at his thumb which was still resting along the edge of my mouth.

Ozzy took in a deep breath and backed away as he pulled his hands to his hips. He let his head hang before shaking it. "You're killing me, Desert Flower." His voice was thick with feeling and I felt a flicker of excitement low in my body.

"Just stay a little longer," I begged.

Ozzy smiled thinly. "Not tonight."

"But, what about your last request?"

A cocky smile replaced the unhappy determination in Ozzy's expression. "I'll keep that one for a rainy day." He rushed forward, grabbed my face in his hands, and pressed a soft kiss to my lips. "Goodnight, Desert Flower. See you in my dreams."

Then he was gone.

CLEO

DELUSIONAL

As tired as I was, I was surprised that I kept up easily with Arabella on the Sunday morning run. After Ozzy left the night before, I spent too much time lying in bed reliving the night and talking myself out of trying to unfold the flowers to read them. I wanted so badly to know what they said, but I couldn't bring myself to destroy them. I only managed to get a few hours of sleep before Arabella was beating on the door and rushing me out to the obstacle course. As we walked back into the Academy after our run, we saw Ms. Petticoat in the hallway heading toward the infirmary, pushing a cart with two trays of food on it.

"I'm going to go see if Ms. Petticoat needs some help with her cart," I said.

"Why?"

"Maybe it'll soften her up so I can see Cassie."

"I don't think pushing her cart is going to do the trick. If Younglove says no, the answer is no."

"We'll see about that. Save me a seat at breakfast," I called over my shoulder as I ran to catch up with the nurse, weaving through the crowd of sweaty cadets.

When I finally rounded the corner, I was happy to see that Ms. Petticoat was having some difficulty holding the infirmary door open and navigating the food cart inside at the same time.

"Let me help you." I grabbed the handle of the food cart and pushed it inside as the nurse held the door open.

"Thank you, Clementine. I have a terrible time getting that thing through the door by myself. I keep asking them for an assistant, but there seems to be too much work detail to go around and not enough Sophisticates."

"Really? Well I'm here now. Is there anything else you need help with?"

"I could always use help, but..." The nurse looked at me. "Nothing you can help me with right now."

I pretended not to notice that "you" was said in a way that meant me specifically.

"Is this for Cassie?" I asked, picking up a tray of food.

"Yes, but..."

"I can take it in to her, I don't mind. Sit down and enjoy your breakfast while it's still hot."

"I appreciate that, but Cassandra isn't allowed to have visitors yet, especially..." Ms. Petticoat paused, looking for the right words. "...especially cadets. Thank you for your help, Ms. Dracone. Go on and hurry up to your shower. You wouldn't want to miss breakfast."

"Come on, Ms. Petticoat," I begged. "Just a quick peek in the door to make sure she's alright. I promise I won't bother her."

The nurse grabbed the food tray out of my hands. "I'm sorry, but the answer is still no. Professor Younglove said you weren't to see Cassandra yet, and even if the professor agreed, Dean Overton forbids it. I'm sorry, I can't let you in. Cadets aren't the only ones around here who can be punished for not following rules. Now go on." Ms. Petticoat put her hand gently on my shoulder and pushed me through the door and back out into the hallway. "Just be patient, dear. You'll get to see your friend soon enough. In the meantime, just behave yourself." Ms. Petticoat gave me a firm look that made it clear that she knew all about the recent accusations against me.

Dejected, I left the infirmary and made my way to the dorms.

"God, I hope they have pancakes for breakfast. I'm starving." Arabella pushed me toward the food line. "I swear I'm putting myself in a carb coma today and then taking a nap all afternoon."

"What about our derby practice? I still don't know if Younglove is going to let me practice with the Damsels this week. You were going to work out with me today, remember?"

"Oh right, I forgot. Well, I guess that depends on just how comatose I am after I get finished with these." She pulled two large stacks of pancakes on her tray along with two bagels, a bowl of fruit, a muffin, and a yogurt.

"There's no way you can eat all of that."

"Ooooh, a dare. I like that."

"I wasn't daring you, I was stating a fact." I reached over, grabbed Arabella's blueberry muffin and took a huge bite right out of the top of it.

"Oh my God! That is not how you eat a muffin! You eat the stump first and save the top for last, it's the best part. Don't you know anything?" Arabella reached for the defiled pastry and dropped it back on her tray.

"You eat the best part first, don't you know anything?" I argued, smiling.

We were still laughing and fighting over muffin remnants when we reached the table where Sterling, Wesley, and Theo were already sitting. The boys were well over halfway through eating their breakfasts. The hushed conversation they'd been having faded immediately and Sterling flashed me a dirty look before standing up, grabbing his tray, and walking away.

I felt as if he'd slapped me in the face.

"What's got his panties in a bunch?" Arabella asked, settling into Sterling's vacated seat.

"Ask Cleo," Wesley answered.

"How would I know? I just got here." I had a feeling I wasn't going to like what would be said next. This reaction from people was becoming all too familiar and Sterling had never been rude to me before.

"Are you seriously going to pretend you didn't insult him in front of everyone this morning?"

A sudden chill flowed through my veins, my heart stuttering and skipping nervously. No. It couldn't be happening again. Not more accusations. Not Sterling. My eyes and throat burned and I couldn't swallow. I was too nauseous to even try to talk. It was bad enough when people I didn't know were accusing me of things. Now my teammates and friends were doing it too? My relationships and reputation were spiraling out of control and I had no idea why or how to stop it.

"What are you talking about? Cleo would never insult Sterling for real, I'm sure she was just kidding," Arabella said. She scooped cut strawberries on top of her pancake, rolled it up, and proceeded to eat it like a taco.

Wesley narrowed his eyes at me. "She wasn't kidding. I was there."

"What did you say to him?" Arabella turned to look at me, her nose wrinkled in confusion as she seemed to be contemplating the strawberry pancake taco she was eating.

I opened my mouth to say I hadn't even seen Sterling this morning when Wesley interrupted. "She was making fun of his Deviation moniker, Hummingbird, in front of the track team."

Arabella stopped chewing and fixed me with a tight glare. "Not cool, Cleo. You know how sensitive he is about that stupid name. Besides, if Younglove heard about it, you'd be in deep shit. We're not supposed to talk about Deviation stuff in front of the rest of the Mandates, remember?"

"You know I would never do that," I insisted. "I didn't even see him this morning. After the run, I went with Ms. Petticoat to the infirmary and when she wouldn't let me see Cassie, I came straight back to my room."

"I know what I saw and heard," Wesley said. "Theo was there, too. Are you calling us liars?" When I just stared at him, he stood up, pushing back his chair with disgusted force. "You're not the person I thought you were, Cleo." He picked up his tray, dumped his unfinished breakfast in the trash can, and then left through the same door that Sterling had.

I looked helplessly between Arabella, who was staring at me with suspicion, and Theo, who was looking at me with pity.

"I need to go talk to Sterling, to explain," I said.

"Maybe I should talk to him first," Arabella suggested.

"I think you might want to consider what Professor Younglove was telling you the other day about using your deviation to relieve some pressure," Theo said. "She might be on to something. It was like you were a totally different person."

Then he got up and left, too.

***

After breakfast, Arabella tried to find Sterling to talk to him, but he went for another run. I tried to track down Ozzy to get his advice on this newest problem of mine, but I couldn't find him. Apparently, he was busy with Rune.

Putting the Sterling problem on the back-burner until she could talk to him, Arabella invited me to come to her room to do homework until lunch time. I knew the invite had nothing to do with homework and everything to do with the newest indiscretion.

It took Arabella a good thirty minutes to work up to the real reason she asked me to study with her.

"Do you want to talk?" Arabella asked, sprawled out across her bed, flipping one of the white butterflies through her fingers.

I was sitting at the desk, diligently working on my Arabic homework. I tossed it to the side and rubbed my eyes, staring at the laptop in front of me. "I don't even know what to say. I keep getting blamed for things I would never do. Things that apparently I've been seen doing, but don't remember at all. I think the Program has finally broken me. I'm totally dysfunctional and clearly delusional. Or maybe I'm just crazy."

"You're not broken and we're all dysfunctional. Look at me, my room is filled with freaking butterflies. And I'm not the butterfly type. I'm more the scary-ass-bird-that-eats-the-butterfly type. And yet, look at this place. It's fluttergasmic in here. That's true crazy right there."

"Yeah, but you're not the one that is doing things—horrible things—you can't remember doing. I'd take fluttergasmic butterflies over sleepwalking delinquency any day. If that's even what it is. I mean, I have no other explanation."

Arabella glanced over at me sympathetically. "Maybe you should give Younglove's suggestion a try. I mean, it makes sense. You've got all that energy building up, which is probably hard to keep under control. You've got to let it out and blow some stuff up. It'd be fun, right?"

I sighed. "Right." I pulled my homework back into my lap and decided to think about it later after I had a chance to talk to Ozzy. When Arabella succumbed to her carb coma and started snoring, I packed up my laptop and books, and went back to my own room to finish my work.

***

"Cleo!" My door swung open with force, slamming into the wall behind it in a shower of cement dust and chips. Arabella's mutant strength was disturbing, especially when she was using it unintentionally.

"Sorry, I guess I lost track of time," I apologized. "Ready to go down for lunch?"

I closed my notebook and set it on top of my desk, turning to get a good look at Arabella who was wild-eyed and manic looking. For once, my tiny friend, who always seemed so controlled and composed, looked frazzled. Arabella's clothes were wrinkled, her makeup was smeared, and her hair was tangled and messy. Arabella could easily change her appearance with just a quick thought, so the fact that she was beyond disheveled was a strange sight.

"Man, you really look like you could use a piece of cake," I said. "And a hairbrush," I added, smiling. It was a little satisfying to be able to use that line on Arabella who always looked like she spent hours getting ready.

"It's gone, I can't find it anywhere."

"Here, you can use mine," I said, grabbing my brush out of my shower caddy and tossing it to Arabella. The brush bounced off her stomach and fell to the floor as Arabella stared, shell-shocked at me.

"Not the brush. I don't need a brush!" Arabella's voice was ratcheting up into a panic and she reached up to clutch at her knotty hair. "I can't find my locket." Her eyes were desperate as if pleading with me to fix the problem.

"You lost your butterfly locket?"

"I looked everywhere, tore my whole room apart. But it's just gone. It was there this morning and now it's missing."

"Don't worry, I'll come help you look. I'm sure it just fell under the bed or behind your dresser. It's in your room somewhere." I came up and put my hand on Arabella's arm. "We'll find it."

Arabella released her breath in an audible sigh, her features relaxing now that she had a solution to focus on.

"I don't know why I'm freaking out about this," she admitted. "It's not like I didn't get along just fine without it for seventeen years." Her arms fell to her sides and she began to pace the room nervously as I searched around for my shoes. "Part of me is embarrassed that I need it so much. A piece of jewelry. Who would have thought? And it doesn't even have a skull on it, totally not my style at all. I mean, maybe it's just junk, maybe it didn't mean anything to my parents at all, maybe—" Arabella's rambling finally cut off. "Cleo?"

"Yep. Just looking for my shoes. Oh, here they are." I got down on my hands and knees and reached under the bed where I'd kicked my shoes earlier. When I sat down on the floor to put them on, I noticed that Arabella was standing at the high dresser, staring at the top of it.

"Cleo, how did this get here?" Arabella reached into the makeup box and lifted her hand. The butterfly locket was hanging from her finger, dangling reproachfully on its golden chain. I stared at the swinging pendant as it seemed to whisper, "Thief! Thief!" with every condemning sway.

"I don't know how that got there." My voice was quiet.

"Did you steal it?"

"No! Of course not. I would never. You know that. Maybe you left it in here earlier."

"I haven't been in your room since I showed this to you yesterday," Arabella accused, her voice hard and clipped in a way that I only ever heard when she was talking to, or about, Quinnie.

Arabella stared at the locket before gathering the chain in her hand and locking the golden butterfly away in her palm. "I know you like it and I know you were jealous that you didn't get something from your parents, but I never thought you'd take it without asking."

Her eyes roamed over me, as if peeling away layers of a disguise. I realized that Arabella was probably remembering every accusation made against me and was finally believing what everyone else was saying.

"Arabella. You know me. You know I'd never steal from you."

"I would've let you borrow it if you asked," she whispered, ignoring my excuse.

"Arabella..."

She put her hand up to stop the denials. "Don't bother. I think you need to get some help, but I can't...I can't be around you right now. I can't trust you." She looked down at the locket in her hand and then back up to me. "I have to go find Sterling. He needs me. Or I need him. I'm not sure."

The door shut behind Arabella and the sudden silence in the room was thick and tangible, pressing on my chest. I could only take shallow breaths because the monster inside was shredding my sanity, trying to claw its way out. Every breath was painful and forced.

I hadn't thought I could ever feel lonelier than I did when I had to leave Cassie behind at the University weeks ago. But now, after making friends and having them taken away one at a time by a dark side of myself that I didn't know existed, and seemingly couldn't control, I felt not just lonely, but alone.

Completely alone.

CLEO

BURN

After Arabella left, I tried to find Ozzy. He promised to help me figure out was going on and I needed to talk to him. I was confused by the accusations, my own belief that I was innocent, and the fact that I had no explanations with which to defend myself. And it wasn't just his help I needed, I needed him. I wanted to know he was still on my side and that I wasn't truly alone.

I looked in all of the usual places I expected him to be, but had no luck. I finally ran into Professor Younglove near the dining hall.

"Shouldn't you be in lunch, Clementine?"

"I was actually looking for Ozzy. Have you seen him?"

"He's not at the Academy right now. He'll be back in time for class tomorrow. Was there something you needed?"

"Uh, no. Um...it can wait." I certainly wasn't going to tell Younglove about my newest problems with Sterling and Arabella. I already had enough strikes against me without giving her more ammunition to be disappointed in me.

Instead of going to lunch, I made my way back down to the infirmary. I knew Ms. Petticoat wouldn't let me see Cassie, but I thought it couldn't hurt to try to get in the woman's good graces anyway. If the nurse had things that needed to be done, I was only too happy to help out and keep my mind busy. I pushed the door open and even though my eyes darted to the back room where I knew Cassie was probably being kept, I went to the main office and knocked on the door, which was open. Ms. Petticoat was busy filing things into a vertical cabinet and looked up in surprise, clearly not used to having people come to her office when they weren't bleeding or otherwise incapacitated.

"Can I help you, Ms. Dracone?"

"You said you needed some help around here and since I wasn't busy, I thought I could help out a bit."

"That's very kind of you," the nurse said, clearly suspicious. "But, you do realize I still won't allow you to see Cassandra."

"I understand, I just need to keep busy today. So, if there's anything I can do..." I spread my arms wide in offering.

She sighed and then led me out of the office and into a storage room where there was a load of sheets, towels, and dressing cloths to fold and put away. The large pile of clean laundry was evidence of just how much traffic the infirmary saw.

As I folded the mountain of stark white fabric, I imagined dozens of conversations with Arabella, trying to find the right words to fix our friendship. Nothing I came up with seemed worthy and when I was still at a loss for how to solve my problem, I asked Ms. Petticoat for more odd jobs. She seemed to have an endless list of ways I could make myself useful, which was good because my hands needed to stay as busy as my mind.

I might have been lost in thought most of the time, but it didn't escape my notice that Ms. Petticoat kept an eye trained on me every second, clearly making sure I didn't try to sneak in to see Cassie.

When it was time for dinner, Ms. Petticoat asked me to fetch some food and when I asked if I could stay in the infirmary to eat with her, the pity in her eyes when she agreed was evident. I stayed in the infirmary doing odd jobs until it was time to go off to work detail.

When I finally got back to my room later that night, I emailed Ozzy asking him to come see me because I needed to talk to him. I stared at the window all night expecting him to climb through with an apologetic cocky smile. Hours later, the sunrise finally began to peek through the glass, throwing warm light all over my tired body.

He never came.

***

That morning, things weren't much better. It was Monday and Arabella didn't meet me at my room for the daily run like usual. Not knowing what to say to fix the issue between us, I didn't even bother to search her out once I got near the starting line. For the first time since arriving, I entered the obstacle course all alone.

I finally made an appearance at the dining hall for breakfast. I knew I couldn't avoid it forever. I had to face my problems eventually. All of my friends were already at the table, but when I sat down no one acknowledged me and one by one they quickly finished their meals and left. I wanted to say something to make things better and I looked at Arabella a dozen times with words of apology on the tip of my tongue, trying to remember the words I had pieced together in my head while helping Ms. Petticoat last night. But, I couldn't seem to make the words form. I didn't remember doing the things I was blamed for doing, so how could I apologize truthfully?

If only Ozzy had been there, I could have asked for his advice. Unfortunately, he still hadn't answered the email I sent him last night. Was he mad at me now, too?

Ozzy was in weapons class when I showed up later that morning, but he was busy setting up and didn't make a point to talk to me before class started. Although the Arabella incident hadn't made it into the rumor mill yet, it seemed plenty of people were talking about how I had allegedly treated Sterling. The rumor of Maya's defiled door was still going strong as well. No one would get within ten feet of me. I wondered if that was why Ozzy avoided me, too.

Now that Rune was in the class and there was an even number of students, there was no need for Ozzy to partner with me. I ended up with Rune and a head full of insecurities. As if weapons class didn't make me feel insecure enough, I was now worried about what I may, or may not, have done to piss off Ozzy.

Surprisingly, despite the assumptions I had that Rune was dangerous, he had yet to live up to that worry. I never thought I'd meet someone who was worse with weapons than me, but Rune surpassed all expectations of mediocrity and fell headlong into complete and utter failure.

We were learning how to use a staff, or as Ozzy pointed out, anything that could be turned into a weapon and wielded as a staff—a broom, a shovel, and a pipe were on his short list. I actually had a little experience with using a staff since I'd learned some bojutsu when I was at the University. Like everything martial arts related, I picked it up quickly, even if it did involve a weapon.

Ozzy showed us how to use the staff to do basic strikes and

blocks. We slowly mimicked each motion several dozen times and then he sent us off in our designated pairs to practice.

"Do you want to block first or strike?" I asked Rune.

If it was possible for someone to look any less interested than Rune, I would've been surprised. He merely shrugged and then pushed his shaggy, golden blond hair out of his cobalt-colored eyes. On most people, that color of blue would've been spectacular—invoking thoughts of bright autumn skies and serene Caribbean waters. But on Rune, that color was deep and empty and utterly devoid of any spark of life. I shivered slightly as I remembered the empty look the rest of the Others had.

"I'll defend," he offered.

The first whack of my staff against Rune's sent his skittering across the floor and into the leg of a Mandate who growled something unintelligible. He gave me a dirty look even though it was Rune's staff, and not mine, that hit him. It went like that for the rest of the class until I was almost ready to strike Rune in the side of the head just so I wouldn't have to watch him chase his staff anymore. Actually, chase was too kind of a word for what Rune did. There was no hurry or worry in his movements. He would slowly walk over to where his weapon had fallen, pick it up, and walk back to me before I knocked it out of his hands again a few seconds later.

Watching turtles race would have been infinitely more exciting.

Class finally ended and I offered to help gather the staffs and put them away. Ozzy was at the weapons cabinet, organizing. I came up behind him with an armload of practice staffs and looked across the training field to where Rune was sitting on a bench, waiting for Ozzy.

"Did I do something wrong?" I asked.

Ozzy turned. "No. Why would you think that?"

"You haven't called or visited. I thought maybe I did something wrong. You know, the other night. When you were in my room..." I whispered the last few words.

Ozzy's eyes darted around the training field as he pulled me behind the door and out of Rune's sight. "Of course not," he said, taking the staffs from me and setting them against the cabinet. "Quite the opposite. You did everything right." He reached up and caught a piece of my hair in his hand and twirled it around his finger.

"I really need to see you. There's so much I want to talk to you about."

He stopped twirling my hair when he heard the tremble in my voice. I refused to break down. I could be strong. I would be.

"What's wrong? Did something happen?"

I took a deep breath to steady my voice.

"Sterling, Wes, and Theo said that I embarrassed Sterling in front of his teammates, that I was making fun of his Deviant name."

Ozzy frowned. "That doesn't sound like something you'd do."

"That's because it isn't. I was in the infirmary at the time, but they swear it was me. I just...I can't even come up with an explanation. On top of that, Arabella accused me of stealing her necklace."

"Why would she think you'd steal something from her?"

My hands dug into the hem of my shirt, twisting it around until my fingers were strangled in the knotted fabric.

"Because she found it in my room."

Ozzy was quiet.

"What's wrong with me?" I whispered.

"There is nothing wrong with you. There has to be an explanation for all of this."

"What if it's all true? What if I'm just as broken as the rest of the Others? What if I'm really doing these things and I just don't remember? What if I'm crazy?"

"You're not crazy. I know you better than anyone else and I know you wouldn't do any of the things you're accused of doing. We'll figure this out together. I promise." His hand slid underneath my chin and he lifted it with a gentle touch of his finger and thumb. He bent down and kissed me softly, so lightly I almost didn't feel it. "I'll come by tonight," he whispered, his lips grazing mine as he spoke.

My lips ached for more, but he pulled away and started stacking staffs again.

"We'll figure out a way to prove you're innocent. Of everything."

But what if I really am guilty? I thought.

***

A few hours later I was on my way to the dining hall for lunch when Arabella met me in the hallway outside. She was holding a white bag and she stared at me as if expecting me to say something.

I shifted nervously on my feet.

"Arabella...I'm really sorry. I can't stand that you're not talking to me. I don't know what's going on with me, but I promise you I'm going to fix it. I'm going to figure out why I don't remember all these things I'm accused of doing. If I have to figure out how to use my deviation, if I have to destroy every single target dummy Younglove has, I'll..."

"Professor Younglove came to the dining hall a few minutes ago. She wants to see you in her office. She told me to send you there."

"Oh." I looked down at my feet. Did this mean Arabella wasn't going to let me apologize? "Did she seem pissed?" I asked.

"Isn't she always?" Arabella pushed a white bag toward me. "I grabbed you a sandwich to eat on the way in case you don't make it back to lunch in time."

"Thanks," I said, holding the bag as if I was holding the last strings of my friendship with Arabella. "You're the best."

"I know that."

"And I'm sorry."

Arabella turned to go back inside the dining hall. I heard her sigh. "I know that, too," she said before the doors closed behind her.

This was progress, right? Arabella didn't say I was forgiven, but she brought me lunch. She still cared about me. I inhaled the sandwich as I made my way through the halls to Younglove's office. By the time I got there I'd eaten the whole sandwich, and I'd also convinced myself that maybe the professor wanted to see me because Cassie was finally well enough for visitors. Of course, that had to be it. I hadn't done anything wrong or been accused of anything all day. The Maya incident was nearly in the past. I only had a few more nights left of her work detail and then, hopefully, things would start to improve and people would forget.

Younglove's door was open, but the room was empty so I walked inside and sat in a chair in front of the desk and waited. I fished an apple out of the bottom of the bag and started eating it. I didn't have to wait long before Younglove entered, picked up her trash can, and walked over to me.

"No food in my office."

I tossed the half-eaten apple into the waste basket and wiped my hands on my pants. Younglove set the can down and sat in the chair. She looked angry, but as Arabella pointed out, when didn't the professor look angry?

"Do you know why you're here in my office?"

"Is it about Cassie?" I asked hopefully.

"So, you don't deny it."

I stared for a moment at the desk before raising my eyes. "Deny what?"

Younglove sighed, exasperated. "What am I going to do with you? You were the most promising one. And now..."

Nervous worry clutched at my stomach.

"Please tell me what this is about." My voice was little more than a whisper.

The chair behind the desk squeaked as Younglove leaned forward to put her elbows on the desktop and rest her chin on the back of her hands.

"I thought you were her friend. I really can't figure out why you would do what you did. It was bad enough that you would target and terrorize a fellow team member, but I just can't understand what would cause you to torment your best friend. And at this point, I'm really not sure what to do about it."

"Torment?" I was shaking my head as it dropped into my hands. A million thoughts spun through my mind, but I couldn't manage to keep hold of any of them.

"Ms. Petticoat caught you in the infirmary. She said you had strapped Cassandra down and were pressing burn marks into her skin with your fingertips." Younglove's mouth twisted in disgust. "I didn't even know you could do something like that."

I was unable to speak, staring in horror at Younglove. Hurt

Cassie? I would never. Ever. Why was Ms. Petticoat lying?

"Well?"

"Ms. Petticoat is wrong. It's not true," I managed to croak. It sounded like I was begging. I could hear the question in my own statement. Even I didn't believe myself anymore. "Professor, you know I wouldn't do something like that."

"If it wasn't you, who was it?"

My mind shuffled through all the possibilities I'd pondered over the last few days. "Persephone?" I said desperately.

"Even if it was possible for Persephone to sneak past our security system, she couldn't have attacked Cassandra. Persephone was seen this morning with a group of Others in Philadelphia near one of the Vanguard Academies. She can't be in two places at once."

I shook my head in disbelief, my heart hammering in my chest. I was so hot that I could feel the sweat trickling down the middle of my back.

"I'll give you one more chance to confess," Younglove said.

"It won't get you out of the whippings, but you can at least avoid solitary confinement," a deep voice threatened. I turned around to see the imposing figure of Dean Overton in the doorway of Younglove's office. I'd never been this close to him before.

"Wh-whippings?" I could barely speak, I was choking on air and words and denials.

Panic slid across Younglove's features. "Do you really think that's necessary?" she asked, looking between the dean and me. "I thought we agreed I would talk to her."

A stern look from Overton struck Younglove speechless. Ms. Petticoat's words from the day before echoed in my ears: *Cadets aren't the only ones around here who can be punished for not follow-*

ing rules. Would the dean really punish Younglove for sticking up for me?

"You've had enough opportunity to get this one under control. It seems extra work detail in the kitchen and detentions with Professor Peck aren't enough of a deterrent. For extreme behavior, we must resort to extreme measures. We had this discussion before with Quinby, did we not? When these Deviants lose control, they have to be punished. They're too dangerous to be allowed to do as they please. They have to be taught respect for the rules of the Program and they need to learn obedience." Overton talked about me as if I were a malfunctioning machine, like I wasn't even in the room listening.

Younglove dropped her eyes to her hands and for the first time I saw regret with the mention of Quinnie and her punishment. She didn't say anything more in my defense.

My gaze was drawn to Overton as he finally came all the way through the door and entered the office. Up close, he was a formidable man. It seemed half the room was filled with his presence—barrel chest, thick mustache, massive arms, large stomach, bald head, bad attitude—there was so much of him. Even when he wasn't speaking he was making a statement. But it was his eyes that were the most frightening part. There wasn't an ounce of compassion in them. This was the man who could read off the names of dozens of young cadets in the middle of the dining hall and send them off to fight in a war without a second thought. This was a man who could order the whipping of a seventeen-year old girl and not regret it.

"I didn't do it, sir." I knew my words meant nothing to him, but I said them anyway because they meant everything to me.

Dean Overton stared at me quietly, my denial fading into the silence of the room as if I never said it.

"Ms. Petticoat saw you, that's all the proof I need. Cassandra was having enough trouble coping and coming to terms with her deviation. All the progress she made in the last week has just been destroyed. Honestly, so has her sanity. I just can't imagine why you would torture her. Why did you do it?"

The world came unhinged as I shook my head frantically. No. Not Cassie. Not Arabella. Not Sterling. Not Maya. Not Michael. I didn't do any of it.

Did I? I wanted to deny it again, but I didn't.

"Very well, then," he said.

He looked toward the doorway and nodded. I turned just in time to see two Hounds enter the room, each of them grabbing me by an arm. They roughly hauled me to my feet. Something sharp jabbed into my upper arm and I flicked my eyes to the side just enough that I could see a needle full of amber liquid sticking out of my muscle, the plunger of it being pressed down by one of the Hounds. I waited for pain or numbness or paralysis to overtake me, but there was nothing but a slight cooling of my body as if ice water had been pumped through my veins.

"Did you give her the counteragent?" I heard the dean ask.

"Yeah. We're cool," the Hound responded.

"Trust me," Overton said to me, "it gives me no pleasure to order this punishment." His smile said otherwise. "I really don't know what else to do at this point. This is far worse than anything Quinby has done. She, at least, has never tied anyone down." He waved to the Hounds, dismissing them and me.

I glanced helplessly to Younglove as I was dragged into the

hallway.

"Professor, please!" I called to her. "You know me. You know I wouldn't hurt Cassie!"

Younglove merely reached to a stack of papers on the side of her desk and pulled them in front of her. She didn't look up as I pleaded, my voice reaching a near scream, begging her to help me. I struggled as the Hounds pulled me down the hall. I reached for door frames or anything else I could grab to slow their progress. I didn't really have a plan for what I would do if I got out of their grip, but I tried anyway.

"Please, don't," I begged.

They ignored me.

"Please! Please!" I screamed.

It was still lunch time, so there was no one in the hallways to hear me as I was carried, kicking and screaming, down a crooked staircase and into the lower levels of the Academy. The hall I was taken down looked vaguely familiar, but I barely registered my surroundings as fear and terror clawed at me. The dark room I was pulled into was grey, stone block. It was mostly empty except for the chains bolted into the far wall, a battered wooden table along the side wall, and a long leather whip coiled on top of the table.

I bucked and struggled as the Hounds calmly led me to the wall and fastened the metal cuffs around my wrists and then pulled the chains taut, hoisting me up onto my tiptoes. I was facing the wall, the side of my face pressed against the rough block as I hung, helpless, from the ceiling. Unable to turn my head to see what was going on behind me, I waited in silence. I couldn't move and I was afraid to breathe.

I heard the flick of a switchblade and then the rip of fabric as the blade tore through the back of my shirt. Tremors of fear rippled through my body as I hung by my wrists. Rough hands pushed the tatters of my shirt to the sides, exposing my back. Another set of thick hands slipped something over my head and then shoved a piece of leather between my teeth, tightening a cord that was attached to either end so that it wouldn't fall out of my mouth.

No one spoke, but the sound of the leather whip as it slid off the table was menacing, like the growl of an animal threatening me from across the room. My breath came in short gasps as I strained to listen.

I waited. And waited.

There was a faint hiss of air right before the pain splintered across my back in an explosion of scorching torment. I screamed, but the sound was muffled by the leather in my mouth. Another hiss and another slash of agony tore across my skin, ripping the screams from my throat. Again. And again. And again. So many times that I thought I'd gone up in flames.

I kept expecting the anger to release me, for my deviation to leave the room a pile of rubble and screaming echoes, but the power never came. The monster had abandoned me and the whip kept coming, leaving me to burn in anguish.

Maybe because my anger wasn't righteous.

Maybe because I really was guilty.

Maybe because I deserved to burn for the monster I was.

Ozzy

Archerfish

Part of me wished I'd never told Younglove about Rune. Actually, there wasn't even a small part of me that was glad I told her. If I'd known she was going to bring him to the Academy, I would have left that boy's ass, and his stupid missing memory, in the hangar.

Why was I on guard duty? It's not like we were at a loss for Hounds to do the job. It's not like my role as leader of the Deviants had any impact on Rune anyway. The kid couldn't remember who he was, why would he care about my status at the Academy? In all honesty, sometimes I thought I scared him more than anything. He never said a word unless I asked him a question first. The way that he followed my every order without question was alarming. I could've told him to drive a nail through his hand and there was a good chance he'd do it without hesitation.

Since coming back from Andrews Air Force Base, it seemed like Rune was always there—a bad decision who was always watching and learning, even if it looked like he was barely existing. Rune put up a good front of being inconspicuous, that's why people usually forgot he was there. He never said anything, just picked at his nails and trailed behind me like a zombie shadow.

I wasn't fooled though, I saw Rune watching Cleo when he thought nobody was paying attention. For that reason alone, I wanted to carve his eyes out of his damn head. It wasn't that I was jealous. Not exactly. I just hated the way Rune looked at her like he was stealing a piece of her, like he was storing her actions and words for later. The little Pistol Shrimp didn't look at anyone else the way he looked at Cleo, and it unnerved me.

She, on the other hand, was completely clueless that he was visually stalking her. Weapons class was a prime example. She was so blind with angry frustration at his lack of effort with the staff that she couldn't see that he was watching her every move, listening to her every word, and taking note of it all.

She may not have noticed, but I did.

I clenched my fists as I was forced, once again, to lead Rune to dinner. I was going to have to come up with a good excuse to get rid of him tonight because I'd promised Cleo that I'd come visit her. I had a feeling if I didn't keep my promise, she just might search me out in my room, and I didn't think either of us was ready for that.

As soon as I walked into the dining hall, it was obvious that Cleo was missing. I hoped she was just late coming from derby practice or punishment with Peck. I felt guilty that I hadn't been there for Cleo. Younglove wanted me to work with Rune one-on-one to see if we could get his memory kick started. If he could remember anything about Delia and the Others, Younglove wanted to know it. In any case, I was so busy with Rune, that I didn't have the opportunity to help Cleo and that royally pissed me off.

I set my tray down at the table and heard the echo of Rune's tray as he followed suit and sat in the chair next to me. What the fuck? There were at least five other chairs at the table. Did he have to sit right next to me?

"Where's Cleo?" I asked before taking a huge gulp of milk. It was a moment before I realized that no one answered me. "Where is she?" I repeated, looking around.

Sterling, Wesley, and Theo shrugged. Arabella was the only one who had the nerve to look up, and she looked guilty.

"Not sure. Younglove sent for her right before lunch. We haven't seen her since," Arabella admitted.

"What do you mean you haven't seen her? She wasn't in the workshop? What about classes and practice?"

Arabella shook her head.

"Well, what did Younglove want?"

"I don't know. Cleo hasn't exactly been herself lately. She's been getting in trouble. A lot. I'm guessing she's being punished."

"Punished as in 'manual labor with Peck' or punished as in 'capital punishment?'"

Arabella was silent for a moment. "If I had to guess, I'd say the latter. There's been a rumor floating around."

"Tell me."

Arabella glanced at Sterling, but he was intent on eating his meal and was clearly not going to be any help in breaking the news. "She snuck in to see Cassie."

"That's a minor infraction, I doubt they'd use capital punishment. Besides, they should've expected she'd eventually sneak in since..." I looked at Rune. The other boy was still looking at the table, but he wasn't eating. I knew he was listening and saving this information in his demented little mind. "Sneaking in to see Cassie is a minor infraction," I repeated.

Arabella looked at Rune warily as if she didn't want to say more in front of him either. "Oh, what the hell," she said, gesturing toward him. "He's going to hear it from someone else anyway. Everybody already knows." She looked back at me. "Apparently, Cleo snuck into the infirmary, tied Cassie down, and tortured her." Arabella glared at Rune. "What do you think about that? Does it make you feel a little homesick?"

Rune used the fork to clean underneath his fingernails. If he heard Arabella, which I was sure he had, he chose to ignore her.

"That's bullshit," I said, standing up. "Cleo would never do that to Cassie. I'm going to find Younglove and straighten this all out. Can you watch him?" I asked, gesturing to Rune.

"No," Arabella said with disgust. "I don't babysit. It's no use anyway. During the workshop I asked Younglove about Cleo and she wouldn't tell me anything."

"Well, I'm not going to sit around and do nothing. I'm supposed to be in charge of the Deviants, I have a right to know what's going on. Come on," I barked at Rune.

I left the dining hall and Rune obediently followed. On my way to Younglove's office, I took a detour past the Hounds' barracks and dropped Rune off. If I was going to confront Younglove, I didn't want him there to hear all the dirty laundry of the Dozen. If he truly was working with Delia Younglove and the Others, he probably knew a lot of details about the Deviants already, but there was no reason to allow him to overhear anything else. Especially not anything that involved Cleo and Cassie.

When I finally reached Younglove's office, I realized how unlikely it was that the professor would be there, since it was still dinner. I knocked anyway, or rather, pounded on her door.

"Come in, Osbourne," Younglove said. For once, her tone wasn't haughty.

"Where is she?" I demanded, slamming the door behind me. Younglove sat at the desk, her head buried in her thin, bony hands.

"I knew you'd come eventually. You can't seem to stay away from her." Younglove looked up. "Where's Rune?"

"With the Hounds."

"Good. It's better he doesn't hear about this."

"Unfortunately, he's heard enough," I growled. "You know I don't trust him."

"And I do? What would you have me do? Keep him locked up in a cell?"

"Why not?" I countered.

"He hasn't done anything wrong."

"Yet."

"We're not monsters," Younglove said wearily.

"Oh, really? Where's Cleo?"

She cringed. "That's different."

"So it's true? She's being punished?"

"It wasn't my decision. It was the dean's."

"We just torture and imprison our own, then? Rune gets to roam free and Cleo gets the whip?"

Younglove stood angrily. "I didn't want to send her down there, but you know I can't defy the dean. She was seen *torturing* Cassie! How can I argue against that?"

"You're her mentor, that's your job!" I shouted.

"If she had listened to me, she wouldn't be having these problems. If she would just accept her deviation and use it, she wouldn't be going crazy and doing things she doesn't mean to do or even remember doing."

"It's your job to guide her," I argued. "You're giving up on her! At least if you don't want the job, let me do it. Take me off Pistol Shrimp babysitting duty. Let me help her."

Younglove rounded the desk angrily, her eyes blazing as she stood in front of me. "I haven't given up on her. I'm doing everything I can."

"Really? Do more. Get her out of the hole now and send her to Ms. Petticoat to get healed. You know how savage those Hounds are down there!" I shook with rage.

"You know I can't send her to Ms. Petticoat; it's against the rules. She has to heal on her own. Even I can't go against Dean Overton on this."

"Well, send her to me then," I retorted. "I can at least help her with the pain." I thought about Ms. Petticoat's miracle cream that I had down in the weapons training area.

God. I was tired of having these same arguments with the professor. Was it less than two weeks ago that I was making the same argument in Quinnie's defense? Although I realized that Quinnie had to be punished for what she did to Katie, there was a small part of me that still cared about her. In the end, I hadn't been able to get her out of her punishment, but I'd been able to help her heal. The cream helped take the edge off the daily agony.

"I can't do that. I can't send her to you," Younglove admitted.

"Why not?" I asked warily. "You let me help Quinnie."

"Because you won't be here when Clementine is released."

Younglove pushed a folder across the desk.

"Another mission? Now? You've got to be kidding me. I'm not leaving."

"You're to take Arabella, Sterling, Sadie, and Evangeline with you."

"You can't do this. I need to be here," I argued.

"I'm not doing this, the dean is. The order came from Headquarters."

"What about Rune?"

"He stays here."

"I'm not leaving him here." I wanted to add "with Cleo" but I knew I wouldn't be doing either of us any favors to admit my affections for her. So far, my interest in her could be interpreted as concern for one of my Deviant Dozen team members. I reacted just as defensively for Quinnie and Sterling when they were both whipped for indiscretions in the past.

"You don't have a choice, and neither do I. The quicker you get this done, the quicker you can be back here and guard Rune."

"I don't want to guard him, I want him gone," I said through clenched teeth.

"Well, we don't always get what we want," Younglove said. "Not when you're in the Program, especially not when you're a Deviant."

***

"You remember what her voice sounds like, right?" I asked Eva. My words sounded tight, even to my own ears. I didn't want to be here on this stupid mission. I wanted to be with Cleo. There was a moment of silence, which I interpreted as an eye roll. If I knew nothing else about girls, I knew that eye rolling was often the first response a female had when a male questioned her ability to do anything.

"It's my deviation, not a hobby. Of course I remember," Eva said, mimicking Delia Younglove's voice perfectly. Eva had been at the Academy for two years and that part of her deviation—her ability to copy someone's voice—never got any less creepy.

We were parked around the corner from a house where the Program's Security Advisor lived. I outlined the plan to everyone an hour ago and now we were watching the house, waiting for the perfect opportunity. I still didn't understand the reason we were being sent to bring this guy in, but it wasn't my job to understand. It was my job to follow orders. Unfortunately, the rest of the Deviants had yet to learn the skill of obedience. There had been too many questions since this excursion began.

"I don't understand, we're just going in to apprehend him?" Sterling was confused and I didn't blame him.

"Those were our orders."

"But, you're an assassin," Arabella pointed out.

I glared at her.

"I mean, it seems a little excessive, don't you think? Why send an assassin and a bunch of Deviants to arrest someone? Why not just send a pack of Hounds?" Arabella asked. "This guy isn't a terrorist or even a Sophisticate. He's just some overpaid, middle-aged Program official who spies on our Internet usage. Don't they usually send you in to do exterminations and whatnot?"

My jaw tightened. "When are you going to stop asking so many questions?"

"Probably when I stop having them," Arabella responded.

I stared at the dark house. Mr. Malleville had turned out the lights ten minutes ago. This would have been easier with Wesley along to use his fancy X-ray vision, but I had a feeling this was some sort of Program test—get the job done with the talents at our disposal.

"Let's get into position," I said, handing the car keys to Arabella. As the rest of us gathered on the sidewalk, she got into the front seat, allowing her deviation to take effect. Her long, wild hair shrank and smoothed itself into a chocolate colored bob and her features elongated and tightened until her cheekbones were more prominent, causing her eyes to look like they were sunken back into their sockets. I stared at the face of Delia Younglove and had to fight the urge to put a bullet through her forehead. *It's just Arabella,* I had to remind myself.

"What?" Arabella asked, frowning back at me.

I didn't answer her. As creepy as Eva's skills were, Arabella's were worse. Watching her change her appearance always made my skin crawl.

"See something you like?" she asked, her voice sliding into a seductive whisper. Arabella's face morphed once more until I was staring at Cleo. Even though I knew it wasn't really her, my heart beat wildly in my chest.

"Stop it," I demanded.

"You're no fun." The vision of Cleo disappeared and the Delia Younglove disguise was back in place.

A disturbing idea gnawed at the edges of my thoughts. "How often do you do that?

"Do what, exactly?"

"Disguise yourself as Cleo."

"That's only the second time I've ever done it. The first time she asked me to. Why do you want to know?" she asked. Her eyes narrowed in suspicion.

"It's just that Cleo has been accused of a lot of things lately that she swears she didn't do."

The Delia Younglove disguise vanished as Arabella's blue-streaked hair and overly dramatic makeup reappeared. She jumped out of the car and approached me, clearly furious.

"Take it back." She jabbed me in the chest with her finger, the keys jangling noisily as they hung from her fist.

"I didn't accuse you; I just asked a question."

"Take it back now or you'll find my foot in a very uncomfortable location. Unlike you, I'm not a liar."

"I'm not a liar, either," I retaliated.

"You don't tell the whole truth."

"Neither do you."

"I always do." Arabella's voice had lowered dangerously.

"Really? What's the truth then? It's certainly not this," I said, gesturing to her face. "What's the real Arabella even look like? You always wear a mask. No one knows what you really look like, or who you really are. How is *that* the truth?"

Arabella shook with fury. "Just because I can look however I want, it doesn't mean I'm a fake. Underneath the hair, I'm still the same me." Her blue-streaked, teased hair changed until it was limp and slightly knotty. It hung to her shoulders in black chunks. "Without the makeup, I'm still Arabella," she said. The black and purple makeup faded until her face was plain, pale, and innocent. Without makeup, she looked harmless. The girl glaring back at me was almost unrecognizable. "Maybe we all pretend to be something we're not, but at least my pretense is only skin deep."

I stared at her as she let the Delia Younglove disguise take shape again.

"Let's get this over with, I want to go back to the Academy," Arabella said, dropping back into the driver's seat of the car and slamming the door behind her.

At least on this point, we could agree. I couldn't believe I'd so easily lost my focus. I was on a mission, I had no business getting into arguments about stuff that had nothing to do with our objective. I needed to get my shit together and stop obsessing about Cleo.

I had a bad feeling about this particular assignment and I wanted to be finished with it. In all the time I'd been going on solo missions for the Program, I had a 100% success rate with no glitches. That was the perk of having perfect aim and the ability to follow orders without question. Success came easily.

However, since the first mission with a team of Deviants, the one where we were sent to rescue Cassie, things never went as expected. I could no longer trust myself to just pull the trigger and end a threat. I hesitated in attacking Persephone the first time I saw her in the basement of The Rink. Then I hesitated in attacking the Others at the hangar at Andrews Air Force Base. If I'd just eliminated the Others like I usually eliminated my targets, things may have turned out differently. My hesitation and inability to focus were causing dangerous situations for me and my team.

I knew part of the problem was that the enemy didn't look like the enemy anymore. They looked like Cleo, myself, and all of the other Deviants I considered friends. In addition, now I wasn't doing the job alone. I didn't just have my safety to worry about; I was responsible for the rest of the Deviants. My attention was scattered and so was my judgment. It was making me a very poor leader and a useless weapon. Perfect aim was pointless when I couldn't be trusted to use it.

I looked at the group gathered around me. Arabella was belted into the black sedan, staring straight ahead, ready to continue on with the plan. Eva and Sadie were leaning on a mailbox, watching me and waiting for instructions. Sterling was standing nearby, his thumbs hooked through the belt loops of his pants, his gaze understandably distrustful after I just insulted his girl.

Despite my misgivings, there was no other option—we had to continue on with the assignment. Now that the Deviants were in training, I knew they'd be sent on missions more often and I might not always be there to keep them safe. No matter how I personally felt toward them, no matter how much I wanted to protect them from this life, I couldn't. That meant I had to get them comfortable with doing the dirty work of the Program.

This job should be easy. Apprehend one, harmless man. How hard could it be?

"Let's go," I said, hooking the headset over my ear and motioning for Eva to get in the car with Arabella. I handed her an extra headset and a cell phone as she lay down in the back seat, pulling a blanket over her head. When I was sure that she was hidden, I motioned to Sadie and Sterling to follow me. I led them down the street at a quick pace, staying in the shadows where we were less likely to be seen. When we reached the side of Malleville's house, I motioned for Sadie and Sterling to guard the back door in case Malleville got spooked and decided to run that way. Between the two of them, they should be able to take him down.

Usually, I was accompanied by a team of Mandates who would disable security systems or incapacitate guards to gain me entry into the places where I eliminated my targets. Unfortunately, the directions I was given this time were to use the skills of the Deviants to complete the mission. Apprehending one man should be no problem, so really it was a test to see how easily my team and I could succeed without using deadly force.

I was curious as to what Janus Malleville had done to earn himself a visit from a pack of Deviants in the middle of the night.

Once I was sure Sterling and Sadie were ready, I positioned myself at the side of the front door where I wouldn't be seen. I touched a button on the side of my ear piece.

"Parrot, you're on," I said quietly, using the code name I'd given Eva.

"Copy that, Deadeye," she responded.

I heard the electronic beeps of a number being dialed over my earpiece as Eva placed the call. Soon the phone was ringing. It only rang four times before Malleville answered.

"Hello?" he answered, sleepily.

"Janus," Eva said in Delia's voice. "It's me. I need to talk to you."

"Not over the phone." His voice was now alert and commanding. It was also laced with a bit of fear.

"I'll be there in a couple of minutes." Eva's tone was clipped and her sentences short, just like I suggested. If she said too much, Malleville might not be fooled.

"You're coming to my house? No!" Malleville said emphatically. "Not now. It's too dangerous."

"It won't take long. I'm alone."

"De..." Malleville cut himself off before saying her name. "It's not good for us to be seen together right now."

"I'm pulling up now. Just let me in."

Headlights broke the darkness as Arabella drove the car

around the corner and pulled up in front of the house.

"Fine," Malleville conceded. "But, make it quick."

"I will."

Arabella parked the car in the driveway. I heard footsteps approach the front door from inside the house as Arabella got out of the car. I pressed myself against the wall as the front porch light turned on and Malleville flicked open the blinds across the front window to watch the person coming up his walkway.

I was impressed with the way Arabella moved. She'd only seen Delia Younglove once, but she seemed to have picked up quite a few of her mannerisms. She was believable, as long as she didn't speak. When she knocked on the door, she avoided looking in my direction, just as I'd instructed. She was like a seasoned soldier—confident and fearless. It scared me. I wasn't scared of her, I was scared for her. She was exactly the kind of person the Program wanted in their war. She had exactly the kind of talents they would use and abuse. I should know.

The sound of the locks on the door turning was a sign that Janus Malleville was fooled by Arabella's disguise. Either he wasn't "in the know" about the Deviants' abilities to suspect her, or he was too confident in his position to think he'd be targeted. Either way, he was a stupid man.

The door opened just enough for him to peek through.

"Delia," Janus said in greeting. "Come in. And hurry before someone sees you."

Arabella nodded in return and pushed the door open as she entered the house. She walked to the center of the room without glancing back, taking a trinket off a bookshelf as she passed it. She turned it around in her hands to inspect it. Malleville was unwilling to take his eyes off Arabella, who was now walking around his house like she owned the place. He absentmindedly pushed the front door, allowing it to close on its own, as he followed her further into the room.

Careless, I thought as I caught the door before it slammed shut. I slipped inside, shut the door, and locked it before Janus realized he and Arabella weren't alone. At the sound of the lock sliding in place, Janus whirled around in horror.

"Euri?" Janus asked. When he saw the gun I was holding, he raised his hands in surrender.

"Wrong," I said, lifting my hand and pulling the trigger.

No hesitation. Not this time. Just perfect aim. Just the way things were supposed to be.

Janus fell to the ground.

Ozzy

16

The Compound

"I can't believe the man doesn't own a car." I stared at the empty garage.

"Explain to me why this is a problem." Sterling glanced at his watch. Again. For someone who did everything at top speed, this night had been more than a little stressful for him. Watching the house for hours, waiting quietly by the back door, watching me restrain an unconscious Malleville. Sterling didn't do waiting. He was bored out of his mind and driving everyone else crazy with his nervous energy. He walked into the garage, picked up a broken broom handle and began tapping it on the top of the plastic trash can.

"It's a problem because there are five of us and we came in a sedan. Despite the fact that we just invaded this guy's home and shot him with a sedative, I wasn't planning on tying him to the roof to get him back to Headquarters. I don't think any of the girls will be too keen on letting him lay across their laps in the back seat. I thought he'd at least have a car we could borrow. Damn!" I said, kicking the trash can and causing it to spin across the empty garage, scattering trash across the floor before it slammed into the wall. "I really don't want to put this guy in the trunk."

Sterling's eyebrows creased. "If I were Janus Malleville and I just got a midnight visit from Perfect Aim, I'd be thanking my lucky stars I was being loaded into a trunk and not a body bag."

I glared at him, hating the fact that everyone assumed I was just a heartless killer. Yes, I was an assassin, but I wasn't heartless. Did they honestly think I would go on missions for the Program if I had a choice? It was easy for others to see the mission papers with pictures of terrorists and the lists of their misdeeds and assume that eliminating those threats was just a simple act of pulling a trigger.

It was never simple.

The lucky ones never saw me coming.

The unlucky ones were the ones that haunted my dreams—the ones that saw me coming and knew they were going to die. Sometimes they pissed their pants. They usually tried to bargain. They always screamed. Nothing they did made a difference, not once they made it into my mission folders. Once they were targeted by the Program, I always pulled the trigger.

Well, until I came face-to-face with Persephone.

"Tell Arabella to pull the car into the garage," I said, tossing the keys to Sterling. "I'm going to take a look around Malleville's house while you all load him up."

"While we load him up?"

"If you think he's so lucky to go in the trunk, you can load him up," I explained.

"Elitist crotch biscuit," Sterling muttered under his breath.

"Did you just call me a crotch biscuit?" I asked.

"No. I called you an elitist crotch biscuit."

"Just load him up," I said, shaking my head.

"Whatever you say, Captain Douche Waffle," he said loudly enough that he knew I could hear him.

I ignored him and went back in the house. It was a bachelor's pad. The windows were covered in blinds, but there were no curtains. The couches were old and the leather that covered them was worn and cracked. I found the home office and shamelessly went through all the shelves. I was searching through the drawers of Malleville's desk ten minutes later when I heard the others struggling to get their unconscious captive in the trunk. I smiled to myself as I heard Arabella cursing at the rest of them.

I pulled on the bottom drawer of the desk, expecting to find more broken pencils and scattered staples. It was locked. Interesting. With a quick movement of my tiny silver tools, I had the drawer open. I hadn't expected to find anything worthwhile in the desk, so I was surprised when I saw that the folders inside the drawer had familiar names on them—Electric Eel, Tiger Moth, Spitfire Caterpillar.

"Ozzy!" Arabella yelled, interrupting my inspection. "He's waking up."

Shit. The sedative hadn't lasted as long as I'd hoped. I wasn't used to knocking out my victims. Usually, one shot from a gun was enough to get the job done. I never had to worry about them moving again after one shot because they were dead.

I grabbed the folders and stuffed them into a messenger bag that was lying on the floor next to the desk. I slung the bag over my shoulder. Before I walked away, I turned back to the desk and grabbed the laptop too, shoving it into the bag along with the folders. The Program hadn't told me to search for any evidence of wrongdoing, but seeing as how Malleville had restricted information in the desk, I wasn't going to take any chances. Janus Malleville may have been the Program Security Advisor, but I was certain that having restricted information in a desk drawer that was easily accessed was not part of Malleville's job description.

"Ozzy!" Arabella yelled again.

"What?" I said, entering the garage.

The top half of Malleville was stuffed halfway in the trunk. His hands were secured with cable ties and the rest of him was hanging out of the open trunk, his legs kicking at anything that came near. Sadie was sitting on the ground, her head tilted back while she pinched the bridge of her nose. The blood all over her chin and shirt were evidence that she had taken a foot to the face.

"You didn't tie up his legs?" I tried not to laugh.

"You didn't tell us to tie up his legs. You told us to search him and then put him in the trunk. You were the one doing the tying up, remember?" Sterling pointed out.

"Why do you think I left the extra cable ties there? Do you expect me to do everything?"

Arabella picked up the cable ties that I pointed to and approached the car. As soon as she got near, Malleville kicked at her. Her arm elongated and she pushed at his foot trying to get it out of the way. It did no good, he was frantic to get free.

"Dude. It's late. Can you just shoot him again or something? For an old fat guy, he kicks pretty hard." Sterling rubbed his ribs on the right side of his body.

I walked over to the trunk and looked inside. "What did you do? Why does the Program want you?" I asked out of curiosity.

Malleville's eyes were wide with fear and he shook his head, kicking out toward me to keep me away.

"Do you want to do this nicely or will I have to shoot you again?" I grabbed the cable ties out of Arabella's hand and approached the car. Malleville began kicking wildly, attempting to get out of the trunk. I sighed and pulled the dart gun out of my pocket, loading a sedative without looking down.

"Remember, I did give you the choice," I said.

I brought my hand up, pointed the gun, and shot him in the neck. A few seconds later the kicking stopped. I secured two cable ties around the man's ankles and then grabbed a length of rope out of the back seat and tied his knees together as well.

"How long will he be out?" Arabella asked.

"I don't know, but we'll probably hear him kicking and yelling long before we get to where we're taking him," I confessed. "Did you search him?"

Arabella nodded uncomfortably. "No weapons. Aren't we taking him back to the Academy?"

"No," I answered. I wanted to go back to the Academy tonight because I was desperate to see Cleo and make sure she was okay, but the Program had a different agenda. "We have to take him to Program Headquarters."

"In New York?" Eva asked.

I was so used to seeing Eva confident and flippant when she hung out with Quinnie that I was surprised to hear fear in her voice. I hadn't known she had any emotion other than cold-hearted bitch. I actually felt sorry for her because I didn't want to go to Headquarters, either. Usually a trip to Headquarters was one way. After finishing at the Academy, Mandates were sent to Headquarters before being deployed on military missions.

"Unfortunately. We're heading to New York right now. Might as well get comfortable," I said, gesturing toward the back seat of the car. I hoped the look I gave them was as apologetic as I felt. If I could spare them the visit to New York, the biggest ghost town of *Wormwood*, I would. But I had orders.

And I always followed orders.

Since it was the middle of the night, I-95 was mostly deserted as we drove north through Maryland. There were a lot of truckers hauling various goods, but even they started to thin out as it got later. It rained during the first part of the trip and the only sound in the vehicle was that of the windshield wipers thumping a weary beat across the wet glass.

As we reached the Delaware state line, however, some kicking and thumping started in the trunk. After only a few minutes of listening to it, I thought I was going to go crazy. I considered pulling over to administer another sedative, but I felt guilty. I didn't know why the Program wanted Janus Malleville, but if the man was being detained and transported to the New York Headquarters, it wasn't for a pat on the back. The least I could do for Malleville was leave him conscious for the remainder of the ride so he could mentally prepare for whatever it was he'd be facing. I wondered if Malleville considered himself lucky. Sure, I didn't put a bullet between his eyes, but there was no guarantee that being questioned and detained by the Program would be a better option.

"You know, it'd be a lot easier to take a nap without all that racket," Sadie complained. "Are we going to have to listen to this all the way to New York?"

"You got kicked in the face not too long ago and you might have a concussion. It's probably better if you stay awake anyway," I pointed out as I turned on the radio to mask the sounds coming from the trunk.

"Maybe you should shoot me with a dart so I can at least be put out of my misery," Sadie suggested.

"Fine by me," I said, pulling the gun from my pocket. "I'll let Sterling do the honors since I'm driving." I handed the gun over to Sterling.

I looked in the rearview mirror and met Sadie's eyes. Despite her scowl, I saw fear. Her eyes snapped over to Sterling who had turned around, grinning. The silver of the gun flashed brightly every time we passed under a light along the highway.

"Never mind," she mumbled.

I held out my hand for the gun.

"Anybody else want to give it a try?" Sterling asked. "Could be fun. At least for me," he said, waving the gun between the occupants in the back seat.

"Put that away before I do it for you. Trust me, you won't like where I put it," Arabella warned.

Sterling put the gun back into my hand.

By the time we reached the New Jersey state line, the noise in the trunk had stopped. Either Malleville was conserving energy, or he finally accepted his fate and was taking a nap. Either way, I was thankful. The annoying noises were gone and the girls had fallen asleep. By the time I saw the road signs for the Lincoln tunnel declaring we had reached New York, it had stopped raining and the sky was starting to lighten. Between the dark shapes of the nearby buildings, thin lines of orange appeared, promising that morning would be here soon. We had succeeded. We had our captive and no one got hurt, unless you counted Sadie's nose.

Up ahead, the tunnel was a yawning chasm of darkness in the dim morning. I flipped the headlights to bright and locked the doors. I was exhausted and looking forward to finally getting some sleep, even if that meant I had to stay the night at Program Headquarters. There weren't many places I liked less than Headquarters. I wanted to get through the tunnel as quickly as possible, but I slowed the car as we were sucked into the mouth of the aging stone. I stayed to the right side of the road.

"What are those?" Sterling asked, slightly horrified. All along the left lane of the tunnel, makeshift tents and shelters stretched as far as we could see. Half of the lights in the roof of the tunnel were broken or burnt out. The Program gave up on trying to replace them years ago, right around the time the tunnel dwellers moved in. As the headlights from the car rippled over the shoddy shelters, people started to emerge and stare at us as we drove by.

"Well?" Sterling asked nervously. "Who are these people, and why are they living in the tunnel?"

"New Yorkers. Or rather, descendants and survivors of New York from thirty years ago."

"I didn't think there were any survivors."

"Technically, there weren't. These are the people from New York City that weren't actually here when *Wormwood* happened."

"Why would they come back?"

"It's their home."

"They're living in a tunnel, that's not a real home."

"They can't get back into the city. The Program owns it now," I explained.

Sterling was horrified. "They own all of it? What does the Program need with an entire city?"

I looked at him. "Where do you think they keep all the Mandates when they're not out on missions?"

"All the Mandates are there?"

"The ones not on missions."

"Why would they keep them all in one place? Doesn't that seem a bit stupid?"

"Not if it's top secret. It's not like they broadcast that information."

"How do you know then?"

I shrugged. "This is where I begin and end almost every mission I do for the Program. I come here a lot."

Sterling was staring at the hundreds of tunnel dwellers that had come out of their shelters to get a look at the intruders.

"How could the Program just take a city like that?" Sterling asked.

"After *Wormwood*, New York City was empty. By the time these people came back to claim it, the Program had already taken control."

Sterling looked at the half-starved, filthy people that stared back at us as we passed.

"Why don't they just go somewhere else then?"

My gaze was caught by a young girl holding her mother's hand as they stood in front of a shelter that was constructed from jagged pieces of plywood.

"I don't know," I admitted. "Maybe they have nowhere else

to go."

"They have an entire country of places to go," Sterling said.

The sound of the back window breaking interrupted our conversation. Eva screamed as shards of glass scattered all over the back seat. I glanced in the rearview mirror to see that several people had moved into the roadway behind us and were throwing rocks at the car.

"Do something!" Sadie screamed as another rock came flying through the back window. She had her arms wrapped around her head and was leaning over with her head between her legs.

Sterling picked the rock up off the floor and inspected it. "They wrote 'thief' on it," he said.

"One of the many reasons I hate coming here," I muttered.

"Is this normal?" Sterling held the rock up for me to see.

"Sometimes. Other times they throw rotten food or trash. The worst is when they throw shit."

"You mean shit shit or junk shit?"

"Shit shit," I admitted, swerving to avoid a sharp looking piece of machinery that had been discarded in the middle of the road.

Arabella groaned. "Then can we get through this tunnel of hate a little more quickly? I don't mind glass all that much, but if I get hit in the head with something that came out of someone's ass, I'm going to kick your ass."

I pressed down on the gas pedal and hurried through the tunnel; not because I was scared of Arabella's threat, but because I didn't want to get hit with anything that came out of someone's ass either.

We emerged from the tunnel and approached the security gate that would allow us entrance into Manhattan. I glanced in the rearview mirror and saw a few children slowly appear at the entrance of the tunnel behind us. Once they saw that the coast was clear, they ran out in a cautious group to play whatever game it was they played in the dusty patch of area outside the wall that surrounded the Headquarters compound. Under the morning shadows of the run-down, deserted buildings at the edge of the compound, the children kicked at discarded cans and hid behind abandoned cars, unaware of how amazing the city had been only a few decades ago. One of the most powerful cities in the world reduced to a nearly lifeless, military headquarters. Millions of deaths certainly left their mark—filthy gouges of decay and desolation that were filled with the presence of the Program. Entering post-Wormwood Manhattan never got any less disturbing. I always felt like I needed a shower afterwards.

I stopped the car at the gatehouse where two guards waited. The gates into the compound were massive, metal structures that blocked out the view of the road beyond. A tall wall extended to either side, rooted to the boundary of the compound by guard towers that stood like sentinels every hundred yards. High above the gates, two guard towers rose into the sky from the other side of the wall, where I knew our arrival was being watched carefully. There were probably no less than a dozen guns trained on us from the moment we came out of the tunnel.

I recognized the guard that came to the car—Jerry. He was a Mandate at the Academy during my first year there. Jerry had the annoying habit of pushing me around a lot. He'd liked to watch me bleed. He was a jackass back then. Still is.

Jerry swaggered to my side of the car. Once the window was down, he leaned on the edge of my door, peering inside the car like he was the King of Manhattan. My fingers twitched as I glanced at the gun on his hip that was pressed up against the edge of my open window. I could have that gun in my hand and a bullet through his heart before he could even blink. I'd dreamt about it many times. He was part of the reason I could turn on the ruthless, monster when I was on missions—my targets always had Jerry's face, right before the life drained out of them. I looked away from the gun and stared ahead at the metal doors.

"Another mission, cheesedick?" Jerry asked.

That nickname wasn't any funnier now than it was seven years ago, but I didn't give him the satisfaction of letting the name bother me.

He looked at his clipboard to see who I was bringing in. "Where is he?"

"Trunk," I responded, hooking my thumb over my shoulder in the direction of our captive.

"You know I have to take a look. I gotta make sure you aren't sneaking anything else in."

Jerry was being a power hungry douche, as usual. I almost warned him to be careful of Malleville as I pressed the button to release the trunk, but then I realized Jerry could use a good kick to the face. More than one if I had my way. Sadly, it was quiet as he inspected our cargo. After a few moments, he came back around to my window, holding the clipboard in front of his face importantly.

"Not as neat as usual," he accused, writing something down.

I shrugged. "He didn't want to come quietly."

"Those are the most fun, aren't they?" Jerry grinned, pushing my shoulder with his hand as though we were buddies. I wanted to put my fist through his front teeth. When I didn't respond, he said, "Head on in, you know where to go."

The gates opened with a noisy groan, and the children playing their games behind us scattered as they ran back toward the tunnel. I drove to what used to be Times Square, listening to the comments of the rest of the Deviants as they saw a dead city for the first time. Their voices were echoes of my own thoughts, lamenting the loss of what had once been. Old signs and billboards were still visible everywhere, but they were advertising businesses that were long gone. The advertisements for Broadway shows were faded and peeling, not worth the effort to take down or fix. Newspaper boxes stood wide open and empty while discarded husks of buses and taxi cabs still littered the streets, battered from use during various Mandate training exercises.

I drove down Broadway and headed for the Empire State Building where the Program held its offices. Even though it was still early, Mandates were out on the streets, doing their morning run. I knew that the Mandates were housed in the other boroughs of New York City—the Bronx, Queens, Brooklyn, and Staten Island—but they came to the Manhattan compound for training. It was such a waste that a city as magnificent as New York had once been was now used for Mandate training and housing.

I had to pass through another checkpoint as we neared our destination. When I pulled into the underground garage, I was met by Dr. Steel, the Program official I checked in with after missions. He was accompanied by half a dozen Mandate guards. They were at least a decade older than me—some of the first Mandates in the Program—and they had been with Dr. Steel for years. He never went anywhere without them.

I got out of the car and motioned for the rest of the Deviants to join me. Dr. Steel and his brawny entourage of guards met us beside the car.

"Osbourne," Dr. Steel said to me in greeting. "I assume all went well?"

I nodded. "We had a little trouble subduing him, it required a few sedatives. We put him in the trunk."

Dr. Steel held out his hand and I dropped the keys in his palm. He then handed the keys to the Mandate on his right who went to the back of the car.

"I heard you let Delia Younglove get away." Dr. Steel said. "Twice," he added, studying my reaction.

There was something about Dr. Steel that made me uncomfortable. He seemed to take my achievements and failures personally. Up until recently, I'd been the Program's most prominent success story and Dr. Steel was proud to show me off at the compound as if he were responsible for pulling the trigger himself. I don't know why anyone would want to take credit for the work I did. Even I didn't want to take credit for it. Right now, however, it was clear that he was unhappy and it was my fault.

"First, you let Delia and the Others get away during the rescue mission, and then you failed to capture her at Andrews Air Force Base. You do realize there will be disciplinary action if you make any more mistakes."

I could feel the gazes of the other Deviants on me as I stared at him. I wasn't used to failure and they weren't used to seeing me fail.

He took a step toward me, his mouth tight with barely disguised disappointment. "I will not tolerate mistakes—"

"Sir?" interrupted the Mandate who had opened the trunk.

"What is it?"

"Janus Malleville is dead."

Ozzy

17

Abandoned

Janus Malleville was dead.

His hands, arms, and legs were bloodied from beating on the trunk trying to get out, but it was clear from the open ring on his finger and the trail of white dust across his cheeks and nose that he finally found a way to escape the Program. In a strange, detached way, I was impressed that he managed to get his bound arms in front of him in order to take the poison. Obviously, he had been desperate.

I just couldn't believe it. I'd been killing people for so many years, it never occurred to me that someone might do it to themselves. Whatever it was that the Program wanted to talk to him about, it must have been worse than death.

"Why didn't you search him? Didn't you check for weapons?" Dr. Steel asked.

"We checked." I looked around at each of my team members who were nodding in agreement. All except Arabella who was staring at Dr. Steel like she was a few pieces short of figuring out a puzzle.

"Well, you didn't do a very thorough job. This entire mission was a failure."

I wanted to remind him that I was usually assassinating people, not kidnapping them. I stared at the mess in the trunk as a group of workers came to clean it out. It's not that I'd never seen a dead body, but to see Malleville still tied up, lying in his own filth—I'd never been more embarrassed to be a Sophisticate. I hadn't pulled the trigger this time, but it was still my fault he was dead.

When I didn't defend myself, Steel let out an exasperated sigh. "Go get some sleep. We'll talk later when I've had time to decide how to deal with you. Go."

Eva and Sadie were still staring into the trunk, horrified by the dead Program security advisor. I grabbed their elbows and led them out of the garage and to the elevators. Sterling and Arabella followed closely, both eager to get away from the scene. Arabella was rubbing her arms as if she could wash the guilt of Malleville's death off. I could've told her that the guilt never went away, that it would be a stain on her soul for the rest of her life. I didn't say anything. She glanced back at the car once, but I stared straight ahead. I didn't ever want to see it again.

In the elevator, Arabella stared at me for a few minutes before speaking.

"That Dr. Steel is really something. Do you know him?" she asked.

"I see him before and after almost every mission."

"He seems familiar."

I shrugged. He was like every other Program official in my

opinion. He always felt strangely familiar to me, but that's because I'd been meeting with him regularly from the time I was ten years old. He's the one that decided to send me to the Academy early. He was almost like my guardian.

"I feel like I've met him before," Arabella muttered.

When we reached the seventeenth floor where the boarding rooms were located, I tried to usher all three girls into one room.

"I'm not sleeping in the same room with them," Arabella said, crossing her arms.

"Why not?"

She rolled her eyes. "Just because we're on a mission, it doesn't make them any less bitchtastic. I'm sharing with Sterling." She grabbed his arm and pushed him through the doorway of the room next to the one Eva and Sadie had entered. "And you're not invited," she said to me, slamming the door in my face.

I was too annoyed to even argue. If Dr. Steel had a preference about who shared rooms with whom, he should've given me instructions.

"You can share with us," Sadie suggested from the doorway of the room next to Arabella's. The offer wasn't given with a come-hither attitude. She and Eva were scared. I didn't blame them, but I still wasn't sharing with them.

"You'll be fine," I assured her. I opened the door to the room across the hall and then locked it behind me once I was engulfed in darkness. I didn't bother to turn on the lights, there was enough light coming through the naked window to find my way to the bed, which was the only thing I needed. I collapsed onto the mattress and fell asleep immediately.

When I woke later that afternoon, one of Dr. Steel's Hounds was waiting in the hallway outside my door.

"Dr. Steel wants to see you in his office."

"Okay, I'll wake the rest of my team and meet you up there."

"I'm supposed to escort you. The others are up there already."

Dr. Steel had Arabella, Sterling, Eva, and Sadie up in his office already? Why? Whatever the reason, it couldn't be good. I grabbed my jacket, pulled the door shut behind me, and motioned for the Hound to lead the way.

The Doctor's office was on the 86th floor where the first observation deck of the Empire State Building was located. He shared the space with another man whom I'd never met. The elevator doors opened and I entered the office, which was richly furnished in dark mahogany wood and shiny glass. Two desks were in the center of the room, surrounded by large windows where the men could oversee the entire Manhattan compound from their lofty position. Beyond the windows, the city sprawled out majestically. It was hard to tell from so far up just how desolate things were below.

Dr. Steel was sitting behind his desk while Eva, Arabella, and Sterling were seated in front of him. Their uncomfortable, straight posture was the first clue that something was wrong. The second clue was that I didn't see Sadie. Then I noticed that everyone was staring up at the ceiling where my missing teammate was dangling by her hands.

I should have known that Dr. Steel wouldn't be able to resist asking for a demonstration of their powers. They'd only recently started formal training in the Deviant Workshops, but I knew that the Program officials were eager to see their experiments in real world situations. I tried to put it off as long as I could, convincing Dr. Steel that the Deviants weren't ready. First, I had to convince the Deviants themselves to keep their powers under wraps and it worked for a while. Now all that hard work was crashing down around me, thanks to Professor Younglove and the Deviant Workshops. I knew she thought she was doing the right thing by teaching the Dozen to use their powers, but I knew it was only putting them in more danger.

Now, Eva, Sadie, Sterling, and Arabella were in the same room with one of the most dangerous men I knew. I should've warned them better. I should've insisted that Professor Younglove send an Academy car to come pick them up right after the mission was over last night. I should not have brought them here. I was stupid. So stupid.

"Ah, Osbourne. So glad you could join us," Dr. Steel said. "I was just getting to know your companions a little better. You can come down, Ms. Dracone," he called to Sadie. She dropped from the ceiling, somersaulting a few times before landing quietly on his desk. Steel whistled his appreciation. "Even more impressive than I imagined," he said quietly. He stood, holding his hand out to her to help her step down from the desk even though they both knew she didn't need the help. "You all may go have something to eat," he said to the four of them. "I need to discuss a few things with Osbourne. Elena will show you where to go."

A female Hound stepped forward and motioned for the Deviants to follow her. I watched my friends go, annoyed that I hadn't been present for the meeting. I had no idea what Dr. Steel had said or what damage had been done in my absence. After they left, I started to take a seat.

"No need for that," Dr. Steel said with a dismissive wave of his hand. "This won't take long, I just need to tell you what I've decided. As recompense for your failures, your friends are going to stay here at Headquarters for a while. I'd like to get to know them a little better now that they're learning to use their deviations. After you've had breakfast, you're free to head back to the Academy."

Shit. I expected punishment, but this was worse than anything I could've imagined. Whipping I could've handled, but my friends in the greedy hands of Headquarters? I couldn't let that happen. I knew eventually, it would, but not yet. Not now.

"They can't stay here, they're not ready," I said.

Dr. Steel smiled. "We'll make them ready. We made you ready."

That's what I was afraid of.

"That was different," I argued. "I'd been exhibiting for nearly six years. Most of them have been exhibiting less than two. They need more time to train at the Academy. They're not ready for real-world application."

"From what I heard, they did just fine last night," Dr. Steel retaliated. "If you had only thoroughly searched your prisoner, he'd still be alive. That wasn't their fault, it was yours."

They did do fine. And I knew it was my fault our prisoner died, but I couldn't let my confidence in them betray their safety. It would cost my friends too much of the little freedom they had.

"It's not just the training, though. With Delia Younglove and the Others on the loose, we need the Deviant Dozen at full strength." It was the only argument I could come up with on short notice.

Dr. Steel was quiet for a moment as he considered what I said. "True," he murmured, tapping his lip with a finger. "But, since you have Rune at the Academy now, I think you can spare one of your companions to stay here."

"We don't know anything about Rune. Not only does he show no abilities, but we don't know his intentions. We'll be lucky if he hasn't wreaked havoc in the short time we were away."

"I assure you, the Academy is fine and Rune is just as you left him."

"Even if he's not a spy—which I'm confident he is—he's not even close to being able to replace any of the Deviant members."

"You just told me that none of your teammates are that far along. Which is it, Osbourne?" Dr. Steel smiled, knowing he was winning our debate, as if I ever had a say in the matter anyway. "I'll tell you what," he said, "we'll compromise. One of your Deviants will stay here and I'll even let you choose who it is."

"I don't know if I can do that."

Dr. Steel shrugged. "Either you choose one, or I'll keep all of them here. As you've pointed out, you know them better than I do. You can decide who is the farthest along and who is the most prepared to do some training. We may even throw in a test mission."

He must have seen my body tense in panic.

"It's no big deal," Dr. Steel said, disregarding my worries. "It won't be anything dangerous. We'd just like to see some skills in action. I will tell you, though," he said, leaning in as if we were conspiring, "if I had my choice, I'd like Arabella to stay. She's a fascinating creature." His voice was greedy.

"Person." My voice was edged with a growl.

"What?" Dr. Steel asked, confused.

"Arabella is a person, not a creature."

His smile was pacifying. "Yes, of course. It was a figure of speech; you know what I meant."

I know exactly what you meant.

"Go ahead and have something to eat with your team. Elena will bring back the one you decide will be staying."

Dr. Steel sat back down behind his desk and I was dismissed.

The others must have known something was wrong because nobody was speaking when I showed up for lunch. I still didn't know what I was going to do. How could I choose one of them to stay? If I could've given myself over, I would have. But, I knew Dr. Steel wasn't interested in something he already had. He knew me. He wanted fresh meat. He wanted fresh skills.

When I finally finished eating, Sterling voiced the question on everyone's mind. "So, what's your punishment?" he asked.

"Why do you think I'm being punished?"

"Because you look like you're in physical pain," Arabella pointed out. "Were you whipped?"

"No."

Everyone seemed to sigh in relief.

"My punishment is far worse than that."

"What is it?" Eva asked, running her fingers through her hair nervously.

"Dr. Steel wants one of you to stay behind for special training when I head back to the Academy. I'm supposed to choose who stays."

If I had punched them in the faces, I don't think they could have been more surprised.

"One of us?" Sadie's voice quivered.

"Who are you going to choose?" Arabella asked.

"I don't know," I admitted. "I can't decide. I don't want to leave any of you behind, but if I don't choose one of you, he'll keep all of you here. It was all I could do to talk him out of that."

"What does he plan to do with the person who stays?" Arabella's voice was wary.

I took a deep breath. "Train you to go on missions like I do."

Everyone found the table top exceedingly interesting.

"Well, maybe we choose the person that has the least chance of getting sent on something dangerous," Arabella reasoned. "Did he give you any specifics about what he planned?"

I shook my head. "No. The only thing he mentioned was that he was particularly interested in you."

Arabella had her derby face on. Although I knew my words must have sliced through her, she didn't show an ounce of fear. She merely nodded. "Fine, I'll stay."

"No!" Sterling yelled, slamming his fist on the table. "I'm staying."

"Don't be ridiculous," Arabella said. "He wants me, I'll stay."

"No," Sterling repeated. "Dr. Steel said Ozzy could choose. Pick me," he pleaded, turning to me. "They can't do much with my speed. I'll be the safest. You can't let them have her." He looked at Arabella tenderly, which seemed to put her over the edge.

"Don't try to be the hero, Sterling. I'm not some sort of helpless girl that needs saving. I can take care of myself."

Sterling ignored her as he came around the table to plead with me. "Choose me," he said quietly. "If it was Cleo, you'd ask the same thing."

I nodded in understanding. Sterling grabbed my jacket off the chair to hand it to me.

"Don't you dare!" Arabella screamed at me. She got up from her seat and came around the table to yell at me some more. "Don't you dare leave him here, Ozzy. I'll never forgive you!"

"I'll never forgive myself no matter who I leave here," I explained, reaching for my jacket.

"Fine, I'll just go tell Dr. Steel that I'm staying. I'm the one he wants. We'll see what he decides once I offer myself up willingly." She started walking toward the elevator, her head held high.

"Damn woman," Sterling muttered. He reached in my jacket pocket, pulled out the tranquilizer gun, aimed, and shot Arabella in the arm with it.

She stopped, looked down at the dart, and then pulled it out, staring at it for a few seconds before glaring at Sterling. The look of betrayal on her features was there for only a moment before she dropped the dart and her body started to buckle in on itself. Sterling ran over and caught her right before she hit the floor.

"Sterling, no," she begged, fighting to keep her eyes open. She clutched at his shirt desperately. "You stupid ass, why did you do that?"

"You know why," he said, kissing her on her forehead. His hand caressed her face, smoothing out the lines of worry as the sedative took over.

Once she was out, Sterling picked her up. She looked tiny and innocent as the wild hair and makeup faded away with her consciousness. He hugged her tightly to his chest as he carried her to me.

"Take care of her," he said, placing Arabella's limp form in my arms.

"I will," I promised.

"Oh, and if you want to make it back to the Academy without her kicking your ass, you better tie her up. Use metal handcuffs, she knows how to get out of plastic cuffs."

"Will do," I said.

Sterling leaned over and brushed Arabella's hair off her face before he kissed her on the forehead again. He whispered something in her ear that I couldn't hear and then he walked over to Elena and turned himself over to Dr. Steel.

It was going to be a long ride home. Especially when Arabella woke up.

Ozzy

18

Roasting Creamsicle

Not only did Arabella know how to get out of plastic handcuffs, but apparently, she could escape regular ones, too.

How could I have forgotten about her ability to stretch her body? I was distracted and making way too many mistakes.

I almost got in a damn accident when she woke up, released herself from the cuffs, and jumped over the seat to try to get control of the steering wheel. I needed Eva and Sadie's help to wrestle her into the back seat while I pulled the car over to the side of the road. Once the car was safely stopped, I shot her with a tranquilizer dart. Again.

I didn't want to have to keep her sedated for the entire ride back to the Academy, but I didn't have much choice. Sterling made the sacrifice to stay at Headquarters in her place and I couldn't let it be for nothing by allowing Arabella to go back. If Dr. Steel wanted her specifically, it wasn't for a good reason.

I called Younglove to warn her of what transpired with Janus

Malleville and our trip to Headquarters. I expected her to be angry, but I didn't expect the distress I could hear in her voice when she found out that Sterling had to be left behind.

"We'll get him back," she muttered. "I'll figure something out. Just hurry back with the girls."

"On my way," I promised. "How is Cleo?"

Younglove sighed. "As good as you can expect her to be," she answered evasively.

"I want to see her when I get back."

Younglove didn't answer.

"Just so you know, I had to sedate Arabella. She was out of control."

"I'll take care of her."

Younglove sounded tired. She usually tried to appear as if she had no emotional connection with any of the Dozen, but deep down, I knew she cared about us. By treating us as tools like the rest of the Program officials did, she was able to keep herself close to help us. She knew that the Program discouraged emotional attachments.

The rest of the Dozen didn't know how much she cared, but I did. She and I didn't always agree on how to keep the Dozen safe, but at least we both agreed that we had to protect them from the Program. She thought that, as Deviants, they should embrace their skills and learn how to use them to defend themselves. I thought laying low and staying under the radar was the best option. But in the end, we both had the same goal: to protect the Dozen.

Sadly, that was impossible. The Dozen could never truly be under the radar. Eventually, the Program would expect them to perform just as they expected me to. They'd invested too much time and money—and an absurd amount of resources—into creating their human weapons. In their opinion, it was time to reap what they had sowed. I knew that losing Sterling to Headquarters was just the beginning.

When I pulled up in front of the Academy, Younglove had a group of Hounds come to the car and retrieve Arabella. Younglove instructed them to keep her under guard in the infirmary until she was sure that Arabella would act calmly and responsibly. Calmly and responsibly—that's what Younglove said. I chuckled to myself. Arabella didn't do calm and responsible. I didn't envy the Hounds who'd be in her presence when she finally woke up.

After Younglove oversaw the safe delivery of Arabella to the infirmary, I cornered her in the hallway outside of Ms. Petticoat's domain.

"How is Cleo? Has she been released from the cells yet? I want to see her."

"She's fine. No, she hasn't been released. And no, you can't see her. You know that."

"I just want to make sure she's okay." I did my best to stay calm, but I was nearly tearing out of my own skin with worry. I couldn't even be bothered at this point with what kind of repercussions there would be for my failure with Janus Malleville.

"I'm doing my best." Younglove frowned at my angry expression. "Don't be upset with me, Osbourne. You know I have no control over punishments that the dean orders. I'll make sure she sees you as soon as she's released so you can help her. Just make sure the dean doesn't find out. Rules are rules. She probably won't be released until tomorrow some time. Right now, I need you to spend some time with Rune."

Could this day get any shittier?

"You can't be serious. I just got back."

"Just for a few hours. He's spent most of the day with Quinby. To be honest, I'm not completely comfortable with that. But aside from you and Cleo, she's the only other person who I feel can handle him one-on-one."

"You mean the only other person that can handle his deviation."

Younglove shrugged. "Assuming he has one, which I'm not entirely convinced of yet. I'm starting to believe he's useless. Why else would my sister get rid of him?"

"Because he's a spy." Why was this obvious only to me?

"Perhaps. Just spend some time with him. See if you can get him to open up."

Pistol Shrimp babysitting duty. Shit. I almost wished I had been able to take Sterling's place at Headquarters.

***

I spent the rest of the day with Rune, trying to befriend him as Younglove asked. I didn't really try too hard. I took him down to Professor Peck's gym for a little weight lifting under the guise of male bonding. When that resulted in an hour of half-hearted questions from me and unintelligible answers from him, I led him out to the course where we did our morning runs. For the first time since coming to the Academy, he showed more than just basic apathy for what he was doing. He actually ran and jumped and climbed with energy. I think I even saw him smile once.

On our way to dinner, I glanced over at him. "Have you been able to remember anything new?"

"No. All I can remember is that night you found me." Rune kicked at a pencil that was in the middle of the hallway and it spun across the floor in dizzying circles before slamming against the wall and coming to a stop.

"What do you think might help you get your memory back?"

Rune took a rare moment to lift his face from its customary downward gaze to glare at me.

"If I knew that, don't you think I'd be doing whatever it was? Do you think I like following you around all day long?"

Asshole. I didn't want him following me, either. If he could be a cocky jackass, so could I.

"Why not? I'm the perfect Sophisticate."

Rune sneered. "Just because you've got perfect aim, doesn't mean you're perfect."

So, he had been paying attention. He knew what my deviation was.

"Same thing," I countered, determined to keep him talking since it didn't happen very often.

He huffed a laugh. "There's no such thing as perfect. Even Sophisticates have flaws. Even you. And since you're deviation is so powerful, it just means your flaws are that much more dangerous," he said cryptically.

"What's that supposed to mean, Shrimp? That's quite a theory for a boy who can't remember anything that happened before last week."

Rune didn't answer. He said too much and he knew it. Damn. If only I hadn't let my pride get in the way, I could've found out more about what was going on in his head. My snarky commentary came too easily sometimes.

Rune didn't talk during dinner, even when Quinnie sat down next to him and started eating food off his plate. She was flirting, but Pistol Shrimp was fully entrenched in the land of mute indifference and ignored her. He didn't even look up when Quinnie took off her sweater, revealing a cleavage-enhancing tank top that clung to her chest and left very little to the imagination. Theo noticed, as did 90% of the rest of the guys in the cafeteria, but Rune stayed strong and had eyes only for the raviolis in front of him. Even when Quinnie leaned forward to whisper something in Rune's ear and brushed up against his arm, he resolutely kept his eyes to the table. I noticed the slight tremor that went through his body, but then again, it was my job to notice everything about him. He wasn't immune to the things going on around him and he wasn't disinterested either; he just wanted the rest of us to think he was.

I was finally able to get rid of Rune right before lights out. I dropped him off with the Hounds before attempting to get down to the cells to see Cleo.

"Sorry, Perfect Aim," the Hound on duty said as he stepped in front of me. "No one sees the girl."

My hands were clenched at my sides, wishing they had a target for my frustration. The testosterone riddled roadblock in front of me could be the perfect release.

"Were you the one who did it, Marcus? Were you the one who whipped her?" I taunted.

He sighed. "Come on man, you know I don't have the stomach for that shit. I get guard duty, that's all. Now go back so I'm not forced to do something you and I will both regret later."

I could've gotten past Marcus, but it would've meant whippings for me, too. I didn't really mind that if it meant I could see Cleo, but I knew Dean Overton well enough to know that Cleo would have suffered additional punishment, as well. I learned that last year when Sterling was punished. When I told him he was a Deviant, he tried to run away. Of course he was caught and brought back to the Academy, and they'd whipped him. He hated me because I tried to force my way in to his cell to see if he was okay. We were both whipped for that. Now that I left him at the mercy of Headquarters, my guilt was compounded tenfold.

"Fine," I said. "But when I find out who it was..."

"You're not going to do anything," the other Hound said. "She did the crime, she had to suffer the consequences. That's just how it is. Welcome to the Program," he said mockingly.

My well-trained brain thought of a dozen ways I could've knocked him unconscious in that moment, just to sate my frustration, but causing Cleo to suffer another round of whippings wasn't something I could live with. I retreated down the hallway, the echoes of the Hound's laughter grating against my self-control. I would just have to wait until she was released. I didn't like it, but I didn't have much choice.

I made it back to my room shortly after lights out and I lay in my bed for hours trying to fall asleep. I tried to convince myself that the quicker I could get through the night, the sooner I'd get to see Cleo, but I was tormented by thoughts of my constant inability to keep the Deviants—my friends—safe.

My self-deprecation became its own kind of lullaby and eventually I fell asleep to the never-ending accusations of inadequacy that plagued my thoughts.

It was still dark when I heard my window sliding open. I sat up in bed, reaching for the tranquilizer gun that had hitched a ride with me all day and was now on my nightstand. The outline of a person was silhouetted against my open window. From the length of the hair and slight body build, it appeared my intruder was female.

"Stop right there." My voice was calm. It was always calm with a gun in my hand.

She stopped with most of her body inside the room and one leg still hanging over the ledge. A breeze blew through the window and her scent hit me, strong and familiar. Roasting Creamsicle. Was I dreaming?

"Cleo? Is that you?"

She pulled her leg through the window the rest of the way and stood tall.

"It's me." Her voice was quiet and strange.

I threw the covers back and started to get out of bed. I didn't care that I was only in my boxers or that she had just climbed into my window in the middle of the night. I didn't care about the reason. I just wanted to take care of her. I had to see with my own eyes that she was all right. I had to get my hands on her before my heart exploded.

"No, don't get up." She put her hands in front of her chest as if to ward me off.

Confused, I sat back down on the bed. Despite the strong urge to gather her in my arms and hold her close, I did as she asked. I didn't want to scare her. She was probably feeling traumatized after what she'd been through and I had to be careful not to make things worse.

"Are you okay?" I asked.

She walked slowly away from the window, stopping in front of me. The room was dark and the moonlight from outside was lighting her edges like a solar eclipse. I couldn't see her face at all, but I was drowning in the smell of her—citrus, vanilla, and a just-struck match. Hesitantly, I reached for her waist, needing to touch her, to know she was real, to know she was okay. Her hand met mine before my fingers made contact with her hip and she gently pushed my arm back down. My fingers flexed, desperate to reach out again after her subtle rejection.

"I don't have much time," she said.

Why was she acting so strangely? Did the Hounds know she was gone? Did Younglove send her? The professor said she would, but why would she send Cleo to my room in the middle of the night?

"Why? Where do you have to go?" I asked.

"Shhhh," she said, gently pushing me back on the bed as she followed my slow recline and hovered over me.

"Be careful. You'll hurt your back." I cringed at the pain that simple movement must be causing her. How had she managed to climb up to my window with the kind of wounds I knew the Hounds had probably inflicted? Hope flared in me that perhaps the Hounds took it easy on her. Even so, she needed to be treated.

"Let me get some medicine for your back, it'll help." I started to sit up but she pressed my shoulder back down to the bed as she continued to climb over me, straddling my waist.

"My back is fine. Just be quiet." She ran her hands up my bare chest, her fingers leaving trails of heat against my skin.

I couldn't think clearly enough to decide what to do. Part of me was desperate to get to the medicine so I could get her some relief. I knew she was strong, but despite what she said, I also knew the whipping marks would still be raw and painful. The other part of me, the part I was embarrassed to admit existed, was happy to do what she said. It was hard enough to resist Cleo's advances when I had an escape route, a plan, and some place to run to. Here in my room with her straddling me on my bed and her scent muddling my senses, my self-control was nowhere to be found.

"Aren't you in pain?" I asked.

"They didn't hurt me," she answered.

I relaxed in relief. They hadn't hurt her. She was fine.

Cleo continued to press her palms against my skin, tracing my muscles with her fingertips. Her hands felt so good that I did as she asked and lay there quietly, staring at the dark outline she cast against the weak light from outside. I wished I could see her face. I wanted to touch her so badly I could hardly stand it.

She slowly leaned down, and her mouth was warm and demanding as her lips made contact with mine. I reached up, wanting to bury my fingers in her hair, but she grabbed my hands again, forcing them over my head. I was so happy to see her that I let her body tell mine what to do. She kept my arms pinned against the bed as she kissed me. It wasn't a sweet kiss, but my kisses with Cleo rarely were. It was all tongue and heat, and heavy breaths that transformed into quiet moans.

Cleo's fingers were usually in a constant state of tracing the edges of my muscles as she explored my body. I loved the way that she liked to whisper my name against my lips between kisses. But tonight, her mouth was frantic and forceful, never once saying my name. Her hands were almost mechanical, moving directly to the places she knew I liked. It was different, and yet the same. I didn't care what it was like as long as I had Cleo safe with me.

Trapped beneath her, my body betrayed any hope of self-control I had as her hands ventured lower. She smiled when she felt what my boxers couldn't hide. I wanted her, badly, and now she knew it. Damn, I wasn't being the hero I wanted to be.

But then again, I rarely was the hero.

Who was I kidding? I never was. I was the villain with perfect aim and a near-perfect record. And right now, I was lost in her, with no way to find my way back to good judgment. She had warned me. She told me she would come to my room and I'd have nowhere to run and hide. As much as I wanted to take it slow with Cleo and make each moment together meaningful, I was a slave to my infatuation.

I'd waited so long for her to finally know me as well as I knew her.

I'd waited so long to have her here like this.

I tried to touch her and she pushed my hands over my head again. I wasn't used to her exerting control over me and I couldn't decide if I liked it or not.

Cleo's hands left mine as she trailed her palms over my forearms, across my shoulders, and down my sides, her mouth leaving smoldering imprints along my jaw and neck as she inched her way lower.

Oh God. I had to stop her before I was incapable of telling her no.

"Cleo," I moaned as her lips reached the muscles of my stomach. "Don't...Stop..."

Pushing myself to my elbows, I tried to lift her up to put some space between us so I could think straight. There was no way I could make good decisions when her lips and tongue were exploring my naked skin.

She shrugged me off and reached up to push my chest back down. I shouldn't have let her, but I did. She slid her fingers inside the edge of my boxers and before I could remember why I wanted her to stop, they were pulled down, just low enough. Her mouth and hands were there. And there. And *there*. I was on fire, my need for her completely out of control. I knew I should stop her, but I didn't because her mouth and her hands and her tongue...*Christ. I was a goner.*

Cleo owned me and she knew it.

***

I was wrecked, flung across the bed like a discarded jacket. My mind was still scattered in a million directions as I recovered from what she'd just done, from what I let her do. Cleo didn't say a word. She merely stood upright, took something out of her pocket, put it on my nightstand, and then went to the open window. Before I could even make the decision to sit up, she was gone.

What the hell?

Gathering my senses, I forced myself to get up, straighten my boxers, and go to the window to call her back. The cool breeze sliced across my bare skin as I gripped the edge of the window and stared out at the grounds below, but she was nowhere to be seen. She had disappeared and become part of the night without so much as a kiss goodbye.

Despite what she'd done and how much physical enjoyment I'd gotten out of her visit, I felt empty. She barely said anything and I was annoyed that she left without a goodbye. Then guilt consumed me as I realized I had basically done the same thing to her—several times.

What kind of jackass was I? How could I let her do what she did and not even insist on checking on her to see if the Hounds had hurt her? I was a selfish bastard, but Cleo seemed physically fine.

Better than fine even, as if the whippings had never happened. Maybe her punishment was all a farce. Perhaps Younglove was able to intervene. That was the only explanation I could come up with for why she hadn't been in pain. Even Quinnie, who never showed weakness, had been a shattered mess when she was released from her cell.

This was so wrong. I had to go find her. She was probably in her room.

I dressed quickly, determined to get some answers out of her. I picked up the object Cleo left on the nightstand and looked at it before putting it in my jacket pocket. The meaning behind the object didn't make any more sense to me than her strange visit. It only took me a few minutes to climb out of my window, cross the dark training field, and scale the tree outside of her room. I lifted the window and crawled inside. It was unlocked, as usual...as if she was waiting for me.

"Cleo?" I whispered, reaching for the light on her desk. I turned it on, expecting to find her curled up in her bed.

Her room was empty and her bed was still made.

Cleo

19

Bed of Lies

It was Wednesday. I think. Two days after my whippings. I spent most of the time lying on my stomach staring at the grey walls, waiting for the burning torment of my lashes to fade. Actually, I couldn't be sure it was Wednesday. I was only assuming it was because of the meals they brought me and the one I expected to come soon. There were no windows in my cell, only rows and rows of rough stone and heavy silence.

It wasn't silent the first few hours I was in here. I screamed a lot, even cried a bit. The pain wouldn't go away and I had bitten through my lip shortly after they took the leather out from between my teeth.

Then time seemed to be suspended as I succumbed to the prison of my own thoughts, trying to ignore the raw slices across my back. Maybe the pain had lessened, but if so, it wasn't by much. It was hard to tell since I refused to move from the bed. My back throbbed and ached in time with my slow breaths. They were constant reminders that the Program owned me, completely.

Someone brought food, but I didn't eat it, preferring to stare at it numbly until the colors and shapes morphed into abstract blurriness. I might have slept. I don't know. It was hard to separate the miasma of my ambivalence with actual sleep. It was only when I remembered to breathe that I realized that I was still alive, in body if not in soul.

I didn't torture Cassie.

That was the 29,232nd time I'd whispered those words in the last two days. I think I was still trying to convince myself they were true.

The door groaned noisily as it opened. Breakfast time, I think. Good, I needed something new to stare at since my dinner from last night was gone hours ago. It didn't take the rats long to find it. I don't even think it had gotten cold before they pounced. Good for them. Somebody should enjoy it.

Heavy footsteps echoed across the room as a pair of boots stopped next to my cot.

"Get up. It's time to go to the infirmary."

I ignored him. If he wanted me to go somewhere, he'd have to drag me because the only plans I had today were to watch my breakfast wilt for the rest of the morning, or at least until the rodents finished it.

He, whoever he was, roughly grabbed my upper arm, jerking me up off the surface of the thin mattress. Pain exploded across my back, pushing a hoarse cry from my throat as he attempted to pull me into a standing position. I didn't have the strength or will to stand and I could feel the delicate scabs on my back break open as my body twisted in his grip. Blood was already trickling down my spine.

"Stop! You're hurting her." Younglove's voice was a cold command. "Put her back down on the mattress. You and Marcus will carry her cot to the infirmary. If I hear so much as a whimper from her, I'll have you chained to the wall next. Do you hear me?"

He didn't respond, but apparently the nameless Hound heard her just fine because he gently laid me back down on the cot. It hurt like hell and I clenched my mouth shut to stay quiet. At least this time, he was trying to be careful. Despite the fact that he'd been a total jackass to me the last two days, I didn't want to be the cause of anyone taking a whipping. Even him.

Did the Program honestly think I was a weapon? A danger to my fellow classmates? I couldn't even intentionally cause pain to people that had tortured me two days ago.

Once I was in the infirmary and the Hounds were gone, Ms. Petticoat fussed over me, gently removing my torn shirt before applying medicine to my back. Professor Younglove leaned against the bed next to mine, watching over me protectively. I couldn't wrap my mind around what it meant that she rescued me from the cells and that I was now in the infirmary. From what I was told, I was supposed to heal on my own as part of my punishment. My gaze locked onto hers. She looked guilty, as if she wanted to look away, but didn't. Ms. Petticoat finished her ministrations and ordered me to lie still while the medicine she applied worked its magic. She gathered up my torn clothing and the cloths she used to clean my back and left.

"Why am I here?" I whispered. My voice was hoarse from the screaming I'd done days ago. The words were quiet, but I knew Younglove heard me.

She didn't answer right away, but when she finally spoke, it was with immense effort.

"Due to recent events, it has become clear to the dean that you were wrongfully accused. Not only of the torture of Cassandra, but of many other things. He ordered me to have you brought here and healed by Ms. Petticoat."

I was wrongfully accused? That meant I was innocent. Of course I was innocent. I knew that. Didn't I?

I didn't torture Cassie. That made 29,233 times I said that to myself. Eventually, I'd believe it.

"I don't understand," I admitted.

"I promise that I will explain everything, but right now you need to rest." Younglove stepped forward and leaned over me before pressing her palm to the top of my head. "I'm sorry I couldn't protect you better," she said quietly. And then she was gone, leaving me drowning in confused thoughts and unanswered questions while the tingling warmth of healing slowly inched across my back.

After the sun spent a couple of hours crawling up and over the windows of the infirmary, slowly spilling light across the floor and walls, Ms. Petticoat came back to check on me.

"How are you feeling?"

I moved my arms, testing the new tightness on my back. It was sensitive, but the pain was barely noticeable anymore.

"Better," I told her.

"Good. I brought you some breakfast. Try sitting up and eating something. Professor Younglove told me that you haven't eaten much the last two days."

With Ms. Petticoat's help, I managed to sit up. When the dizziness subsided, she slipped a hospital gown over my front and quickly fastened it to cover me. She placed a tray in front of me and my stomach growled. I was starving.

"After you're done with breakfast, I need you to rest a little longer. That will help speed up your healing. Professor Younglove asked that you attend your workshop after lunch, so you'll remain here until that time. I'm certain you'll be feeling almost normal by then. I have to go check on my other resident," she said, heading toward the back part of the infirmary. I assumed she was talking about Cassie. There was a door at the other end of the room that was flanked by two Hounds. I understood their wariness, but they didn't have to worry. I wasn't going to try to get back to see Cassie. I was still trying to decide if I trusted myself enough to be around her.

I didn't torture Cassie. I reminded myself. That made 29,234 reminders now.

When I finished eating, Ms. Petticoat took away my tray and I stretched out on my stomach across the bed, sleep overtaking me before I had an opportunity to ask her why I'd been released and healed. I'd have my answers in a couple of hours. All I needed now was the complete and utter nothingness of deep, painless sleep.

***

I left the infirmary right after lunch started so that I could go back to my room and clean myself up before the workshop. Ms. Petticoat tried to clean me up, but my pants were filthy, I was still wearing the hospital gown as a top, and there were spatters of dried blood on my skin. I also wasn't too quick to forget that I shared a cell with rats for almost two days.

My thoughts were as quiet as the hallways as I made the walk alone. I was amazed at just how effective Ms. Petticoat's treatment was. I felt almost normal, at least physically. Emotionally, I was numb. The time I spent in the cell seemed to have robbed me of the ability to agonize and worry over things. I survived the whippings, and even though I still didn't know why I'd been released and healed, I didn't seem capable of caring. I felt like my emotions had seeped through my wounds like air out of a punctured tire, leaving me flat and empty. Maybe it would just take time for me to get back to normal. Or maybe I'd turn into the careless monster that I feared already lived inside me.

I cleaned up quickly and it was early when I made my way down to Younglove's office for the workshop. Everyone was still eating lunch and I had the hallways all to myself again. I was the first one in the office and since Younglove wasn't there, I decided to have a seat and wait. A dozen chairs had been added for the meeting so I grabbed one and pulled it to a dark corner of the room. It was as if the shadows welcomed me.

When the other Deviants started to arrive, I made sure my face was a mask of ambivalence. I knew it was too much to hope that the accusations about Cassie and my subsequent punishment were secret. Word would have gotten around. It always did; especially when it involved misdeeds and punishments.

It wasn't long before Quinnie arrived with Sadie, Eva, Marty, and Dexter. As soon as she saw me, Quinnie's face lit up with knowing satisfaction and she mouthed the words, "How's your back?" before giggling and turning to her friends. They sat in the chairs at the front of the room and were soon lost in a conversation that included much staring in my direction.

Wesley and Theo arrived soon after and also took seats, but not close to me. They looked over at me frequently, almost guiltily, but neither said anything. I couldn't tell if the looks on their faces were pity or disgust, but it was pretty clear they didn't want to talk to me. I wondered when Sterling and Arabella would show up and if they'd be ignoring me as well.

I was surprised when Ozzy came through the door with Rune. He rarely came to the workshop. As soon as he saw me, he gestured for Rune to go sit with Wesley and Theo before heading back to the corner where I sat. He dragged a chair so it was positioned in front of me and then he sat down, straddling the back of the seat. He didn't look as relieved to see me as I hoped he would. He looked angry and frustrated. Maybe he believed I was capable of hurting Cassie. Maybe he thought I got what I deserved.

My stomach clenched in embarrassment. It seemed my ambivalence was wearing off.

"Where were you last night?" he asked.

Where did he think I was? I stared at him, confused as to why he needed to ask me that. Surely everyone knew where I was.

"I figured the rumor had gotten around," I admitted. I still couldn't get a read on what he was thinking.

"I went to your room after you left but you weren't there. I couldn't find you anywhere." Confusion briefly wrinkled his forehead.

What was he talking about? Of course I wasn't in my room. I was in a damn cell with the skin almost completely flayed off my back. I rubbed the side of my face with my left hand before allowing my fingers to secure a chunk of wayward hair behind my ear. Did he just want to hear me say I was in the cell suffering from my punishment? That seemed a little cruel, even if he did think I was capable of torturing my best friend.

"I was in the cell most of the night," I admitted in a whisper. "Then I spent a few hours in the infirmary." I spoke quietly, not wanting the others to hear any of the details.

"The infirmary? Was that before or after you came to see me?" The harsh look on his face melted away and was replaced by worry.

I was definitely out of it last night, but I was certain I hadn't seen Ozzy. Did he come to my cell when I was unconscious? Wait, no. He said I came to see him. He answered his own question before I had a chance.

"Dumb question," he said. "Obviously you went to the infirmary before you saw me. No wonder you weren't in any pain." He reached forward and grabbed my hand. "I wanted to talk to you about what happened last night."

My confusion faded as my curiosity was piqued. "What happened?"

His smile was awkward and his face flushed with color. "I shouldn't have let it go that far. I mean, it was amazing...you were amazing...I just didn't mean to let it go so far."

"Okay..." I had no idea what he was talking about. Maybe the Hounds had hit me a little too hard. Ozzy wasn't making any sense at all.

He took a deep breath. "I'm screwing this up. I don't want you to get the wrong idea. I've been looking forward to being with you like that, you just caught me off guard last night and I sort of lost control. I didn't want you to think..." He looked down briefly before returning his gaze to mine. "It's just that I didn't get a chance to make sure you were okay or to talk to you. You...well you know what you did. And it was great. Better than great. But afterwards, you left so fast and then when I came to look for you in your room, you were gone." He was rambling. It wasn't like him. He reached into his jacket pocket and pulled something out. "You left this on my nightstand and I have no idea what it's supposed to mean." Ozzy held out his hand and put the object in my palm.

I looked at the strange item—a glossy black ball with a window to see the mysterious answer block inside. I knew what it was. I'd just never seen this particular one before. He thought I left this on his nightstand? Last night? My eyes struggled to leave the smooth black surface of the ball and meet Ozzy's stare.

"What exactly do you think I did last night?" I asked quietly, handing the ball back to him.

Before he could answer, Younglove entered the office.

"Oh good," she said. "Everyone is here on time. We have a few important items to discuss before we begin the actual workshop."

I looked around the room. What did she mean everyone was here? Where were Arabella and Sterling?

Ozzy reached over to grab my hand and pull my attention back to him. "We'll talk later. Don't run away after the workshop," he whispered.

"Okay."

"First of all," Younglove announced, "I have some great news. Cassandra, the last member of the Deviant Dozen, is now ready to join us." Younglove turned her gaze to the open door of the office and beckoned with her hand.

My breath jumped back in my chest as a familiar figure entered the room. Seeing Cassie was both wonderful and terrifying. Wonderful because she looked strong, healthy, and totally healed...and because I missed her. But, terrifying because I didn't know how she felt about me anymore. Her eyes surveyed the room and trapped me immediately, as if our souls knew exactly where to find one another. She didn't glare hatefully like I feared she would. Cassie came through the doorway and stood at the front of the room next to Younglove, her gaze never breaking contact with mine.

"Cassandra, otherwise known as Horror Frog, has healed from her experience with the Others and is ready to join us for the workshop to work on her deviation."

"Her code name is Horror Frog?" Quinnie jeered. "What exactly is her deviation?" It was obvious that whatever Younglove's answer was, Quinnie doubted that Cassie could live up to the name. Cassie was petite, pretty, and one of the most harmless looking creatures I'd ever seen. From all appearances, there was nothing at all horrifying about her.

Cassie's gaze broke from mine to fix a glare on Quinnie that would have made any normal person flinch. Before Younglove could answer the question, Cassie leapt the five feet separating her and my nemesis and perched on the arms of Quinnie's chair. Bone-white blades protruded from the backs of her fingers and were crossed in front of Quinnie, pressing against the delicate skin of her throat. It happened so quickly, Quinnie never had a chance to defend herself. Cassie hadn't even flinched when her hands transformed. Did that mean it no longer hurt her, or had she just learned to suffer through it?

Quinnie's fingers sparked blue arcs of electricity. "Get off now, before I show you how I got *my* name," she growled. Despite the menace dripping from her words, there was a tremor in her voice that I was only too happy to hear.

"Cassandra," Younglove warned. "We talked about this."

Cassie merely turned her mouth into a smile that curled her

upper lip, showing her teeth in an unfriendly way.

"She asked a question," Cassie said. She was calm and controlled as she stepped off Quinnie's chair with her characteristic dancer's grace. "I was just giving her an answer." The white blades receded and disappeared back into Cassie's skin, which was now marked with red, vertical welts on her knuckles.

"Well, now she knows. Can you please find a seat? Preferably one not next to Quinby. I would like to get through this meeting without anyone needing to go to the infirmary." Even though Younglove didn't look at me, I squirmed in my seat.

Cassie took her time as she walked around the occupied chairs and found an empty one. She then dragged it back toward my corner, allowing the legs to screech in protest as they skid along the floor. I had to force myself to breathe as she set the chair next to mine and then confidently took a seat, never taking her eyes off my face.

"Hi," she said.

"Hi."

"We have to talk." Her eyes narrowed and I knew this was an order, not a request.

I nodded.

"May I continue?" Younglove asked, looking at Cassie as if needing permission. I thought I could see the ghost of a smile tugging at the corners of Younglove's mouth. It looked like Cassie had worked her charismatic magic on the professor already, because the woman was clearly a fan of my best friend.

Best friend. Was I even allowed to still call her that? I glanced sideways at Cassie wondering how much damage was done to our friendship and if we would ever be able to overcome it.

"Please continue, Professor, it's your workshop," Cassie answered. "I'm here to learn, correct?"

Younglove tilted her head at the question. "Yes. First thing you need to learn is that we don't attack or threaten other Sophisticates." I could almost hear Arabella making some sort of sarcastic comment in response to that. We all knew that Quinnie hadn't quite learned that rule yet. The silence that followed Younglove's remark was a painful reminder that the Dozen was not at full capacity. No Arabella or Sterling to whisper hilarious insults about our frenemies.

"Good to know," Cassie said in her best prim and proper voice. "It won't happen again."

Younglove's face became serious as she walked around her desk and leaned against the front of it. "Cassandra was our good news. Now on to the bad news, and unfortunately, there's plenty of it. You may have noticed that we're missing a few members. Don't," she said, turning to Quinnie and putting her hand up. "I'm not in the mood for any insolent remarks. I'm well aware that you know who is missing and why. I don't want to hear your opinion." She paused as if waiting for Quinnie to defy her. When it was clear Quinnie was going to follow directions for once, Younglove continued.

"Two nights ago, Osbourne was sent on a mission with a team of Deviants—Sterling, Arabella, Evangeline, and Sadie. Their mission was to take Janus Malleville, a Program Security Advisor, into custody and deliver him to Program Headquarters in New York."

That name sounded familiar.

"I don't know exactly why Mr. Malleville was wanted by Program Officials," Younglove continued, "but I do know that he has connections with Delia Younglove. It may be that he had information about the Others. In any case, although the mission went as planned and Malleville was successfully detained, he managed to commit suicide on the way to New York to avoid interrogation. Obviously, the Program officials in charge were not pleased and blamed Osbourne for the accident. As punishment for the perceived failure, Dr. Steel, the official in charge of the mission, wanted to keep Osbourne's team at Headquarters so he could study their deviations while undergoing further training."

I glanced at Ozzy, hoping for an explanation, but he merely looked at the floor as he leaned forward, elbows on knees, hands turning the black ball.

"Osbourne was able to convince Dr. Steel that with Delia and the Others still on the loose, we need to have the Dozen at full force. Dr. Steel eventually agreed, but insisted that one member of the team remain behind for testing and evaluation." Younglove took a deep breath. "Sterling offered to stay behind."

Sterling offered to stay? Oh God. No. Why did he do that?

"What about Arabella?" I interrupted. "Where is she?"

"She is here at the Academy. She's recovering."

"From what?" I asked.

Younglove sighed and explained what had occurred. "Arabella was understandably upset when she regained consciousness," Younglove said. "She is being kept under careful watch in the infirmary until we can be sure that she can deal with the situation calmly."

Nobody said a word.

Holy shit. I thought my suffering over the past two days was bad. Sterling was at Headquarters. Alone. Knowing the Program, he wasn't there on vacation. As awful as Sterling's situation was,

Arabella's guilt and anger probably had her in a far worse hell. Sterling sacrificing himself for her was something she would punish herself—and others—over for a very long time. At least now I knew who was on the other side of the guarded door in the infirmary this morning. It must have been Arabella, not Cassie.

"What about Sterling?" I asked. "You're not going to just leave him there, are you?"

Younglove's gaze hardened and the skin around her mouth tightened. "No, we won't. I don't know how yet, but we will get Sterling back to us soon. I promise."

The room was quiet. Even Quinnie was smart enough to keep her mouth shut.

"Now," Younglove said, breaking the awkward silence. "We have one more order of business and this one will most definitely not be pleasant." Her eyes cut to me.

I wasn't surprised. The Program didn't do pleasant. At this point I really couldn't expect anything even closely resembling pleasant.

"As some of you may know," Younglove continued, "Clementine has been accused of a number of abhorrent activities in the last week or so. Even though she repeatedly proclaimed her innocence, evidence proved otherwise."

Christ Almighty. Did Younglove need to do this now? With Cassie here? I took my whippings, why rub salt in my wounds in front of everyone? My fellow Deviant members turned in their seats to look at me, most with looks of disgust. I wanted to disappear.

"Per Academy rules, Clementine was punished for her indiscretions as they occurred. That is, until this morning when it became clear that the evidence wasn't what it seemed."

What? I looked at Younglove expectantly. "Are you saying you finally figured out I wasn't lying?" My voice was clipped and bitter, but I didn't care. I just spent the last two days recovering from torture, I had every right to be angry.

"We caught the person responsible for all the trouble." Younglove leaned back and reached for her intercom. She pressed the button and then said loudly, "Bring her in please."

Outside of the office, I could hear orders being barked and a familiar voice throwing back nasty replies.

No. It couldn't be.

Cassie reached over and grabbed my hand. "Don't let go," she whispered.

The door opened and a Hound walked in, dragging a girl by her arm. I could see from where I was sitting that her arms were slashed with jagged red marks that looked like they were in various stages of healing and I wondered if she just came from being disciplined. Another half a dozen Hounds followed, all pointing weapons at the girl in their midst. She was wearing a wrinkled St. Ignatius uniform that was torn in places and stained with what looked like dried blood. Her brown hair was tangled and matted at the edges of her face, but her shoulders were thrown back in defiance. Her eyes immediately found me and her lips peeled back in a satisfied smile.

Persephone. Everyone told me it wasn't possible for her to be at the Academy. But, here she was.

I was definitely going to be sick now.

She let her gaze slide from me and over Cassie where it finally rested on Ozzy.

"Hey, loverboy," she called. "I'd like to have my lucky 8-ball back now."

Ozzy's shocked gaze bounced between me and Persephone, realization crashing over his handsome features in a tumble of horrified emotions. After staring at us in disbelief, his tortured gaze finally settled on Persephone as his fingers released the black ball he'd been holding. It fell to the tiled floor with a loud crack and then slowly rolled across the room and came to a stop at my double's feet. She tried to bend over to pick it up, but the Hound holding her arm wouldn't allow it. Instead, she licked her lips and pinned Ozzy with a malicious smile.

"Thanks," she said. "For everything."

CLEO

20

NEW BEGINNINGS

Oh God.

Persephone and Ozzy. Ozzy and Persephone.

They'd been together last night and Ozzy let it go too far. That's what he said: *"I shouldn't have let it go that far...I sort of lost control."*

His words tumbled over and over in my mind as the truth slammed into my heart like a wrecking ball. He thought she was me and he went too far. What exactly did they do? What was "too far?"

I forced my eyes to find his, but Ozzy refused to look at me. He was staring at Persephone as if his life depended on it.

"Ozzy?" I asked quietly.

"Take her to her cell," Younglove ordered the Hounds. "They've seen enough. We'll bring her back out when we make the announcement to the rest of the cadets. For now, I want her out of my sight."

Persephone continued to grin at Ozzy as she allowed the Hounds to drag her out of the office.

"Ozzy?" I asked again, reaching for his arm.

He flinched at my touch and when he looked at me, I saw nothing but torment. He swallowed hard.

"Cleo." My name was a strangled apology when it finally fell from his lips. Ozzy got up from his seat and hurried toward the door. He stopped just long enough to pick up the magic 8-ball from the floor and then he was gone.

***

"Give me the skinny on all these douche canoes," Cassie said.

Younglove left with Ozzy and the Hounds to take Persephone back to wherever the hell it was they were keeping her. Thankfully, they took Rune, too. The professor told us to use the training arena to do some reading while she was gone. She even suggested we could practice with the dummies if we were careful, but everyone separated into their cliques to discuss what just happened. Quinnie was with her group at a table and none of them even bothered to get out their text books. Wesley and Theo were off on their own as well, but they were staring at me and Cassie, and not even trying to be discreet about it.

I was still trying to process what was going on with Ozzy and I wasn't too proud to admit that I was devastated that he left without an explanation. I was sure my chest was being crushed by the pressure of my emotions, but I couldn't think about that right now. Cassie was here. She was talking to me. I could deal with Ozzy and Persephone later. There was no use worrying about it now without knowing all of the facts. I rashly blamed Ozzy once without getting all the details. I wasn't going to make the same mistake twice. I mentally boxed up my insecurities and sadness, shoving them into the back of my mind to deal with later.

All I could do at this point was answer Cassie's question. She wanted to know all about the douche canoes. Part of me wanted to smile at her crudeness. Sterling would've loved her choice of words.

"That's Quinnie," I said, pointing in the direction of my least favorite person in the room. "Her code name is Electric Eel and she can manipulate electricity."

"She was the one the professor called Quinby."

"Quinby, as in Queen Bitch. You don't want to mess with her. She's probably going to get revenge for the humiliation you bestowed upon her in the office."

Cassie huffed, unworried. "She can try, but I'm pretty sure she'd like to keep that pretty face in one piece." White slivers poked out from her knuckles before receding back into her skin like a cat stretching its claws. She seemed completely unaware of it.

As if Quinnie heard Cassie's threat, she looked over her shoulder at us with a hate-filled glare. Cassie waggled her fingers in a parody of a wave, allowing the blades to slide out of her knuckles just enough to let her girlish gesture turn into something sinister. Quinnie rolled her eyes and put her back to us.

"You're kind of evil," I said.

"Thank you."

I was quiet for a moment. "I really missed you," I admitted.

"I know," Cassie said. "I missed you, too."

I raised my eyebrows.

"Once I realized you weren't the one beating the shit out of me in that hell-hole or tying me down to burn me with your fingers, I missed you," she clarified. "And, I missed you like crazy when you left the University. Why else would I come looking for you? Twice, I'd like to remind you." Cassie absentmindedly grabbed my hand again. "Okay, so what about the rest of them?" She gestured to the table where Quinnie was now ignoring us.

"The girl with brown hair is Eva. They call her Tiger Moth and she can do all sorts of stuff with radio and sound waves. She can make her voice sound like anyone else's that's she's heard. It's really creepy. The other girl at the table is Sadie. She's got wicked acrobatic skills and they call her Ring Tailed Cat. The African-American guy is Dexter and he spits out venom that pretty much melts anything it lands on. It's as gross as it sounds," I assured her. "They call him Spitting Cobra and the other guy at the table is Spitfire Caterpillar. His real name is Marty and he can make the hairs on his body turn into deadly, sharp, projectiles."

Cassie's face scrunched in disgust.

"I know. It's as bad as it sounds."

"What about those two over there?" She motioned to Wesley and Theo.

"They're twins, obviously. Their names are Wesley and Theo. They call Theo Bull Shark and his ability is electroreception. He can navigate pretty much anywhere; he never gets lost. Or so they say. Wesley's code name is Bald Eagle and he can see really far."

Cassie shrugged. "Not a bad power, but pretty benign."

"He can also see *through* things."

"Like what?"

"Everything."

"Even..."

"Yeah, even your clothes. If he wanted. Says he doesn't do that though."

Cassie laughed. "Yeah right. Like he could resist this," she said, gesturing to her body. I didn't want to justify her joking by pointing out that Wesley already seemed to have trouble resisting her. His gaze was practically glued to her.

She leaned back into her chair and continued her boasting, gazing around the room as she ran her fingers through her hair. "It's hard enough to look at myself in the mirror every day without falling in love; I don't know how the rest of you can resist."

"You're not that hot," I taunted, smiling because we both knew it was untrue. She was gorgeous.

"Please." Cassie rolled her eyes. "I make fire sweat I'm so damn hot."

It was good to have Cassie back. Overly confident, bossy Cassie. Even though my heart was still slightly crumpled over Ozzy and Persephone, I felt like I could face anything now that Cassie was here. I knew it was insane to measure my inner strength by the absence or presence of another person, but she'd been my cornerstone for so long it was a wonder I managed to survive at the Academy without her. I knew I had Arabella and Sterling to thank for that.

"What about the ones that are missing? The professor mentioned Sterling and Arabella. Plus that other guy that left with her. He's the one that found me in Baltimore. What was his name again?"

"Ozzy. His code name is Archerfish and he has perfect aim and insane tracking abilities."

"Right. I think I heard something about that. You seemed close at the meeting. Is there something going on between you two?"

"Sort of."

"Sort of as in yes there is, or sort of as in you want there to be?"

"Sort of as in yes there was, but I think something happened between him and Persephone. I don't know what, and just thinking about it makes me sick. Can we talk about something else?"

Cassie stared at me. "For now. We'll come back to it later," she promised. "So, what about the other two Deviants?"

I gave her a grateful smile, relieved that for now, I could refrain from torturing myself with jealousy and speculations. Ozzy had proven that he cared about me, I just needed to be patient until we could talk.

"Sterling and Arabella are the ones that are missing. Sterling has super speed and they named him Hummingbird. Arabella is the Mimic Octopus. She can change her appearance, stretch her body, and has preternatural strength."

"Preternatural?"

"She's scary strong."

"Got it."

For a few minutes, Cassie considered what I told her, taking the time to look around the room and watch everyone as they interacted. Wesley and Theo weren't talking much because Wesley was spending so much time stealing glances at Cassie.

"So, who do we like?" Cassie asked.

"Well, two weeks ago I would've said everyone but Quinnie's group."

"What about now?"

I shrugged. "I still like everyone else, I'm just not sure if they like me."

"Because of that crap the professor mentioned?"

I nodded and I was angry that I could feel the burn of tears threatening at the corners of my eyes. Why was I such a damn baby all the time? I could cause things to explode, and yet losing the trust of my friends made me feel worthless. I needed to get a backbone. Pronto.

"Tell me about it," Cassie encouraged, putting her arm around me.

So I did. All of it. I was surprised how much more it hurt saying everything out loud, realizing that my friends thought I was capable of all of those horrible things Persephone did.

"That's some messed up shit," Cassie said when I finally got through my story.

"I just don't understand what she was doing here."

Cassie sighed. "My guess would be that she was sent here to spy, or at the very least, find me. None of these strange things you were accused of doing happened until after you and your team rescued me, right? I bet Delia Younglove sent Persephone here to get intel."

"Obviously, but how did she get in? And why would Persephone risk getting caught by causing trouble and framing me for it? That kind of defeats the whole purpose of spying."

"She probably couldn't help herself. The Others? They're all insane," Cassie muttered. She went quiet and her features clouded over.

By the look on her face, I knew she was remembering her time at The Rink with Delia Younglove and Persephone.

"So," I said, nudging her with my elbow to bring her back to the present. "I heard about how you ran away and got caught the first time. How did you manage to go off the grid and get away from the University the second time?"

"A taser." She groaned. "Trust me, it wasn't fun or pleasant, but it did the trick."

"Who did you tase?"

"Myself."

"You tased yourself? Why would you do that?"

"It was the only way to escape. I found out that our tattoos are tracking devices and that electrical shocks can disarm them."

"Seriously? How did you find that out?"

"I had a meeting with Delia Younglove. When I got to her office, I was outside and I overheard her talking about you on a call with Professor Younglove. She had it on speaker phone and I could hear everything they said. The professor told Delia that you suffered an electrical shock and it caused your tracking tattoo to go on the fritz and stop working. She said they had to inject your tattoo with something to jumpstart it again because it had basically shorted out. I didn't know that the tattoos were tracking devices the first time I ran away, but that's how they found me so quickly. I barely made it to Baltimore. Anyway," Cassie continued, "I didn't know exactly how the tracking tattoos worked or how to short it out, but I figured tasing myself was the only option if I wanted to run away again."

"And?"

"And it hurt like hell!" She laughed. "Man, did it hurt. But, it worked. I called a cab and walked right off campus."

"But the cabbie took you to The Rink."

She nodded. "Professor Younglove and I have discussed it. We're pretty sure that Delia meant for me to overhear the conversation about how an electrical shock could disable the tracking tattoo. That way, she could let me think I was escaping, but kidnap me without the Program knowing what happened. I guess she didn't think you guys would find the cab company I called."

A shiver ran through me at the thought of what would have happened to Cassie if we hadn't found the information in time. Delia and the Others had been packing up to leave The Rink. If we hadn't quickly pieced together all the small clues to find Cassie, she might have been gone forever. She might have become just like Persephone—a vicious, mindless, demon. Cassie's hand reached out for my arm.

"Hey. You rescued me. It's going to be fine. Calm down," she said.

"I just was thinking about what if..."

"It doesn't matter. We're together again. Everything is going to be fine."

She was right. We were together. We could do anything together.

"It's good information to have," I said.

"What is?"

"How to disable the tattoo," I whispered.

She looked around the room. "It is."

"We could do it again," I suggested.

"We could," she agreed. "But I think this time, we escape en masse."

"En masse?"

"It's not just about us," she said, staring off into nothing. "Sophisticates deserve to be free."

Professor Younglove returned to the workshop before it was over, much to the dismay of the entire group who had just gotten used to the idea of some free time. She came alone, and gave no excuse for the absence of Ozzy and Rune.

"Join us," she said, motioning Wesley, Theo, Cassie, and me to come to the table where Quinnie and the rest of the group were already gathered. "Now that Persephone and Rune aren't around, I wanted to see if you had any questions."

"Should we be worried?" Marty asked. "If that girl can do the same things Cleo can, what's to keep her from turning this whole place into a war zone?"

That was a good point; I hadn't thought of that. Maybe it's because I thought of my deviation as more of a curse than a tool.

"That's a valid worry," Younglove answered, echoing my thoughts. "Thankfully, the Program has created a few...antidotes, if you will, for your deviations. I can assure you that Persephone is not a danger right now. At least not as far as her deviation is concerned."

An antidote? As in Younglove could give me something to take away my deviation? I noticed the other Deviants shifting uncomfortably in their seats at the mention of the antidote. They clearly didn't like the idea that their powers could be taken away, but for me it was like a dream come true.

"Actually, antidote isn't really the right word," Younglove corrected herself. "Her deviation won't be cured, just subdued. What we've given her is called a counteragent and it must be given consistently to be effective. It just makes it so she's unable to use her deviation for a certain amount of time."

"Have any of us ever been given counteragents?" Dexter asked.

"All of you have. When you were younger, they were given to you as safety precautions so you wouldn't start to exhibit your deviations before you were old enough to learn how to use and control them. Ozzy's counteragent was experimentally removed when he was 10 years old. Even though he adjusted fairly well, it was decided to wait a little longer for the rest of you. Even after the counteragent was removed, most of you took quite a while to start to exhibit. That might have been a result of prolonged exposure to the counteragent or it might have just been a natural progression of your deviation. We still don't know. You, and the Others, are the first of your kind," Younglove reminded us.

I remembered the night of the Autumn Formal when Quinnie attacked Katie and Ozzy pulled Quinnie away with something pressed to her neck. I'd bet my charred alarm clock that Ozzy had given Quinnie her counteragent. I also remembered the guards mentioning giving me a counteragent before they whipped me. Now, at least, I knew why my deviation didn't show up to rescue me in the cells.

"Professor," I said, drawing her attention to me. "How did you discover Persephone was on the Academy grounds and that she was doing the things I was accused of doing? Where has she been hiding all this time?"

"Theo was the one who discovered her presence," Younglove said.

I stared in disbelief at Theo. The guy we always teased, the one that never seemed to have two brain cells to rub together. He was the one who saved me?

"Theo was convinced of your innocence," Younglove continued. "He hacked into the Academy surveillance system to look for discrepancies in the footage of the events in which you were accused. He was the only one who noticed that in the videos, you were missing your tattoo." Younglove crossed her arms, shook her head, and stared down at the floor. "I'm disappointed that I didn't notice that detail on my own. I just couldn't believe that one of the Others might be here. Persephone and the Others had been seen at Andrews Air Force Base and the security system at the Academy is the highest that the Program has to offer. Persephone should not have been able to enter the grounds unnoticed. We're still questioning her to find out how she accomplished that feat." She looked back up at me. "In any case, Theo was scanning the video footage last night and found evidence of Persephone sneaking through the grounds while you...while you were..." Younglove paused in embarrassment.

"While I was in the cell," I offered.

Younglove met my gaze apologetically. "I'm sorry," she offered. "I should have tried harder to stop the dean from following through with the punishment. I should have looked more closely at the evidence. I should have known you were innocent."

I knew she wanted me to tell her it was okay. But it wasn't. It would never be okay that I had been whipped for something I didn't do. I didn't blame her, but I also wasn't going to act like I merely got a slap on the wrist.

"One thing I don't understand," I said. "Persephone was seen in other places while she was actually here doing all of those awful things. How is that possible?"

"It wasn't actually Persephone seen at all of those other places. It was Ambrosia, Arabella's twin, disguised as Persephone. The only place Persephone was ever really at was Andrews Air Force Base. She came here directly after the confrontation and has been here since."

"How do you know?" Cassie asked.

"Persephone was only too happy to tell us how easy it was to outsmart the Program by having Ambrosia pretend to be her in Washington D.C. and Philadelphia."

"Did she tell you why she was here or how she got past the security system?"

"Not yet," Younglove admitted, "but I intend to find out."

The bell rang and it was time for us to go to our next class. Dutifully, we all got up from our seats, grabbed our bags and jackets, and headed for the door. Younglove stayed at the table, for once not shouting out assignments to have done for the next workshop. I hurried to catch up with Theo before he could leave since we didn't have our next class together.

"Hey, Theo!" I called as I jogged across the gym and into Younglove's office. He turned and waited for me to catch up. Wesley waited too, although I could tell he was waiting for Cassie.

"What's up?"

"Thank you." I dropped my backpack and threw my arms around his neck, hugging him tightly. I surprised myself by following that up with a kiss on his cheek.

"Settle down, Tigress. Don't go trying to lay claim on the Bull Shark. I'm not a one-woman kind of man." He pried my arms from around his neck and gently pushed me back. Despite his bravado, I could tell that he was embarrassed by my affection.

"Not a one-woman kind of man? Who says shit like that? Is this guy for real?" Cassie asked.

"Totally real," I said. I leaned in to hug him again, even though he was doing his best to avoid me. I finally managed to get my arms around his neck. "Thanks for believing in me," I whispered.

"Yeah, yeah, whatever." He peeled my arms off his shoulders and turned me toward the door. "Get to class, Dracone."

He was flustered. The overly confident troublemaker who spent most of his time arguing with Arabella was flustered because of a hug. Theo was used to being the jerk, not the hero, and he had no idea how to deal with positive attention. Despite all of the horrible things that had happened in the last few days, the temptation to mess with him was too good to pass up.

"Just one more hug," I begged, arms outstretched.

"No way. You'll get your ugly all over me. I don't hug ugly girls."

"You think I'm beautiful," I pestered.

"I think you're crazy." He avoided another attempt at a hug and brushed his arms with his hands as if I'd gotten him dirty. "When is Arabella coming back? I miss her."

"Don't reject my gratitude, Theo," I crooned.

"Dude, I'll see you later," Theo said to Wesley, dodging another hug from me. "I gotta hit the head." He shouldered his pack and jogged through the door, apparently on his way to the bathroom.

Wesley stared after him, a smile on his face. "I never thought I'd see anyone break his cool. That was kind of awesome." He looked back at me and his smile faltered. "Cleo, I'm sorry I didn't believe you. I feel like such an ass."

I shrugged because I was still hurt that he believed the worst of me. "The evidence was stacked against me," I admitted, letting him off the hook. "I just can't believe that out of everyone, Theo's the one that believed in my innocence," I mused, amazed that I was just now realizing that the real Theo was a caring, intelligent person hidden beneath layers of asinine comments and stupid actions. "He really is a sweet guy."

"If you really want to thank him," Wesley said, "keep that to yourself. I think he likes being known as the insensitive jackass."

"Don't we all?" Cassie asked sarcastically. She turned to Wesley who immediately blushed under the power of her attention.

"Hi, I'm Cassie," she said in greeting. "You're Wesley?" She held out her hand to him.

"You can call me Wes," he said, wrapping his fingers protectively around hers. He shook her hand reverently like she was the goddess incarnate. I was half surprised he didn't drop to one knee in adoration. Wesley was definitely worshiping at the church of Cassie.

"Nice to meet you, Wes. What class do you have next?"

"Conditioning with Professor Peck. What about you?"

Cassie looked questioningly at me. "Whatever Cleo has. I'm supposed to go where she goes. Professor Younglove's order."

"History of Wormwood with Professor Lawless," I told her. "Speaking of class, we should be on our way or we're going to be late."

"Want me to walk you there?" Wesley eagerly asked Cassie.

"Yes, thank you," Cassie said at the same time as I said, "No, that's all right."

I looked at my best friend. Her eyebrows lifted and her eyes widened in a plea. I groaned inwardly. It seemed as if I could look forward to Wesley walking me to all of my classes again. Well, not walking me, walking Cassie. Either way, it was more of Wesley, the lovesick puppy. I huffed in agitation. I deserved sainthood for the sacrifices I made in the name of friendship.

Then again, Cassie had tased herself and survived torture at the hands of Persephone in her effort to find me. The least I could do was suffer through Wesley's drooling. The important thing was, we were still friends and we were together again. It was time for some new beginnings.

CLEO

21

MISSING IN ACTION

Ozzy was avoiding me. At least I thought he was. I didn't see him the rest of the day. That wasn't too strange considering the only time I would've been able to see him was at dinner, but he skipped it all the same. Rune hadn't been there either. I tried not to worry about it, and focus instead on making sure that Cassie was adjusting well to life at St. Ignatius.

It was difficult to keep speculations about Ozzy and Persephone from poisoning my thoughts. It was the not-knowing exactly what happened that bothered me. I was desperate for any distraction that would keep my mind from thinking the worst. Unfortunately for Theo, he had become my distraction. At dinner, it was just the four of us: Cassie, Wesley, Theo, and me. Wesley monopolized Cassie's attention and Theo spent the entire meal threatening me every time I moved.

"I saw that," he said through a mouthful of food when I shifted in my seat. "I swear if you come over here and try to strangle me again with those twiggy arms of yours, I'll kick you in your whisker biscuit."

Whisker biscuit? His insulting names were even worse than Sterling's.

"Don't be so vulgar, Theo. I wasn't strangling you, I was hugging you." I blew him a kiss. The one thing I'd learned was that Theo liked to flirt inappropriately as long as he was ultimately rejected. When the flirting was turned around on him, he didn't know how to handle it. He glared at me and it reminded me of the way Arabella usually looked at him. Oh, how things had changed in just a few days.

"As a very wise woman once said, a hug is just a strangle you haven't finished yet."

"What wise woman?" I laughed.

"Jenny Lawson. She's the hero of the eccentric."

"You know you're my hero." I leaned toward him.

"I'm serious, Dracone. I have access to the entire video surveillance system," he threatened. "I can find out secrets you don't want me to know."

That sobered me up.

"That's right," he said with a triumphant smile. "Consider me the eyes and ears of this place. Don't force my hand."

"Fine," I surrendered. "You're no fun."

"You're no fun either. Just ugly as hell."

I smiled. "You love me."

He grunted and tried to pretend he wasn't blushing. "I can't wait for Arabella to come back," he said.

I had to agree with him. It felt odd that Sterling and Arabella were both missing. I was torn between my need to be with Cassie and the duty I felt toward Arabella, even if I wasn't sure where our friendship stood. She probably still didn't know that it was Persephone, and not me, who stole the butterfly necklace out of her room, but I didn't care if she was mad at me. I wanted to make sure she was okay.

What was I thinking? Sterling, her secret little romance, had sacrificed himself for her. Of course she wasn't okay.

I wondered if Ms. Petticoat would let me see her if I went down to the infirmary. Doubtful, but maybe I could try after work detail. Once I had Cassie settled in her room, I'd have an hour or so before lights out.

There was a loud banging noise.

"Oh no," Cassie said, interrupting my thoughts.

"What's wrong?"

"It looks like the professor is about to clear your name." She pointed across the dining hall.

Younglove sure knew how to make an entrance. The doors to the dining hall had been thrown open dramatically and she walked purposefully into the room, followed by a group of familiar people. As she paraded down the aisle between all of the tables, silence preceded her like a fog rolling in over a valley. Just when the room had gotten so quiet that I was worried I'd gone deaf, the incessant whispering began; then the pointing. Everyone saw who was following the professor.

Persephone was wearing a self-satisfied smirk, even though she was surrounded by a group of Hounds.

"Quiet down, everyone," Younglove ordered. "Since I know you only have about ten minutes before you head out to your work detail, I'll make this announcement as quickly as possible. I want to clear up a few rumors. Clementine Dracone has been accused of a number of egregious events lately. Regrettably, she has also been subjected to the punishments for these atrocities, despite her claims of innocence. Last night, we caught the person responsible for the aforementioned infractions. This is Persephone," she said, motioning to the girl I could only refer to as my evil twin. "Yes, she looks like Clementine. No, I will not give you any details as to why she is here. For now, all you need to know is that Clementine is completely innocent, and the guilty party," she motioned to Persephone again, "will be punished. Please enjoy the rest of your dinner."

The professor finished her short speech and turned to leave. The noise in the room rose in volume like a wave, peaking and cresting behind Younglove as she left the dining hall. The Hounds followed Younglove, leading Persephone out as well. She turned to look at me, her wicked smile never slipping from her lips. The marks on my back seemed to ache in sympathy for all the trouble she'd caused me. I never wanted to use my power more than I did at that moment. The monster snarled in my chest, waking the flame inside me until my skin hummed with the need for release. I wanted to attack her for ruining my reputation. I wanted to hurt her for what she did with Ozzy. I wanted to destroy her for what she'd done to Cassie.

"I think I need some fresh air," I said, standing.

"I'll come with you," Cassie offered.

"You should stay here."

"Don't even bother arguing with me, you know it's pointless." She grabbed her St. Ignatius hoodie, which was slung over the back of her chair, and slipped her arm through mine. "Let's go."

Cassie desperately held on to my elbow as I ran in a near panic through the hallways, making my way to the training field where weapons class was held. I barely made it outside and shed Cassie's arm from mine before I was sprinting across the field and toward the edge of the woods. I couldn't hold my breath any longer and when I finally exhaled, a rush of heat tore through my body like water sucking away from a sandy beach just before the crash of a huge wave.

The ball of fire burst out of me and slammed into a nearby tree, sending flames into the sky, and devouring the few dry autumn leaves that still clung to the branches. Pieces of smoldering leaves fell through the darkness like delinquent fairy dust before winking out into nothing. The flames that had erupted into the tree eventually disappeared and I could see a hole in the trunk where my anger had hit. The edges of the hole glowed with the remains of the fireball, and ragged fragments of bark fell to the ground in a charred pile.

"Well," Cassie said, coming up next to me as she examined the burning consequence of my rage, "that was interesting. I guess I should apologize for not believing you back at the University."

A small smile crept across my mouth. "You should."

Cassie nodded and then grinned. "But, you know better."

"I do."

"Do you feel better?"

I took a deep breath and thought about it. For once I felt cool, relieved, and almost carefree. "Yeah, I think I do. Maybe Younglove's right. Maybe I need to do this more often."

***

"This is yours," I said, leading Cassie to the door of the room that used to belong to Maya. My name had been cleared and my reputation was on its way to repair, but Maya's old room had already been set aside for Cassie. And even though I hadn't done any of the things Maya accused me of doing, I was happy that she wasn't returning to her room. The wounds were still too raw for both of us.

"At least our rooms are close to each other."

"If you need anything, you know where I am," I said, pointing to my door down the hall. "Are you going to be all right?"

"I'll be fine." Cassie put the key in the knob and unlocked her door. She turned around before going inside. "We're going to have to do something about Wesley."

"What do you mean?"

"Did you not notice how desperate and annoying he was?"

"I did try to keep him from walking us to class. You were the one that did the big pleading-eye thing."

"He's cute," Cassie said defensively. "How was I supposed to know he was a stage-five clinger?"

"Next time, just trust my judgment. You better get some rest," I suggested. "The morning run comes really early and the first day sucks major donkey balls. Trust me."

Cassie rolled her eyes. "I can't believe they're going to make me run. I'm going to have to find a way to get out of it."

"Like cramps?" I said, smiling.

"Exactly."

"Don't bother. I tried that excuse a few weeks ago. I ended up unconscious."

"Do I even want to know?"

"No." I grinned, giving her a hug. "I'm so glad you're here."

"Me too." She gave me one more tight squeeze and then slipped into her room, shutting the door behind her.

I hurried down the hall toward the stairwell, hoping to make it to the infirmary before lights out.

"Hey! Where are you going?"

I turned around to face the familiar voice. "To visit you, actually," I admitted.

"You're going the wrong way."

Arabella was standing in her doorway. She looked normal, not at all like the unstable girl Younglove had described earlier in the day.

"How are you doing?" I asked, crossing my arms and rubbing them nervously.

"Want to talk?" she asked.

I nodded.

She looked up at the camera mounted at the top of the wall. "Come on in, we have some time before lights out."

I briefly entertained the worry that maybe following Arabella into her room, and out of the view of the cameras, might not be in my best interest. She probably didn't know about my innocence and Persephone's guilt since she'd been in the infirmary all day, and by all accounts, she was half-crazed over what happened with Sterling.

But her friendship meant too much to me not to risk her anger.

As soon as I entered her room, I questioned my decision. All of the white butterflies had been ripped from the ceiling and were scattered across the floor. The carpet was littered with so many little white carcasses that it looked like they had all just dropped dead mid-flight.

"I didn't take your necklace," I blurted. "Persephone did."

"I know. Younglove told me everything."

I wasn't sure what to say, so I stared at the butterflies near my feet, waiting for Arabella to speak.

She cleared her throat. "I'm sorry I accused you of stealing from me. I should have known better."

I drew a circle on the carpet with the toe of my shoe. "The evidence was pretty damning," I admitted. I was still hurt that she hadn't trusted me, but she was hurting now, too. Holding on to a grudge would be stupid. "We're good now, though. Right?" I asked, looking up at her.

Relief flashed through her eyes and she rushed forward to hug me. When she finally let me go, I nudged one of the butterflies with my foot. "What happened in here?"

"I was doing a little rearranging," Arabella explained.

"It looks like you might have had a wee bit of a temper tantrum," I said, bending over to pick up the bent butterfly that was near my foot.

Arabella scrunched her nose and looked around. "Better than losing my shit in the infirmary and getting confined there for the foreseeable future."

I nodded, waiting for her to say something else. She just stared at me. "Are you okay?" I asked finally.

Arabella sighed. "No. But I will be." She bent down and started gathering the discarded butterflies and I squatted down to help her. "We're going to get Sterling back," she said.

I didn't point out that it was impossible; I merely continued to pick up the butterflies.

"I have a rough plan, there are just a few small details I have to iron out," Arabella continued.

I figured her small details were probably pretty big ones, but I wanted to get Sterling back safely, too.

"We don't even know exactly where to find him," I said. "I mean, I know he's at Headquarters, but from what I've heard, that place is huge, filled with Mandates, and surrounded by a huge wall."

"I should clarify. Sterling has a plan." She held up her phone and waved it at me.

"You've talked to him?"

Arabella smiled. "Being a favorite of Lawless has been quite beneficial. He got me a pair of phones months ago that weren't registered with the Program. I guess Dr. Steel never bothered to worry that Sterling would have an unregistered phone. They never took it from him. Maybe they didn't bother to do a search because he stayed there willingly."

"You've really talked to him? Is he okay?"

"He's fine. He just wants a little more time before we put the plan in motion."

"Why more time?"

Arabella smiled. "Because he found some top secret information about the Deviants and he's trying to gather more. As soon as he gets what he wants, we'll put the rescue mission in motion. Our biggest problem will be the tracking tattoos. We need to find a way to disable them and that's what he wants me to figure out. Sterling's plan won't work if the Program knows where we are after he escapes."

"So, what's the plan once we rescue Sterling? If we're able to disable the tracking tattoos, then what?"

"Then freedom. We do whatever we want. We get as far away from the Program as we can and we live our lives like we want. I'm tired of living by the Program's rules, aren't you?"

Freedom. Had there ever been a more beautiful word?

"Count me in," I said.

"All we have to do is turn these bastards off," Arabella said, pointing to her wrist.

I smiled. "Arabella, today is your lucky day."

Ozzy

22

Coward

I knew I was being a coward, but how could I face Cleo when I couldn't even face myself? She deserved an explanation and I wanted to give it to her, I just didn't know what it was yet. The truth was, I couldn't come to terms with what I had done.

I enjoyed it.

Persephone and I...we had been together...and I enjoyed it.

Resisting the urge to take a sledge hammer to the weapons cabinet, I nocked another arrow and let it fly. It hit the bulls-eye, just like the dozens before it had. It was dark out and I wasn't even sure how much of the bulls-eye was left. The small circle was now a forest of ruined arrows embedded one on top of the other, a collection of shattered wood and misplaced anger.

How long had I waited to meet Cleo in person? How long had I imagined what it would be like to talk to her? How long had I waited to be the reason she laughed and smiled? How long had I dreamed about holding her? Kissing her?

It felt like I'd waited my whole life for her.

I was pretty sure that I'd fallen in love long before she claimed any of my top days. I'd waited so long and in a matter of one night of thoughtless decisions, I betrayed all of it. I ruined it. If I had just listened to my mind instead of my body, I would've realized something was wrong. I would've realized that it wasn't Cleo in my room.

I'd been weak and now I couldn't see how I was going to fix my betrayal. What I had done with Persephone was worse than not telling Cleo about Cassie. It was worse than the picture from Quinnie. I'd been intimate with another girl and liked it—a lot.

A small growl escaped my throat as I shot off another five arrows. The sounds of the splitting wood echoed the splintering of my guilty heart.

***

The next morning, I still couldn't face Cleo. Not yet. I told Younglove that I wasn't feeling well and, surprisingly, she didn't ask questions. She got a Hound to teach the weapons classes for me and ordered Quinnie to babysit Rune for the day. Younglove didn't try to stop me from heading down to the training rooms in the lower level of the Academy. I appreciated that she could give me the small feeling of freedom that was always in short supply as a Sophisticate.

As I kicked off my shoes inside the door, I was flooded with memories of the last time I'd been down here—when I forced Cleo to make up the weapons class she missed. I glanced around the room, counting off each memory just as I had counted off each triumph back then.

I kissed her right there in the middle of the mat after I let her kick me in the face. One. I kissed her again on that part of the floor after I tackled her. Two. I kissed her against that wall. Three. Oh, and that's where she kissed me back, right before the alarm on my watch went off. Four.

I stalked across the room to the heavy punching bag.

The first time my fist hit the bag, I felt the force of the impact shudder all the way up to my shoulder. I hit it again and again. When my arms got tired, I kicked it, feeling satisfaction in the groan of the chains as my foot made contact over and over. I didn't stop when my breath came in ragged pulls that burned my lungs. I didn't stop when my muscles were aching and too heavy to command. I didn't even stop when the skin on my knuckles started to peel away. I only stopped an hour later when my body dropped me to the mat with nothing more to give.

I lay on the floor, concentrating on the way that my breath filled my aching lungs and then rushed out just as quickly as it had come.

The truth? I was still angry. Everything that I had been confident about was crumbling around me and it was all Persephone's fault. Everything I had come to depend on about myself and my deviation was no longer trustworthy. I couldn't trust my eyesight because I couldn't tell Persephone and Cleo apart. They sounded the same, they smelled the same, and clearly, after the midnight visit, I couldn't trust my judgment at all because they even felt the same. My tracking abilities were shit when it came to telling them apart.

It wasn't just my tracking skills, either. I couldn't even trust my perfect aim, the skill I counted as my most dependable trait. I'd proven twice now that I couldn't take a shot at Persephone. My inability to do what I was designed to do was putting everyone in danger. My feelings for Cleo and my confusion over Persephone overruled my common sense. And if I couldn't trust my deviation, what was left of me? It had been part of me for so long that I no longer knew who I was without it. My perfect aim had always defined me, and everything else had always paled in comparison.

Or, was I ever anything else but perfect aim? Maybe that was the problem. Without my deviation, I was nothing.

As if my own personal crisis wasn't bad enough, I knew that I still needed to get Sterling out of Headquarters. I owed it to him and he was depending on me. I had no idea how I was going to accomplish that, but it seemed an easier task than trying to repair the damage I'd done to my relationship with Cleo.

Once my breathing was back to normal, I pushed myself up to standing and walked over to the punching bag. I imagined that it was Persephone and that she was staring at me with that triumphant, deadly smile. I raised my hands in front of my chin in the ready position, pulled back my arm, and twisted my torso as I slammed my fist into the heavy red canvas. It felt good. I would win this battle of my confusion over her. At least it was a step in the right direction. The next time I saw her, I wouldn't hesitate. I'd take the shot.

My arms began swinging a steady rhythm, beating my frustration and failures into the bag. My leg flew up and kicked squarely in the middle. The bag swung and when it came back toward me, I kicked it again. And again. My fists and feet were punishing the bag—and my body—but I couldn't stop myself. I felt the pain and the fatigue, but it was minor compared to the madness that drove me to keep swinging and kicking.

When the bag ripped off the chain and flew across the room, crashing into the wall, I finally allowed myself to rest. After ten minutes, I went to the storage closet down the hall, got another heavy bag, hung it from the ceiling, and started all over again.

I decided it was time to head to my room after I ripped the second bag off the chain. I still didn't have any idea how to rescue Sterling and my hands were so torn up I could barely bend my fingers, but at least I was too tired to care about any of it. It was past the time for lights out and I planned to crawl in bed, fall into sleepy oblivion, and continue to ignore my problems for the rest of the day. Night. Whatever.

As the weapons instructor, I'd been given the option to move into the wing where the rooms for the professors were located. The suites were larger and had their own bathrooms, but I declined. At the time, I didn't like the thought of being so far away from the rest of the Deviants, especially Cleo. I might need to reconsider that decision as the thought of my old room brought back memories of Persephone and what had happened. Her hands, her mouth, my...no. It made me sick just to think about it. I wouldn't think about it.

I pushed open my door and tossed my duffle bag to the floor before collapsing on the bed.

"Where have you been?" The voice was familiar, demanding, and unexpected.

The anger of the last few hours rushed through me and I grabbed the gun off my nightstand and fired at my intruder before I gave myself a chance to think twice about it.

Finally. I'd let instinct take over and do what my mind and body knew how to do. I shot her. Maybe the third time was the charm. I almost patted myself on the back.

Her eyes were wide in fear as she reached up and grabbed the dart that was sticking out of her arm, exactly where I'd aimed.

"Ozzy?" she asked, pulling the dart out of her skin and looking at it in confusion. She looked up at me once more before she slumped over into unconsciousness.

Hearing her say my name nearly crippled me. I'd convinced myself that there was no difference between her voice and Persephone's, but in that moment I realized that was just an excuse I told myself as justification for what happened two nights ago.

I just shot Cleo with a dart.

Fuck.

***

I wanted to hold her in my arms the entire time she was unconscious, as if that would somehow negate what I'd done. My fingers ached to touch her and I felt like all might be right with the world if I could just have her close to me, just where I needed her. But I knew that holding her was no longer a privilege of mine. It killed me to think it might not ever be my privilege again. I had no idea why she snuck into my room, and now I had to wait for her to wake up to find out. I laid her on my bed and then sat in the chair, thankful that I'd taken the time to shower in the locker room before coming back up. At least I could make her comfortable without covering her with blood and sweat.

I don't know how long Cleo was out, but as soon as she started moving, I sat up straighter and fought off the exhaustion that clung to every part of my body.

Her eyes fluttered open, causing her eyelashes to scatter thin shadows across her cheeks. She was confused when her eyes finally managed to stay open, but when she saw me in the chair next to the bed, awareness settled in. She stared at me while I waited for her to speak.

"What the hell, Ozzy?" her voice was raspy as she forced the words out, but it was still Cleo's voice. No matter how raspy it was, I could tell it was Cleo.

"How do you feel?" I asked, inching toward the bed, careful not to touch her.

"Like I just got shot with a dart. How do you think I feel?" Cleo reached up to touch her shoulder where the dart had hit her and she winced when she rubbed the spot.

"Sorry. I thought you were someone else." I felt my mouth curve into a smile, desperately hoping that there was something between us that I could still salvage. Humor had always been my go-to response when I didn't know how to act.

"Well, at least you actually tried to shoot her this time," Cleo deadpanned.

The smile fell off my lips in an avalanche of crushed hopes. I leaned back into the chair, giving Cleo the distance I was sure she needed. She was right. The one time I actually got the nerve to shoot Persephone and it wasn't Persephone at all.

"Oh crap," she said. "I'm sorry. I'm moody when I wake up. Come here," she said, motioning weakly with her hand.

My eyebrows raised in question as I tilted my head, wondering if she was going to land a right hook to my jaw as soon as I got close enough. If that was her plan, I had to admit that I deserved it.

"Come lay down next to me," Cleo clarified, patting the space next to her on the bed.

"I don't think that's a good idea."

"I promise I'm not trying to seduce you. Even if I were, I'm still too sluggish to do it properly. I only seduce when I'm at 100%

effectiveness," she joked.

I still didn't move.

"I promise I'm not going to hurt you either. Look, no weapon," she said, showing me her open palms and smiling.

She had plenty of weapons she could use to hurt me. Her touch, her kiss, her trust...every single one could bring me to my knees. Every single one of those things hurt when I knew that I'd betrayed her.

"Just lay down. I swear I have a good reason."

I wanted to. Oh God I'd never wanted anything in my life as much as I wanted to lay down next to her. I just hadn't earned the right.

"Cleo, we haven't had a chance to talk about...what happened—with Persephone."

"Ozzy," she warned. "I don't want to talk about that right now." She started to push herself up on her elbows. "If you don't get your ass over here on this bed right now, you're going to be very sorry."

I hesitated.

"Please," she said.

I walked around to the other side of the bed and gingerly lay down on my back next to her. She scooted closer to me and then sighed as her arm touched mine. I didn't say anything because I was afraid to ruin the sense of comfort that washed over me at that simple touch and sound.

She rolled slightly toward me as she reached into her back pocket. As she settled onto her back again, she brought her hands on top of her stomach and I could see that she was holding the pieces of paper I had written my top five days on. Last time I'd seen them, they were lying on her desk still folded into the flower origami I had made for her. It was clear that the flowers had been opened, read, and refolded many times. The crisp folds that were once in the paper were now softened and the writing was smudged.

"I read these," she sighed. "A couple times." She paused as she lifted the papers. Cleo stared quietly at each paper before shuffling to the next. I turned my head so I could see her. Her eyes were sliding back and forth beneath the edges of her lids as she reread the papers again.

"I know you," she said once she finished the last one. "I know you're punishing yourself over what happened with Persephone."

I started to interrupt her and she clamped her hand over my mouth.

"It doesn't matter. Not right now. Not to me." She reached down and gently grabbed my hand, bringing it up where she could see it. She carefully inspected the raw wounds on my knuckles and fingers where the skin was barely intact.

"I don't want to talk about what happened," Cleo continued. "I know you're hurting and upset over everything, and I know my face is probably the last thing you need to see right now because it just reminds you of...her. But I'm selfish and I want to be the one to comfort you."

"Cleo, it's not like that. It's just..."

"Close your eyes," she demanded.

I did what she said only because I was ready to let her take the worry away from me. I felt the mattress shift and my body tensed, nervous that she might try to kiss me. Or worse, touch me like Persephone had. I wanted to kiss Cleo and make the memories disappear, but that would only be a patch on the issue at hand, it wouldn't solve anything. It'd probably make things worse, for her and for me.

Instead of a kiss, I felt Cleo turn so she was facing me. She rested her cheek against my shoulder, draped her right arm over my chest in a half hug, and slowly brushed through my hair with the fingers of her left hand. My body relaxed in the luxury and comfort of her simple touch and I sighed.

"When was the last time someone just held you?" she asked. "Touched you with compassion or sympathy?"

"Never."

Cleo pulled me closer. "That's what I thought. Go to sleep, I'll protect you," she whispered.

She didn't have to explain any further. We both knew it was my heart she was protecting. I fell asleep knowing that no matter what dangers awaited us as Deviants, my heart at least would always be safe with Cleo, even if I didn't deserve her.

Cleo

Kicking It

I didn't want to get out of the bed and leave Ozzy there alone, not after I'd seen how broken he was last night. But, it would be time for the morning run soon and I had to get back to my room. I gathered my papers with his top five days written on them and tucked them in my pocket before setting my I-had-to-go-I'll-see-you-later note on the pillow next to his head. Pressing my palms against the edge of the window, I gently pushed it up and lifted myself over the ledge. At least the obstacles on the morning run had done some good—they'd given me the strength and skills to climb into and out of a second story window. As I scaled down the side of the building, I giggled to myself. If this whole Sophisticate thing didn't work out, at least I'd have a bright future as a cat burglar.

Cassie's second day on the morning run didn't go any better than mine had. At least she had two people to hold her hair back as she puked. Arabella was doing her best to keep her mind off

Sterling by helping me get Cassie acclimated to life at St. Ignatius. Mostly that meant dragging Cassie through the morning run. She had to be forced through every single part of the course because she hated getting dirty only slightly less than she hated running. Together, we got her through, though.

We showed up early for weapons class and Ozzy was already there with Rune. I nearly had a heart attack when I saw all of the rifles lined up on the table near the weapons cabinet. I thought handguns made me nervous, but rifles were downright terrifying. I'd fainted just touching a small handgun, there was no way I was going to make it through class if rifles were involved.

"Wow. We get to use guns?" Cassie asked. "That's kind of cool."

"Not the word I'd use," I mumbled.

"Clementine, could you come here for a minute?" Ozzy called out. Hearing him use my full name like the rest of the professors set off warning bells.

"I'll be right back." I said to Cassie.

"Don't worry, I'll keep her company," Wesley offered.

I glanced back at Cassie who glared at me with a look that demanded I return as quickly as possible. It had only taken a day for Wesley to completely ruin his chances with her. Cassie hadn't come out and told him to buzz off yet, but she was pretty damn close to it. She had a little more restraint than Arabella when it came to telling people how she honestly felt, but not much.

I made my way across the training field, worried about the guns, worried that Cassie might physically hurt Wesley before I got back, and worried about what Ozzy wanted to discuss with me.

"Cleo." He said my name like it was a breath he'd been holding in too long.

"You okay?"

"Thanks for staying last night. It was exactly what I needed. And thanks for the note. I panicked at first when I woke up and you were gone."

"I'm sorry. I didn't want to wake you."

"Your note was more than I expected and last night was more than I deserved."

"Ozzy," I said in a warning tone.

"Look, I need you to do me a favor," he said, changing the subject.

I looked over my shoulder at the table filled with all of the rifles. "Please tell me it has nothing to do with those."

"I know you hate guns." He smiled. "I have no intention of having you pass out again, so I'm not going to make you train with them today. I also have no intention of letting Rune anywhere near those rifles. Younglove insists that he take a weapons class, so I was hoping that since you're experienced in martial arts that you could take him to the training room and do a little sparring with him."

"Really? I thought you didn't trust him."

"I don't, but I trust you. And I know that you can protect yourself."

"If it'll get me out of handling a rifle, I'll do anything you want."

I shouldn't have been surprised when a wicked smile appeared on Ozzy's lips. He might still be feeling guilty about Persephone, but he was still Ozzy.

"Right. Well, thanks. I even give you permission to kick him in the head."

I laughed. "Hopefully it won't come to that. What about Cassie?"

"It looks like Wesley will be only too happy to partner up with her," he said, nodding to where Cassie stood.

I glanced over at my best friend and the look she gave in return spoke volumes. She was close to losing her self-control.

"You might want to partner her up with Theo," I suggested.

"But, Wesley likes her."

"She doesn't feel the same way. If you force her to partner up with him, I can't be responsible for what she does."

Ozzy nodded in agreement. "Theo could use a challenge."

"She's definitely your girl."

Ozzy turned back to me and held out a key, which I took. "I hate to ask you to babysit Rune, but I have to teach this unit and I can't have him here."

"I can't be here, either."

"I know," Ozzy admitted. "Ask a few of the Hounds to go with you so you'll be safe."

"Sure," I agreed, knowing that I wouldn't bother. As much as I didn't trust Rune, I also wasn't scared of him. Besides, this was my chance to get some information out of him. If he knew anything about Delia and the Others, maybe I could get him to tell me. "I'm just going to go tell Cassie where I'm going. I'll be back after class to take her to conditioning."

"No problem. And Cleo?"

"Yes."

"Can I see you again tonight?"

I hated hearing the uncertainty in Ozzy's voice. He was never uncertain. I blamed Persephone for his missing confidence.

"You don't have a choice. I know where you sleep."

Ozzy's lips curved into a devastating smile and I wanted to rush forward, grab his face, and kiss him senseless. "Maybe I'll give you a reason to make another flower for me," I said instead.

"I already have plenty of reasons," he said in a low voice.

I grinned like a fool as I headed back across the training field. Cassie rushed over to me.

"What was taking you so long?" she demanded through gritted teeth. "I was seriously two seconds away from committing homicide. If I have to look at his adoring eyes a minute longer I'm going to throw up all over myself. You know how I hate ruining a perfectly good outfit."

"Good outfit? You're wearing a uniform," I pointed out.

Cassie looked down her nose at me. "I make this plaid look good."

"Sadly, that's true," I agreed. "You're probably going to hate me for this, but I've got some bad news. I have to take Rune for some personal martial arts training. Ozzy doesn't want him in class today."

"That's fine. I could use a little martial arts training, too. I doubt my ballet skills will do much good in a fight."

"Sorry...you're not going." I winced, expecting her to yell at me. Before she got a chance, I continued. "Don't worry, I told Ozzy not to pair you up with Wesley."

She squinted her eyes at me. "Who'd you tell him to pair me up with?"

"Theo?" My voice lifted into a question because I wasn't sure if she would consider Theo a better option.

Cassie bit her bottom lip and glanced over at Wesley's twin. "Bull Shark Boy? He's cute, too. I guess that'll work."

I sighed in relief. "I'll be back before class is over so I can walk with you to conditioning, okay?"

"Take your shoes off before you come inside," I told Rune.

"Why?"

"Because this is a dojo and it shows respect."

I expected him to argue, but instead he took off his sneakers and set them on the floor next to mine. I shut the door behind him and then sat down on the floor, leaning against the wall.

"You can sit if you want," I offered.

Rune looked around the room. "What are we doing here?"

I closed my eyes and leaned my head against the wall. "Skipping class."

He was quiet for a moment and when I didn't give him any further explanation, he spoke again. "What are we supposed to be doing here? Why aren't we in weapons class with everyone else?"

I was pretty sure that was the most he'd ever said at one time to me.

"I'm supposed to be teaching you some basic martial arts skills. We're not in weapons class because they're learning about rifles today. I don't like guns and Ozzy says you can't be trusted with one, so here we are." I opened my eyes to look at him. "Sorry. Hate to break it to you, but it's true."

He shrugged. "So, are you going to teach me basic martial arts skills or what?"

"I don't think so."

"Why not?"

"Because I pretty much suck at teaching anything physical. Want to learn a new language? I'm your girl. But if you want to learn a sport, I'm the last person for the job. I can perform the skills, I just can't teach them. I would probably end up using you as a punching bag and, just so you know, Ozzy gave me permission to kick you in the head. So, I guess the question is, do you feel like getting your ass kicked for the next hour?"

"I'll pass."

"That's what I figured. I'd hate to have to mess up your pretty face."

He huffed. "You think you're that good?"

"I know I am." I leaned my head back against the wall.

"You don't know anything about me."

"According to you, neither do you. You've got amnesia, remember?"

"Maybe I'm really good at martial arts."

"You don't know what you're good at. And, if your martial arts skills are anything like your staff skills, you're better off just taking a nap."

Rune didn't reply. I was hoping that if I kept him talking, maybe he'd slip and let out some important nugget of truth about his past. Unfortunately, he didn't fall for it. Either he was trained well, or he really was clueless about himself.

"So, have you remembered anything else since you've been here? School? Friends? Family? Pistol Shrimp skills? Banks you've robbed?" I asked.

I felt Rune's eyes on me, but I refused to look at him. He had a bad habit of staring and if I let him know it bothered me, I'd give him the upper hand. That was the last thing I wanted to do when I was alone with him.

"Nothing worth remembering," he answered.

I noticed he didn't just say no.

"Want to talk about it? Maybe if you talk about it, it will help you regain your memory more quickly."

"Actually," he said, standing up. "I think I'm ready for an ass-kicking."

Clearly, he didn't want to talk.

"Great." I stood up and brushed the back of my pants with my palms out of habit. Maybe if I gave him what he asked for, he'd realize talking was a better option than martial arts. "I'm ready to give an ass-kicking then. How do you prefer to be defeated? Aikido? Judo? Karate?"

"I think I know a little Karate."

"Well, let's find out." I took off my hoodie, dropped it on my shoes, and walked to the middle of the room. I turned and motioned him forward by hooking my first two fingers. "Just remember, I warned you. I'm a sucky teacher, but I'm really good at Karate. Really, really good."

He tossed his jacket down and walked confidently toward me.

***

Rune groaned as he lay on the mat, clutching his ribs with his right hand.

"The bell's about to ring," I said, throwing his jacket on top of his prone body. "I have to get you back to Ozzy so I can get to class on time."

"I think you broke a rib."

"Don't be such a baby. I didn't even kick you that hard. It's probably just bruised."

"You didn't even try to take it easy on me."

"You told me you knew Karate."

"I said I *thought* I knew a *little* Karate."

"You told me you were ready for your ass kicking. I was just giving you what you wanted."

"That was a joke."

"Well, now you know better than to request an ass kicking from someone who can give it to you."

He glared at me. "I've never seen a girl fight like you."

"How do you know?"

His eyes widened as he was caught off guard. "I don't know for sure, but girls aren't supposed to fight like that."

"Now you're just being a chauvinist pig, and I'm tempted to kick you again. Get up or we're going to be late."

Rune grimaced. "The least you can do is help me up."

He held his hand up and I grabbed it to pull him to his feet. Once he was vertical, he forced a smile. I saw his fingers twitch long before he threw the punch at me. I spun, ducking away from his fist before ramming my elbow into his ribs. He dropped to his knees with a growl and I had to force myself not to laugh.

"Done?"

"Yes," he moaned.

"Good. Don't try a sucker punch on me again. I'll actually kick you in the head next time."

***

I ended up dropping Rune off at the infirmary with Ms. Petticoat. I may have gotten a little bit over zealous with our work-out. It was possible I really had broken something. At the very least, he needed some of Ms. Petticoat's miracle healing cream. It was his own fault. If he hadn't kept trying to punch me, I wouldn't have been forced to defend myself.

I had to wait for a group of Hounds to show up and watch

over him before I could head back to weapons class. The second bell rang as I was on my way. Great, Cassie was going to kill me. We were going to be late to Peck's class, which meant extra squats. Peck nearly had heart failure when she saw Cassie yesterday since her legs are even more spindly than mine. Peck had made it her personal mission to rectify our lack of leg strength, which meant that our class period was one never-ending squat-fest.

"Where have you been?" Ozzy demanded as I jogged into the training area. "And where's Rune?"

"Infirmary. Don't worry, I left a group of Hounds to watch over him."

"What did you do?" Cassie asked as she handed me my backpack.

I shrugged. "He asked for an ass kicking. How could I say no?"

Ozzy couldn't hide his smile. "I hope your feelings aren't hurt, but I think today might be one of my top five days," he said wistfully.

I leaned in, "I promise that tonight I'll make sure it is."

Ozzy's smile faltered and I reminded myself that he was still suffering from Persephone's deceit. I had to seriously tone down the flirting.

"By the way," I said, changing the subject. "Rune remembers a lot more than he admits."

"I know." Ozzy frowned. "I don't think he has amnesia at all. But, try telling that to Younglove."

"The good news is that you don't have to watch him for the rest of the day. I'm sure he'll have to stay in the infirmary."

"Thanks to you."

"You can thank me later," I suggested.

"You better get to class," Ozzy reminded me, avoiding the opportunity to flirt with me. "Peck will be waiting."

"No good deed goes unpunished," I complained.

Ozzy

24

Last Request

Should I sit on the bed or in the desk chair? What time is it? Why isn't she here yet? Did she get caught trying to sneak over? Maybe I should just go and find her. No, maybe I should email her. Did she still want to see me? Maybe she changed her mind.

I sat down on my bed and got out a book to read. Rather, I got out a book to pretend to read. I hated that I'd become so unsure of myself. I hated that Persephone had done so much damage to my confidence.

I'd never been so nervous in my life. I knew it was because I was in love with Cleo and I was afraid I was going to ruin it. It was almost absurd to say I was in love with a girl that had barely known me a few months, but I'd known her for years. Loving her was the easy part. The hard part was earning her love and trust. Recently, I hadn't done a very good job of that.

I had to tell her about Persephone. Cleo had to know exactly what happened.

She was probably in her room by now. I could be over there in about five minutes.

Just as I was pushing up the edge of my window, I heard her voice.

"I'm coming," she said quietly. "Sorry it took so long, Cassie was bitching about Wesley."

Her thin fingers appeared over the window ledge as she pulled herself up and I could see her face lit by the light in my room. It was flushed with the exertion of the climb and the cool weather of late autumn. I reached out to help her climb over the ledge and she stumbled into me all quiet giggles and chilly air.

"I didn't think you were going to come," I admitted.

"I told you I would. Have a little trust."

"How do you manage to get over here without getting caught?"

She smiled. "I have my ways. I know people."

"Theo?"

Cleo shrugged. "He wants me to make sure you're okay. He feels protective of you."

"Theo?" I repeated.

"You'd be surprised what you find when you look a little deeper. Besides, I kind of have him wrapped around my little finger," she added, wiggling her pinky.

"Apparently."

Cleo took off her jacket and laid it across my chair before leaning against the desk.

"So, you wanted me to come. I'm here. What should we do?" There was a playfulness in her smile that was reflected in her eyes.

What did I want to do or what did I have to do? They were not the same thing.

"I need to talk about what happened."

Her smile disappeared. "Ozzy, you don't have to do that. Whatever happened is in the past. I think I'm better off not knowing the details." She shifted nervously and looked down at the floor, biting her lip.

"I didn't have sex with her," I blurted.

Cleo's eyes darted up to mine, relief clear in them.

"We didn't go that far," I continued. "She just...you know...with her mouth...and I...well I..." I couldn't say the words. It seemed imperative for Cleo to know how far things went, but I couldn't say the words.

Cleo closed the distance between us and put the tips of her fingers over my mouth. "You've confessed enough. I don't need to know anymore and you don't need to tell me. Don't let her take away anything we have."

"What do we have?" I searched Cleo's eyes hoping that they reflected some of the feelings I had for her. I knew they couldn't be as strong, but just seeing a hint of what I felt would change everything.

"Each other," she said simply. "What else do we need?"

My mouth crashed into hers and there was no hesitation when she kissed me back, her lips meeting mine with feverish need. Our mouths were frantic and a little mad, as if they'd forgotten what it felt like to be together and they had to discover it again, all at once. With my hands on her shoulders, I guided Cleo back and she sat on top of my desk, blindly pushing papers and books out of her way. They tumbled to the floor as my lips found hers over and over again—pleading, claiming, owning.

Cleo pulled away, taking a deep breath and licking her bottom lip. She hooked her fingers in the waistband of my jeans and pulled me forward so that her knees were on either side of my thighs. She was still wearing the plaid skirt of her St. Ignatius uniform and I almost stopped breathing when I saw the bare skin of her knees brushing the denim of my legs. I held her face in my hands, worried that if I put them anywhere else, I might lose control. I had to be in control of myself tonight.

I tilted Cleo's chin up and kissed along her neck, down to her collarbone where her creamsicle scent was strong. I ran my nose along the delicate skin around the bottom of her throat, taking long, leisurely breaths of her before allowing myself to kiss the skin there. Each time I touched her, it was slow and deliberate, my tongue taking a small taste before my lips pressed against her hot skin. Her hands ventured inside my t-shirt and her fingers traced up my ribs, leaving a trail of heat in their wake. My own hands had fallen from her face and were wrapped around her upper arms, anchoring my fingers in a safe zone, trying to convince my brain that touching her there was enough. It had to be enough because I wasn't sure how much more I could take. I wanted to take it all, but knew I couldn't. I promised myself that tonight, just holding her would be enough.

Deep down I knew it'd never be enough. I'd never have enough of her. I would always want to kiss her, touch her, smell her, taste her...have her. My heart was hammering so hard and fast inside my chest, I knew she could feel it as her palms rubbed their way up my torso, taking the time to explore every inch. Her thumbs pressed small circles into my skin, sliding along my body with deliberate slow pressure that left me feeling starved for more of her touch.

Tiny, breathy words were slipping from between her lips. I couldn't understand what she was saying, but the plea was clear. She wrapped her legs around mine, hooking her feet behind my knees so she could pull me closer. Cleo's hand was in my hair, pulling my face up from her neck, bringing my lips to hers with a need that I mirrored. There was so much heat between us as we traded breaths, melded our lips together, and tasted each other's desperation.

"Cleo," I said, pulling away from her. "You're smoking."

She took several deep breaths as a smile hooked her mouth into a wicked grin. "You're smoking hot too, Ozzy."

"No, I mean, you're literally smoking. Your clothes are smoldering," I said, lifting her arm so she could see the tendrils of smoke coiling from the fabric of her clothing. Touching her arm, I realized the heat between us wasn't just the desire of being together. Her skin was so scalding hot that one carefully placed breath could set her on fire like a pile of kindling.

Cleo lifted her arm and inspected the smoking fabric. "That's new." She frowned. "And not welcome. This usually only happens when I'm angry."

"Are you angry?"

A tight laugh escaped her throat. "No, not at all. Quite the opposite, in fact."

"Well, maybe it's a good thing," I offered.

"Is this a way of saying you hope my clothes catch on fire and leave me butt ass naked in your room?" she joked.

I coughed. "Not a bad visual," I said, attempting not to envision her without clothes. "I just mean, maybe it's a sign we need to slow down."

"Right. Well, these clothes can go to hell because I was quite enjoying myself." She reached for my waistband again and a rush of hot air billowed off her, causing me to flinch when it hit my bare skin. I felt sunburned.

It was a sign. We had to take a few steps back and slow things down a bit.

She growled her displeasure when I backed away, disentangling myself from her leg lock. A sudden gush of cool air seemed to surround me once I was a little farther away from her.

"We just need some time to cool off. You're really putting out some heat."

"Okay," she agreed, looking at her skin as if it was betraying her.

I reached forward to grab a strand of her hair and coil it around my finger, wanting to touch her and knowing this was as close as I was going to get until things calmed down. We stood quietly, watching each other for a few moments.

"I want to use my last request from the two truths, one lie game," I finally said.

Her smile was just the answer I was hoping for and she licked her lips in excitement. "I'm all yours."

"Sleep with me?"

Her smile faltered briefly. "Tonight? I'm not sure I'm ready for that," she said.

"Not like that," I assured her. "I just want you to sleep in bed with me tonight."

She relaxed. "Ozzy, all you have to do is ask. It doesn't have to be a reward. I'll gladly sleep with you any night."

"I'm not just asking you to sleep in my bed. I want to be the one protecting your heart tonight."

Her smile turned shy, but she didn't say no. She merely pushed off the desk and walked to the bed, crawling across it before flopping over into a sitting position. She kicked off her shoes, pushed down the blankets with her feet, and looked up at me expectantly.

"Ready," she said. Her voice faltered a little, which surprised me since what we'd been doing just moments before was a lot more intimate than cuddling.

I lay down next to her and gently coaxed her onto her side so I could pull her back into my stomach. Once her back was flat against me, I pulled the blankets over top of us, and pushed her hair away from her neck so I could rest my head behind hers. I pressed a soft kiss at the back of her neck, which sent a shiver through her body before she relaxed back into me.

"Good night, Cleo," I murmured, running my fingers along the soft curls of her hair.

"It sure is," she sighed.

Cleo

Everything Burns

Once again, I had to slip out of Ozzy's bedroom while he was still sleeping so that I could make it to the morning run on time. I left another note letting him know that I wish I didn't have to leave. When he showed up to breakfast, his smile was genuine and directed at me. Memories of the night before—the naughty and the innocent—warmed my cheeks and my heart.

Even with Cassie and Ozzy now joining us at our table, Sterling's absence was felt. I stopped by Arabella's room to get an update on Sterling and his progress. She'd said that he told her it wasn't time to stage the rescue; that the information he was gathering was too important to abandon just yet. There was pride in Arabella's voice when she told me that Sterling was memorizing all the information he had uncovered. Apparently, he had a photographic memory.

For now, Sterling was safe, Ozzy was happy, Cassie was turning her attention to Theo, and Rune had abandoned our table to sit with Quinnie. All good news. I didn't know if Rune was truly interested in sitting with Quinnie and her friends, or if he was just avoiding me since I kicked his ass in the training room yesterday. Either way, I was glad he was preoccupied for a while.

Ozzy leaned over close enough to whisper in my ear. "I need another favor."

"I'd be happy to sleep in your bed again," I whispered back. "Or maybe you could come visit me this time."

He thought for a moment and then smiled. "In that case, I need two favors. I need you to do something for me right after breakfast. Younglove wants me to take the Deviants down to the weapons arena and do some firearms training today. I need you to take Rune down to the training room again."

"But, it's Saturday."

"I know, but with everything that has happened with Delia and the Others lately, she thinks it's important for the Deviants to get some extra firearms training. Especially Cassie, since she's only been here a few days."

I sighed. "Okay. I guess babysitting Rune is better than playing with guns." I looked over to Quinnie's table to find that Rune was staring at me as if he heard what we were talking about. If his scowl was any indication, he didn't agree with me.

"So," I said, once we entered the training room. "Did you bring a book?" I kicked my shoes off and sat down against the wall, pulling a book out of my bag. "If not, you can borrow one of mine."

Rune toed off his shoes and walked to the middle of the training room, curling his fingers to beckon me like I'd done to him the day before.

"I want to train," he said.

"Anxious to spend the afternoon with Ms. Petticoat again? She is a fetching woman," I teased him.

"Stop talking and start punching," he ordered.

Geez. This guy was a glutton for punishment.

"Rune, I don't think it's a very good idea. I mean, I was holding back yesterday."

"I've got to learn basic self-defense. Ozzy certainly isn't going to teach me anything."

"Rune..."

"Hit me!" he yelled.

Wow. Rune rarely talked. He certainly never yelled or ordered anyone around. Fine, whatever. He wanted an ass-whooping? I'd be happy to give him one. It's not like I couldn't use the exercise and training, too. I stood up and tossed my book on top of my bag.

When it was clear I was going to give him what he wanted, he charged me, trying to catch me off guard. He threw a right hook and when I ducked it, he attempted to kick me. That was new. He hadn't tried that yesterday. Unfortunately for him, I dodged his foot with a spin, grabbed his leg, and slammed my elbow into his upper thigh. He let out of a grunt of pain and hobbled away from me. And then he rushed me again.

I easily beat him again.

At some point, he'd have to realize that rushing me wasn't going to get him very far. Until then, I was happy to give him a dose of hard knocks.

After twenty minutes of nearly identical spars, we took a break to get a drink of water.

"Maybe if you'd break down the moves and show them to me,

I'd be able to learn them," he complained.

"I told you yesterday that I'm not a teacher."

"You are for today."

"As far as I'm concerned, I'm only down here to avoid the guns," I explained. "As far as Ozzy is concerned, I'm only down here to keep you away from the guns." I set my water bottle down and walked to the middle of the room. "Are you ready for more or do you want to call it a day?"

"More," he said, his voice gruff and angry.

I allowed him to make the first move and he didn't waste time in throwing a cross punch at me. I dodged it and threw a round house kick to his ribs—the ones that had been injured yesterday. I knew it was a dirty move, but either he was going to learn to defend his weak spots or he'd take the hit. This time, he took the hit.

Rune hissed as he grabbed his side with his other arm. The hiss turned into a seething growl as he turned his angry glare on me.

"You want to learn?" I asked. "Learn to protect it or I'm just going to do it again. The first rule to any fight is to take down your opponent as easily as possible. You're not even bothering to look for my weak spots, you're just trying to use brute strength to overcome me and it's not going to work."

We circled around each other. I was fresh and ready. Rune was limping and sweaty. He lunged forward, kicking his leg toward my stomach. I spun out of his reach and at the same time brought my leg up into another round house kick, hitting him in the same exact place I had a moment before. He dropped to the floor groaning.

"Protect yourself, Rune! You have to protect yourself!"

His head lifted up quickly, the look in his eyes so vacant and vicious, it nearly took my breath away. He thrust his hand in front of his body and made a quick motion with his fingers. A loud crack, like the sound of a large tree splintering in half, filled the room as some invisible force hit me in my torso. It knocked me off my feet and I slid across the floor, banging into the wall and gasping for air. It felt like someone had hit me right in the stomach—with a boulder. Rune's eyes flew wide open as the vacancy that had been there before was replaced with panic.

Son of a bitch. He used his deviation on me.

Heat rushed through my body like a blow torch, setting my skin on fire from inside. My rage was ignited and the only thing keeping it in check was the fact that I could barely breathe.

Rune raised his hand again, reaching out to me as he tried to stand up. I put my hands up in defense and exhaled. A wall of scorching heat rushed out of my pores, nearly screaming as it unfurled from me. Rune threw up his arms, covering his face. The wall of heat was a shimmering rush of air that rolled over him like a wave crashing on shore. He yelled out in pain as it passed over him, and when he dropped his hands from his face, I could see that his clothing was singed and the tips of his hair were blackened. Any exposed skin was red and covered in what looked like sunburn.

He flinched and I put my arms up again, ready to unleash something even worse if he made any kind of move. Rune glared at me, assessing my intentions as I still struggled to get my breathing under control.

"So," I managed to say through broken breaths. "You really are the Pistol Shrimp."

"I didn't mean to do that," he growled.

"It looked like you meant to do it," I snapped back.

"I just wanted to retaliate. I wasn't trying to do that. You told me to protect myself. It...I...You don't understand. You told me to *protect* myself."

"Not by trying to kill me, you asshole."

"It was an accident."

"I have to tell them, you know."

Rune's eyes hardened, almost gaining that vacant look again.

"You can't," he demanded. "They'll lock me up, just like Persephone."

"Maybe they should," I countered.

"Maybe they should lock you up, too," he argued, showing me the raw skin on his arms. "You're no less a monster than I am."

***

You're no less a monster than I am. I knew he was right, but honestly, I was beginning to depend on my monster. It made me stronger, more confident. It protected my friends. It protected me.

I took him to the infirmary again because his ribs were hurting and he had minor burns all over his hands and arms. The entire walk to the infirmary, Rune continued to declare that what he'd done was an accident. Of course, I didn't believe him. At the same time, I felt bad for him. He seemed to be genuinely sorry for what he'd done, even after I gave him a terrible case of sunburn and ruined his clothes.

When Ms. Petticoat asked Rune what happened to his arms, I was momentarily worried that he would rat me out and I'd get in trouble for attacking him with my deviation. I couldn't bear going to the whipping cells again. Instead, Rune told Ms. Petticoat that his burns were from being outside too much and that his bruised ribs were an accident. He didn't tell her that I used my deviation against him, although she probably suspected as much. I didn't mention that he'd attacked me either. I called for a couple of Hounds to take over for me before I headed back to the weapons arena. On my way out of the infirmary, I chanced a look back at Rune. He met my gaze and with a few small movements of his hands, I saw him give me the signs for "silence" and "promise."

He knew languages were my expertise. All languages.

I wasn't sure if he was asking me to promise to keep silent, or if he was promising to keep silent about what I'd done. I decided it was an agreement that we'd keep each other's secret. I nodded and signed back the word "promise" to him. It looked like we were going to protect each other for now.

"How'd it go?" Ozzy asked when I returned to the weapons arena to find him locking up the guns and ammunition. "I don't see Rune. Does that mean he made another trip to the infirmary?"

"He did." I knew I had to tell Ozzy what happened, but something was stopping me. Rune's actions proved that he was dangerous, but there was a small part of me that worried he'd be punished if I admitted he attacked me. I wasn't so much worried about him being locked up, but I couldn't bear it if they sent him to the whipping cell. I couldn't bring myself to sentence anyone to what had been done to me.

I said nothing. When Ozzy looked back at me, the guilt settled low in my stomach because I felt like I was lying to him. And as much as I owed him the truth, I felt like I owed it to Rune, and myself, to not condemn him to torture.

***

At lunch, Arabella sat right next to me. She was so excited she could barely sit still.

"Sterling said he'd be ready soon," she whispered. "Maybe in a few days. We should talk to Ozzy and make a plan about who will be coming with us."

I nodded in agreement. We had to talk to Ozzy. I knew he'd come and that he'd support the idea. It was just a matter of finding the time and opportunity to talk to him and everyone else.

"This is it," she hissed. "In a few days we'll have Sterling back and be free of the Program."

I didn't mention that even if we disabled the tattoos, we'd never really be free. We might escape from under the Program's thumb, but we'd always be on the run. That wasn't true freedom. I still thought we should leave. I knew we had to, if for no other reason than to rescue Sterling, but it was still not a decision to be made lightly.

"Can I come by your room tonight?" I leaned over and asked Ozzy.

"I'll come to yours," he promised.

Good. Maybe when I talked to him tonight we could find a way to have everyone to meet after lights out. I also had a few hours between now and then to decide how I was going to tell him about Rune and what had happened in the training room. Once my initial surprise had worn off, I realized that Rune probably wouldn't be punished for what he'd done; at least not whipped. He might be put under stronger surveillance like Persephone, but perhaps that wasn't a bad thing.

Katie interrupted my thoughts when she came up to our table and stood behind me and Arabella. "Younglove wanted me to tell you that we have a scrimmage today."

"It's Saturday," Arabella pointed out. "We never practice on Saturday."

"I know, but the team has been screwed up with so many of us missing practices lately."

That was true. Katie had been injured by Quinnie and missed several days, Quinnie had missed practices when she went to The Rink, I missed practices because of my punishments, and Arabella had missed time because of her secret mission to get Janus Malleville. We'd be lucky to survive a regular practice, let alone a scrimmage. What was Younglove thinking?

Katie looked at Cassie. "You've been practicing with us for a couple of nights, how do you feel on skates?"

Cassie shrugged. "Fine."

She was better than fine. Just as she had with ice skating, Cassie had picked up roller derby fast. She still hadn't quite gotten the hang of blocking, but her skating was top notch.

"Good. Susie tore her ACL on the run this morning. Stepped in a damn hole and ripped her knee to shreds," Katie lamented with a shake of her head. "Younglove wants you to pivot for me in today's scrimmage."

"No problem," Cassie said, taking a bite of her sandwich and turning back to her conversation with Theo.

I remembered my first scrimmage against Quinnie's team when I was a mess of nerves. Not Cassie. She was fearless. She was the girl who tased herself and ran away twice to try to find me. That girl had nerves of steel and I was proud to call her my friend. I needed to learn how to get nerves like that.

"Scrimmage is at four," Katie said. "See you there."

***

The scrimmage turned out to be a total disaster. It should have been called "Cassie Target Practice," because Quinnie's team was taking cheap shots every chance they got. Each time Cassie got shoved to the track, her eyes blazed with hatred. I wondered how much effort it was taking to restrain the urge to let her blades fly loose. With Eva and Sadie on Quinnie's team and Cassie, Arabella, and me opposing them, the scrimmage was constantly a breath away from becoming a full-fledged battle zone. One wrong word, one miscalculated move, one over-reaction, and someone would end up in the infirmary—or a wooden box.

On the next jam, Cassie and Katie took a break while Arabella took pivot and I lined up next to Quinnie as jammer.

"Stealing one boyfriend wasn't enough for you?" she snarled.

"I didn't know you even had a boyfriend to steal, let alone two."

"You knew Ozzy was mine."

"I didn't steal Ozzy. He came to me all on his own." I refused to look at her.

Quinnie hissed. "Stay away from Rune. He's mine."

I couldn't stop myself from laughing. "I'm not trying to steal Rune. I want nothing to do with him."

"I know you've been alone in the training room with him the last few days."

"Yeah. Kicking his ass, not sucking his face. Get your facts straight."

"Stay away from him," she warned again.

"My pleasure," I retorted.

The whistle blew and we both surged forward in anger. As I came up behind Maya, I instinctively slowed. I knew that Younglove told everyone what happened, and Maya had even apologized, but things were still strained between us. Even in practices, we seemed to have invisible force fields around us that prevented us from getting too close. Normally, I would have skated close to Maya and used her bulk as a shield, or allowed her to help by pushing or pulling me ahead of her, but the awkwardness remained. I tried to change course slightly to find a different way through the pack and Quinnie shot past me, pushing me into Maya with her shoulder. We tumbled into the track in a heap of graceless body parts.

Quinnie wasn't finished there. As she came up behind Arabella, I could see that she said something to her. Arabella lost her focus and instead of just bumping into Quinnie, she tackled her. The ensuing pile-up that resulted after that left only two girls standing, both watching helplessly as my pivot and the other team's jammer rolled around on the floor trading punches. Quinnie's skin was sparking like it was covered in glitter and Arabella's arms were constantly looking too long, or too bent, or too rubbery. It took both teams to pull the girls off each other.

"Don't you say his name!" Arabella was screeching. Her arms were being held by Katie and Maya and she was kicking out with her skate, trying to make contact with Quinnie who was being pulled away by two Mandates from her team.

A burst of the whistle informed us our jam was over. No one was sent to penalties since it seemed there were too many offenders in that particular fight. Younglove and Professor Jediah switched groups and I found myself back on the bench with Arabella.

"You okay?" I asked, hesitantly.

"Not even close."

I scooted closer to Arabella and put my arm around her shoulder. I didn't say anything because there were no words to make the situation right. There was nothing I could say that would ease her fears for Sterling or take away the pain of his absence. All I could give her was the comfort of my presence. It wasn't much, but she laid her head on my shoulder and exhaled, which was as close as I'd get to an admission that she needed the comfort.

During Cassie's jam, Katie failed to outscore the other jammer and we were falling behind. Younglove sent me out for the next round and kept Cassie in as pivot. Younglove seemed to have a hard time deciding which pivot was more dangerous with Quinnie—Arabella or Cassie—but ultimately she told Cassie to keep the pivot helmet panty she was wearing.

As the first whistle blew, I heard the ringing of a cell phone. Younglove reached into her pocket to pull out her phone. The second whistle blew, sending me and Quinnie into action. I risked a glance over at Younglove and noticed her hurrying out of the arena.

Quinnie must have noticed it, too, because Younglove's absence was all it took for her normal shoulder bumping to turn into all-out shoving. I struggled to stay upright and when I finally gained my balance, I chased after Quinnie with no goal other than to catch her. I didn't care about the score, all I cared about was catching up to her. I didn't know what I'd do when I caught her, but I'd figure it out. Sadie was playing pivot for the other team and when Quinnie came up behind her, they joined hands and clotheslined Cassie from behind. Professor Jediah blew her whistle to call a penalty on her skaters, but it was too late. No one was paying any attention.

Cassie's blades were out, electricity was arcing from Quinnie's fingertips, and Arabella was rushing off the bench and barreling into the commotion as both teams pushed and shoved one another. As the normal Mandates began to notice the abnormal things going on between the Deviants, they stopped struggling and backed up. Cassie jumped toward Quinnie, the blades on the back of her fingers were streaks of white as they swiped. Blue energy jumped from Quinnie's hands, bouncing off Cassie's shoulders and knocking her to the ground. I was already pushing my way toward the center of the melee to try to stop the fight, but when I saw Cassie's limp body falling backward, my insides caught on fire as I screamed in rage. I grabbed the arm of a Mandate from the other team and pulled her out of my way until I was standing in front of Quinnie.

"It's about time you showed up," she sneered.

"Stop it." I forced the words past the heat in my throat, sure that small flames were licking past my lips and across my tongue with each word.

Quinnie raised her hands, her body humming with the force of her anger. Before she had a chance to unload her fury on me, I released the hold on my protective rage. A cone of fire erupted in front of me, separating me and Quinnie with a wall of scorching heat. I saw her throw her arms in front of her face and stumble backward to get away. The flames leapt to the ceiling as a few lights above us shattered under the heat of the sudden blaze. Once the fire had started though, I couldn't seem to reel it back in or stop it. I could hear screaming and shouts, but they seemed far away, echoes of reality. The only reality I had right now was the fire and my rage, both of which were hungrily feeding on one another.

"No!" The scream was torn from Younglove's throat as she reentered the arena. "Stop! Now!"

Another light burst as Younglove rushed toward me. I saw her frail body and dry skin heading for my wall of fire and that was all it took for my anger to disappear, taking the heat with it. I sank to the floor, which was little more than charred wood and coils of smoke.

Ozzy

26

The Dam

Once I dropped Rune off with the Hounds, I rushed to the training field where Younglove asked me to meet her. Her voice had been agitated over the phone and I could hear shouting in the background. I wasn't sure what I was going to be walking into, but it sounded like a fight. When I walked out onto the dark training field, however, I noticed it was just a gathering of the Deviant Dozen: everyone except for Sterling and me. The group was separated in the usual way—Cleo, Arabella, Cassie, Theo, and Wesley on one side and Quinnie, Eva, Sadie, Marty, and Dexter on the other. The girls were dressed in their roller derby training clothes.

What I really found confusing, however, was the state the girls were in. Clearly, their scrimmage hadn't gone well. At the very least, an altercation of some sort had occurred, which probably had been the sounds I heard in the background during Younglove's phone call. Quinnie, Sadie, and Eva were wearing clothing that was ripped and looked like it had been burned. They also had bloody cuts on their arms that they were in the process of bandaging up. Cassie was holding an ice pack to her head and Arabella had one on her shoulder. Cleo was the only one not visibly using first aid, but she was slumped in a chair as if she couldn't hold herself up any longer. All of them were sporting hairstyles that resembled a basket of yarn left to the whim of a dozen feral cats.

Younglove was at the weapons cabinet, frantically pulling out hand guns and ammunition, setting them on the table next to her.

"What's going on?" I asked.

"Oh good, you're here," Younglove answered, turning away from the cabinet to look around at the group. "We have an emergency. I hoped we'd have more time, but no such luck." She set the gun she was holding on the table and clasped her hands in front of her. "Delia Younglove finally called. She wants Cassandra returned to her tonight."

"And what was your response?"

"That we would meet her."

"What are her demands?"

"She wants Cassandra brought to the Conowingo Dam at the county border tonight."

"We're not going to give Cassie to her," I stated.

"Of course not," Younglove agreed.

"And if we don't show up or bring Cassie?" I asked.

"What do you mean if we don't?"

"Did she make any threats?"

"I'm assuming she'd destroy the dam," Younglove said evasively.

"That seems a little anti-climactic after she blew up a hotel in Vegas and attacked Andrews Air Force Base. She didn't give you any exact threats? She just said bring Cassie and you agreed? Why would we bother to show up?"

"Conowingo Dam is not only a working dam, but it's also a hydroelectric plant and a bridge to cross the river. Destroying it would be disastrous to travel and utilities in the area, not to mention the danger it would pose to the people downstream."

I'd traveled over the dam before and what Younglove said was true, but it still didn't seem to fit. Why would Delia choose a dam out in the middle of nowhere after attacking high profile targets? Destroying a Las Vegas hotel was momentous. If she was going to choose a dam, why not the Hoover Dam? Why some small dam that only locals knew about? It made no sense to me.

"Did she actually say she was going to destroy the dam if we didn't show?" I asked.

"Not exactly," Younglove said. "But it was implied."

"How would she do that? She doesn't have Persephone," I pointed out.

"There are traditional ways of blowing up a bridge, as you well know, Osbourne." Younglove was flustered. "The point is, we know what she and the Others are capable of and we have to meet her. This could be our chance to stop her from further terrorist attacks."

Younglove wasn't being logical. The Program didn't negotiate with terrorists, but that's exactly what she was doing. Even if we didn't actually plan to turn Cassandra over to Delia Younglove, we were acquiescing to her demands to show up when and where she dictated, which was stupid. We had no idea what we'd be walking into.

"She wants to meet at the dam at 8:00," Younglove continued.

"Who are you planning to send?"

"I'm sending all of you. I don't want to, but the Program is getting impatient and wants her apprehended. This could be our chance. Without Persephone, she only has ten Deviants. There are eleven of you with Cassandra."

"So, you do plan to send Cassie."

"As a Sophisticate, not as a sacrifice."

Sophisticate. Sacrifice. It was the same thing in my opinion. To be honest, we were all being sent as sacrifices.

"Does Overton agree that this is the right thing to do? What about Dr. Steel?"

Younglove's expression was angry. "The Deviant Dozen is my responsibility, as is Delia."

"You can't make this personal," I said carefully. "You can't make this decision without talking to the Program administrators." Even I knew that.

"You may be the weapons instructor, Osbourne, but I'm still in charge here. You will go to the meeting and you will capture Delia and the Others."

"What about Persephone and Rune?"

"They'll stay here in custody," Younglove answered. "With the counteragent in her system, Persephone is not a concern while you're away."

"We could be walking into a trap," I said. "I don't think we should go."

"And miss the opportunity to stop the Others?"

"Delia doesn't have Persephone, who is probably her strongest weapon. She chose an unimpressive location, and she hasn't made any direct threats. I think it's too much of a risk." It just wasn't adding up for me. Delia was the type who liked flair and big messages. Conowingo Dam was neither.

Younglove ignored my arguments. "Please take the Dozen to the Hounds' storage facility and have them outfitted for the mission. I'll gather maps and building plans for the dam. We'll have about twenty minutes to plan before you have to leave."

All of the reasons Younglove gave for why we should go were the same reasons I thought we shouldn't. Delia was smart enough to know she was outnumbered and that she had no leverage. It made no sense, but Younglove had made up her mind.

I followed orders, because that's what I always did.

***

We had to take two SUVs and a van to the dam. The SUVs were for basic transportation and the large van was for bringing back our captives. The Program would want to interrogate Delia, and I assumed there would be plenty of tests and experiments planned for the Others. It would probably be more humane if we just killed them all rather than handing them over to the Program.

Younglove gave me the counteragents for each of the Others, so that we could eliminate the threat of their powers and make transporting them safer. Honestly, the chance of us successfully administering ten counteragents without anyone getting hurt would take a goddamn miracle.

I was driving one SUV with Cleo, Cassie, and Arabella. Marty was driving a second with Dexter, Quinnie, Eva, and Sadie. Wesley and Theo were driving the van. I didn't know if it was a good idea to put those two together, but it was too late to change my mind since we were almost to the dam.

Cleo had been quiet and withdrawn since we left the Academy. I figured she was scared and I didn't blame her. She was sitting in the passenger seat studying the blueprint of the dam. Younglove went over it with us before we left, but the perfectionist in Cleo wouldn't be satisfied until she had memorized every bit of information the drawing had to offer.

"What are you thinking about?" I asked Cleo.

When she inhaled, there was a nervous shudder to her breath. "I just hope everything goes as well as Younglove thinks it will." She was silent for a moment and when she spoke again, she turned to look at me. "Do you think we did the right thing leaving Rune and Persephone at the Academy?"

Her question caught me off guard. Of all the things I was worried about, I hadn't really thought much about them since we'd left. "We couldn't bring them with us," I reminded her.

"I know, but maybe we should have left some Deviants to guard them. You know, to make sure they don't start trouble while we're gone."

"It'll be fine," I assured her. "Like Younglove said, Persephone has the counteragent in her system. And Rune won't even know we're gone. He's been spending a lot of time under the guard of the Hounds. He'll probably be glad to have a break from us."

"I know, it's just—"

"Don't worry. Besides, it's too late to do anything about it anyway. We're here."

As we neared the bridge that led over the dam, I slowed the vehicle. I pulled to the side of the road and the other two vehicles quickly parked behind me. Ahead, I could see the powerhouse that housed the turbines and the operations for the dam. It was built to the right side of the bridge that spanned the dam on the end closest to us. The woods around us were dark and the only light was from the moon and the exterior lights of the powerhouse.

"Wesley? Theo? See anything?" I said into my tactical headset.

"Nothing yet," Theo replied.

"Everyone exit your vehicles roadside. Wesley take point with Quinnie and me. Theo and Cleo will guard the rear. Everyone else, position like we discussed." I knew that Cleo was probably our most powerful weapon and it made sense to have her up front, but I also knew that she wasn't in complete control of her deviation. Admittedly, I also wanted to keep her as far from danger as I could. Besides, I knew I could count on Quinnie to attack if needed. She was nearly sparking with eagerness as it was.

After I adjusted my headset to make sure that I could easily communicate with the rest of the group, I checked my weapons. Cleo was the only Deviant who hadn't taken a gun. She had reluctantly taken a few throwing knives, but she was essentially relying on her deviation if we needed to attack, or worse, defend ourselves.

Younglove told us that we were supposed to meet Delia inside the powerhouse. As we made our way toward the building, I was surprised that even at 8:00 in the evening, there was no traffic traveling over the bridge. It wasn't a major highway by any stretch of the imagination, but the road was usually well-traveled. The bridge was empty. Even Delia's vehicles were nowhere to be seen.

Soon, we reached the dam and followed the walkway around the right side of the powerhouse, away from the road. The building was on our left, and to our right, the walls of the dam plunged into the river below. The windows of the powerhouse were at least thirty feet high, but we couldn't see into them from the walkway since they were about twelve feet off the ground. Wesley and I climbed to the top of the short wall underneath the windows and cautiously peered through them. All of the lights were on inside and the turbines were spinning, but it was empty—no workers, no Delia, no Others. That wasn't much of a surprise since I hadn't expected Delia or the Others to be standing out in the open where they'd be easy targets, but it also made it difficult to decide how to enter the building. I didn't want to be the easy target, either. I wondered where the workers were and if they'd become hostages or if they were already dead.

"I don't see anyone in hiding," Wesley said.

"We're still a little early so we'll walk around the building before going inside," I said into the mouthpiece of my headset so that everyone could hear me.

"Should we split up?" Wesley asked. "I could take half of the group and go around the other side," he offered.

"No. Let's stick together," I said. "That's our best strength. We might not surprise them, but it gives us a fighting chance, at least."

We walked along the powerhouse wall and around the corner to the other side. Overhead, on the upper portion of the building, large neon letters flickered ominously with the words "Conowingo Hydroelectric Plant." The top of the building was covered in a complex metal structure that looked a little like boxy electrical towers that gave the entire place an unfinished, dangerous look. We were on the northeast side of the powerhouse and there was a set of stairs leading up to a door. The neon letters overhead cast a sickly orange glow over us.

"Wesley? See anything?" I asked, gesturing to the wall in front of us.

"Nothing. We should go in this way. We'll be able to see down to the main floor where the turbines are."

I climbed the stairs and tried the door, which was unlocked. On a second inspection, I noticed that the lock had been melted away by acid. The metal sagged down the door in oozing droplets that fell away from a gaping hole underneath the doorknob. That was a pretty good sign that Dexter's twin had been here.

"Weapons, everyone," I advised, drawing my own before opening the door and entering the building. I quickly scanned the area. There was nothing but the overwhelming sound of the turbines and the vibration they created. I checked my watch.

"It's 8:07. Where are they?" I asked.

"Only one way to find out," Wesley responded. "We have to go in."

"Quinnie, how big of a shield can you create and how long can you hold it?" I asked, referring to the electromagnetic shield she'd created at Andrews Air Force Base.

"Big enough to protect all of us, but only from one side. I can't bend it in an arc yet. I can hold it for a while as long as it's not hit too many times."

"I don't think it's necessary," Wesley interjected. "I don't see anyone nearby."

I didn't sense anyone either, but I wasn't willing to sacrifice the safety of my team by being careless. In the end, however, I decided not to have Quinnie waste energy until I knew we needed her shield. We descended the steps and walked the main floor, checking behind all of the turbines. Nothing. Not a trace of Delia or any of the Others. Aside from the turbines, the room was empty and still. At the other end, beyond the last turbine, there was another set of stairs that led to a lower level where it appeared there were two more turbines.

I motioned to Cleo, Cassie, Marty, Dexter, and Theo to guard from the top while the rest of us checked the lower level. We descended the second set of stairs and began the painstaking task of checking everything.

"It looks like there are two people on the other side of that turbine on the right," Wesley said nodding to the turbine in question. "They're tied up and not moving," he noted quietly.

Beside me, Quinnie started moving her hands in front of her body and I saw the blue light of her shield spin into existence, growing until we were safely behind it. I motioned for Arabella, Sadie, and Eva to guard our backs as Wesley, Quinnie, and I rounded the turbine. On the floor, two men in tan coveralls were lying on the ground, bound and gagged. One was an older black man with glasses and intelligent eyes. The other was a balding white man with a ruddy brown mustache and a stomach that pressed his uniform tightly around his middle. They were conscious, but looked like they were too scared to move. Quinnie allowed her shield to blink out of existence and both men cringed away from her.

"Pull off their gags," I told Wesley.

He holstered his gun and bent down to do as I ordered.

"Who are you?" I asked when both men were un-gagged.

"I'm Randall and this is Dan," the man in glasses stated haughtily. "We're the night staff. But, you already know that."

"Who did this to you?" I asked. "Did you see them?"

"Is this some kind of joke?" he retorted.

The balding man, who Randall had called Dan, cowered away as if afraid of being associated with him. When Dan turned his head, I noticed that there was a bruise forming on his left cheek.

"No, just a simple question. Did you see who did this to you?"

I asked again, as the rest of the team came down the stairs and joined us.

"Of course I did. I might be wearing glasses, but I'm not blind."

In another circumstance, I might have liked Randall for his bravado, but I was in a hurry and he was being awfully mouthy for someone who was tied up and surrounded by nearly a dozen armed people. "Can you describe them to us?" I asked impatiently.

"Don't need to. They're standing right behind you," he said, nodding his head beyond me.

I whirled around worried that the Others had snuck up behind us, but all I could see was my own team members. And then I realized that he was talking about my team: the ones who looked like the Others. Of course he would think we were the same people.

"I see. Can you tell me what happened?" There was no point explaining things to him. The best I could do was get basic information and hope it helped. If the bruise on his coworker's face was any indication, the Others hadn't been easy on them.

"Around 5:00, your friends there stormed in and attacked us. They beat Dan up when I tried to fight back. They tied us up and put us here. Then an older woman with short hair told us that they'd release us in a few hours as long as we were quiet and didn't try to escape. So, are you here to release us? What did you want with the powerhouse anyway?"

I ignored his questions. "Have you seen anyone else in the last three hours?"

"Why are you interested in this place, son?" he asked instead.

Randall wasn't going to answer my questions, so I turned to Dan. "Have you seen anyone else in the last three hours?"

He shook his head.

"I don't think they're here," Wesley said. "I've seen no trace of them."

Not here? Why would Delia demand we come if she wasn't even here? Oh shit. What if they asked us here because they were planning to get rid of us in one act of terrorism? All they had to do was set off an explosion here at the dam and they'd easily eliminate us.

"We need to untie Randall and Dan and get out of here now," I ordered. I bent to undo the bindings on Dan's wrists as Quinnie and Wesley worked on Randall's bindings.

"Can you show us the quickest way out?" I asked Dan. He nodded, getting to his feet as soon as he was free.

"This way," he motioned, leading us to a set of stairs along the far wall that led to a door. He hurried up the stairs and I motioned Randall and the rest of the Deviants forward, as I took up the rear. I scanned the powerhouse room one more time as we rushed outside. Our vehicles were within sight.

"Head for the SUVs," I ordered, ushering Dan and Randall along with us as we ran.

I expected to hear an explosion or some other disastrous event as we sprinted away from the bridge and into the darkness, but there was nothing. As we ran, Cleo turned to look at me, fear clear in her eyes.

"Why are we running?" she asked.

"If they're not here, I'm guessing they plan to take us out another way," I answered.

Several of the Deviants looked over their shoulders at the powerhouse, finally understanding why we were running. We slowed as we neared the SUVs and van and I asked Wesley and

Theo to check the vehicles and surrounding area for any threats. We quietly waited as the brothers walked around and peered into the darkness.

I'd never been on a mission this confusing. This was not how my assignments normally went. Usually, everything was researched and planned down to the tiniest detail. My teams and I got in and out with efficient success. Sophisticates were never sent into a situation with so much uncertainty. There were so many things wrong. In fact, there was nothing right about this mission at all. If Delia and the Others didn't plan to meet us here or destroy us in an act of terrorism, then why did she demand that we come?

The sudden ringing of my phone caused Arabella and Quinnie to swing around, their guns pointing at me.

"It's just my phone," I said, reaching into my pocket as they lowered their weapons.

Jesus. We were all on edge.

"Hello," I said into the phone.

"Osbourne," Younglove yelled. She was breathing hard and it sounded like she was running. "They're here. Delia and the Others aren't at the Conowingo Dam. They're here at the Academy. It's all my fault..."

Cleo

Dangerous Secret

Conowingo Dam was a trap, just not the kind we were expecting.

The line went dead after Younglove's desperate plea and none of the other numbers Ozzy tried were successful. We had no details about what was going on, but one thing was clear—Delia lured us away from the Academy so that she could attack it. Without the Deviants around for protection, the Academy would be easy pickings for the Others. Leaving Rune and Persephone behind was like giving Delia two huge gifts. All they were missing were big red bows around their necks.

Losing Rune and Persephone as captives took away any leverage we had. The bigger problem was that I was the only person at the Academy who knew Rune could use his deviation. I hadn't told anyone what he could do. In trying to protect him, I put the entire Academy at risk. Just thinking about the carnage we'd be facing at St. Ignatius made me sick to my stomach. If anyone was hurt, it was my fault because I chose to keep a very dangerous secret.

Ozzy sped down the dark roads. The Academy was thirty minutes away and we all knew just how much damage the Others could do in that time. How long would they stay? How vicious would they be? Were they just there to get Persephone and Rune, or did they have another purpose?

I wrapped my arms across my chest, willing Ozzy to drive faster. The sooner we got to the Academy, the sooner we could help and I could start to alleviate the guilt that consumed me.

The SUV careened around a corner. Ozzy was driving so recklessly that I found myself gripping the middle console and the handle on the door until my fingers were white. I peeked in the mirror on the passenger side door and could barely see the headlights of the other two vehicles behind us. We rounded another bend in the road and Ozzy slammed on the brakes.

"Shit!" he yelled.

The back wheels of the car fishtailed as my body was thrown into the seatbelt with so much force that the air was knocked out of me. Arabella screamed as she slid off her seat and slammed into the back of mine.

"Christ on a cracker! What is your problem, Ozzy?" she snapped, struggling to get off the floor as the car slid to a stop.

Mere feet in front of our vehicle, a massive tree stretched across the road. I looked at the end where the roots should have been and could see that the tree trunk was sheared in two. It appeared to have been struck by lightning. The edges were black and ragged. On the other side of the tree, cars were backed up as far as I could see and state highway vehicles were at the front of the line. Workers were attempting to cut the huge tree into smaller pieces to move it out of the way.

"Well, now we know why there weren't any cars coming this way," Arabella said.

"Delia and the Others did this," Ozzy growled.

"I bet they did the same thing on the other side of the bridge, too," Arabella said. "That's why we didn't see any cars crossing the bridge while we were there."

"Cleo," Ozzy said, turning to me. "Do you think you could make a hole through this for us?" His eyes had a desperate, manic glare to them.

I shook my head vehemently. "No. It'd be too dangerous."

Ozzy ground his teeth together. "Everyone back at the Academy needs us now. What about Younglove? Katie? The rest of the girls on the team? No one will even bother to try to defend themselves until it's too late because they'll think the Others are us."

Anger flared inside me at his accusation. Even though I knew he was right, I knew I was right, too.

"This isn't the kind of job for my skill, Ozzy. If I blew a hole in that tree, I'd send wood shrapnel all over the place and probably kill or injure most of the people nearby. I'm not going to risk the lives of everyone here. You and I both know we're already too late to catch Delia. Me risking the lives of the people on the other side of that tree isn't going to change that. We'll find another way to get through."

I reached for the car door handle just as Dexter knocked on the window. After the stress of the night, seeing his face unexpectedly on the other side of my window almost gave me a heart attack. I could feel the heat of my fear flare through my skin, but I reined it in to keep from losing control. He motioned for me to roll down the window, which I did.

"Want me to make a path through that?" he asked Ozzy, tilting his head toward the tree.

Right. Dexter. The Spitting Cobra and his corrosive saliva. Everyone was always quick to turn to me when something needed to be destroyed, but, each one of us had our own ways to cause damage. In this case, Dexter's skill was the perfect answer—controlled destruction via acid.

"Good idea," Ozzy agreed, avoiding looking at me. "I'll come show you where to burn through to make pieces small enough to move out of the way." He got out of the car and met Dexter by the tree. I watched in silence as Dexter leaned over various parts of the tree trunk. Every time he moved, he left behind smoking splits in the trunk that were almost surgically precise.

"Why are you so scared of using your deviation?" Arabella asked me.

"Same reason as always. I don't want to lose control and hurt anyone," I answered.

"What if people get hurt because you don't use it?" Arabella countered.

"So, it's my fault the Academy is being attacked?"

"I didn't say that, but why do nothing when you can do something?"

"Because I don't trust myself."

"You did just fine in the woods a few days ago," Cassie responded, referring to the first time she saw me use my deviation.

"You do just fine every time you use it," Arabella added. "You might not realize you're controlling it, but you are. Every time. You use just enough to do what you need to do."

"What about Quinnie and the exploding lights during derby

practice?" I asked. "I went overboard that time and she got hurt."

Arabella waved her hand dismissively. "She healed just fine, some minor flesh wounds, no permanent damage. She deserved much worse for what she did to you in the bathroom. Trust me, if you hadn't been in control, all of us would have taken glass shards to the face that night."

I looked out the front window and watched as Dexter continued to burn the huge tree trunk into smaller slices with his methodic and careful aim. Maybe Arabella was right. Maybe sometimes there was no way to avoid the fact that people were going to get hurt, it was just a matter of making a decision I could live with. I thought about what happened between me and Rune in the training room and how I'd kept it a secret to keep him from being punished. Now he was at the Academy probably helping Delia and the Others do God only knows what to the unsuspecting Mandates and professors there. My silence had become even more harmful than my deviation. Keeping that one dangerous secret made this entire night even more disastrous than it should have been.

"At some point, you're going to have to trust your deviation and yourself," Arabella said, interrupting my thoughts as she opened her door. "Now that we're dealing with the Others, you need to act, not just react." She got out of the SUV and went around the front to help push the chunks of tree to the side of the road.

Arabella was right. I needed to act. I needed to take control of my deviation and stop being scared of the monster inside. It was part of me whether I wanted it to be or not. I could either be afraid of it for the rest of my life, or use it.

"She's right, you know. You've got to rule your fear," Cassie said as if she could read my thoughts. She had said that phrase to me so many times over the years it that it had become our mantra. "Come on," she said, reaching over the seat to muss up my hair. "Let's go help. It looks like Dexter is done."

Moving the tree out of the road only took about fifteen minutes, but that was fifteen minutes too long. Ozzy didn't speak as we drove the back roads to get to the Academy. I wondered if he was angry with me for not doing as he asked and then I wondered if he had a right to be angry. I did know one thing for sure. If there was any possibility that Delia and the Others might still be at the Academy when we got there, I had to confess my dangerous secret now. I had to tell Ozzy about Rune.

"Delia will want to take Rune with her," I said into the silence.

"Probably," Ozzy agreed. "Good riddance."

"No. It's a bad thing. Rune is the Pistol Shrimp."

"So Younglove keeps telling us," Ozzy said, staring out the window.

"It's not just a name. He can use his deviation." My voice was quiet, but it still seemed to shatter the silence of the car.

Ozzy didn't say anything immediately. "How do you know he can use his deviation?" he finally asked, warily.

"He used it this morning in the training room," I admitted.

"He attacked you?" Ozzy's words sliced through the darkness and I cringed at how sharp they were.

"I wouldn't say attack. Not really. I was provoking him. He defended himself."

Ozzy's knuckles turned white as his hands squeezed the leather of the steering wheel. "Did he use his deviation first or did you?"

"He did, but..."

"He attacked you and you weren't going to tell me?" Ozzy interrupted.

"It's not that I didn't want to tell you. I was scared because I retaliated and used my deviation on him. I can't go back to the cells."

"Did you honestly think I'd turn you in? Or that Younglove would send you back there for defending yourself?" Ozzy looked hurt.

"No." Of course I didn't think Ozzy would turn me in, but I had been worried he'd tell Younglove about Rune's deviation just to prove Rune couldn't be trusted.

"I can't believe you didn't trust me. How could you not tell me?" Ozzy's voice rose in anger.

"I'm sorry. I was going to tell you."

"When?" The word snapped out of his mouth angrily.

"That's enough, Ozzy," Cassie said. "Stop yelling at her. You think she doesn't regret her decision? That's why she's telling you now. Remember who the real enemy is and leave her alone."

Ozzy's gaze flew to the rearview mirror where he could see Cassie. "He could have killed her."

"She could have killed him," Cassie reminded him. "She's not exactly defenseless."

"I'm going to kill him," Ozzy said under his breath as he returned his gaze to the road.

There was nothing to say after that. We rode in silence the rest of the way and when we reached the main gates, none of us were surprised to see that they were gone. The once imposing gate to St. Ignatius was now nothing more than twisted fragments of metal scattered around the ground outside of the wall. It looked like the earth was littered with the deformed skeletons of tortured beasts. Most of it was still smoking and tiny fires burned in the dry grass at the sides of the road. It wasn't clear how Delia and the Others had gotten inside the gates, but it was obvious that they blasted their way out.

It was eerily vacant as we followed the driveway around to the front of the Academy. The doors were wide open, hanging crookedly from their hinges. Windows along the front of the building were broken as flames licked through the jagged openings of some.

Ozzy motioned us toward the front doors. "If you see any survivors, help them to safety. We have no idea what we're walking into, so be careful and stay together."

I started to make my way forward and Ozzy grabbed my hand, pulling me back to his side.

"Stay close to me. I'll be useless unless I know you're safe."

"I'll be fine," I assured him, moving toward the door again. He kept his grip tight on my hand, angling his body so that I was mostly behind him.

"Just stay near me," he growled.

As we entered the building, I noticed Arabella and Cassie were nearby and I felt a protective urge to push them behind me like Ozzy had done to me. The rest of the Deviants had drawn their guns and the only sounds were our careful steps, our nervous breaths, and the hunger of the fires that fed on the old wooden furniture and heavy drapes in the foyer.

"Where to first?" Marty asked as we slowly crossed the marble floor that was cluttered with shards of wood and broken glass. In several spots, the marble was cracked and cratered as if a bunch of small meteors had slammed into the floor.

"Let's find Younglove," Ozzy said.

Ozzy took the lead and I stayed beside him, guilt tearing at my insides as I gazed at the destruction around us. We still hadn't seen a single person, even though some of the dark patches on the floor looked suspiciously like blood.

My thoughts of self-condemnation were interrupted by a loud crack that echoed through the vast hall. I didn't have a chance to register what the sound was before I was knocked off my feet and on my back. I was staring up at the ceiling, which was blackened by smoke, and I couldn't breathe. My chest felt like it had caved in and no matter how hard I tried to pull breath into my lungs, I couldn't. Pain stretched across my chest, the worst of it centered on the right side of my body. I reached up and grasped at my shirt, trying to get it off, trying to free my lungs to breathe.

"Cleo!" I heard the tortured sound of my name ripped from Ozzy's throat.

There was shouting and a blue light lit up the room. I couldn't hear anything but my own panicked thoughts and I couldn't see anything as blackness swam across my eyes while I struggled to find my breath. Finally, I saw Arabella's face drop into the hazy darkness in front of my eyes. She gripped the edges of my shirt, ripping the fabric in two. Once I was free of the shirt, she grabbed the velcro of my bulletproof vest and pulled the straps apart, releasing me from the jacket's tight embrace.

"It's okay, Cleo," she assured me. "It hit the vest. Calm down. You can breathe. Just try." She ran one hand down the side of my head to calm me and her other hand over the spot where I was shot. Her gaze and calm words were a lifeline as I felt my heart rate slow down and a sliver of fresh, precious air trickled into my lungs.

More shots echoed through the hall followed by the sound of bullets ricocheting and more shouting.

"Don't shoot! Hold your fire," Ozzy yelled, stealing a worried glance down at me.

As I slowly found the ability to breathe, I allowed Arabella to help me sit up. A blue, glowing circle of light was spinning in front of us, crackling with energy as it appeared to funnel outward from Quinnie's hands. The rest of the Deviants were behind the shield of light, pointing their guns in different directions. I turned my gaze to where Ozzy was pointing his weapon—a wall on the other side of the room where a hallway led deeper into the Academy.

"It's us, Professor Lawless," Ozzy shouted, holding up his forearm so that his tattoo was visible. He also lifted his other hand so that the gun was pointing in the air, proving he was no longer a threat. After a few agonizing moments in which I managed to get my breath under control, Professor Lawless finally inched his way out from behind the wall.

"Ozzy?" he asked.

"Yes, it's us," Ozzy responded. "Stop shooting."

Without waiting for Lawless to respond, Ozzy dropped to his knees in front of me and pulled the vest completely over my head before forcing me to lie back down.

"Where were you hit?" Ozzy asked as he began to pull off the thin tank top I was wearing under the vest.

I pointed to the spot and winced, realizing how tender it was. "It's sore, but I'm fine," I assured him, pulling my shirt back down so that I didn't end up half naked for no reason. "We've got more important things to worry about right now," I managed to say through painful breaths.

"Nothing is more important right now. Not to me," Ozzy said quietly, his eyes burning protectively as I attempted to sit up again.

"Oh my God," Lawless said as he hurried across the entryway. "Is that Clementine? Did I hit her? Is she hurt?"

"I'm fine," I said again. "I was wearing protection. Just a little sore."

I noticed Quinnie's shield disappeared once Lawless abandoned his weapon.

"I thought you were the Others," Lawless explained apologetically. "I'm sorry."

"What happened?" Ozzy asked the distraught professor. "We went to meet Delia and the Others at the Conowingo Dam like Younglove ordered, but they weren't there. We got a call from Professor Younglove that the Others were here attacking the Academy."

"That's true. It was during work detail. I don't know much about what happened except that I heard explosions and a lot of screaming. And when I came to investigate, the place was in chaos," Lawless explained.

"Where is everyone?" Ozzy gestured to the empty, demolished room around us.

"Most of them are safe, but not all," Lawless admitted. "Delia took Persephone and Rune."

"We assumed she would."

"They killed the Hounds guarding them." Lawless's voice broke on the word "killed," but he managed to get the sentence past his lips.

"What about the rest of the Hounds? Did any survive?" Ozzy

barely kept his own voice controlled. He knew the Hounds better than any of us. To most of us, they were our guardians—merely a presence to thwart any ideas of misbehaving and to punish us when necessary. To Ozzy, some were his loyal companions during years of missions. He had trusted his life to them and they'd trusted theirs to him.

"A handful. They're with the cadets," Lawless said.

"Any other casualties?" I could tell Ozzy didn't want to ask the question, but did so out of duty. We had to know all of the details.

"Overton was killed. It appeared that he was specifically searched out."

Ozzy wasn't nearly as affected by this fact as he was by the death of the Hounds. I didn't want to hear about anyone dying, but I'd be lying if I said I was heartbroken. Overton was the man who sent me for whippings in the cells, and although I wasn't glad he was dead, I also wasn't sad.

"That's unfortunate," Ozzy answered, diplomatically.

"For the most part, it looks like the main purpose was to get in and rescue Persephone and Rune. They had a very specific agenda and they weren't here long at all."

"Can you take us to Professor Younglove? Since Dean Overton is no longer in charge, we need to speak with her to see what she'd like us to do."

"I'm sorry," Lawless said, as he reached into his pocket, pulling out a black device that he handed to Ozzy. "Younglove isn't here. Delia took her."

Ozzy

28

Osmium Box

"What's this?" I asked Lawless, staring at the tracking unit he just handed me.

"I tuned it to track Twyla Younglove, so you can find her. If you find her, you find Delia and the Others."

"But, she doesn't have a tattoo," I pointed out. As far as I knew, Twyla and Delia were both failed experiments. They worked for the Program, but were not marked and tracked like official Sophisticates.

"No, she doesn't have a tattoo because she wasn't officially fit with a tracking device. But unbeknownst to the Program, she had one put in her arm. You have to find her. She has information Delia wants."

I nodded and gripped the tracking unit in my fist. I owed it to Younglove to rescue her from her sister. Of all the officials in the Program, she was the only one I trusted. Not to mention the fact that what Lawless said was true—Professor Younglove had important information that we couldn't let Delia get her hands on. I probably didn't even know half of what she knew about the Dozen.

"First, I want to check out the video footage of the attack," I told Lawless. "I need to see exactly what happened here." I pointed to Theo and Wesley. "Can you secure that for me?"

"No problem," Theo said. "I'll sync it up to a tablet we can take with us."

"You four," I said, indicating Marty, Dexter, Eva, and Sadie. "Pull the fire alarms and get the sprinkler system on so we can put out any fires."

"That won't work. The Others disabled it," Lawless said. "After I made sure that the remaining Hounds took the faculty and cadets to safety, I came back to try and put the sprinklers on. I'd just discovered that it wasn't working when you came into the Academy."

"Where is the worst damage?" I asked. "Is the entire building on fire?"

"No. Overton's office, the cells, and the foyer received the worst damage. Persephone wasn't capable of much more than walking out when they rescued her, so thankfully the attack was limited."

"Sadie and Eva, go to Overton's office. Find some fire extinguishers on the way and see if you can get the fires near his office under control before it spreads. Marty and Dexter, you do the same in the cells. Quinnie, Arabella, and Cassie, I need you to take care of the fires here in the foyer."

There was no hesitation as the group split off to do as I ordered. I was surprised that even Quinnie didn't complain, especially about being paired up with Arabella and Cassie.

"Is Ms. Petticoat around?" I asked Lawless. "I'd like her to take a look at Cleo before we leave."

"She's with the cadets taking care of the injuries some sustained. I'll go get her." He looked guiltily at Cleo. As angry as I was that she'd gotten hurt, I couldn't be angry at him. At least when push came to shove, he took the shot when he thought it was Persephone.

"No need," Cleo said as she forced herself to stand. "I'm fine." She steadied herself on her feet, clutching her ribs with her left arm.

"You're not fine. You might have a broken rib." I gently grabbed her shoulders to prevent her from going to help Arabella and Cassie.

"I'll get Ms. Petticoat. Be right back." Lawless hurried through the doorway where he'd been hiding when we first came in. The sounds of his footsteps were soon lost as the girls returned with fire extinguishers and began suffocating the many fires nearby. The coils of smoke that reached for the ceiling were soon snuffed out as well.

"I'm fine," Cleo repeated, the soft brown of her eyes blazing into a dark molten color.

I pulled her into my arms, not even caring if anyone else saw, and kissed the top of her head. "When I saw you having trouble breathing, I was sure he hit someplace you weren't protected by the vest. I thought you were dying and I felt a piece of me dying, too."

My continual failure to protect her was eating away at me. When she first told me about Rune attacking her in the training room, I could think of nothing but how I was the one that asked her to go down there with him. If he had seriously hurt her, it would have been my fault. Finding out the truth about the danger I'd put her in had scared me shitless. I'm not sure my heart could survive if something happened to her. I cared about her too much.

No. I didn't just care about her, I loved her. The worst part? I couldn't tell her I loved her because I knew it would sound crazy. I kissed the top of her head again to keep myself from blurting out the words my soul was screaming to her. I love you, Cleo.

She gazed up at me, her eyes a storm of emotions. *I didn't say that out loud did I?*

"I'm sorry for not telling you about Rune. I didn't mean to lie," she said.

"It doesn't matter." I put my hands on either side of her face and brought her lips to mine, grateful that I hadn't lost her. She kissed me back greedily and an unexpected warmth enveloped us as she clutched my jacket, her lips begging me for forgiveness. Cleo's hands slid up my arms and over my shoulders and when her fingertips touched the skin of my neck, I flinched away from her.

"What?" she asked, surprised at the sudden distance between us.

I reached up to my neck where her fingers had just been, where it felt like I'd been burned with a dozen hot pokers.

"Nothing." When I lowered my hand, Cleo gasped.

"Did I do that?" she asked, leaning in to look at my skin.

"What?"

"You have burn marks where I just touched you." She was frightened and I remembered the uncomfortable heat between us while we kissed the last time she'd been in my room. I remembered the way her clothes started to burn and smoke.

Before I could answer her, Quinnie sauntered up to us, a fire extinguisher swinging from her hand.

"Fires are out." She glared at Cleo, who didn't notice. Cleo was too busy staring at her own hands as if they didn't belong to her body.

"Got the footage," Theo called, waving a tablet over his head as he and Wesley came running into the room. "Lawless is right behind us, he's bringing Ms. Petticoat."

I didn't have time to worry about what was going on with me and Cleo and the new side effect of her deviation. We had to look at the security video and go rescue Younglove. The rest we could deal with later when we had time.

Theo put the tablet in my hand and pressed a couple of icons to bring up several views from different cameras. The first view showed Delia and the Others coming through the front doors of the Academy as if they belonged there. As their progress through the Academy moved from camera to camera, I could see that although some people were curious about the large group of people moving as one, no one tried to stop them. Why would they? They looked like us.

Theo stood next to me tapping the icons of various camera views and dragging different images to the center of the screen so we could see Delia's movements through St. Ignatius.

Ms. Petticoat arrived and told Cleo to lie back down on the floor so she could check out her injuries. Cleo grumbled again about being fine, but agreed to be examined after I gave her a stern look. Confident she was in good hands, I turned back to the tablet to see the next camera view Theo had pulled front and center. It showed Delia and the Others entering the common area where the Hounds were gathered. Rune was there, too, just where I'd left him.

The Hounds were scattered around the room, some watching television, others sitting at tables playing cards. A few looked up when the door opened and most turned their gaze to Euri, my twin. Of course they'd look to him. They were used to dealing with me. They probably thought I had come back to get Rune.

The image of the video was small, but it was clear enough to see the events unfold and there was also sound so we could hear what was being said. Marty's twin and Elysia struck first—Spitfire Caterpillar daggers and Electric Eel bolts of lightning struck the chests of the closest unsuspecting Hounds. Chaos immediately ensued, the Hounds attempting to subdue the Others and the Others showing absolutely no mercy. A couple of the Hounds stood apart from the melee, protecting Rune.

"Rune," Delia said, gesturing to the Hounds on either side of him, indicating that she wanted him to attack them.

Rune shook his head. "I can't. They gave me a counteragent." He continued to stand behind the Hounds. Delia merely shrugged and motioned for Euri to dispatch the two men, which he did with two perfectly placed shots from a hand gun.

Rune glanced up at the camera with an apologetic look.

That couldn't be right. It was clear that he was part of Delia's team. He was the spy we always feared he was, but were too ignorant to treat like one. I couldn't understand it. Why did Rune tell Delia that the Hounds had used a counteragent on him? There wasn't even a counteragent developed for his deviation because his twin Deviant hadn't survived past exhibition. It made no sense.

Rune's gaze dropped away from the camera as a Hound fell at his feet, screaming and clutching his face where Dexter's twin attacked with his acidic spit. Rune's face was unreadable, but it was clear he was neither helping nor stopping Delia and the Others.

"Where is Persephone?" Delia demanded from Rune once all

of the Hounds were eliminated.

He looked up from the injured Hound and pointed toward the door that led to the cells.

"Show us. I don't want to be here any longer than necessary."

It had taken only a few moments for all of the Hounds to be disabled. Most lay still. Those who were moving were incapable of defending themselves.

"Go take care of Dean Overton," Delia said, sending half of the Others away. Theo split the screen for me so that we could see where they were headed. Once we realized they were going straight to Overton's office, I asked Theo to close the window. We knew the outcome of that part of the mission and I didn't particularly enjoy watching an execution. I never had, even when I was the one doing the execution.

We watched as Delia, Rune, and the remaining Others entered the cells and extracted a smug looking Persephone from her cell.

"Did you find the counteragents?" Delia asked.

"No," Persephone said. "I think they might be in the Restricted Section. I was trying to get inside when they discovered me."

"What about the rest of the things we discussed?"

Persephone shook her head no.

"She was too busy stirring up trouble with Cleo," Rune said.

"And what's your excuse? You were supposed to be helping me," Persephone countered.

"I was under constant guard," Rune explained. "They didn't exactly trust me."

"Enough. We don't have time for this," Delia growled as she turned to Persephone. "Take me to the Restricted Section. Pollux, you come with us. I need you to find where they hid it." Delia motioned to a guy who looked like Wesley before following Persephone back through the common room, not at all careful as she walked past the fallen Hounds, kicking them out of her way.

"No need to watch the rest of that," Lawless said, indicating the video. "They didn't find what they were looking for. It was never in the Restricted Section and they ran out of time to search other places." He handed me a metal box. "This is what they wanted."

"What is it?" I asked.

Instead of answering, Lawless turned his gaze to Wesley who looked at the box intently. His curiosity turned to frustration as he stared.

"What is it?" I repeated, but to Wesley this time.

"I don't know. I can't see inside." Wesley looked at Lawless. "It's made out of osmium, the only substance I can't see through. Why do you have an osmium box?"

"To keep someone like you from looking inside. This was hidden in my office. Thankfully, they didn't check there before leaving."

"What do you want me to do with this?" I asked, lifting the box.

"I'm trusting you with it. It holds Deviant secrets that only Twyla Younglove and I know. If something happens to her, or me, I want to be sure you have that information. It belongs to you." He handed me the key to the box. Not that we needed it. Dexter could open it as easily as his twin had melted the lock on the powerhouse door.

"Thank you." I was dying to look inside, but Ms. Petticoat was helping Cleo to her feet and it was clear that the remaining video would only show more destruction. I'd seen enough to get a good idea about what happened. I could watch the rest in the SUV. The most important thing now was finding Professor Younglove, Delia, and the Others. They already had a head start on us, but at least they didn't know that we could track them. That is, we could track them as long as they kept Younglove alive.

"I know you don't have many Hounds to spare," I said to Lawless, "but I need at least two drivers."

"I can get you that," Lawless said. "Have you checked where she is yet?" he asked, nodding toward the tracking device in my hand.

I powered it up and watched as a red dot began to flash on the map in the middle of the screen.

"It looks like we're heading to Baltimore City."

CLEO

29

BATTLE AT THE HARBOR

As the SUVs took the exit ramp from I-95 to the Inner Harbor of Baltimore, Ozzy sat next to me watching the videos on the tablet. He was busy memorizing Delia's movements through the Academy. I, on the other hand, couldn't bear to watch as people we knew were injured. If I'd just told the truth about Rune to someone, we might have avoided the entire situation. Younglove might have been able to guess that her sister was setting us up.

I bit my lip, wondering how Younglove was doing; if she was being tortured for her secrets.

I wondered how in the world we were going to get her back without any Deviants getting hurt, or worse, killed.

I wondered if I would be able to act, or just react.

"We should be on our way to save Sterling," Arabella said, turning around. She was sitting in the passenger seat up front and was speaking to me, but glaring at Ozzy. "If something happens to us, who will help him?"

Ozzy looked up from the screen. "I promise we'll go get him as soon as this is over. You have my word."

"Yeah, like that's worth anything," she growled, turning back around.

"We can't let the Others get away when we have the ability to find them tonight. Besides, we owe it to Younglove to help her."

Arabella huffed in annoyance.

Ozzy lifted the black tracking unit to look at the screen. "It looks like they're in the Power Plant building down on Pier 3," he said to the driver. "You can let us out at the intersection of Pratt and Gay Street. Park nearby and keep your headset on in case we need you."

The Hound nodded and navigated the SUV through traffic, which wasn't too bad since it was nearly midnight. Both of the SUVs pulled over at the intersection Ozzy had indicated. When I got out of the vehicle, I felt a pinch of pain in my chest from my bruised ribs, but I knew I was lucky that it hadn't been worse.

As quickly as possible, the eleven of us gathered in a tight knot on the sidewalk. We weren't wearing our headsets yet and our weapons were tucked away since we didn't want to draw attention from passersby. Ozzy led us across the street and down Pier 3 where the warehouse was located. From what I could tell, however, the Power Plant was no longer a warehouse. It was refurbished into a large book store, a restaurant, and a sports bar. There were lights all over the building and people were everywhere, still enjoying their late Saturday night.

"Why would they bring her here?" I asked Ozzy. "You'd think they'd go someplace less public. Are you sure that thing is working right?" I pointed to the tracking unit he still held.

"I'm not sure of anything," Ozzy admitted. "I'm trusting Lawless on this one."

I didn't like that at all. I felt like I'd trusted one too many people in the Program and I was constantly being punished for that misplaced trust. Ozzy directed us to go behind the building where our movements were less likely to be noticed. Despite my desire to run in the opposite direction, we followed him.

Once we were behind the building, we put on our headsets and the red armbands Ozzy brought for us so that we'd know friend from foe.

"What's the plan?" Marty asked.

"We're going to split up," Ozzy answered.

"I thought you said at the dam that splitting up was a bad idea."

"I did, but this is a different layout and they have a hostage. Besides, they're not expecting us this time. Theo and Wesley, I want you stationed outside, watching who is going in and out of the building. Wesley, I want you in the back, Theo you're up front. I'm sending Marty and Dexter with you as protection."

"We can protect ourselves," Wesley argued.

"I need you watching the building. Marty and Dexter will be watching your backs. I don't care how you pair up, just do it and get in position. Make sure your headsets are working before you leave. Sadie and Arabella, I want you two to scale the building and get a good look in the windows on the top floors. That's probably where they are. If there is a basement, I doubt they'd use it because it would leave them without an escape route. The rest of us will enter the building and try to find Younglove. Hopefully, from your vantage point, you'll see something and be able to give us an idea of where to go or what we might be facing."

Those not entering the building went to their places as Ozzy directed. While I was putting on my headset and everyone else was checking their weapons, I watched as Arabella and Sadie climbed the building, heading for the lit windows of the warehouse several stories above. Wesley watched them as well, ready to warn them if he saw danger. Arabella had no difficulty keeping up with Sadie as they scaled the outside of the warehouse using hand and footholds that were invisible to me. They were like two tiny bugs clinging to the wall, moving from brick to brick and ledge to ledge.

My nerves were shredded. I couldn't stay still and my thoughts were racing a million miles a minute, bouncing through my mind until I thought I'd go crazy with the clutter of the many worries I had for everyone. To add to my problems, I was still in pain. Even though Ms. Petticoat had given me some of her miracle cream for the discomfort in my ribs, I wasn't feeling a hundred percent.

"Ozzy," Theo said over the headset. "We're in position out front and six of the Others just left the building."

"Which six?"

"The ones that look like Sadie, Dexter, Arabella, Wesley, Sterling, and me."

"What are they doing?" Ozzy asked.

"They're heading down the pier toward the water."

Ozzy was quiet for a moment. "Marty, I want you to follow them to see where they're going and what they're doing. Don't let them see you. If they do, hopefully they'll just think you're one of them, but do your best to stay hidden."

"Got it," Marty said. "On my way."

"Theo, I'll send someone out front to protect your back," Ozzy said.

"I'll go," Cassie offered.

"No." I grabbed her arm, desperate to keep her with me. I couldn't bear the thought of something bad happening to her and me not being there to help.

She pulled the headset away from her mouth and leaned in to speak quietly to me. "Look, Theo needs someone to watch his back and I want to be the one to do it. We'll be fine. You just do what you need to do, okay? Take care of yourself. Rule the fear." She leaned in to hug me and then jogged off through the darkness around the building to find Theo.

We were now down to four in our group—Ozzy, Quinnie, Eva, and me. It didn't seem like nearly enough to overcome the Others and rescue Younglove. Especially since each of our own twins were still unaccounted for and probably inside, along with Marty's twin and Rune.

It was going to be a freaking disaster. If it came down to a fight, would we even have time to look for arm bands to see if the person in front of us was friend or enemy? We should have come up with a better way of identifying one another.

"This is probably the entrance they would have used," Ozzy said, indicating a door with a complicated digital lock. He motioned to Dexter who briefly left Wesley's side and came forward to spit on the keypad, causing it to smoke and disintegrate into a puddle of melted plastic and metal.

Ozzy tried the door and it opened easily. He peered inside.

"We're heading in," he said into the headset. Before entering, he grabbed my hand, gave it a tight squeeze, and said, "Stay close."

He turned and handed the tracking unit to Eva for safekeeping, and then we entered the dark hallway beyond the open door. There was a set of stairs that zigzagged blindly up several flights. We went slowly, Ozzy clearing each set of stairs as we came to a landing. I followed behind him and Quinnie took up the rear.

My headset crackled, followed by the sound of Arabella's voice.

"We found Younglove. She's on the top floor. Rune, Persephone, Elysia, and Eva's twin are in there with her."

"What about Delia, Euri, and Marty's twin?" Ozzy asked quietly.

"I don't see them. Do you want us to check some of the other rooms?"

"Yes. But, do it quickly. We're almost to the top floor."

We passed a door at each landing, but hadn't tried any of them yet. Ozzy was convinced we had to go to the top floor so we hadn't bothered with investigating the other floors. Now that Arabella confirmed that Younglove was on the top level, he thought it best to avoid an altercation for as long as possible. A fight with the Others before we found the professor would only make it more difficult to get her, and the rest of us, out alive.

As we rounded another set of stairs, the headset crackled again and Ozzy stopped to listen to who was checking in.

"It looks like the Others who left the building are at the dock getting a boat ready," Marty said.

"What kind of boat?" Ozzy whispered.

"Some sort of small yacht kind of thing. They're taking off all of the canvas coverings and loading things onto it like they're preparing to leave."

"Then we strike now while they're at half strength and before they can move the professor. If they get her to the boat, we may never catch them. Arabella and Sadie, have you seen anything through any of the other windows?"

There was a grunt and heavy breathing followed by Arabella's voice again. "Nothing yet. Either they're not here or they're in an interior room with no windows."

"Okay. Head back to the room where they're holding Younglove. We'll need your help to get the professor out of the window and lower her to the ground where the Hounds will be waiting. Think you can do that, Arabella?"

"No problem," she said. "Give us a minute or two to climb back over there and find a good foothold."

"Dexter, contact the Hounds and make sure they're ready to pick the professor up."

"Sure. What about Delia and the Others? Should we assume we're taking them captive and will need transportation for them, too?"

"We'll do our best to subdue them and take them into custody, but at this point, Younglove is our priority."

"We're back in position," Arabella said. "Delia and Euri just entered the room. Still no sign of Marty's twin, though."

"We're coming," Ozzy said. We were at the top of the last flight of stairs and he pushed the door at the landing open, revealing a hallway with a number of closed doors on either side. Six of the Others were at the boat and five were in the room with Younglove and Delia. Marty's twin was still unaccounted for, so we needed to be careful.

We crept down the hallway with our backs against the wall until we reached the door where Ozzy could hear voices inside. He motioned Quinnie to the front and she started moving her hands in a circular motion.

"Stay behind Quinnie," he reminded us. Just as blue light

started to swirl outward from her palms, Ozzy kicked the door open and he and Quinnie rushed through the opening. Eva and I followed them in and I quickly took stock of the situation.

Younglove was seated on a couch along the far wall with Rune at her side. I couldn't see any signs of physical abuse on the professor, although her hands were tied together. Persephone, Euri, Elysia, and Eva's twin were standing near a table and it appeared that they had been in discussion with Delia. As soon as we entered the room, Euri drew his weapon and fired at the same time that Elysia loosed several bolts of electricity at us. I winced as both the bullets and bolts bounced off the circular light Quinnie was creating. She faltered on her feet and the light flickered as she took the hits, but she increased the speed of her spinning arms and the shield lit up to full force again.

Hidden behind the safety of Quinnie's light, Ozzy took a shot at Euri, a dart hitting the other boy in the neck and causing him to stumble into the table before falling to the floor.

Persephone flipped the table over and dropped behind it before Ozzy had a chance to fire at her. Elysia threw another streak of electricity at us and Ozzy shot a dart at her. Elysia's bolt of electricity bounced off Quinnie's shield and hit the wall to the right, leaving a jagged hole. Ozzy's aim had been true and Elysia dropped weakly to the floor, trying to pull the dart out of her neck.

Delia ducked behind the table with Persephone. "Rune! Hit the shield!" Delia screamed.

Rune stood up and Ozzy swung the gun toward him at the same time that Eva yelled, "No, Rune. Don't!" in Delia's voice.

Confused, Rune halted, his eyes finding me as he flexed his hands. Before Ozzy had a chance to shoot him, a huge concrete block came flying in through the window, causing glass to explode inward toward us. Shattered glass shards hit Quinnie's shield and although it wasn't as powerful as the electricity or bullets, the sheer amount of glass that hit the shield seemed to weaken it. I briefly saw the long, stretched arms of Arabella come through the hole in the window, wrap around Younglove, and pull her outside into the darkness.

Everything was happening so fast. We'd only been in the room for about thirty seconds and I didn't know what to do. How could I subdue the Others without putting everyone in danger? Which one should I focus on? It was a freaking free-for-all with gunshots, electricity, and broken glass flying through the room.

"Ozzy!" Marty called through the headset. "The Others left the dock and are returning to the warehouse. Should we engage them?"

"No. Wait for us. Let us take care of this confrontation first."

Behind me, I heard Eva scream and turned to see Marty's twin in the doorway. Eva stumbled into me, a large black dagger protruding from her shoulder. I held her with my good arm, trying to carefully lower her to the floor.

"Pirro," Delia yelled. "Euri is down. Take the other three out."

Pirro, Marty's lookalike, swung his arm and without a thought, I thrust my hand in front of me and a fireball flew from my palm. Before it hit Pirro, it was knocked aside by another fireball. The collision caused a small explosion that rained tongues of flame around us. I spun around to see that Persephone was standing behind the table and sending a barrage of explosions around the room. Several of Persephone's fiery projectiles hit Quinnie's shield and it finally disappeared as she sank to her knees in exhaustion.

The room exploded in chaos. There were at least three bodies on the floor now and Delia was nowhere to be found. Fire and blasts of air echoed in the small space as wood splintered, gun shots rang out, and people screamed.

Pirro regained his senses and as he swung his arm toward me again, I spun around, kicking the back of his elbow hearing it crack.

"Persephone!" someone yelled.

I looked away from Pirro just as my twin rushed past us and ran through the door. I pushed Pirro and his broken arm out of the way and followed Persephone. When I finally managed to make my way out of the room and into the hallway, she was already pulling open the stairwell door and disappearing through it. I flung my arm toward the door, releasing a blast of heat, but she was already gone and the heat only managed to knock the door wide open again.

As I ran down the hall to chase Persephone, I could hear Ozzy shouting my name and I hoped he would trust me to take care of this. It was Persephone who tortured Cassie. It was Persephone who turned my friends against me. It was Persephone who stole an intimate moment with Ozzy and tarnished his trust in himself. Persephone was my problem and I was the one who was going to stop her. The monster inside me roared in approval.

My feet pounded the stairs and at each landing I recklessly swung myself around the corner trying to make up ground on Persephone's head start. It was a different set of stairs than we'd taken to get up to the top floor, so I had no idea where it would take me. I just knew I had to follow her. I should have been worried and careful, but all my monster could think about was revenge.

At the bottom of the stairs, a heavy door was still closing so I knew that Persephone wasn't too far ahead of me. I kicked the door open and had just enough time to duck as flames came hurtling toward me, shattering on the wall above my head. We were out in front of the building and people were screaming and running away from where I crouched. Persephone turned to run across a small bridge and I pushed myself to my feet to chase her, determined that no one else would get hurt.

"Cleo!" I heard Ozzy yelling through the headset. "Where are you?"

"I'm chasing Persephone," I managed through labored breaths. My ribs were killing me. "We just crossed a small foot bridge. She turned left toward a big glass building. It has a triangular roof," I panted.

"That's the National Aquarium. Just stop. Wait for us."

"Don't worry, Ozzy. I've got this," I told him.

"The Others from the dock are coming, Cleo," Theo warned through the headset. "Wait for backup. I repeat, wait for us or you're going to be outnumbered seven to one."

"Rune and Marty's twin are out there somewhere, too," Ozzy said. "Fall back, Cleo. Wait for us. Please." His last word was a strangled plea, but I knew I couldn't stop.

If I stopped chasing Persephone, I'd lose her. I could still see her in front of me and I was gaining on her. Maybe those morning runs were good for me after all. There were no tourists down at this end of the pier so instead of answering Ozzy, I flung my arm forward and released a blast of anger. It was a wavering ball of nearly invisible heat that rolled over the bricked walkway. It hit Persephone in the legs, knocking her down. She spun around and up onto her knees, a scream of fury wrenching from her throat. Behind her, I could see the six Others that had been down by the boat rushing to her rescue under the shadow of the strange building.

Persephone reached into her pocket holding something dark and round. She lit it up like a torch and hurled it at me. I was already attacking, this time with my own fire. The roaring blazes we created slammed into one another and detonated outward in an enormous explosion. It looked like napalm as sticky tongues of fire lashed out at everything around us.

Persephone threw her arm out and attacked me again. Just as I retaliated with even more energy than before, I was hit with an invisible force on my left side. I vaguely saw the fiery explosion I released rip through the one Persephone had thrown. It caused a massive eruption overhead and I heard the sound of shattering glass as my body was thrown over the side of the pier. I hit the water below so hard that it felt like all of my bones had been crushed with the impact. My breath burst out of me in one last blast of heat and I floated for a moment before the cold water crept up over my limp body and started to drag me under, steam rising from my skin as the harbor swallowed me.

Unable to move, I stared up through the water as fire tore across the sky and flaming diamonds rained down.

I couldn't move or fight the grip of the water as it pulled me under.

Ozzy

30

Shattered Heart

Her hand was still so cold, but at least she was breathing on her own now. When we first pulled Cleo's lifeless body out of the water, my heart shattered into a million tiny slivers.

She hadn't been breathing then, but she was now. Her heart was still beating, which meant mine could still beat, too.

I held her small hand in mine and reached up with the fingers of my other hand to brush her dark hair away from her face. I was used to feeling heat with Cleo's touch, but her fingers were cold and still.

The hotel suite was large, but it felt cramped. Cassie and Arabella were curled up in armchairs near Cleo's bed, neither willing to leave her side. The other rooms were filled with the rest of the Deviants, everyone catching up on sleep and recuperating.

We survived.

Most of the Others hadn't been so lucky.

The Program sent a team of doctors to our hotel suite. Cleo and

Eva had the worst injuries, but according to the physician in charge, they would both be fine. They just needed to rest. Eva was quickly recovering, but Cleo was still unconscious. Younglove went back to the Academy with the Hounds to assess the damage there, but she told us we might as well stay in the hotel suite while everyone healed. It made no sense for us to go back to the Academy right now since it was in disarray anyway. Besides, I made a promise to Arabella, and myself, to rescue Sterling from Headquarters, which meant that I wasn't planning to go back to the Academy at all.

I stroked the skin on Cleo's arms and face, concerned that the excessive warmth that seemed to usually surround her was completely gone. I wasn't going to lie. It didn't seem natural and that worried the hell out of me. Wanting to warm her frigid body, I climbed on to the mattress next to her and pulled her to my side, yanking the covers higher over her, and rubbing her arm to get the circulation going.

The door to the room creaked open.

"Should we order some food?" Theo asked.

"Yeah," I mumbled. "It's dinner time. Might as well."

Theo closed the door and I heard the television turn on in the living room. Cleo shivered in my arms and I pulled her closer as she finally opened her eyes.

"Where am I?" she asked, her breath raspy and quiet.

I leaned up on my elbow to look down at her, running my hands along her hair.

"In a hotel room in Baltimore."

"Am I dead?"

"How do you feel?" I asked instead.

Her eyes blinked slowly.

"Like someone removed all the bones from my body, crushed them with a sledgehammer, and then put them back inside."

I couldn't resist leaning down to kiss her, to feel the life in the lips I thought would be still forever.

"If I am dead," she mumbled, "this isn't a bad way to go. Except for the crushed bones part."

"You're not dead," I told her. "But, you were close."

"I don't remember anything."

"We went to rescue Professor Younglove. We fought the Others and you chased Persephone."

"Oh, right. I remember that part."

At the sound of our voices, Cassie woke up and turned her head toward the bed. "Cleo? Is that you? Are you okay?"

"Yeah. I think so," she said in a rough voice.

Cassie jumped up from her seat, waking up Arabella in the process. Both girls rushed over, fussing over Cleo while they tried to order me out of the bed. No way was I moving, now that I had her safely in my arms again. They settled for sitting on the mattress on the other side of Cleo.

"So what happened after I chased Persephone?" Cleo asked. "I'm a little fuzzy on that part."

"Your deviation kicked her deviation's ass," Cassie bragged.

"You blew up a monument," Arabella added.

"You nearly died," I said.

"Details. I need details." Cleo sighed.

"After you knocked Persephone down, you attacked each other," Cassie explained. "When the power of your deviations collided, yours steamrolled hers. You were winning. The problem was that Pirro had followed you out of the building. He threw one of his knives at you from behind and Rune saved you by hitting you with a blast of air and knocking you out of the way."

"You mean knocking her into the harbor where she almost drowned," Arabella interrupted.

"Well, he didn't mean to do that," Cassie said.

"That's his version," I growled. I still didn't trust that boy, but I couldn't deny that without his actions, Cleo would have been dead.

"Rune saved me?" Cleo was disbelieving. "Where is he now?" she asked.

"We don't know. He ran off with the surviving Others," I told her. "We were too busy trying to save you to worry about them."

"Survivors? Do you mean someone...died?"

"Most of them did," Arabella admitted. "Delia and Eva's twin were killed in the room where Younglove was being kept. It looked like Delia was killed accidentally by Rune. Eva's twin was killed by a stray blast of fire. Almost all of the Others died when Rune knocked you out of the way and one of your fireballs went awry. It destroyed most of the National Aquarium and the six Others that had been down at the boat were crushed under the broken glass and building fragments. Marty's twin, Pirro, fell on one of his own blades when he was hit by one of Rune's blasts of air."

"I killed people?" Cleo asked, horrified. She was shaking.

"It wasn't your fault." I tried to comfort her.

She stared at her hands and I thought I heard her mutter the word "monster."

"It was an accident," I told her. "Your fireball ricocheted off Persephone's. If you hadn't stopped her, innocent bystanders could have been hurt. Think of all the people the Others have killed just to make a statement."

Cleo was quiet as she rubbed her hands together, as if trying to get them clean. “Who survived? Which Others?”

“Rune, Persephone, Elysia, and Euri,” I said.

“Only four?” Her voice was small.

“Four very dangerous Others,” I reminded her.

“And they’re missing now?”

I nodded.

“If Rune ran off with the Others, why did he bother saving me?”

“He said he owed it to you for not turning him in.” I was forever in debt to that asshole now, but I’d take it. To have Cleo alive and well, I’d make any sacrifice; put myself in debt to anyone.

“So, you talked to him?” she asked, looking between the three of us.

“I wouldn’t exactly call it talking,” Arabella said. “He sort of just yelled at us as he was running away. He said to tell you that you guys were even now.”

Cleo was thoughtful for a moment. “How are the rest of the Deviants? Is everyone okay?”

“Eva is recovering from a stab wound, but everyone else is okay,” Cassie explained.

“Except for Quinnie,” Arabella reminded her.

“What happened to Quinnie?” Cleo asked.

“Broken heart. Rune chose the Others over her,” Cassie said. “I feel kind of bad for her. She’s too upset to even act like a bitch right now.”

***

When room service brought up dinner, Arabella and Cassie went out into the main living area to eat.

I stayed in the bed, running my fingers through Cleo’s hair. I’d be happy to lay here for the rest of my life as long as Cleo was with me. Fuck the Others. Fuck the Program.

While Cleo had been unconscious, Arabella told me about what Sterling had been up to at Headquarters. He'd be making an escape attempt soon and we would go get him. Apparently, he had a plan to get out, we just had to get him once he was on the outside. I had a hard time believing he'd be able to escape Headquarters, but Sterling sacrificed everything for Arabella and saved me from the difficult choice of who to leave behind. I had to trust him on this.

I'd done a lot of talking with Arabella and Cassie since we arrived at the hotel, and we made the only decision we could. We'd pick up Sterling and then face a life on the run. Once we defied the Program, there'd be no going back. I only had a little time left to convince the rest of the Deviants to join us. I'd give them the choice—return to the Academy or join us for a chance at freedom. The Program had never given us a choice in what to do with our lives, but I'd give it to them, even if it meant they might choose the Program and would some day be sent to hunt down those of us who chose to run.

"Are you hungry?" I asked Cleo.

"No, I'm feeling a little nauseous actually."

"It's probably all the filthy harbor water you swallowed."

"Or, it might be the fact that my actions resulted in the deaths of seven people."

"It's Rune's fault Pirro is dead. You can't feel bad about protecting yourself. If it had to be you or them, I'm glad it was you that survived."

She sighed. "Me too, I just feel...sad. It's not like they knew any better. They were just doing what Delia told them. How are we any different? We just do what the Program tells us. Don't get me wrong, I hated them. I wanted revenge, but I didn't want any of them to die."

I pulled her tighter and kissed the top of her head.

"Does it get any easier?" she asked. "Taking someone's life. Does it get easier?"

"No."

"How do you do it? I feel like a piece of my soul has been ripped out. Six pieces actually. How can I keep doing this and stay whole?"

"You won't have to keep doing this," I reminded her. "We're going to be free."

"I still feel broken...like I'm splintered." Her breath shuddered as if she were holding back tears.

"I'll always be here to help hold you together."

Her eyes finally found their way to my gaze right before her lips pressed against mine. Her kiss was full of need. It felt like a plea for me to never let her go, to always make things right. When I reached up to hold her face in my hands, I could feel the tears sliding down her cheeks. I pulled back to look at her as I wiped them away with my thumbs.

"Promise?" she asked.

"Promise."

Cleo tucked her head into my shoulder, and after a few minutes, I could hear her breathing returning to normal as I continued to comfort her with gentle touches of my fingers. There was a knock on the door before it opened.

"Ozzy?" Theo asked. "Younglove's on the phone for you."

He brought the phone over and handed it to me.

"Professor Younglove," I answered in greeting.

"Osbourne," she said frantically. "Do you still have the osmium box that Professor Lawless gave you?"

"Yes, it's in the SUV that the Hounds left for us."

"Retrieve the box and then leave. Immediately. Don't take the SUV."

"Leave? Where do you want us to go? Why can't we take the SUV?"

"Osbourne, the Program has given the order to terminate the Deviant Dozen experiment."

"I don't follow."

"When the Program found out about Delia and the Others, I was told that I needed to have the Others apprehended. After the attack at Andrews Air Force Base and your failure to capture the Others, there was serious concern about the danger both groups posed. It was made clear to me that if the Deviants couldn't handle the Others, there would be consequences. That's why I was so intent on having you meet them at the dam. I thought it was our only chance to keep the Dozen safe from the Program. Now, after the attack on the Academy and the destruction at the Inner Harbor last night, the Program has decided that you're all too dangerous. I've been instructed to order you back to the Academy and have you terminated."

"Terminated? The Program wants to kill us?" I couldn't believe it. I knew we'd never been anything but a tool for the Program, but how could they make the decision to kill a dozen teenagers because they were afraid of us? We'd never done anything but follow their orders. I'd done everything they ever asked me to do. Even though I'd been discussing plans with Arabella and Cassie to defy the Program, I'd never considered that they might terminate us.

"Osbourne, you have to run. When you don't come back, they'll come for you."

"Where do we go?"

"First you have to go to New York. I was just informed that Sterling has disappeared. That, along with everything else, has the Program scared. You need to find him and then find a safe place to hide. Go through the information in the osmium box. There is contact information in there about people who can help you. The first thing you need to do is disable the tracking tattoos, Cassandra knows how."

"I know, we've already discussed it," I admitted.

Younglove was quiet for a moment, but she didn't ask why we'd been discussing the tattoos. "I'm sorry," she said. "I have to go. You need to run now. Disable your tattoos and get the hell out of there. You don't have much time."

"What about you? Won't they know you warned us?"

"That's a risk I'm willing to take. You have to leave now. Please."

The phone went dead and I sat up in bed. The door suddenly banged open. Cassie and Arabella were in the doorway.

"Sterling just called," Arabella said, holding up her phone. "He escaped Headquarters. We have to go get him now."

Cassie held up a taser and squeezed the trigger once, allowing electricity to dance between the pins on top.

"Time to go off the grid," she said with a smile.

ACKNOWLEDGEMENTS

After months of writing late into the night, agonizing over plots and characters, and dissecting my manuscript from every angle, I finally get to send my story out into the world. There is a huge supporting cast of people who have helped make *Conviction* possible. Whether reading, editing, or just cheerleading for me, your support has meant more than I can say.

Johnny Manzari...you are my partner, my love, my future. Your support for my dream has always been unwavering and unmatched. The fact that you don't even really like books makes it even more special that you encourage my dream of being an author. You can't imagine how much I rely on your faith in me, your unconditional love, and your humor. I'm so lucky to have you: "You don't marry the person you can live with, you marry the person you can't live without."

Many thanks to my beta readers: Laurie Marin, Amber Hodgson, Laura Ward (author of Not Yet to be released July 2014), Dani Fisher, and Tina Bland for taking the time to read the first draft of Conviction and for giving me valuable feedback on everything from the manuscript to the synopsis.

Laura, Dani, and Tina: our writing group has been such a wonderful blessing and I look forward to our weekly conversations about books and writing. I love being able to email you for virtual support and encouragement and I look forward to all the wonderful books you all are working on. A huge extra sparkly thanks to Laura Ward for coming up with the brilliant title for Conviction. It's so perfect!

From the bottom of my heart I want to thank my generous friends who took the time out of their busy lives to thoroughly edit my manuscript. Thanks to Eva Gerald (author of Peacemaker), Rich Sanidad, and Shelly Burch for your brilliant red pens and thoughts. You asked the questions that were difficult to answer, but in the end made my book so much better.

I want to thank the bloggers who read Deviation and reviewed it for me: Lindsay Self from Broke Book Girls (thebrokebookgirls.blogspot.com), Tahlia Newland from Awesome Indies (tahlianewland.com), Elizabeth Mallack from Reader Views (readerviewskids.com), Amanda from Of Spectacles and Books (www.ofspectaclesandbooks.com), and Satarupa from Curse of the Bibliophile (curseofthebibliophile.blogspot.com).

I can't have a proper acknowledgment section without thanking the two people who created the weird little monster that I am today. Mom and Dad, thank you for being the kind of parents that let me believe I could do anything (no matter how weird or crazy that thing was) and for always being there (no matter how far you had to travel to support me). You let me know it was okay to be different and I'm forever thankful for the beautiful, unconditional love you've always given me.

Special thanks also to the rest of my family...Pop, Honey, Mimi, Kay, Johnnie, Mary Ann, Jason, Fili, Lisa, Jeff, Joe, Jen, Angel, Ryan, Andy, and Jenn for asking me for updates and being supportive.

My deepest gratitude goes to all my friends who have been there to give me virtual high fives or words of inspiration in person and on social media. Thank you for buying my first book, reading it, reviewing it, and suggesting it to others. Here is a special thank you to all those who supported me by becoming my fans via facebook and instagram (I hope I spelled your names correctly): Abigail Davis, Alexis Hall, Alfred Hall, Alicia Burn, Amber Hodgson, Amy Blades, Andrea Shreni, Angela Paolatonio, Angie Zavaglia, Barbara Dean, Bekky Levesque, Bobby Cogan, Brad Opel, Brittany Lindsey, Carrie Sanidad, Carrie Kemether, Cate Katergaris, Catherine Howard, Chad Lawton, Charles DeWeese, Chelsey Warfield, Christy Pantazelos, Cindy Stanley-Lee, Cynthia DeWeese, Dana Shetzler, Danielle Mallon, David Bozak, Dawn DeVoe, Deanna Ashenfelter, Dina Justice, Divya Burton, Elizabeth Kefauver, Elizabeth Helen, Elizabeth Shaw, Emily Jeffries, Emily Gehart, Erin Hromada, Felix Wang, Fran Diaz, Glennen Greer, Hailea Cole, Haley Bug, Haley Lewis, Heather Harmon, Heather Szczytko, Heather Swyka, Hermano Talastas, Jacki Poore, Jacki Manzari, Jaime Zicafoose, James Greso, Jane Baker, Jamie Falcon, Jason Hurlock, Jenny Hutton, Jen Mabry, Jennifer Swayne, Jennifer Tuff, Jennifer Caggino, Jennifer Schmoll, Jennifer Shade, Jeremy Dukes, Jessica Holmgren, Jessica Wilson, Jill Hall, Jim Phillips, Joanna Chaffee, Jonathan Szczepanski, Jose Teneza, Justin Fazzio, Katy Wilcox, Kelli Eastburn, Kelly Herdrich, Kelly Otto, Kelly Soltysiak, Kevin Preston, Kris Miller, Kristen DeMarino, Kristina Gaston, Laura Marin, Laura Ward, Laura Mueller, Laurie Amici, Lawanda Summers-Stephen, Leah Shepherd, Lee Miller, Leila Swyka, Lindsay Self, Lisa Malin, Lisa Sutton, Lizet Christiansen, Lou Hromada, Marcia Rosa, Margaret Sommerman, Matt Hodgson, Maureen Cogan, Maureen Barnes, Maureen Pietschmann, Meaghan Vance, Megan Diaz, Megan O'Bryan, Melissa Giambrone, Michelle Ward, Michelle Cassels, Molly Buckmeier, Morgan McKay, Nadja Greso, Nicole Eury, Noel Lloyd, Ozana Jovanovic, Patti Blakeney, PJ Klavon, Rapid Reviewer, Rebecca Roese, Reka Montfort, Rich Sanidad, Riq Parra, Rob Matthews, Robert Carroll, Rosey Matthews, Ruth

Dumer, Salvador Orochena, Sam Richardson, Sandy Vogelman, Scott Pyle, Sharon Thorpe, Shannon Guisto, Shelly Burch, Stacey Britton, Stef Dykes, Stephen Clugston, Susan Longo, Tamara Calloway, Theresa Carter, Tiffany Hromada, Tiffini Crown, Timothy Preston, Tom Husfelt, Tracey Carroll, Wendy O'Bryant, Yuri Achille.

Thanks to Cassie Sanidad for the awesome Deviant artwork. You're so talented.

Lastly, a special thank you to Chay Rojas. You rock!

DEVIANT DOZEN / BAKER'S DOZEN CODE NAMES

Clementine/Cleo – (Malaysian Fire Ant)

Twin Other: Persephone/Effie

Cassandra/Cassie – (Horror Frog)

No Twin Other

Arabella – (Indonesian Mimic Octopus)

Twin Other: Ambrosia

Quinby/Quinnie – (Electric Eel)

Twin Other: Elysia

Sadie – (Ring Tailed Cat)

Twin Other: Daphne

Evangeline/Eva – (Tiger Moth)

Twin Other: Echo

Osbourne/Ozzy – (Archerfish/Coondog)

Twin Other: Euripides/Euri

Sterling – (Hummingbird)

Twin Other: Aison

Dexter – (Spitting Cobra)

Twin Other: Egan

Marty – (Spitfire Caterpillar)

Twin Other: Pirro

Theo – (Bull Shark)

Twin Other: Castor

Wesley – (Bald Eagle)

Twin Other: Pollux

Sebastian – (Pistol Shrimp) died before exhibiting

Twin Other: Rune

CONVICTION PLAY LIST

Monster by Paramore
Counting Stars by OneRepublic
Still Into You by Paramore
Do I Wanna Know by Arctic Monkeys
My God is the Sun by Queens of the Stone Age
Dirty Little Secret by The All-American Rejects
Harlem by New Politics
Up in the Air by 30 Seconds to Mars
A Beautiful Lie by 30 Seconds to Mars
My Songs Know What You Did in the Dark by Fall Out Boy
Radioactive by Imagine Dragons
Dream On by blessthefall
Paint it Black by VersaEmerge
People Are Strange by Echo & The Bunnymen
...Baby One More Time by Bowling for Soup
Stronger (BBC Live Version) by 30 Seconds to Mars
Pain by Jimmy Eat World
Bleeding Out by Imagine Dragons
Love Don't Die by The Fray

ABOUT THE AUTHOR

The first thing Christine does when she's getting ready to read a book is to crack the spine in at least five places. She wholeheartedly believes there is no place as comfy as the pages of a well-worn book. She's addicted to buying books, reading books, and writing books. She even turned her dining room into a library—reading is more important than eating. She also has a weakness for adventure and inappropriate humor. Christine is from Forest Hill, Maryland where she lives with her husband, three kids, and her library of ugly spine books.

CONNECT WITH CHRISTINE MANZARI:

Website: www.christinemanzari.com

Facebook: www.facebook.com/ChristineManzari

Twitter: www.twitter.com/Xenatine

Instagram: http://instagram.com/xenatine

Pinterest: www.pinterest.com/xenatine

Goodreads: www.goodreads.com/Christine_Manzari

BOOKS BY CHRISTINE MANZARI:

Deviation (The Sophisticates Book 1)

Conviction (The Sophisticates Book 2)

Redemption (The Sophisticates Book 3)

Hooked (Hearts of Stone Book 1)

Hitched (Hearts of Stone Book 2)

The Pledge (College Bound Series Book 1)

The Color of Us (College Bound Series Book 2

61690943R00195

Made in the USA
Lexington, KY
17 March 2017